MARY HIGGINS CLARK

DEATH WEARS A BEAUTY MASK
AND OTHER STORIES

**SIMON &
SCHUSTER**

London · New York · Sydney · Toronto · New Delhi

A CBS COMPANY

First published in the US by Simon & Schuster, Inc., 2015
First published in Great Britain by Simon & Schuster UK Ltd, 2015
A CBS COMPANY

This paperback published, 2015

1 3 5 7 9 10 8 6 4 2

Simon & Schuster UK Ltd
1st Floor
222 Gray's Inn Road
London WC1X 8HB

www.simonandschuster.co.uk

Simon & Schuster Australia, Sydney
Simon & Schuster India, New Delhi

A CIP catalogue record for this book
is available from the British Library

Paperback B ISBN: 978-1-47114-322-9
Paperback A ISBN: 978-1-47115-212-2
eBook ISBN: 978-1-47114-323-6

Acknowledgments

In 1972 I began a novella that I called "Death Wears a Beauty Mask." After fifty pages I was not sure how I would end it and put it aside to write *Where Are the Children?*

Going through old files, I came across it, decided I liked it and finished it this past summer. It was fun to work on it from the perspective of its setting in 1974.

This collection contains nine of my short stories including my first published story, "Stowaway." This book represents my early years as a writer but I hope not yet the end.

Along the way there are people whom I am happy to recognize for their assistance. First and foremost, my editor and dear friend since the beginning, Michael Korda. He has steered the ship for all my writing and is indispensable.

I want to thank Marysue Rucci, V.P., editor-in-chief at Simon & Schuster. It has been wonderful working with her these last few years.

My home support group is Nadine Petry, my assistant; my son David Clark and my daughter Patty Clark. Thanks for all your support and suggestions.

And, of course, to my spouse extraordinaire, John Conheeney, who listens patiently as I tell him, "This book is not going well." His response is, "I've heard that for the last thirty books."

And many thanks to you, my dear readers, without whom I would not exist as a writer. I value each and every one of you. I hope you enjoy "Death Wears a Beauty Mask" and the other stories in this collection.

Cheers and Blessings,
Mary

IN MEMORY OF ANN MARA

Dear friend and magnificent lady

Contents

Death Wears a Beauty Mask

June 1974

The Pan American Clipper began its final descent into Kennedy Airport at 8:00 A.M. Janice pressed her forehead against the window as she tried to peer through the grayish clouds. Mike leaned over, fastened her seatbelt, gave a quick pat to her thigh and said, "You won't be able to see your sister from here, honey."

He stretched out his legs, which felt too long and cramped in the meager space allotted by the airline as suitable for tourist-class passengers. At thirty, Michael Broad, a deputy district attorney in Los Angeles, had retained the muscular leanness of his college track-team years. His brown hair was already showing liberal streaks of gray . . . a hereditary manifestation which secretly delighted him. His low-key personality didn't fool the discerning for too long. His gray eyes had an almost constant expression of quizzical irony. Defense witnesses being cross-examined had come to fear the steely, penetrating quality of those eyes. They would not have believed the expression of tenderness he invariably showed when he looked at the girl sitting next to him.

Janice, his twenty-two-year-old bride of three weeks, was tanned, slender, narrow-hipped and long-legged. Her dark blonde hair stopped three inches past her shoulders. They had met a year ago when she escorted him to the stage at the University of Southern California, where he had been invited to lecture on student safety.

She smiled at Mike as she settled back in her seat. "You can't see a darn thing," she complained. "It's so cloudy or smoggy or whatever. Oh, darling, I just can't wait to see Alexandra. Do you realize it's been nearly a year and she's the only relative I have in the whole world?"

Mike pointed to his brand-new wedding ring. "What about me?" he said dryly. She grinned at him, then restlessly turned back to the window again. She knew it was hard for Mike to understand her eagerness. With a mother, father, two brothers and two sisters, he had always been surrounded by family.

With Janice it had been different. Her mother died when she was born. Her sister, Alexandra, older by six years, had taken over as substitute mother. Alexandra left Oregon and went to New York when Janice was twelve. For a long time she had managed to get home every few months. But then as her modeling career zoomed, the get-togethers became more and more scattered. The last one had been in New York when Janice had spent ten days with Alexandra last summer.

Alexandra had planned to attend Janice's college graduation from USC. But she'd phoned to say that she had to go to Europe to do a commercial. When Janice told her that she and Mike had decided to have a small wedding—Mike's family and twenty of their close friends—at the Church of the Good Shepherd church in Los Angeles right after her graduation and use Mike's vacation time for a honeymoon, Alexandra made Janice promise that they'd spend the last week of it with her. This was the ideal time to visit. Mike would be going back to work and Janice would start her master's degree in English in July. Since she was a child she had known she wanted to be a teacher.

"I'll be at the airport with a brass band, darling," Alexandra had said. "I've missed you so much. This damn, rotten job . . . I pleaded with them to delay the shoot but they can't. I want to see you so much and meet Mike. He sounds wonderful. I'll show you New York."

"Mike knows New York inside out," Janice said. "He went to Columbia Law School."

"Well, I'll show you places you just don't go to when you're a student. All right, darling . . . that's June 24. I'll be at the airport. Just look for the brass band."

Janice turned back to Mike. "I can't wait for you to meet Alexandra. You'll love her."

"I'm anxious to," Mike said. "Although I must say I haven't exactly missed having other people around the past few weeks."

They'd spent the past three weeks in England and France. Janice thought of the out-of-the-way inns in Devon and Brittany with Mike's arms around her. "Neither have I," she admitted.

Thirty minutes later they were at the head of the line. An inspector studied their passports and stamped them. "Welcome back," he said with a hint of a smile.

They hurried to the baggage area. "I know ours will be the last to come in," Janice lamented as she watched bag after bag tumble onto the conveyor belt. She was almost right. Theirs were the next to last to arrive. Finally, as they came to the doors of the main terminal, Janice raced ahead. Friends and relatives of their fellow passengers were gathered in small welcoming groups.

Alexandra would have stood out in the crowd. In one this small it would be impossible to miss her. But she wasn't there.

Janice's look of anticipation wilted. Even her shoulders sagged as she said, "I guess the brass band got held up in traffic or something."

Mike replied good-naturedly, "Lateness seems to run in your family." Her habit of being at least fifteen minutes behind schedule everywhere had improved only slightly after a series of lectures when she'd kept him waiting.

The suggestion restored some of Janice's equanimity. "Alexandra always is a little late," she admitted. "She'll probably be along any minute."

But half an hour passed . . . then an hour. Three times Mike phoned Alexandra's apartment. An answering service volunteered to take a message. He got coffee for them and they sipped it from paper cups, afraid to leave the area. At noon Mike said, "Look, honey, it doesn't make sense to keep waiting. We'll leave a message for Alexandra here and take a cab to her apartment. We can probably get the superintendent to let us in."

Alexandra lived in an apartment building bordering the Henry Hudson Parkway on 74th Street. She had a private entrance and a terrace. Janice described it to Mike in the cab. "It's just gorgeous. Wait until you see the views of the Hudson."

The decision to go to the apartment had obviously picked up her spirits. Mike nodded encouragingly when Janice said that undoubtedly Alexandra had gotten stuck on an out-of-town modeling job and had probably sent a message they didn't receive. But he had already sensed something could be very wrong.

When the cabbie reached 74th Street, Janice directed him around the back of the building where the private entrances faced the river. "Maybe she just got back from Europe and overslept."

When Mike rang the bell, a short, stocky woman opened the door. Her hair was tied in a knot at the top of her head. Her blue eyes flashed like searchlights anchored in her plump face.

"You've got to be the sister," she said abruptly. "Come in. Come in. I'm Emma Cooper." The housekeeper, Mike thought. Janice had talked about her. Last year when she'd been in New York to visit Alexandra, the housekeeper had been on vacation, so they had never met.

Janice hadn't exaggerated when she'd enthused about the apartment. Lime walls and carpeting made a subtle and elegant background for fine paintings and obviously expensive furnishings. Mike whistled softly. "Too bad you're so homely, honey," he said. "I'd send you out to model too."

Janice wasn't listening. "Where is my sister?" she asked the housekeeper eagerly.

A frown that might have been disapproval or worry added creases to the other woman's forehead. "I don't know," she said. "I know she got in Monday evening but she didn't come home and didn't call. She was looking forward so much to your visit and talked about nothing else. I don't know what she expects me to do. She redid the guest bedroom for you. The painter was here two days ago. 'Was this the right shade?' he asks me. What am I supposed to say? I told him to go ahead. She'll probably decide it's all wrong. Phone's driving me crazy. Every ten minutes it's been ringing. I stopped picking it up. Let the answering service have the job. Yesterday, Mr. Wilson, the agency guy, was practically shouting at me."

"You mean my sister arrived in New York three days ago and you haven't heard from her?" Janice demanded.

Emma shook her head. "She was due in from that Beauty Mask trip Monday evening. When that Wilson fellow called, he said that they all arrived on the chartered plane but separated at the airport. He told me Miss Alexandra was supposed to be driven home by the owner of the charter airline. He hasn't seen her since. Nobody has. Not that that's so unusual. Sometimes when Miss Alexandra has had enough of all the fuss, she takes off and gets a rest. One time it was to Cape Cod, another time to Maine. Then she shows up like it was yesterday she took off. A little inconsiderate when she's doing all this decorating."

Mike stopped the flow of words. "Is it possible Miss Saunders went on another job?"

Emma shook her head. "That Beauty Mask thing was all she was doing these past couple of months. Lots of pictures for magazines and them commercials."

"Has she been reported missing?" Mike asked.

Emma shook her head vehemently. "Course not."

"What are you trying to say?" Janice demanded.

"Nothing. I'm trying to say nothing. Please don't go 'round reporting Miss Alexandra missing. Like I said, she sometimes ups and takes off and no explanations given or asked. . . . She don't like anyone messing around her with questions."

Janice turned to Mike. Her eyes seemed even larger when they were frightened. "Mike, what should we do?"

"First, get the messages from the answering service. See who's been calling."

The answering service at first refused to give any information about Alexandra's phone messages. "Even though you are her sister," the authoritative voice of an operator said, "we always give the messages directly to her. She has told us never to give them to anyone else who claims to be calling in her name."

Mike took the phone from Janice's hand. "This is Alexandra Saunders's brother-in-law. She has not been heard from for three days and her family is terribly worried. Answer this, has she phoned in for her messages in these past three days?"

There was a pause. "I really don't know if we should share that information—"

Mike interrupted. "If you don't share it and if you don't give me what messages she received, I am an attorney and I will get a court order to get them. Miss Saunders is missing. Can you understand that? She is missing! I am calling from her phone. You can call me back to verify that I am in her apartment."

There was a notepad and pen by the phone. Less than a minute later he was jotting down names and phone numbers.

When he put down the phone, he said, "Grant Wilson called

on average three times a day. So did a Larry Thompson—about the same. And several calls from a Mark Ambrose. Most of the others seem to be invitations to charity dinners, salon appointments, etc."

Emma knew who the men were. "Grant Wilson. He's the owner of the Wilson Modeling Agency that books Miss Alexandra. Larry Thompson, he's the guy who does all those photo shoots and the commercials. Marcus Ambrose, he owns the charter plane service that took them over and flew them around in Europe."

"We'll start with Wilson," Mike decided.

"Don't worry about your bags," Emma said. "I'll put them in the guest room."

"I don't know what salary arrangements you had with Alexandra, but I want to make sure—"

"Don't worry," Emma interrupted, "I'm paid through the end of the month."

Twenty minutes later they were at the General Motors Building on Fifth Avenue. As they stood at the entrance, Mike looked at it appreciatively. "They were just building this when I was in law school."

Janice smiled forlornly. "When I was here six years ago, Alexandra took me to lunch at The Plaza." She stared at the impressive old hotel across the street. "It was such fun; celebrities kept coming up to our table."

Grant Wilson sat behind the massive desk in his corner office. The windows commanded a breathtaking panoramic view of Central Park. The office was furnished like a living room: deep blue carpeting, sofa and chairs covered in the same expensive brocade as the draperies; good paintings, a well-equipped bar, bookcases. It was the kind of office that signified top-of-the-ladder success in the Madison Avenue world. Grant had been successful. He'd come to New York twelve years before when he was twenty-eight. In those years he'd worked himself up to executive vice president in one of the most important modeling agencies in New York. Three years ago he'd opened his own agency.

Grant had a high-bridged nose, light brown eyes, the trim build of a man who works out frequently at the Athletic Club and a head of graying but abundant hair.

Right now he was badly frightened. He'd been at lunch at the Four Seasons. His meal had consisted of salmon with a salad and two gin martinis. The martinis were to calm his nerves. When he got back to his office, his secretary gave him several messages. The first was that Alexandra's sister and her husband were on the way to see him. What did that mean? He'd forgotten Alexandra had said her sister was married. He had thought she was some college kid. What kind of questions would she ask about Alexandra? How should he answer them? He'd tell her he couldn't understand how the hell anyone as familiar as Alexandra could just disappear. He'd say that you couldn't open a magazine without seeing her face. And all those guest appearances on Johnny Carson and Merv Griffin. Surely somebody would notice her somewhere. But she might as well have fallen through a crack in the earth.

There were other messages. Ken Fowler from Fowler Cosmetics, the company that owned Beauty Mask, had phoned three times. He still hadn't paid the last invoices they'd submitted. If they didn't immediately reshoot that last commercial in Venice, he would refuse to pay any of the outstanding invoices.

The intercom on his phone buzzed. It was the receptionist. "Mr. and Mrs. Broad to see you. Mrs. Broad is Alexandra Saunders's sister."

"I know who she is," Grant snapped. "Bring them in immediately." He slammed the phone down, rubbed his hands together to dry them and waited.

When his secretary came in with his visitors, Grant stood up, every inch the welcoming, gracious executive. He took both of Janice's hands in his. "My dear, I'd have known you anywhere. You're the image of your sister." Then he shook Mike's hand warmly.

He was, as a matter of fact, thrown off base by the appearance of the young couple. God knows what he'd expected—a pair of lunatic college kids with shaggy haircuts, flowers on their toes and granny glasses. But this Mike Broad was no lightweight kid. And as for the sister, he studied her carefully. What a knockout; not that ethereal look of Alexandra . . . more of a healthy kind of beauty. A bit taller . . . probably five or six pounds heavier but it looked good. He'd been warning Alexandra that you could overdo the stringbean look.

Janice was protesting. "Oh, I'm nothing like Alexandra. Well, there's just no comparison." Next to Alexandra's chiseled beauty she had always felt like a peasant. "Do you know where my sister is?" she demanded.

As she finished the question, she realized that simultaneously Grant Wilson had been asking one of her. He'd said, "I hope you're bringing news of Alexandra."

Grant studied the narrowing of Michael Broad's eyes, the crushing disappointment in the girl's face. He felt the muscles in his own throat constrict.

"Let's all sit down." He waved his hand toward the sofa. They sank into it and he decided to jump right into the subject they'd come to discuss.

"I'm not going to pull any punches," he said. "I'm worried about Alexandra. I wasn't at first . . . for reasons I'll explain. Quite frankly I thought it was just possible that she'd made arrangements to join you, my dear." He nodded to Janice.

Mike leaned forward. "Mr. Wilson, when was the last time you saw Alexandra?"

For an instant Grant had the feeling he was on a witness stand. There was something professional about the way the question came. He looked directly at Mike.

"Three days ago, on Monday evening, a group of us returned from Venice on a chartered plane. We had gone to Europe to do television commercials and photography for a very important new campaign featuring Alexandra. As you may know, Fowler is one of the largest cosmetic companies in the world, on the level of Elizabeth Arden and Helena Rubenstein. Beauty Mask is a new product of the company. Very simply, it's probably the most exciting new product in the cosmetic industry . . . which I might add is a multibillion-dollar business."

He nodded to Janice. "As this young lady will probably verify, some days a girl just doesn't look her best. She may have circles under her eyes from being out half the night or studying late, or she may have tension lines in her face. There are any number of creams on the market to hide those lines and shadows. Beauty Mask is different. It simply eliminates them. Facial masks are usually messy to put on and have to stay on for half an hour at least to be effective. Beauty Mask comes in a jar. You rub it on your face, as you would cold cream, and it hardens in seconds. Leave it on while showering, wash it off with warm water and a cloth, and your face will look as though you've spent a week at Maine Chance. I can't be sufficiently enthusiastic."

"But what has this to do with Alexandra?" Janice demanded.

Grant's tone suggested he was not used to being interrupted. "Very simply this. In an unusual arrangement, my modeling agency was chosen to provide the models and to oversee the implementation of the Beauty Mask introduction. We've prepared a saturation series of magazine ads and television commercials. The client deferred to my suggestion that Alexandra be the model for the entire campaign. In terms of television residuals alone, the booking is worth a fortune to her. However, because of the amount of money Fowler has allocated for this campaign, the Beauty Mask people are incredibly demanding. We've already had to redo several of the commercials at great expense. The one we just completed in Venice was quite difficult. We had weather problems . . . camera problems . . . and Alexandra just doesn't look that great in it. As a result, Alexandra was very tired and rather uptight when we got off the plane. I was rushing to a dinner engagement. My baggage came out first. I grabbed it and ran. When I heard she was missing, I thought she was someplace like Gurney's in Montauk relaxing for a few days. But I don't believe that anymore."

"What do you believe?" Mike asked.

Grant Wilson turned the paperweight on his desk. "I don't know. I simply don't know."

"How did you know she's missing?" Mike persisted.

"She was supposed to be at my office on Tuesday morning with the director of the commercials and the photographer to go over the footage but she never showed up," Grant replied.

Janice tried to keep her voice steady. "I understand you've left many urgent messages for my sister to phone you. Why?"

Grant's expression became grim. "Because the client has not approved the commercial we did in Venice. Because the great probability is that we'll have to redo it. Alexandra looked fabulous in the three other commercials, but she doesn't look that good in the final one. All the others are a buildup to it. That's why she can't look tired and drawn in it, when it's the climax of the Beauty Mask effect. We've got to reshoot immediately. Fortunately, we have enough Venice background that we can redo it in New York. The campaign is due to break in the August issue of *Vogue* and that will be published in a few weeks. We can't use anyone except Alexandra because she's in all the print ads and in the other three commercials. But the client insists that they okay the Venice one before they pay the final invoices. The progression of the publicity campaign has her photographed in New York, Paris, Rome and finally Venice."

"What will happen if you don't locate Alexandra in time to reshoot?" Mike asked.

Grant stood up. Unconsciously he was gripping the edges of his desk. "The client is threatening to scrap the entire campaign, to introduce its product for Christmas with a new agency and a new model . . . and in that case would refuse to pay us one cent more."

Mike stood up too. With one hand under her elbow, he drew Janice to her feet. "I think it's time we called the police," he said.

"You can't do that!" Grant said violently. "Do you realize what a scandal would do to this campaign? Can you see what Suzy or Rona Barrett would do in their columns with a juicy item like Alexandra Saunders being listed on a missing persons bulletin? As I told you, she has been known to disappear for a few days when she needed a break."

"If that is the case," Mike said slowly, "I would say that Alexandra will be showing up very soon. There's no doubt that she wanted to see Janice and was planning to be here to meet us."

"That remains the single shred of hope," Grant agreed.

"Then, against my better judgment, we'll wait another twenty-four hours before we call the police," Mike said, "but no more."

Janice thrust her hand out. "Good-bye, Mr. Wilson," she said, turning toward the door as she spoke. She desperately wanted to get out of this office. She wanted to be alone with Mike, to have a chance to think.

"My friends call me Grant." He attempted a smile. "I am very much in love with Alexandra and have been pressing her for some time to accept an engagement ring from me. She and I are right for each other. She has always said that she wasn't ready to marry. Frankly, I think your marriage might have started her thinking. I asked her again in London and in Venice. But that's another reason why I didn't worry too much when she bolted. I knew she'd want a little time to herself . . . to test her feelings. I honestly think this time she might be ready to say yes."

Mike said, "I see why you've hesitated to take action. Let's leave it at this. We're in Alexandra's apartment. Call us there if you learn anything or hear from her . . . and of course we'll do the same."

"Agreed."

They turned to go. For the first time Janice noticed that a large portrait of Alexandra was hanging on the wall by the door. She was wearing a pale green Grecian-style gown. Her long, blonde hair was hanging loosely to her waist. She looked enchantingly lovely. Grant studied it with them. "Alexandra posed for that several years ago. Larry Thompson took the pictures. He's a great photographer and a very good artist and drew this portrait from the stills he'd taken. He did one for himself. I saw it, and at my request, he did one for me."

Larry Thompson, the photographer. He was the next name on the list of people Mike and Janice had decided to see. He was the director who had filmed all the Beauty Mask commercials.

They said good-bye to Grant, walked down the long corridor and made a right turn toward the elevators. Mike stopped just as he was about to push the down button. "Honey, wait a minute. I just want to check something."

"What?"

"Nothing much. Be right back." He hurried back to the office they'd just left; the door was slightly ajar.

He could see Grant Wilson standing in front of Alexandra's portrait. With both hands he was grasping the frame. He was staring at Alexandra's face. Then with a gesture of futility he clenched one hand into a fist and slammed it against the wall.

Mike hurried back and rejoined Janice at the elevators. "What did you want to check?" she asked.

"I wanted to ask what exactly is the last date they have to reshoot the Venice commercial. But I decided not to ask him now."

As he took Janice's hand with a reassuring smile, he wondered what impression was seared most on his mind . . . the beautiful smiling face of Alexandra in the portrait . . . the face so like Janice's . . .

or the despair-ridden eyes of Alexandra's would-be fiancé as he stared at it.

Outside the building Janice expected Mike to signal for a cab. Instead he steered her across the street to The Plaza Hotel. "We haven't had any lunch. That pre-landing breakfast was pretty small," he said firmly.

An hour later they were reading the very small nameplate above the bell of Lawrence Thompson's 48th Street town house. Together they studied the exterior of the brownstone, noticing the graceful latticework around the windows and the small upstairs balcony which was bordered with geraniums.

"This is the Turtle Bay section," Mike told her. "One of the lawyers who lectures at Columbia has a place here. Only he's on the next block. Calls it mock Turtle Bay. This house would probably sell for twenty or thirty thousand dollars."

"I wouldn't be the buyer," Janice said. "I think it looks gloomy." She pushed the buzzer hesitantly. No one answered. After a moment she looked at Mike. He shrugged, turned the handle and opened the door. They went into a small, stark, untidy reception room. A rickety desk strewn with models' pictures was at an ungainly angle in one corner. Camp chairs stood folded against a wall. A few others had been opened haphazardly and were the only available seats. A large sign announced: MODELS ARE SEEN ONLY BY APPOINTMENT. PLEASE DO NOT RING THE BUZZER. LEAVE YOUR COMPOSITE. WE'LL CALL YOU.

Janice said, "I can tell you already I won't like Larry Thompson." Leaning over the desk she pressed the buzzer firmly. From inside somewhere she heard the faint sound that assured them it was working. Through thick double doors that led to the next room they could hear children shouting and a dog barking.

Minutes passed. No one came. "If at first you don't succeed,"

Mike murmured. He reached past her and firmly thumped the buzzer again.

One of the double doors opened slightly and a distracted-looking fortyish woman with large owl glasses poked her head through.

"For heaven sake, can't you read the sign?" she demanded. "Just leave your composites. We're in the middle of a shoot and no one's going to see you now."

"This is certainly our day for welcomes," Janice whispered.

Mike stepped forward. "We want to see Larry Thompson," he told the woman. "We'll wait till midnight if necessary. It has nothing to do with modeling."

The eyes behind the owl glasses narrowed thoughtfully as they looked at each of them and then fixed on Janice.

"You look familiar. Ever work for us?"

Mike said, "Please tell Mr. Thompson that Alexandra Saunders's sister is here to see him."

Even with the racket coming from behind the partly opened door, the woman's gasp was distinct. "I thought . . . You can tell." She looked at them shaken. "I'm Peggy Martin. Of course Larry will see you. We've been moving heaven and earth to find Alexandra. Look, why don't you just come in here if you don't mind and sit in a corner until we finish this blasted shoot."

She opened the door wider. "We're doing a floor wax ad and it took the whole damn morning to wax the set with the product. Then one of the kids spilled a bottle of milk on it before she was supposed to. The dog knocked it out of her hand and we had to start all over. Took two hours to redo the floor. . . . It was all gummy from the milk. We'd no sooner finished when the dog peed on it. God, what a day."

They followed her inside. The studio was a huge, cavernous room. At one end cameras were gathered around a simulated kitchen. Four little boys and three girls in rain gear and boots were scampering around the edge of the set. An energetic-looking Saint Bernard was racing back and forth, barking furiously.

Peggy waved them to chairs and hurried across the room. "Now look, kids," she said firmly. "Larry wants to get this shoot finished. Come on, all of you. Calm down!"

Four women were sitting in a corner near the cameras. One of them got up and started toward the children, a washcloth in her hand. From behind a camera a shout came. "What do you think you're doing, lady?"

The woman turned. She threw back impressive shoulders and jutted out her jaw. "Harold's face looks dirty. I thought I'd give it a wipe with the cloth."

Peggy blocked her way. "Mrs. Armonk, please. Harold is supposed to look dirty and muddy in this shot. The whole idea is that no matter how many kids or dogs come through your kitchen, your Superb-Waxed floor shines on. Which of course is a lot of hogwash. Look, why don't you and the other kids' mothers wait in the dressing room . . . all of you."

Disgruntled, the woman turned and Janice and Mike watched as she and her companions reluctantly went out a small door behind the set.

"Lights okay, Larry." A gray-haired man with a creased face and an eyeshade made the statement with resignation in his voice.

The camera was facing the set, and the man behind it was standing directly opposite Janice and Mike. He was wearing a sports shirt. Dark brown hair framed a classically handsome face. About six feet tall, he had a sinewy build that combined with a determined jaw to give an unmistakable impression of latent strength.

"Okay. Hey kids, no more horsing around. This time we're really going to get the shot. Now, all of you go over to the door, and when I yell, come running across the kitchen floor and make sure that mutt is on the side near the camera. Harold, you hold his leash. Kathy, you carry the milk bottle and don't drop it again."

"Okay, Larry." The chorus of treble voices sounded cheerful. For an instant there was dead silence, then one of the little girls called, "Larry, is it okay if I go to the bathroom first?"

"God . . ." the lighting man sobbed.

Larry climbed out from behind the camera. "Honey, if you just hold it for another five minutes, I've got a great prize for you, that teddy bear you like so much."

"Then I'll wait," she promised.

He squinted into the camera, made a tiny adjustment, then shouted, "All right, ready . . . RUN."

Shouting and pushing, the models ran across the set, the dog under their feet barking furiously. Janice and Mike watched as Larry Thompson repeatedly clicked the button in his hand.

"Great," he yelled, "you're great. Now come back from the other side. Faster. The dog . . . get him on your right, Harold. Kathy, drop the bottle now . . . okay . . . good . . . that's it. You're all swell kids. Now get out of here."

He turned to his assistant. "Remind me never to buy any of that lousy wax for myself, will you."

Mike leaned over to Janice. "Right now I'd like to be prosecuting a truth-in-advertising case."

Janice smiled fleetingly, then tensed. Peggy had gone over to Larry Thompson and was whispering to him.

It was interesting to Mike how the news that Alexandra Saunders's sister was present could make so many people so disturbed. Larry Thompson straightened up, glanced hurriedly in their direction and just as quickly turned away. He strode through another door out of the studio without looking at them again. Peggy Martin came back to them.

"Larry will be right with you. He's supposed to be at a meeting at the agency in a couple of minutes and has to make a phone call."

They watched as the model children came out from the dressing room. Peggy Martin hurried over to them. "Mothers, don't forget to sign releases," she ordered. "That will be for . . . let's see . . . what time were you booked . . . eight this morning . . . that's eight hours at thirty dollars an hour."

One woman said, "Scott's rate is forty dollars an hour."

"Yes," Peggy reminded her briskly, "but on this booking we set a limit of thirty because we knew it was going to be an all-day job. Check with your agent. She okayed it."

Then they were gone. As the children passed, they gave Janice and Mike a friendly wave. "Two hundred and forty bucks," Mike muttered. "I worked a construction job all week every summer through college and law school and thought I was a big deal making one hundred a week breaking my back. And they made that in eight hours . . . my God."

"Don't forget Scott's usual rate is forty an hour," Janice pointed out. "His mother's disappointed he didn't make three hundred and twenty."

Mike shook his head in disbelief. Peggy was hurrying back toward them. Without the children and the dog the huge room felt suddenly quiet and empty. She took off her owl glasses as she flopped in a chair next to them. "Your sister is one of my favorite people in this whole world," she said.

Janice leaned forward eagerly. "Do you know her well?"

"Oh, sure. Larry uses Alexandra all the time. He does loads of high-fashion ads as you may know. Now he directs a lot of television commercials. He's been going abroad with the Beauty Mask bunch, and Alexandra is their model for their big campaign. She is the nicest person. Most of the gals in this business who do well begin to take themselves too seriously, but not Alexandra. But where the heck is she now? I've got to warn you; Larry's doing a slow burn. They need to do a retake on the commercial they did in Venice. The client is screaming. Grant Wilson is a wreck. Larry's got a boiling point of minus two where work is involved."

Janice glanced at Mike. "I think we'd just be wasting Mr. Thompson's time seeing him. I was hoping he could tell me where my sister might be."

Peggy looked alarmed. "For Pete's sake, don't go until you've seen him. He'll have a fit. Let me check and see how long he's going to be."

As she reached for the extension phone, the intercom buzzer sounded. "There's Larry now." She spoke into the phone. "I'll send them right up."

"Larry's waiting," she said. "He lives on the upper two floors. Better take the elevator. The stairs are steep."

The elevator was in the foyer. They stepped into it and Peggy reached over and pushed one of the buttons. "I'm going to scram," she said. "This has been one hell of a day. Tell Larry he can get me at home if he asks you where I am. And give my love to Alexandra when you see her."

Larry Thompson finished the last of the sandwich that was his belated lunch. He braced himself as the whine of the elevator informed him that his visitors were on the way up. He was sitting in his study, and it was a far cry from the frenetic confusion of his studio below. Oak floors glowed with a soft patina. Dark brown bearskin rugs lay in front of the fireplace. Gothic windows opened onto the balcony. The massive armchairs had a Spanish motif. White walls served as a quiet background for oil and watercolor paintings. Most of them were Larry's own work. The one over the fireplace was of Alexandra.

The elevator stopped moving. The door slid open and the young couple stepped out. Larry felt as though he'd been hit by a thunderbolt. He'd hardly glanced at them sitting in the corner of the studio, but now he could see that this girl was breathtakingly like Alexandra. That hair, and those eyes and the straight nose . . . but there was a difference. She had more of a vibrant quality. Her skin tone was not better than Alexandra's, just different. They both were beautiful women.

Larry realized he was staring. He jumped to his feet. "I'm sorry. But when you think your eyes are playing tricks on you, it doesn't help your manners much." He extended a hand to Mike. "Larry Thompson."

Mike shook his hand. "Mike Broad. Janice Broad, my wife. Janice, as I guess you know, is Alexandra Saunders's sister."

Larry smiled tightly. "If I'd met her in Hong Kong, I wouldn't need to be told that." He motioned them to a seat.

Larry remembered Alexandra had said a few weeks ago that her kid sister was getting married. They would be on their honeymoon. Young love. And if they were real lucky, they might be happy a good six months, he thought bitterly. "Okay, what's the deal with Alexandra?" he demanded. He could swear the look on the girl's face was genuine. Sheer astonishment. The guy, Mike Broad, was cagey. His expression didn't change.

"What's that supposed to mean?" Mike asked quietly.

Larry realized his hands were clenched, almost into fists. He knew Mike Broad was scrutinizing him as though he were a bug under a microscope. What was he seeing? "It's supposed to mean that I assume you have some message from Alexandra . . . or at least know where she's hiding. . . . From all she's ever said about you"—he looked at Janice—"I know you're very close. Did she let you in on whatever is bugging her?"

Before Janice could answer, Mike asked, "Why do you think something was bugging her?"

Larry looked weary. "Mike . . . It is Mike, isn't it? I've known Alexandra for ten years, ever since she came to this town. The Dorothy Lohman Agency sent her to the studio where I was working, and I got the job of doing some test shots of her. I could tell she was lying when she said she had experience. I've always been able to tell when she's faking it. And I can tell you now that the last time I saw her in that airport three days ago I knew she was upset about having to do the retakes. She looked exhausted. If I'd had the brains to follow my hunch, I would have driven her home myself."

"Where do you think she went?" Janice asked, her voice rising.

"I thought she might have gone to a spa for a few days to get some rest and calm down. But that doesn't explain why she hasn't called anybody."

"But why would she run out on anything that important?" Janice sighed.

"Because she never should have accepted that booking in the first place," Larry snapped. "Fowler Cosmetics has a terrible reputation in the business. They offer big money, but they're never satisfied with the results. Then they pick a fight with everyone—agency, talent, production company, PR firm—everybody who is associated with the campaign.

"Alexandra was doing fine. She didn't need this job. It was all about Grant Wilson's ego and desire for big commissions. He strong-armed her into doing it. Because of the bad deal they agreed to, Grant Wilson and the ad agency will be paid only a fraction of the money they spent producing the commercials until they're all okayed. Now he's worried about losing his fees, to say nothing of the fact that Alexandra's reputation will be badly damaged if they dump the campaign.

"We've been given an ultimatum. Either we reshoot the last commercial or we forget the whole damn deal . . . and what's more, we have to do the shoot by next Monday. The one good thing is that we have enough background footage of Venice that we can finish it in New York."

"But Alexandra must realize that," Janice protested. "Don't you know her well enough to believe she'd never walk away from that responsibility?"

Larry stood up and looked at Alexandra's portrait. A moody frown creased his forehead. "I turned your sister from a high school kid from small-town USA into a top model. The first day I met her, she knew all the dumb tricks in the book and thought she was so smart. She still thinks she learned to pose in front of a mirror."

Irritably he turned the dial on the air conditioner. "I recommended her to editors. I took her around, introduced her to people, got her on the right accounts, kept her away from the sleazes, and she was doing great until . . ."

"Until what?" Mike asked.

"Until she got involved with the biggest sleaze of all, Grant Wilson. Three years ago her agent retired and Wilson persuaded her to go with him."

Janice sprang up. Larry Thompson's words seemed to be beating against the sides of her head. "We'd better go, Mike," she said. "It's obvious Mr. Thompson doesn't know where Alexandra is. It's equally obvious that although he's worked with her for ten years, he doesn't know that she's incapable of letting anyone down. She'd die rather than have that happen. We're just wasting our time here."

Larry Thompson reacted as though she had slapped him. "Perhaps, Janice," he said defensively, "the reason I choose to believe that Alexandra is deliberately staying away is because I don't want to face the alternative."

Janice's eyes widened. "What do you mean?"

"That's enough, Thompson," Mike snapped.

"It would seem obvious that you've just put your finger on what I mean if we accept the premise that Alexandra would rather die than let her friends down." Larry's expression changed, became bleak. His voice was suddenly husky. "I keep asking myself if there was any reason she was looking so exhausted, even unfocused, those last days in Venice. She looked terrible. A year ago some nut was stalking her. Leaving messages on her phone. Pasting notes on her front door. They never caught him. Was she afraid that he was shadowing her again? And if so, why in hell didn't she turn to me for help?"

Emma was just getting ready to leave when they arrived back at Alexandra's apartment. She looked at them and said, "You don't know where Miss Alexandra is." It was a statement of fact. After a brief hello to her, Janice headed to the bedroom. Mike suspected she was close to tears.

"Seems sort of foolish to come in every day when Miss Alexandra isn't here." Emma sighed. "But that's the way she wants it. Today I did all the windows and took the brass fixtures off all those tables and the desk and shined them up. They look real nice. Place always looks good. Then she has a party and some of those friends of hers . . . I'll tell you. Cigarette ashes all over and spilled drinks."

Mike studied the woman carefully. She'd obviously been trying to pass the working hours by doing unnecessary housework. He made his tone conversational. "I guess Alexandra has lots of friends," he said.

"Some might call it lots of friends. I call it a lot of leeches."

"Well, surely there are some close friends. . . . Grant Wilson?"

"He's a mean one."

"Mean?"

"Treats a person like dirt under the feet. Heard him tell Miss Alexandra she should have a bell to ring for me to come running. A bell. Bet the only bell he's used to is a cowbell. Comes from some hick town . . . so does Miss Alexandra. But at least she don't act like she was born in the White House. He's a phony."

"Who would you consider a close friend? Maybe someone she would turn to if she was upset?"

"Oh, let's see. She's got dozens of friends. The kind you read about in the gossip columns. But she wouldn't go to any of them, I don't think, with a problem. They're not the kind you tell your secrets to."

"Emma, think. There has to be someone," Mike insisted.

"Oh, sure, she has women friends—real friends. Why shouldn't she? But the one she was really close to . . . That would be Nina Harmon, and she got married last year and lives in London," Emma responded.

"There's no one else in particular?" Mike pressed.

"Let me think about it," she replied.

"Who else is here often?" Mike asked.

"Mark Ambrose. He owns that plane they chartered for all these Beauty Mask commercials they done this year. Fact he owns a bunch of planes. Has one of those charter airlines, it's called Executair. Miss Alexandra said he could probably buy and sell the lot of them. He's sweet on her, that's for sure. But she's not interested. At least if she is, I haven't noticed it. But on the other hand, you never know. Miss Alexandra is very private."

"How about Larry Thompson? Does he come here much?"

"Oh, he's around. They go out to dinner. What a good-looking guy! He used to be a child actor, you know. He's a funny one. Not a big talker but takes everything in. Looks bored when he comes to parties. Did a beautiful sketch of Miss Alexandra last year. Gave it to her. She started to rave about it. Then he said that he wanted to capture her before the wrinkles got too deep. She started to cry and threw it at him. Then he started making apologies. Said he was just teasing. That she had to realize he was just joking. He said, 'Just look in the mirror, for God's sake, Alexandra!' "

Emma shook her head. "Well, I'll see you tomorrow. You didn't say nothing about dinner. But if you want, I'll stay and fix you something."

Mike shook his head. "No. We'll be going out. Thanks."

After Emma left, Mike phoned Executair Airlines. The office was at Kennedy Airport. He was told that Mr. Ambrose would be returning from Chicago late that afternoon and would be in the office until between seven o'clock and seven-thirty. The receptionist was very definite that she knew Mr. Ambrose would want to see Alexandra Saunders's sister.

"We'll be there at seven," Mike said.

He went into the guest bedroom. Janice was lying on the bed. As he'd expected, her eyes were swollen with tears. She tried to hide them from him. He sat next to her and put his hand under her chin.

"Something in your eye?" he asked.

Her arms went around him as she threw her head on his lap. "Oh, Mike. Something's happened to Alexandra. You believe it too."

He bent down and kissed the back of her neck, then deftly unzipped her dress. Tenderly he massaged her back. "Baby, something's wrong, that's for sure. But it may be as simple as the fact that Alexandra took off because she's not sure about wanting to marry Wilson or that she's worried that she can't ever do that repeat commercial to the client's satisfaction. If we don't hear from her soon, as I said, we'll contact the police and report that she is missing. But in the meantime I want to see the guy who has been flying them around. According to Emma, he's pretty crazy about Alexandra. Maybe he can tell us something. We don't have to leave for the airport until six-thirty. But right now what you need is a shower and a nap and . . ."

Janice turned over and looked up at him. She smiled faintly. "And . . ."

Mike pulled her up. "Guess," he whispered, his lips against hers.

They drove to the airport in Alexandra's blue Lincoln convertible. Mike had talked the garage attendant in the building into letting them have it.

"You're very persuasive, Counselor," Janice said. "I never thought he'd give it to you." She sat very close to him.

Mike glanced at her. "You look good," he said. "I like that dress."

Janice looked down at the blue-and-green print. "It is pretty, isn't it? It's a Pucci. Alexandra sent it to me for Christmas. She told me she bought the same one for herself."

The airport had seemed huge to her that morning. Now, seeing the lines of passengers waiting to check in and the arriving passengers struggling to carry their heavy suitcases, and hearing the recorded announcements of flight arrivals and departures, it seemed to her like the hub of a private universe.

Mark Ambrose's unpretentious office was on the second floor of the main terminal. The receptionist at Executair Airlines, a woman perhaps in her late fifties with graying hair, introduced herself as Eleanor Lansing. "Mr. and Mrs. Broad . . . Mr. Ambrose just arrived. I'll tell him you're here. I know he's very anxious to see you."

Janice wasn't sure what she'd expected the owner of Executair Airlines to be like. Whatever her mental image, it didn't fit the man who strode into the reception room. Marcus Ambrose looked more like a bouncer at a bar than a pilot. His shoulders filled the doorway as he came through it. Reddish brown hair with a tendency to curl lay damp on his forehead. His eyes were dark brown and accentuated by heavy dark eyebrows. Separately, none of his features was outstanding. Together they formed a ruggedly attractive face.

His gasp was audible as he stared at Janice. His face paled and he came forward quickly. "For a minute . . . I thought . . . You're so like her. And that dress . . . It's hers, isn't it?" He grasped Janice's arms. "Where is she?"

"Take it easy," Mike said curtly. "You're hurting my wife."

"Oh." Slowly Ambrose released his grip. "I'm sorry . . . It's just . . ."

He suddenly seemed aware that the receptionist was staring at him. "Come inside." As soon as the door was closed to his private office, he turned to them. "Have you heard from her? Has she been with you? Do you know where she is?"

Wearily Janice stared at her hands as Mike explained Alexandra's failure to meet them. Like the others, Marcus Ambrose knew their arrival was expected and anticipated by Alexandra.

"I just can't figure it out," he said. "Everything was fine in London and Paris. Then in Venice trouble started. The first few days there was a lot of technical stuff to do—product shots, background, that sort of thing. Alexandra had a little free time. She and I went sightseeing together. She was in great spirits. Talking all the time about you two . . . how anxious she was to see her sister and meet the guy she'd married. I bet I could write your biography."

"How well do you know Alexandra?" Mike asked.

Marcus Ambrose smiled. "I've known her for a couple of years, ever since Grant Wilson started chartering one of my planes for his location shots. I piloted the flights myself and had such a ball that ever since I always keep those bookings for myself if I possibly can. And, I admit, for the past year Alexandra has been the real reason."

Another worshipper at the shrine. Janice wondered, with all the men who claimed to care for her, why would Alexandra have wanted to disappear?

Mike said, "Grant Wilson told us that while they were in Venice, he proposed again to her and he felt that this time she might be more receptive."

"I doubt that. She wouldn't be crazy enough to get stuck with that cranky, uptight jerk. But Alexandra was getting tired and she didn't photograph well the last few days."

"Were you at the shoots? Did you see her being photographed?" Mike asked.

"As a pilot, I have a lot of downtime. I enjoyed watching the shoots. She was on the set that last day and had to open that jar of Beauty Mask and start to smear it on her face. Well, they had her opening jar after jar. But when she took it off, they didn't get the effect they wanted and she started getting nervous. Then Grant Wilson and Larry Thompson started shouting at each other. Between them, they had Alexandra too upset to pose. Finally she just ran off the set."

Janice studied her nails. For the moment she simply didn't want to react emotionally to what she was hearing. Later on she'd think about Alexandra being screamed at by all those precious friends of hers who claimed to be so worried about her.

"What happened then?" Mike asked quietly.

"I followed her out." Marcus Ambrose pushed his chair away from the desk and stood up. The chair almost toppled backward. "I followed her out and caught up to her at the door. The poor kid had that slimy goo all over her face and she was trying to rub it off before it hardened." He winced as though distressed at the memory. "Larry Thompson was right behind me. He grabbed her arm, said something about finishing what she started. I told her to tell them to go to hell, but she just shook her head and went back into the studio. I took off. That night we all had dinner together. Alexandra didn't eat anything. Finally she got up and left the table. I went looking for her to see if she'd go out to the Piazza and have a drink. She liked listening to the violins there."

Janice said, "She'd written to me about St. Mark's Cathedral and the outdoor tables in the Piazza. Venice was her favorite city in Europe."

"I found her on the hotel steps with Wilson. I guess they'd been quarreling. She was saying that he must have known all along she was wrong for this Beauty Mask thing. He said something about wanting her to make the money . . . about a fortune in television residuals. They both shut up when they saw me. But the next day they did finish the last commercial, then we all packed up and boarded my plane early Monday morning. I could tell no one was happy about it."

"Did you talk to Alexandra alone at all after that?" Mike asked.

"Before we landed I had offered to drive Alexandra to her place. She said okay. . . . She seemed . . . well, distracted and preoccupied. When our bags came out I gave them to a porter. I wanted to check the office for messages. I told her I'd meet her in the terminal. I wasn't gone longer than ten minutes, but when I came back she was gone."

"She was gone!" Mike and Janice exclaimed together.

Ambrose frowned and shook his head. "I've been trying to decide if I should have gone to the police. And there's one more thing."

Janice stood up. She pressed both hands, palms flat, on his desk. "What else could there possibly be?" she demanded.

Marcus Ambrose strode over to the closet in his office. He pushed back the sliding door. Janice and Mike stared at the floor of the closet. Side by side, almost completely filling the available space, were two large blue suitcases engraved with the initials A.S.

"They were outside with mine in the terminal. The porter was waiting with them. She had told him that I'd be right down to collect them. And then she disappeared."

"It sounds as though she ran off in a panic," Mike said tersely, not wanting to look at Janice. "It may be that she just takes off sometimes and she was terribly upset about the commercials."

"And the other possibility is that she spotted paparazzi in the terminal and didn't want to be photographed," Ambrose said, a note of hope in his voice.

Alexandra's luggage in the trunk, they rode away from the airport in brooding silence. Janice sat rigidly straight, her hands locked together in her lap. Mike glanced at her, started to speak, then thought better of what he'd been about to say, that Marcus Ambrose looked vaguely familiar to him. That's impossible, he thought, and turned his full attention to the driving. The clouds that had been hovering overhead became a persistent driving rain that slapped against the windshield. Mike waited until they'd gotten well away from the airport traffic before he reached over and covered Janice's hands with his own.

She raised his hand to her lips and brushed it against her cheek. "Oh, Mike," she said. "I'm so scared. It's such a horrible night. I keep wondering where Alexandra is right now and imagining those people all trying to find her. They want her because she means money to them. They must have hurt her so much to make her just run away like that."

"Janice," Mike said. "Think carefully. How well do you really know your sister?" He felt her body stiffen. "Now, don't get mad. Think. You've got a preconceived notion of a sister who was the most important person in your world while you were growing up. Right?"

"Yes." Janice's voice was thoughtful. "Daddy was wonderful but remote somehow. You could never talk to him easily. For years after she left, Alexandra would phone once a week and I'd tell her all about school and everything I was doing. When I was in high school, all I had to say was I was going to a dance or a party and there would be a dress special-delivered in time for it. This is the last one she sent me for Christmas. She paid my way through college and paid all of Daddy's bills when he got sick."

She hesitated, then demanded, "Mike, what are you trying to make me say? I know you. You're getting at something."

Mike nodded. "Just answer me a couple of questions. What's Alexandra's favorite drink? . . . How much does she drink? Has she ever told you about any steady boyfriends? How much money has she got? Did she ever tell you she had a problem with a stalker last year?"

"She never even hinted it!"

"Well, that's my point. Honey, you see your sister as an all-generous, all-beautiful fairy godmother. You don't really know her as a person. From everything we heard today, I'd say she needs you badly."

They drove over the Throgs Neck Bridge, through the Bronx into Manhattan and down the FDR Drive in silence. Then Janice said, "There's just one thing I remember. When I was starting the spring semester this year, my tuition check was late. When Alexandra paid it, she sent me a note saying she was sorry it hadn't been on time but she'd been away and didn't have her checkbook with her. I didn't think anything of it then but now I wonder, could it have meant she was short of funds?"

"As soon as we get back to her apartment we'll go through her desk and see if we can find anything to indicate where she might have gone. Damn . . ." Mike suddenly reached up and adjusted the rearview mirror. "That idiot behind us has his brights on."

"Why doesn't he just pass?" Janice asked. She glanced over her shoulder, then cried, "Mike, be careful!" Through the now torrential rain, the lights suddenly weren't being reflected in the rearview mirror. The car that was tailgating them had pulled out and was weaving next to them, forcing them against the guardrail on the right side of the Drive.

Janice screamed.

A short distance ahead of them was the solid mass of a concrete stanchion. Mike wrenched the steering wheel to the left but the other car prevented him from turning. Their car hit the barrier head-on. The impact threw them forward, then back. Janice smashed her head against the windshield, then snapped back against the headrest. As she slumped down, she felt Mike reach for her, but it wasn't his voice that sounded in her ears as she drifted into unconsciousness. Instead it seemed that far off in the distance she was hearing Alexandra cry, "Janice, help me, help me."

Sirens . . . a light shining in her face . . . voices . . . "Mike."

"Just stay still, honey, don't move."

The feeling of being lifted out of the car . . . rain pelting on her face. The ambulance pulling away with the sirens screeching in her ears.

Mike was beside her. She tried to sit up and felt him gently hold her down. "Mike, are you all right?"

"Fine, honey. Just a few bumps. We need to get you X-rayed. That was a pretty hard bang your head took."

"Mike, I think that car tried to cut us off. I saw the way he turned the wheel."

"I think so too, honey."

"I'm not staying in a hospital. I'm all right."

"You won't have to stay unless it's absolutely necessary. I promise."

Janice felt the dizziness begin to recede. Her head throbbed violently and her back and neck were stiff. But she could think clearly. Had someone really tried to cut them off? Or was it a careless or drunk driver? Alexandra calling to her . . . She had to get to Alexandra's apartment. She had to go through her desk and try to find out where Alexandra might be.

But any hope she had of getting out of the hospital quickly was dashed. The emergency room doctor at Mount Sinai insisted on a complete set of head X-rays. It was a full two hours before she was told that she'd been lucky . . . she was all right except for a mild concussion. The doctor suggested she stay overnight in the hospital but agreed to let her go home as long as she promised to go directly to bed.

"She'll be very sore tomorrow," he warned Mike. "Incidentally," he added, "there's a policeman waiting outside who wants to talk to you. He has to make a report on the accident."

In the lobby the policeman asked Janice how she was feeling. "From the look of that car, it's a miracle either one of you is alive," he said. "We have the driver who sideswiped you. He was extremely intoxicated. When he wakes up, he will find out how much trouble he is in."

"I hope his insurance is up-to-date," Mike said tersely. He brought out his license and the registration, silently thanking the fates that Alexandra had kept the registration in the glove compartment.

"It's not only that he nearly killed us. This isn't our car. It belongs to my sister-in-law."

Mike hailed a cab outside the hospital. He opened the door for Janice before putting Alexandra's luggage, which the police had removed from their car, in the trunk. The rain had diminished and now it was a thin, chilly drizzle. Mike gave the cabbie Alexandra's address. The man was just starting to snap the flag down to begin the meter. When he glanced in the mirror and saw Janice, he spun around. He flipped the backseat light on and stared at her. "What's the matter?" Mike demanded. "Don't you know where that address is?"

The cabbie snorted. "Are you kidding, mister? I drove the young lady here only a couple of hours ago. Don't you remember me, miss?"

Janice gripped the seat. A wave of dizziness washed over her and she was afraid she was going to faint. "What did you say?" she demanded. To her own ears her voice sounded hoarse and strained.

The cabbie pulled away from the curb, then glanced into the rearview mirror. "Gee, miss, don't put me on. I even said how much I liked that dress and asked you if it was real expensive or would I be able to buy it for my wife, remember? You told me it was a . . . some foreign name."

"A Pucci," Janice whispered. "Alexandra," she said. "Mike, he must have driven Alexandra today. Remember I told you she bought the same one for herself."

"Where did you pick that woman up?" Mike demanded.

The cabbie sounded uneasy. "Wow, maybe I'm wrong. It's just you look so much alike . . . and that long blonde hair . . . and that dress . . . and you're going to the same place. Say, could you be related to her?"

Janice felt her knuckles whiten as she dug her nails into her palms. "Please," she said. "Please. Where did you pick up the woman who looked like me?"

"At Kennedy Airport. Tonight . . . around eight o'clock. I'd just dropped a fare off there and she hailed me. Was I glad that she was coming to my territory. Told her what a break it was for me. That's how we got to talking."

"Kennedy Airport," Janice said. "Could we have just walked past Alexandra? We were all there around the same time."

"Yeah. This lady asked me to take her to the address on Riverside. She looked all upset and worried, so I kept up a conversation. I'm kinda good at getting people to talk and relax. Anyhow, she said she was meeting two people on the London flight. They were supposed to come in at eight this evening from Europe but never showed. She told me she checked at the airline and found out that their flight came in at eight this morning."

"Eight this evening . . ." Janice felt giddy. She remembered that last phone conversation with Alexandra. Alexandra had been so distracted and upset about not making the wedding. Janice remembered how she'd repeated the airline and the time twice.

"Anyhow, she was rushing home to see if you were waiting at that apartment. Just dropped her off around nine o'clock. So you're the people from London. How about that? Wait till I tell the missus. Believe me, miss, New York is just a little town after all. I'm not kiddin'. There's more of this sort of thing than you'd guess in a hundred years."

Alexandra was home. Alexandra was home. She'd just been away and she'd come home in time to meet the flight that she'd expected Janice to be on. Janice felt hysterical tears of relief crowding her throat. She forced them back. Everything was all right. Everything was fine. In just a few minutes they'd be laughing about the mix-up. She leaned back and closed her eyes, aware of the throbbing in her forehead.

In less than fifteen minutes the cabbie said, "Here we are." He turned into the driveway and went around the building to the first private entrance. Two steps led to the enclosed terrace of Alexandra's apartment. When Janice looked up, she saw a light in the living room window.

She almost fell in her rush to get out of the cab. Mike caught her as she tripped. "Easy, honey." He paid the driver as Janice hurried up the stairs. She became aware of the ache in her back and shoulders.

The door of the apartment was locked. Impatiently she waited while Mike reached in his pocket for the key. He turned the key and opened the door. Janice rushed past him. She started to call Alexandra's name but it froze on her lips. From the foyer she stared into the living room. The lamp on the table next to the club chair was on and like a spotlight it illuminated the figure in the chair.

Alexandra was wearing the Pucci print. But she wasn't waiting for anyone. She was slumped back in the chair, her beautiful blonde hair tousled around her neck and shoulders, a narrow cord around her throat. Her face was white, thick chalk white. Little droplets of blood had dripped from her lips. Her huge blue eyes were open and staring at Janice . . . through Janice.

Janice opened her mouth to scream but no sound came. She tried to move but could not. She raised her hand to hide the nightmarish sight. But when she touched her forehead she vibrated to the soreness there and knew this was no dream. She felt Mike's arms go around her, but tore herself away from him. She began to scream, a shrill tearing sound as she stumbled across the room, threw herself down in front of the chair and reached up her arms to embrace her dead sister. The still warm body crumpled against her shoulder. As she screamed Alexandra's name, she was barely aware of Mike's strong hands grasping her fingers, forcing them open and half carrying, half dragging her out of the room.

"I'm so sorry, honey. You shouldn't touch the body. We have to call the police."

Hubert Twaddle, age fifty-two, a big man, stout without being fat, with a shining dome rimmed by mostly salt-and-pepper hair, was the head detective in the Manhattan District Attorney's Office.

He knew that his name, Hubert Twaddle, made the people he met for the first time try to conceal an involuntary smile. They didn't know that Twaddle was a familiar name in Scotland. Twaddle chuckled to himself as he recalled voting for Hubert Humphrey solely on the basis of their shared first name.

People didn't realize that by their inclination to smile, they were also psychologically relaxing. Hubert Twaddle found that fact enormously helpful when he was questioning a family member, friend, associate or enemy of a murder victim.

They had been called back to the office earlier that evening to interview a witness in a homicide case. Moments after they had finished, a call had come from the local precinct of West 74th Street at 11:30 P.M. Famed Alexandra Saunders, the beautiful fashion model, had been found murdered in her apartment.

Hubert Twaddle did not waste words. "I will be there directly," he said and hung up the phone. "Ben," he called to the younger detective, his partner, who always accompanied him on his cases.

Bennington Lyons sprang up from his chair. His desk was next to Twaddle's. He looked even younger than his twenty-nine years. He had bright red hair, a cherubic face and a gym-toned body. Already a legend in the department, he had been promoted to Detective second grade after having been shot and nearly killed when, in his patrol car, he'd come upon two longtime felons breaking into Tiffany's, the famed jewelry store on Fifth Avenue.

A bullet to his shoulder, another to his leg, lying on the sidewalk, he had returned fire, wounding both suspects, preventing their escape. Few besides Twaddle knew that Ben was the heir to the Lyons oil refineries and had been brought up on Park Avenue, gone to Harvard and gotten his master's at John Jay College.

To avoid the limelight he now lived in a rental apartment in Queens, happily pursuing his career in the police department.

Twaddle was sure that one day Bennington Lyons would be police commissioner.

When they arrived at Alexandra's apartment, they found that the medical examiner's van was already parked and a crowd was gathering outside the building. The doorman, his voice shaken, directed them to Alexandra's pied-à-terre. There, a policeman was outside, guarding the door.

When he saw Twaddle and Lyons he stood aside to let them in. Twaddle stepped forward, his eyes narrowed as they registered the crime scene. At least six policemen were in the room. Even so, it was eerily quiet. A police photographer was snapping pictures. The medical examiner, Milton Helpern, was bending over the figure of a woman leaning to one side in the large club chair.

Even Twaddle, as he came closer, was startled out of his usual calm when he saw that the victim's face was covered by a chalklike mask.

It was obvious that the knotted cord around the victim's neck was the cause of death.

"The lock on the door to the terrace was jimmied. My guess is the victim was sitting in this chair and may not have even heard the perpetrator come in behind her until it was too late. There is no sign of a struggle," Helpern said.

"When?" Twaddle asked.

"Not more than three hours ago. Maybe less."

"Who found her?"

"Her sister and the sister's husband. The sister went into shock.

They're in the guest bedroom. There's a doctor who lives in the building. He came up and gave the sister a sedative. The victim was supposed to have met them at the airport. I got that from the sister's husband."

Briefly he recounted what Mike had told him, including the fact that a cab driver claimed he had driven the victim home.

Ben voiced the thought that was on Twaddle's mind. "Then someone either followed her or was waiting for her."

Twaddle's eyes went from one end of the room to the other. Nothing seemed to be out of place. Under different circumstances he would have admired the tastefully furnished room, but now he was only looking for any sign of a struggle.

There was none.

The layout of the apartment was easy to perceive. The double glass doors led to the terrace where the killer must have waited for Alexandra. To the right he could see a small dining room and knew that the kitchen would be connected to it.

The hallway off the living room obviously led to the bedrooms. With Ben behind him, he headed there. They passed the master suite, then farther down the hallway, knocked on the closed door of the guest bedroom.

Mike, red-eyed from lack of sleep, opened it. For the second time in a few minutes Twaddle was startled out of his usual impenetrable calm. The slender young woman, blonde hair spilling on the pillow, her eyes closed, was wearing exactly the same dress as the victim. She appeared to be asleep.

In the next few minutes, with step-by-step clarity, Mike told Twaddle the events of the day, starting with Alexandra not meeting them, the answering service giving them the name of the three associates who had been frantically calling her, and the cab driver who claimed he had driven her home.

Finally Twaddle asked Mike how long he and his wife had been planning to stay in New York.

"We were to stay here with Alexandra for the next week," Mike said quietly.

"Are there any other relatives?" Twaddle asked.

"My family—by that I mean my parents, two brothers and two sisters in Brentwood, California. Janice's only relative was her sister."

"In that case, we will need you to stay here for at least a week. There will necessarily be an autopsy and we will need to question your wife in depth to learn anything her sister might have said to her that would have meaning to us."

Twaddle paused, then added, "The body will be moved in the next few minutes. My team will be finished processing the scene in about an hour. Do you plan to stay in the apartment tonight?"

"I hadn't thought about it," Mike said. "Our luggage is here." Unconsciously he blinked and rubbed his eyes. "We have just been in an automobile accident. It will be easier for my wife if we stay here."

"Mr. Broad, I won't trouble you anymore tonight. You are obviously very tired."

He turned and, Ben behind him, left the room. As he had expected, the body was in the process of being removed.

Ben had been making notes, as Twaddle, in a gentle voice continued to zero in on the sequence of events as dictated by Michael Broad.

Ben was a faithful follower of the *New York Post*, which not only had an excellent business section but also kept him *au courant* of the news on current celebrities, some of whom his playboy cousin knew intimately, though Ben avoided personal publicity like the plague.

The minute he heard the name Alexandra Saunders, he remembered that about five years ago, his cousin had dated her briefly and had a serious crush on her, but she had given him the brush-off.

Ben remembered he had thought that she was one smart lady.

Emma Cooper arrived at the apartment, her face already settled in lines of grief. She realized she had inadvertently reached into her pocketbook for her key.

"I'm the housekeeper," she told the patrolman at the door. "They sent for me."

Bracing herself, she was about to go in when she had to step aside. A gurney with a body bag on it was being rolled out of the apartment.

Her mind filled with visions of beautiful Alexandra and the three years she had worked for her. It had started when Alexandra bought this apartment.

Alexandra had been twenty-five then and had just signed her first major modeling contract, to be the spokesperson for a perfume company. Her old agent had retired and she had gone with the Wilson Agency. That Wilson fellow had been around all the time, meeting here with the decorator, telling Alexandra that he'd make the final decision on the décor—that she had no experience with choosing furniture and wall covering and carpeting.

Alexandra had clearly been in awe of him. But after he left, she had asked the decorator to stay. "Tell me where you think he's wrong," she had asked him.

"I think that you would want some antique accessories but a comfortable couch and chairs."

"You're absolutely right," Alexandra had said.

Emma knew that day that, mingled with her insecurity, Alexandra could be bossed around only to a certain point. Was that what had happened here?

Why am I thinking that? she asked herself. Unable to resist the temptation, she touched her hand to the body bag, ignoring the disapproving expressions of the cops pushing the gurney.

The living room seemed filled with policemen. But it was the man who stepped forward to greet her who commanded her immediate attention.

There was a sympathetic expression on his face and a gentleness in his tone when he said, "I am so sorry about this, Mrs. Cooper. Why don't you step into the dining room with me? We can sit and talk without interruption. I am Detective Hubert Twaddle."

My God, what an awful name, Emma thought, forcing back an inadvertent smile. Beyond her shock and grief she steeled herself to be questioned about Alexandra.

Before Twaddle's hand under her arm guided her into the dining room, she absorbed the reality of that fine powder over Alexandra's favorite chair and the fact that the door to the terrace was open.

"I got a call saying that she was dead," Emma said, her voice a whisper, still unbelieving. "I saw her body being wheeled out just now."

"I know," Twaddle replied as he pulled out a chair for her at the dining room table.

"Somebody killed her, right?"

"Mrs. Cooper, wasn't that your first question when you were called to inform you about Miss Saunders's death?"

Emma realized that someone else was entering the room, a boyish-looking younger man with red hair. He was carrying a glass of water and placed it in front of her.

To her satisfaction, he was carrying a coaster to put under the glass. Nothing bothered her more than when a slob of a guest set a glass down on this table and the ones in the living room. They ought to know better, she thought, when they're putting stuff down on a valuable antique table.

Why was she thinking that? she wondered. Oh, Miss Alexandra . . .

"Let me introduce Detective Ben Lyons," Twaddle was saying. "If you don't mind, he will be taking notes of our conversation."

Emma nodded. "Okay."

The questioning began.

Emma did not know that everything she said was being compared with what she had told Janice and Michael.

"When were you expecting Miss Saunders to be home?" Twaddle watched closely as a momentary look of irritation crossed Emma Cooper's face.

"Last Monday. Now, I know these—shoots, they call them—can take a couple of days or a week. Usually it's quiet when she gets back from a big job. She was supposed to get back Monday night. But this time the phone never stopped ringing on Tuesday. Everybody who was on the plane with her was looking for her."

"Weren't you afraid that something might have happened to her?"

"Only yesterday I started to worry. It wouldn't be the first time Miss Alexandra skipped town after she finished a hard job."

"You used the word 'hard,'" Twaddle said.

"Yes, I did." Emma's voice became steely. "That Grant Wilson is a mean one. Alexandra's his top model but she didn't want to do that Beauty Mask job. She hated to put that stuff on her face. She said it felt like putting on one of those masks they used to make impressions of dead people's faces."

"She said that?" Twaddle asked calmly.

"Yes. I could see why she might want to get out of town, but at first I thought it was rude not to call me. It made it real tough for me what with the painter coming and making me say yes to the color. But when she was a no-show to meet her sister, I thought that don't sound right."

"Did you know that she left the airport without her luggage?"

"No one told me that! Why would she do something like that?" Emma demanded.

"From what her sister was told by Mr. Ambrose, he had run up to check his office. Miss Saunders was to wait in the terminal for a few minutes. When he returned, he found the porter with both his luggage and hers. She had tipped the porter generously to wait with it."

"That don't make sense," Emma said flatly. "She must have had a good reason to just run away like that."

Hubert Twaddle nodded. "Mrs. Cooper, you are a very observant woman and you obviously dislike Grant Wilson. Tell me more about him."

"Bad tempered. A bully."

"If this is true, why would Miss Saunders have continued to work for him?"

"I think it's 'cause he has the biggest modeling agency and gets his people the best jobs."

"How well do you know Larry Thompson?"

"Oh, he's her favorite photographer. He's a hard one to figure out. He kind of sits back and takes everything in, if you know what I mean. I know he had a hard time for a while. He and his wife split up. Then she got sick and they got back together. She died last year. But if you ask me, he's another one who is sweet on Miss Alexandra. But then they all are."

"Have you ever met the pilot of the plane, Marcus Ambrose?"

"Oh, he's been around. He calls her a lot."

She frowned and bit her lip. "There's one thing you probably already know because we spoke to the cops about it. Miss Alexandra had someone stalking her last year. He'd leave creepy messages on the phone saying how much he loved her. Then he pasted notes on the terrace door at night. It was scary. The calls and notes just stopped. They never found him."

"Mrs. Cooper, thank you. You've been a great help. Those young people are resting in the guest bedroom. By now the police will have completed this phase of the investigation. May I suggest that you tidy up the living room and, late as it is, prepare a light snack for them? From what Michael Broad told me, they have not eaten since lunch."

Emma sprang up. "Happy to help. When you think that poor girl is still on their honeymoon . . ." Obviously grateful to be able to take some action, she got up and with purposeful steps left the room.

Twaddle had stood up with Emma. He waited until she was out of earshot, then said, "We will interview the building employees who were on duty. I suspect they will not be able to tell us anything. The door to the back terrace cannot be seen by the doorman. Tomorrow morning we will interrogate the three men who seem to be most closely involved with Alexandra Saunders: Grant Wilson, Larry Thompson and Marcus Ambrose."

Friday

Grant Wilson lived on Fifth Avenue, in the apartment house next to the one where Jackie Kennedy had moved shortly after her husband's assassination. It gave him a secret thrill to occasionally leave it at the same time she was leaving hers and have a chance to wish her a pleasant day.

It had just happened this morning, and he was savoring the memory of the glamorous former first lady as he started his mile-and-a-half walk to the office. Then he was stopped by the doorman running after him to say that two detectives from the District Attorney's Office urgently needed to see him.

His mouth suddenly went dry with fear. He turned. They were

standing at the entrance to the apartment building. Not wanting to say anything in the presence of the doorman, Wilson invited them up to his apartment before he demanded to know why they were there.

Before they had a chance to answer, he burst out, "It can't be that something has happened to Alexandra?"

Hubert Twaddle had already wondered if this might not be the response from the head of the modeling agency. After all, Wilson's star model had been missing for three days. He had left countless messages begging her to be in touch and reminding her that the Beauty Mask campaign was in jeopardy. Now, seeing the sudden pallor that came over Wilson's face, Twaddle concluded that the man might be genuinely afraid of what he might hear.

"Clearly you have not heard the news, Mr. Wilson," Twaddle said. "Miss Alexandra Saunders was murdered in her apartment last night."

Wilson sank into a chair and buried his face in his hands. "Not Alexandra," he said, his tone unbelieving.

For the next hour, step by step, Twaddle and Ben Lyons heard from Grant Wilson the same story they had heard from Michael Broad. Alexandra had not been seen since Monday night when their chartered plane had landed at Kennedy Airport. Wilson had been in constant touch with both Larry Thompson, the photographer, and Marcus Ambrose, the owner of the charter airline, as to where Alexandra might have gone.

"Where were you last night from seven o'clock on?" Twaddle asked.

"I was at a black-tie dinner at the Lotos Club. It's on 66th Street just off Fifth Avenue."

"Were you there all evening?"

"Yes, of course. It began at six-thirty."

"What time did you leave?"

"When the dinner was over, about ten o'clock. I went directly home from there."

Ben knew what his partner was thinking. If Wilson had left the Lotos Club around 10 P.M., he had plenty of time to go to Alexandra's apartment around the time of the murder.

"Do Thompson and Ambrose know about Alexandra's death?" Wilson asked dully.

"I do not know if they have heard it on the news," Twaddle answered. "If they haven't, they will hear it from me very soon."

Larry Thompson had a late breakfast meeting with an account director of Lehman Advertising Agency and his two assistants. Over eggs Benedict, coffee and cigarettes they informed him that he had been chosen to be the producer of a series of commercials for the most popular breakfast cereal in their client's array of products. It would be a lucrative engagement for Larry except for the fact that all the commercials would involve having young child actors in them. Thinking of the chaos of yesterday's shoot, he knew it would be a difficult assignment but career enhancing.

He also knew that for the money he would be getting it would be worth it. Even so, Larry was barely able to contain himself as the account director and his assistants decided to again refill their coffee cups.

Had they found Alexandra? he kept wondering. When would they find her? It was a question that haunted him as he said a final good-bye to the agency men and took a cab to his townhouse on East 48th Street. At the front door, he found a note taped to the doorknob. Detective Hubert Twaddle requested that he phone him immediately.

It was a warm morning, but even so, as Grant Wilson had earlier, Larry found himself breaking into a cold sweat. Impatiently he turned the key in the lock and, not waiting until he went up to his apartment, grabbed the phone in the studio and dialed the number on the card.

Unable to reach either Thompson or Marcus Ambrose at home, Hubert Twaddle and Ben Lyons had returned to their desks in the detective section of the District Attorney's Office. Ben studied Twaddle's face as he told Thompson that Alexandra Saunders was dead. But, as usual, neither by voice nor demeanor did he give Ben the slightest hint of what kind of reaction he was getting from Thompson. It was the kind of inscrutable expression that Ben wanted to develop for himself.

"We will be at your studio in twenty minutes," Twaddle concluded, and hung up the phone. He turned to Ben.

"A second grief-stricken and shocked associate of Miss Saunders. This one claims he was home all evening," he said dryly. "Now, since Mr. Ambrose's secretary has just left word that he will be in his office at one o'clock, we will go directly to Kennedy Airport after we see Mr. Thompson. The Medical Examiner's Office said that the autopsy will be completed and the body ready for formal identification by three o'clock. We will pick up Miss Saunders's sister and brother-in-law at two-thirty. And now let's pay Mr. Thompson a visit."

Larry Thompson's assistant, Peggy Martin, came to work at 10:30 A.M. happy in the fact that it was going to be a normal business day. Not that yesterday's models had been bad kids. It was just that Kathy dropping the milk bottle too soon had caused a delay while they cleaned and rewaxed the floor.

Peggy went inside and to her surprise found Larry sitting by the phone in the studio, his hand still on it. For a moment she thought he might have had a stroke. She rushed over to him and shook his arm. He turned to look at her, his eyes staring. He said "Peggy" tentatively, as though he wasn't sure who she was.

"Larry, what's the matter?" Peggy demanded.

"Alexandra is dead," he said, his voice a monotone. "Peggy, Alexandra was murdered last night."

"No, that's impossible," Peggy said, then recognized the futility of her words. She realized that there was nothing she could say to him now. Instead she took the phone from Larry to call the modeling agency and cancel the afternoon booking.

"Peggy, that's going to cost Larry plenty," the agent said. "When you don't give twenty-four hours' notice, you pay full rate."

"So bill us," Peggy snapped and slammed down the phone. She turned to Larry as the buzzer sounded. She rushed from the studio through the foyer and opened the door. Two men, their expressions hard to read, were standing there. They wasted no time on pleasantries.

"We are Detectives Twaddle and Lyons," Ben said. "We are here to see Mr. Thompson."

Peggy led them into the studio and placed two folding chairs across from where Larry was sitting.

"I'll be right outside if you need me," she said, her eyes now filling with tears.

Larry Thompson did not greet them. Twaddle told him who they were as he scrutinized Larry's expression. Before they began to question him, Larry said, "You told me Alexandra was murdered. How?"

"Miss Saunders's body was found in her apartment. We are speaking to anyone who might have seen or spoken to her Monday evening. Was there anything unusual in her mood or behavior after she got off the plane?"

"At first I thought that the strain of the Beauty Mask campaign had gotten to be too much for Alexandra. But when I heard that she didn't meet her sister's plane yesterday, I couldn't believe it. She talked about nothing but how much she wanted to see her and meet her new husband. When she didn't come to the airport, I knew something was terribly wrong."

"Did you see or hear from Miss Saunders after leaving the airport Monday evening?"

"No, I did not."

"Where were you last evening starting at seven o'clock?"

"I was home by myself."

"Did you to speak to or telephone anyone from seven o'clock on?"

"No, I didn't. We'd had a rough day on the set and I was worried about Alexandra. I wanted to be here in case she phoned." Then he burst out, "Have you any idea who could have done this to Alexandra?"

"Not yet," Twaddle told him. "But I assure you we will soon."

He got up and Ben followed suit. "We will be in touch with you, Mr. Thompson," Twaddle said. As they walked to the curb and got in the car, Twaddle commented, "Such a splendid performance from a former child actor. But no supporting cast to verify that he was home last night."

Promptly at one o'clock Twaddle and Lyons arrived at the Executair Airlines office at Kennedy Airport. As they took in the décor of the reception area, their thoughts were interchangeable. One didn't need a decorator's eye to see that every piece of furniture—the desk, chairs, bookcases, filing cabinets—had been ordered from a catalog. There was not a single picture on the walls. The thin, faded blue carpet was of the indoor/outdoor variety. Certainly any profits from this airline were not wasted on frills.

Ambrose's secretary, Eleanor Lansing, had an anxious expression on her narrow face. Mr. Ambrose was on a long-distance call, she told the detectives, and would they mind please having a seat. As

Twaddle and Lyons waited, they heard Miss Lansing answering inquiries on the phone. She ended each conversation with the same tagline: "We have a perfect safety record." In between calls, Twaddle attempted to engage her in conversation and learned that Marcus Ambrose had started the business six years ago. There were six other pilots and yet it was Ambrose's hobby to frequently take the controls himself when interesting people booked a charter.

"Wasn't it awful about that beautiful model, Alexandra Saunders, who was murdered?" She sighed. "I heard it on the radio when I was having lunch. She was part of a group that regularly chartered our planes . . . just shows you never know.

"I never met her. I wish I had. Someone else made all the arrangements for that trip. The charter Miss Saunders was on was booked by the Wilson Modeling Agency."

The door of the inner office opened. Ben was sure Twaddle would have loved to continue talking with Eleanor Lansing, even though he would never give the slightest hint of disappointment that a conversation was over. Instead, Twaddle rose to his feet and solemnly acknowledged the muted greeting from Marcus Ambrose. The man's face was flushed, his eyes were half-closed and his hand was trembling when he extended it.

Ambrose's private office had been furnished with the same disinterest as the reception area. He waited until he'd closed the door before turning to the detectives and asking, "Do you know who did this to Alexandra?"

"The investigation into her murder is continuing. We are trying to discover where Miss Saunders might have gone when she left the airport on Monday evening," Ben replied.

"I had offered her a ride home and she accepted it. But then after I stopped here for ten minutes, I returned to meet her at the terminal, in the arriving passengers area. She was gone."

For the next half hour Twaddle and Ben repeated the questions they had asked earlier that morning. Ambrose's statements were identical to those he had given to Mike and Janice. He had been at the filming of the final commercial in Venice. Alexandra neither looked nor felt well.

"Do you have any idea why she would have left the airport without taking her luggage?" Twaddle asked.

"I thought she might have seen one of the paparazzi and didn't want to be photographed looking the way she was. She certainly knew I would take care of her luggage."

"Were you and Miss Saunders personally involved?" Twaddle asked.

"I only wish. I won't deny that I was trying, and as I told her sister, in her free time we did some sightseeing together and I was beginning to think she enjoyed being with me."

Fifteen minutes later when Hubert Twaddle and Ben Lyons were in the car, Ben volunteered, "I don't think we got very much out of that interview."

"Let us not be too sure of that," Twaddle answered. "But I believe the background investigations of Mr. Wilson, Mr. Thompson and Mr. Ambrose may make very interesting reading when we get back to the office."

Even though Emma had prepared scrambled eggs for them after the police left last night, Michael had decided not to awaken Janice. He had covered her with a blanket and let her sleep through the night.

At nine o'clock on Friday morning she opened her eyes and then closed them again. She had had a nightmare. In it, Alexandra had died. No, she had been murdered. And her face was covered with chalk—no, it was a beauty mask.

It wasn't a nightmare. It had happened. Alexandra was dead. "No, no, no," Janice murmured. She looked up. Mike was sitting on a chair next to the bed. "Who?" she demanded, anger in her voice.

"Janice, we don't know yet. But I believe the detectives who were here last night will find some answers for us."

"Where is Alexandra's body?"

"The medical examiner took it."

"They'll do an autopsy, won't they?"

"I'm afraid that's necessary." Mike was tempted to say, "Try not to think about it," but did not. Of course she was going to think about it. Of course she was going to grieve for her sister.

As she had promised, Emma Cooper had arrived to make breakfast. She could be heard moving around in the kitchen. The living room was in perfect order, except for the armchair that had replaced the one where Alexandra's body was found. The police had taken it as evidence.

Emma had explained that to Mike last night. "It looked so empty here without that chair where . . ." She did not finish the sentence. "I brought in one from the dining room."

Mike opened Janice's suitcase and took out her warm bathrobe. He realized that she was still wearing exactly the same dress that Alexandra had been wearing when she was murdered, that it was bound to be a fresh shock for her. He helped her to slip it off then replace it with her robe.

It was like dressing a child. She stood mutely as he tied the sash around her waist and put her bedroom slippers on her feet. Then, his arm around her, they went into the kitchen, where Emma had the table set and an omelet bubbling in the pan.

The comforting scent of brewing coffee welcomed them as they sat down. "I hope you had as good a sleep as you could get," Emma said.

"Yes, I did," Janice murmured, her voice composed but filled with sadness. They ate silently, grateful for the food but still overwhelmed by what had happened only hours ago.

After breakfast they went back to the bedroom, showered and dressed. At ten-thirty Twaddle phoned. "The autopsy has been completed," he said. "I will pick you up at two-thirty and take you to the Medical Examiner's Office."

As the hours passed, Mike could see that Janice was on the verge of losing the fragile composure she had managed to display. By the time the detectives arrived, silent tears were running down her cheeks. In the car on the way over, Twaddle asked only one question. "Did your sister always wear a wig?"

Startled at the question, Janice said, "I know she has a collection of wigs. She wrote to me about them. She said that they were great for when the weather was bad and her own hair got too curly."

"I see."

They did not speak again until they got out of the car in front of the grim-looking building on East 30th Street that was the Medical Examiner's Office. They walked through the sterile lobby and were taken to the morgue. Mike felt Janice begin to tremble as they approached a gurney with the outline of a body visible beneath a sheet.

Taking care to be certain that Michael Broad was holding his wife tightly, Twaddle lifted the sheet from the victim's face. He had expected anything from an outpouring of grief to watching Janice crumple in a faint. He had not expected to hear a shriek and then hysterical sobs of relief as Janice screamed, "THAT'S NOT MY SISTER. THAT'S NOT MY SISTER!"

For a moment Mike and the two detectives thought that Janice was in denial, but then through her sobs they could make out what she was saying. "Alexandra has natural blonde hair. It's as long as the wigs she wears. I don't know who this is. I don't know who it is. But it isn't Alexandra. Thank God, thank God it isn't Alexandra."

The detectives leading, Mike half led, half carried Janice to the medical examiner's offices. There they waited while she managed to calm herself as she alternated between relief and panic that Alexandra might have been murdered as well.

Twaddle did not try to soften what he needed to say. "Mrs. Broad, it seems almost certain that this young woman was murdered by mistake because the killer thought she was your sister. What we don't know is whether the killer realized he had made a mistake before he left the apartment.

"The question is why would this woman, who dressed to appear like your sister, have gone to the airport, according to the cab driver, expecting to meet you."

Twaddle continued. "Would your sister, or for that matter any woman, be likely to have applied the Beauty Mask after she was fully dressed?"

"Of course not," Janice said. Alexandra is alive. Alexandra is alive, she wanted to shout out, but then became terrified as the conversation continued.

"Then we must assume the killer applied it, probably to delay our investigation, if only for a short time," Twaddle said, and then he continued.

"And there is one other very disturbing aspect. What would be the killer's next move if he realizes that the woman he killed was not your sister?" Twaddle paused.

"So you are suggesting that whoever murdered this woman, if he realized his mistake, since last night has been out there searching for Alexandra or—" Mike stopped before he said what they were all thinking: "Or may have already found Alexandra."

"That is what I am telling you. Mrs. Broad, did your sister mention a close friend in any of her letters to you?"

Janice shook her head. "No one whose name came up enough for me to really notice."

"Then we must talk immediately to the housekeeper again. Would she be at the apartment?"

"She was planning to stay until five."

The answering service picked up on the first ring. Twaddle instructed them to let the call ring through to the apartment. "If she doesn't pick up, we'll phone the building superintendent and get him to knock on the door."

But Emma Cooper answered the phone. When Twaddle identified himself, she asked anxiously, "How is Miss Janice, poor thing? I've been praying for her all afternoon. To think of her having to look down at Miss Alexandra's dead body."

"Mrs. Broad is doing very well under the circumstances," he said, "but now it is important to our investigation to know where Miss Saunders was staying since Monday. We need you to give us the names of close friends of Miss Saunders, either male or female."

"Male, I'd say no one close. Sure, she has a lot of girlfriends. What with her being so nice and friendly and kind."

"Mrs. Cooper, can you give us some names?"

"Let me see. Her address book is here."

Ben knew that when Twaddle bit his lip he was wildly impatient. But then he began to write names on the pad he always carried, repeating them as he wrote, "Joan Nye—Lee Rush—Irene Brady—Alice Kohler—Lisa Markey."

"Mrs. Cooper, this is very helpful. Which of these women most resembles Miss Saunders in appearance?"

On the other end of the phone Emma Cooper frowned. "Well, let's see. There's Joan. She's a television producer. She's shorter than Miss Alexandra and her hair is real dark. Miss Rush—" Emma interrupted herself, "Oh, of all of them I'd say Miss Markey. She's a model too. Sometimes she wears a blonde wig in her pictures. When she does, she sure looks like Miss Alexandra. Looks like her but not anything as gorgeous as Miss Alexandra—"

Twaddle cut off the flow of words. "Mrs. Cooper, do you know if Miss Markey worked at the Wilson Agency?"

"No. She worked for the Ford Agency. She was always telling Miss Alexandra to dump Wilson and sign up with Ford. Oh, and I should tell you I was cleaning out the medical chest in Miss Alexandra's bathroom. I swear there were two unopened jars of Beauty Mask there. Now one of them is gone."

"Mrs. Cooper, thank you very much. We will pick up the other jar. And I must tell you something in deepest confidence. The following is information you cannot share with anyone. The body that was found in the apartment was not Alexandra Saunders."

He heard a gasp on the other end of the phone. "Oh, thanks be to God."

Twaddle continued. "Mrs. Cooper, again it is crucial to our investigation to know where Miss Saunders has been staying since Monday. If you hear from her, you must notify us immediately."

"Of course I will," Emma said. "Thanks be to God."

Twaddle broke the connection. Without looking at the others in the room, he dialed information and asked for the number of the Ford Agency. When he inquired about Lisa Markey, he was put through to her booking agent. In an irritated voice the agent told him that Lisa had not arrived this morning where she was scheduled to pose for the fall line of a designer. "Do you know where I can reach her?" she asked.

"I'm afraid not," Twaddle said.

He hung up the phone and looked at Janice, Mike and Ben.

"I believe it is possible we have learned the identity of the young woman who was murdered last night," he said.

On Friday morning in Windham, New York, a popular Catskills ski resort, Alexandra stirred, then opened her eyes. She blinked to orient herself. She looked at the clock and was shocked to see that it was almost noon.

She sat up and swung her legs to the floor. Her long blonde hair spilled around her shoulders and she brushed it away from her face. She stood up and reached for the robe she had borrowed from Lisa. Putting it on she realized that this was the day she would finally see Janice and Mike. Lisa had promised to pick them up at the airport last night, take them to the apartment, and tell them to meet Alexandra up here. How great it would be to see them and meet Mike! They probably slept late because of the time difference between New York and London. They should be here by mid-afternoon.

I want to tell Mike what's been happening to me. From everything Janice has written and said about him, he'll make sense of what's been going on. I just don't trust myself anymore.

She walked unsteadily the few steps into the hall to the only bathroom. She turned on the light and looked into the mirror over the sink. She studied the face staring back at her. Her skin that had been pasty gray and blotchy when she was in Venice had now fully returned to its normal healthy glow. It was in her eyes that she saw the greatest change. They had been so heavy-lidded and dull but were now completely clear. Alexandra remembered that only a few months ago a gossip columnist had referred to them as "intensively blue and unforgettable." I look like myself again, Alexandra thought. I could redo that commercial in a heartbeat. The only difference, she realized, was the feeling of fatigue she had not been able to shake off since she had been in Venice. I need a cup of coffee, she thought.

When she had fled to Lisa's apartment on Monday evening, it wasn't necessary to explain that she wasn't well. Lisa had taken one look at her and said, "What's the matter with you? You look terrible."

Alexandra had told Lisa that she just needed to get away from the pressure. "Damn this Beauty Mask booking," she had told her. "I know they'll want to do retakes quickly and look at me."

She walked into the small rustic living room/den, realized how dark it was and turned on the light. She glanced out the window, looked at the sky and noticed that a storm was gathering. So gloomy looking, she thought. Not like last year when she had come here for the first time on a skiing weekend with Lisa. Lisa had told her she had just inherited the house from her grandfather. "The cabin isn't much, I assure you," she had said, "but the skiing is great." Lisa was right. The skiing was great fun. They had had a terrific weekend.

Lisa is such a good friend, Alexandra thought gratefully as she went into the kitchen, took a jar of instant coffee from the refrigerator and turned on the kettle. As she waited for the water to boil, she thought again about Monday evening.

That was when Lisa had suggested that she spend a few days in Windham. She had promised to meet Janice and Mike at the airport on Thursday evening and take them to her apartment. Alexandra then realized that she did not have a picture with her of Mike and Janice to help Lisa recognize them.

Lisa had solved the problem. "I'll wear my blonde wig and the Pucci dress you gave me. Don't worry. They'll recognize you/me.

"I'll tell them that you asked that they stay at your apartment on Thursday night and drive up on Friday. They'll probably appreciate a chance to sleep in. Sorry, my cabin phone is turned off after the winter."

The kettle was boiling. Alexandra measured coffee into the cup and stirred it.

She had slept at Lisa's apartment on Monday, and early Tuesday morning she had driven up in Lisa's car. It should have been only a two-hour ride, but several times she'd had to stop, rest and get more coffee. The minute she arrived, she had thrown herself on the bed and fallen into a deep sleep.

And I've been asleep almost the whole time since then, she thought. What is the problem that I need to sleep so much? Is what

I suspect possible? Did I jump to conclusions at the airport? Thank God I've given myself some time to rest and think.

She brought the cup into the den, turned on the television and settled on the couch. And then she saw her face on the screen and in horror listened as her murder was reported.

For long minutes she sat trying to absorb what she was hearing.

The broadcaster was saying, "According to police, Alexandra Saunders had gone that evening to meet a flight at Kennedy Airport. She had been mistaken in that the flight had actually arrived in the morning. She then returned to her apartment. Apparently, while sitting in her living room, she was murdered by an intruder. Police are asking that anyone with any information relevant to Alexandra Saunders's whereabouts beginning on Monday evening contact them at . . ."

My God, it must have been Lisa's body they found at my apartment. She must have still been wearing that blonde wig that made her look so much like me.

I didn't warn Lisa that I thought someone might be trying to harm me, she thought. I just told her that I was at the end of my rope and couldn't face trying to redo that last commercial. I know I looked terrible. I was afraid she'd think I was paranoid if I said that I thought Marcus Ambrose might be drugging me. Oh, Lisa, I'm so sorry. This is my fault.

Whoever killed Lisa wanted to kill me. Probably still wants to kill me.

Where were Janice and Mike? She had to let them know she was alive. She'd call the apartment and hope Emma or Janice would pick up. She couldn't leave a message with the answering service. But Janice must know by now that I wasn't the one who was murdered. But how could she *not* have known? Unless . . .

Alexandra stood up and quickly grasped the arm of the couch to keep from falling. The thought that had caused her to become weak-kneed with horror was that someone might have mutilated Lisa's face, if he realized he had killed the wrong person.

Steadying herself, she walked into the kitchen, where the only phone in the cabin was kept.

She picked up the receiver and listened for the dial tone.

There was none.

Too late she remembered that Lisa had told her that she turned off the phone after the ski season.

I'll drive into town, she thought. Lisa and I had dinner at that little Italian restaurant in the center of town. I'll use the phone there. She went into the bedroom, looked down and with wrenching pain realized she was wearing the robe and pajamas she had borrowed from Lisa. She considered skipping a shower but decided not to do that. She knew that a shower would refresh her and would take only a few minutes.

Fifteen minutes later, dressed in Lisa's slacks and a short-sleeved shirt, Alexandra went outside. She opened the door of Lisa's car and turned the ignition. The motor started to engage, then sputtered and died.

No matter how often she turned the key, the engine refused to start. I can walk, she thought, then realized with dismay that she had not borrowed shoes from Lisa and only had these three-inch heels. She would start down the road, and if she passed another cabin, she would ask to use their phone.

She got out of the car just as the dark sky exploded into torrential rain. She made a dash for the house and got back inside as the yard was brightly illuminated by a bolt of lightning. A loud bang was followed a few seconds later by a clap of thunder. With horror, she watched as a massive oak tree collapsed and fell across the gravel driveway.

I can't go out in this, she thought. Then, as had been happening since the last few days in Venice, an overwhelming feeling of drowsiness washed over her. Stumbling, Alexandra made her way into the bedroom and threw herself on the bed. "He's probably still looking for me," she mumbled. "He knows about this cabin." As she fell into a deep sleep, the electricity in Windham went off.

A search warrant in hand, Detectives Twaddle and Lyons were let into the studio apartment of Lisa Markey by the building superintendent, a Hispanic man in his early forties.

The walls of the small interior were painted bright red and the ceiling borders were stark white. Together they made a suitable background for the Picasso prints on the walls.

A couch with red-and-white-printed upholstery was undoubtedly a pullout, Twaddle decided.

Everything was in perfect order. It was obvious that Lisa Markey had been a tidy young woman.

There were framed pictures on the table next to the couch. One of them was of Lisa at a restaurant with a couple who were probably her grandparents. Twaddle picked up the frame and studied it. Lisa Markey bore a great resemblance to the pictures he had seen of Alexandra. In this photograph Lisa's hair was a light shade of brown, but he could see that if she was wearing a blonde wig she could easily have been mistaken for Alexandra, especially from a distance.

And the intruder had come up to her from behind and probably did not see her face until it was too late.

What a terrible waste of a young life, Twaddle thought, but a sense of urgency made him put the photo down quickly.

Ben was opening the door of the closet, which turned out to be unexpectedly large. The clothes were hung in groups of blouses, jackets, skirts, slacks and dresses—most of them for cocktail wear. Across from the hanging garments a row of shelves held shoes and pocketbooks. A rack over the hanging clothes was the place where Lisa had stored her luggage.

"It's impossible to tell if clothes are missing," Ben observed. He pointed to the shelf over the hanging garments, where two suitcases, one large and one small, were stored. "The question is, is anything missing? Look at those two suitcases—there's an empty space between them. Maybe there was a third one."

Hubert Twaddle nodded, pleased with Ben's observation. "Let us visualize this. Alexandra took a cab from Kennedy Airport to the home of her good friend. Why didn't she go home? Because she was afraid. Where is she now? Where would she have gone?"

"You mean she came here and Lisa Markey helped her to hide somewhere?" Ben asked.

"Yes, that's what I mean. Alexandra left her suitcases at the airport. We know that she was visibly upset and nervous, but Ben, think—to leave her luggage was an act of desperation, nothing more, nothing less. She wanted to hide. Her good friend Lisa lends her clothes and promises to meet her sister and her sister's new husband at the airport. We need to have another talk with the building superintendent now and learn as much as we can about Lisa Markey."

The superintendent lived on the ground floor.

"Something happened to Miss Markey, didn't it?" he asked bluntly when they pressed the doorbell of his apartment on the lobby floor.

"I am not at liberty to discuss our purpose in being here," Twaddle answered. "There are some things we need to know about her. First, does she drive a car?"

"Yes, she keeps it in the garage here in the building. You can't miss it. It's an old Chevy. I don't know why she doesn't get rid of it and lease a new one. Does pretty well as a model, I think. She seems to me to keep pretty busy."

"Can you ascertain as to whether her car is in the garage?" Ben asked.

"Sure, I'll phone down."

As they waited in the hallway the super stepped back into his apartment. Not more than a minute later he was back.

"Miss Markey took it out Tuesday morning. But she didn't get into it. She gave it to another lady."

"I think we'd better talk to the garage attendant," Twaddle said quietly.

They went outside onto the street. After the heavy rainstorm last night the weather had turned pleasantly warm again. Now the street was crowded with pedestrians, some strolling as though enjoying the sunshine, others darting in and out in a hurry to their destinations.

Twaddle and Lyons went down the ramp to the garage. It was not a large one and the single attendant was sitting in the booth reading the newspaper. A short, bald man with a drooping mustache, he looked to be in his late sixties.

The superintendent must have already alerted him that they were coming, because his first greeting was a question.

"Is anything wrong? Did something happen to Miss Markey?"

"As I explained to the superintendent, I am afraid I cannot answer any questions," Twaddle said firmly. "But I need some information from you. We understand that Miss Markey checked her car out but did not get in it. Can you describe the woman she lent it to?"

"She was blonde, about Miss Markey's height. Slender like Miss Markey. I couldn't see her face. She was wearing big dark glasses."

Twaddle and Lyons exchanged glances.

"I think that description is sufficient," Twaddle said. "But I have another question. Was either woman carrying any luggage?"

The garage attendant frowned.

"Let me think. Oh, sure, Miss Markey's friend had a suitcase. Not a big one. Miss Markey had a heavy insulated bag—the kind you put food in. I took it from her and put it in the trunk. It was heavy. I kind of joked about it, asked her if she was going on a picnic."

"And what did she say?"

"She said her friend was just getting away for a few days. Then I told her that I didn't like the fact that when I tried to start the car, it took a few times to get the engine to turn over. Maybe she should have it checked."

Ben Lyons looked up. A car was coming down the ramp to the garage. The attendant and certainly Hubert Twaddle heard it too.

"Did you hear them discuss where Miss Markey's friend might be going?" Twaddle asked quietly.

"I can't be sure, but Miss Markey has some kind of place in the Catskills. She loves to ski, so maybe her friend was going there, because Miss Markey said to her something like, 'If you can find any snow, my skis are in the closet.'"

As the attendant turned away to give a ticket to the new arrival, Twaddle hurriedly asked, "Are we the only ones who have asked if Miss Markey's car was here?"

"Yes, only you guys."

Twaddle handed him his card and a ten-dollar bill.

"This is very important. If anyone else asks about Miss Markey's car or where she might have gone, call me immediately. It is imperative that you not give out any of the details you have told us. If anyone asks, just say that you are not permitted by building management to provide information about tenants."

After leaving the Medical Examiner's Office, Janice and Mike returned to Alexandra's apartment. Janice's fleeting hope that her sister would be there was dashed when they entered the quiet living room. Emma Cooper had already left for the day.

Mike said, "Let's go through all of Alexandra's papers and also her luggage to try to find some clue as to where she has gone."

A quick look through the suitcases revealed nothing.

In Alexandra's bedroom, they began going through her desk. Mail that had arrived since her departure to Europe three weeks ago had been sorted by Emma into neat piles on the surface.

But as they opened the drawers, they realized that Alexandra was the kind of person who tossed letters and pictures and memorabilia she had received into haphazard piles. Playbills from Broadway shows, gossip columns torn from newspapers, guest lists from affairs she had attended, photos of herself with friends and old appointment books were all jammed into the desk drawers.

"We'll never find anything here," Janice said, her voice strained with anxiety.

But in the bottom drawer she found a handsome, leather-bound book. Opening it, she realized it was Alexandra's journal.

Feeling that she was violating her sister's privacy, Janice opened it and began to read. The entries were brief and had begun ten years ago when Alexandra first arrived in New York.

I had read about the Dorothy Lohman Agency, that she didn't mind people who walked in off the street to see her. She would say yes or no just like that! She looked at me and said "I can use you!" She called up Larry Thompson and he said to send me over. I thought he'd probably be an old man, maybe fifty or sixty, but I don't think he's even thirty.

His fiancée was there. Her name is Audrey. She's a model and absolutely gorgeous. I felt like such a hick out of the cornfield next to her. But then he started to take pictures of me and he asked if I had been posing in front of the mirror. Before I could answer, he said, "Don't bother to lie." Then he started barking orders. "Look this way, turn that way, smile, stop smiling, look over your shoulder. Now I want a deer in the head-lights expression." When he was finished he said he'd send the pictures to Dorothy.

The next entry was weeks later.

Dorothy told me that I was damn lucky that Larry Thompson was interested in me. He's been recommending me to big-time clients. I told her that I was scared of him and she said he's like that with everybody— it's just his way.

Janice skimmed through the entries, smiling at some, including when Alexandra did a car commercial.

It was a Buick commercial in Maine. And it began with the an-nouncer saying, "It's a beautiful day filled with sunshine and the newly-weds are going for a ride in their new Buick."

The male model and I were to come out of the house together beaming at each other. The car in the driveway with a white bow on the hood. It rained for four days straight. We sat around and played Monopoly and watched television. God knows what it cost the Buick people.

Three years ago, Alexandra had written about her agent's retirement.

Dorothy's been like a mother to me. I may be signing with Grant Wilson. Larry is furious. He hates Grant Wilson but I think he's wrong. Wilson's proposing me to the Hammer and Stone Furniture Company for a series of ten commercials. If they want me, it's too good to turn down but I've heard that Grant Wilson has a nasty temper.

A few weeks later Alexandra had written, *I think Larry and his wife are having problems. She's been seen with some multimillion-dollar corporate executive but claims it's just a business relationship.*

A month later Alexandra wrote, *To quote Rona Barrett, "by mutual agreement Larry Thompson and his wife, Audrey St. Clair, are filing for divorce. They insist it is amicable. But rumors are that tycoon Nelson Sheridan is waiting in the wings."*

Nine months later Alexandra wrote, *Larry and Audrey have recon-ciled. She has been diagnosed with pancreatic cancer. Nelson Sheridan disappeared from view. Larry insisted she come back home so that he can take care of her.*

As she read Janice felt as though she was walking with her sister through the ten years they had seen each other so little.

Alexandra could be caustic when she wrote about celebrities— and sympathetic to others whose careers were not working out. She mentioned helping out some friends who were having money problems. *I know they'll probably never be able to repay me but that's not what it's about.*

Sometimes there were no entries for two or three years. And then an entry would start, *I'm mad at myself that I didn't keep up with more frequent entries but nothing particularly new to report. As usual I go out a lot but so far nobody I can visualize looking at over the breakfast table for forty or fifty years.*

But the entry of two years ago was the one Janice had wanted to find.

Met Lisa Markey at a shoot today. Genuine, funny and honest. She told me she knows she'll never be another Suzy Parker but she gets lots of jobs posing for the Sears and Roebuck catalogs. She said it's a riot the way the fashion editor will pin a dress or a jacket or slacks so they look great on camera. But when they take out the pins! Talk about a bunch of shapeless rags.

A year and a half ago Alexandra had written, *Audrey died today. I am so sorry for her. She was so furious at what was happening to her that she made Larry's life hell. I saw him yesterday. He looks twice his age.*

A week later she had written that Lisa Markey told her that her grandfather had died and left her his ski cabin.

Alexandra had gone skiing and loved it. She hadn't said with whom. I even thought it might have been with a guy, Janice recalled.

Janice continued reading from the diary.

Lisa was so excited. She had her first helicopter ride. Said it was thrilling. They were shooting a Sea and Ski commercial in the Catskills. Told her I was jealous. I've always wanted to ride in a helicopter.

There were more and more references to Larry Thompson, Janice observed.

Larry looks better. He went to visit some friends in France and I think it did him a world of good.

Larry and I went out to dinner. I started to complain about how miserable it is to work for Grant Wilson. If I expected sympathy, I didn't get it. He said "I was trying to warn you." I was ready to throw something at him, but then he smiled. And I knew that as usual he was trying to get a rise out of me.

Another entry read, *Audrey has been gone a year. Larry was at dinner at 21 last night. And according to Rona Barrett he was paying special attention to socialite Robin Reeves.*

I wonder if Alexandra is in love with him, Janice thought. It certainly sounds like it to me.

Mike had dumped the deep top drawer on the bed and had been going through it item by item. She began to close the diary as Mike handed her a picture of Alexandra and another pretty woman holding their skis. Their resemblance to each other was remarkable. It was taken while they were in front of a ski lodge. Over the lodge was a sign that said WINDHAM.

"Mike, if Lisa Markey has a ski house in Windham—"

Mike cut her off. "I was thinking the same thing. That could be a place to look for Alexandra."

Hubert Twaddle and Ben Lyons had just reached their desks minutes earlier when the call from Mike came in. Twaddle had just finished ordering a squad of detectives to immediately start ringing the doorbells of all the apartments in Lisa Markey's building to see if anyone knew the address of the cabin.

Twaddle did not waste time.

"What kind of picture is it?"

"It's the kind of picture they take at resorts and sell to you. It's in a cardboard frame. It has a 'Welcome to Windham' sign on it."

"Windham, are you sure it says Windham?" Twaddle asked urgently.

"Yes, of course. It's spelled out. W-I-N-D-H-A-M. According to an entry in her diary, Alexandra was there a year and a half ago—"

Twaddle interrupted him.

"Mike, that is very important information. Thank you for it."

He hung up abruptly and turned to Ben.

He had earlier left instructions that the backgrounds of the three men who had arrived at the airport with Alexandra on Monday be thoroughly checked. They were still waiting for the reports.

Twaddle's phone rang again. It was the garage attendant at Lisa Markey's building.

"You asked me to call you if anybody came asking about Miss Markey or her car. Someone did."

"Did you get his name?" Twaddle snapped.

"No, I didn't."

"What did he ask about Miss Markey?"

"He said he had a lunch date with her and that she didn't show up. He said he rang the doorbell of her apartment and nobody answered. He said he was worried about her and asked me if she had taken her car out. Just like you told me, I said that I was not permitted to give out personal information about the tenants."

Twaddle detected a hesitation in the man's voice. "Did you give him any information at all?"

"He was so upset. He was afraid something had happened to Miss Markey. He said he worried about her driving that old car. I told him she lent it to a friend who hadn't returned it. So don't worry about her."

"Did you say anything about where Miss Markey's friend may have gone?"

"I didn't say anything, but then he asked if the friend might have gone to the ski house."

"And what did you say?" Twaddle asked.

"I told him the cops said I'm not allowed to say that."

"What did he look like?"

"He was a big guy. Looked like a football player. Reddish brown hair. Kinda curly."

Ben had moved closer to Twaddle to hear both ends of the conversation.

Twaddle hurriedly thanked the garage attendant and put down the phone. They looked at each other. "Marcus Ambrose," they said in unison.

Twaddle ordered, "Ben, find out if there is a phone number for Lisa Markey in Windham."

Thirty seconds later Ben said, "There is no such listing."

"Then phone the town clerk in Windham and ask him to check the records for a property listed in Lisa Markey's name. We have to find the address of her cabin. Thanks to that loose-lipped garage attendant, Marcus Ambrose may be headed there now."

Rapidly, he continued to bark orders.

"Contact the local precinct in Windham to see if they know where her home is. She's not an ordinary owner of a ski cottage. Lisa Markey was a beautiful young woman and would have been noticed if she was there every season."

The lead detective who had been probing further into the backgrounds of the people who had flown with Alexandra in the chartered plane—Marcus Ambrose, Grant Wilson and Larry Thompson—appeared at Twaddle's desk. "We found something, Hubert," he said.

Twaddle scanned the reports. "It is exactly what I suspected. As always, it's about money."

He fished in his pocket and found Marcus Ambrose's business card. He waited as the phone rang twice before it was picked up.

"Executair Airlines. Good afternoon."

Recognizing her voice he said, "Good afternoon, Miss Lansing. This is Detective Twaddle. Am I right that your firm has a helicopter for hire?"

"Oh, indeed we have."

"Is it available right now?"

"I'm so sorry but Mr. Ambrose just took off in it."

"Oh, I am sorry," Twaddle remarked mildly. "Do you happen to know where he is going?"

"No, I don't. He doesn't tell me his comings and goings." Miss Lansing giggled. "After all, he's a bachelor and good-looking and rich. I only wish I was twenty years younger."

Twaddle had no interest in responding to inane chatter.

"Miss Lansing, did Executair provide a helicopter to take a party to Windham, New York, last winter?"

"I think so. Let me look." A minute later she was back on the phone. "In February of 1973 we brought a party to Windham, New York. The client was the Ford Modeling Agency."

"Do you keep a log of which of your pilots flew on each reservation?"

"Of course we do. On this flight Mr. Ambrose, himself, was the pilot."

"Thank you, Miss Lansing," Twaddle responded crisply and hung up the phone.

"Ben, call the Windham Police Station. Tell them that a potential murderer is on his way to Windham. They must find the name of the grandfather who died and left his cabin to Lisa Markey. I will have a police helicopter waiting for us at the heliport. We have got to get there on time."

In murky darkness, Alexandra got off the bed and reached to turn on the lamp. It didn't work. She then flipped the wall switch for the overhead light. Again, nothing. She felt her way into the living room. The rain was beating savagely against the windows and roof. She had noticed there was a flashlight on the shelf over the kitchen sink. Her foot hit the ottoman in front of the television and she lost her balance but managed to steady herself before she fell. Disoriented in the unfamiliar surroundings, she made herself stand perfectly still and think. The entrance to the kitchen was on the right side of the living room. The couch was facing the television and was across the room from the ottoman. Extending her arms, she sidestepped until she felt the wall and then went forward, making her way into the kitchen.

She moved forward until she felt the wooden door frame at the entryway. Steadying herself against it, Alexandra visualized the layout of the kitchen. The refrigerator was on the right. The sink was just past it. Once she had the flashlight, she would be all right. Praying that the batteries would work, she moved slowly until her fingers touched the cold steel of the sink. She reached up and felt the shelf and then groped until she felt the cool plastic frame of the flashlight. Afraid she might drop it, she wrapped both hands around it. Probing the surface, her thumb found a switch that she was able to slide forward. The welcome beam of light brought a huge sigh of relief.

She knew there was nothing she could do until either the electricity came back on or it was light in the morning. Feeling famished, she opened the refrigerator door and shined the flashlight inside. Taking an apple, she padded to the big chair in the living room. She felt herself shivering and realized how cold the room had become. The flashlight's beam revealed a blanket folded on the ottoman. She wrapped the blanket around her and shined the beam on her wristwatch. It was only 5 P.M.

She finished the apple, put the core in an ashtray and closed her eyes. She was so tired again. So unreasonably tired. She started to drift off, unable to fight the overwhelming fatigue.

A patrol car, its siren screeching, raced Twaddle and Lyons to the heliport on East 34th Street.

"We don't have much time," Twaddle said. "And we still don't have Lisa Markey's address in Windham. But while they are searching for it, we will be on our way there. By the time we get to the helipad, Ambrose, if that's where he's gone, will already be at least thirty minutes ahead of us."

The pilot was already at the controls of the helicopter when the squad car pulled up. Twaddle and Lyons scrambled aboard.

"There is a major storm in the Windham area," the pilot informed them. "If it hasn't passed, we may have to circle around until it does."

"That could work to our advantage," Twaddle said. "Pray God, it does."

The next hour was spent in silence, broken only by Twaddle's one remark. "I should have known immediately," he said. "Why else would she have fled the airport without her suitcases? Ambrose was the one she was afraid of. And now looking at his dossier, we have the whole picture."

Finally they spotted the emergency landing lights of the Windham helipad.

Janice and Mike found nothing else in Alexandra's papers to suggest where she might have gone. At six o'clock they tried to concentrate on the evening news. The Watergate scandal was the top story.

A harried-looking President Nixon was being threatened with impeachment. The calls for his resignation were growing louder.

The Big Apple's steady drumbeat of fiscal problems was raising the possibility of bankruptcy.

A neighbor had reported a new piece of evidence against a young mother who was under suspicion for the murder of her two children.

When the doorbell rang, a persistent demanding ring, they both were startled. Michael sprang up to answer it. Larry Thompson was at the door.

"I thought she was dead," he said in a near shout. "A newspaper reporter who has sources inside the police department told me that when they removed the Beauty Mask, you said the dead girl was not your sister." His face was deadly white, his tone of voice ragged and demanding. "You've got to tell me. Is Alexandra alive? Is she alive?"

They had promised Twaddle that they would not reveal the truth to anyone. But looking at the tortured expression in Larry Thompson's eyes, Janice was compelled to answer. "Yes, she is," she said flatly.

The icy calm she had managed to maintain broke.

In a burst of words, she sobbed, "The police believe that whoever murdered Lisa Markey did it by mistake and is stalking Alexandra. The detectives are on their way to Windham in a helicopter, hoping that she is staying in Lisa's ski cabin. But they're not sure that she is there. And they still don't know the exact address in Windham."

Thompson stared at her as wildly conflicting emotions played out on his face. He grasped Janice's arm. "Why didn't they ask me?" he demanded. "I know the address. I KNOW IT."

Alexandra opened her eyes. Although it was still raining, it was not the torrential rain of the early afternoon. Without the flashlight she could see the bare outlines of the furniture in the room. She was still exhausted, but the consuming fatigue that had kept her sleeping almost round the clock since she had arrived here three days ago was diminishing.

It was in London that it had started. She had almost been hit by a car. She had blamed herself for not being careful to look to her left as she crossed the street. But it wasn't like her to do that. She had begun feeling light-headed that day. Why?

In Venice she had barely made it through the magazine shoot, unable to give Larry the wide-eyed expression he had been looking for. "Come on, Alexandra, you have been doing this for years. Did you stay up all night?"

I knew that Grant Wilson had taken out a three-million-dollar policy on me, she thought. He was worried about the Beauty Mask campaign, that the client wouldn't be satisfied. He's been losing clients. I wonder how badly he needs that insurance money to stay afloat.

But it was when they came back to Kennedy Airport that she began to suspect who was responsible for what was happening to her. When Marcus Ambrose offered to drive her home, she had accepted. They were behind the others leaving the baggage area. For some reason he had been stopped at the baggage exit and ordered to open all of his luggage.

When he unzipped his shaving kit, the agent reached in, pulled out a prescription bottle and examined it. "I assume as a pilot you know you can't take these for forty-eight hours before you take the controls. Barbiturates as strong as these can make you very drowsy."

It was at that moment that she knew she could not get in the car with him.

Alexandra shivered. She wanted to be home. Janice and Mike were surely waiting for her there. She wanted—at last Alexandra allowed herself to face the reality that she had resisted. She wanted desperately to be with Larry.

When they stepped out of the helicopter, two uniformed policemen were waiting for them. "I'm Captain Rawley," the older one said to introduce himself. "Officer Jennings is our driver. Let's get out of this rain and into the car."

The news that Twaddle had been hoping to hear had not come. Lisa Markey was not in the Windham town register.

To find her address, they needed to know the name of her grandfather. She might not have switched the title to her own name.

"We got a warrant for her apartment," Twaddle explained. "We found nothing related to her cabin. So far we haven't been able to locate any relatives who could help us."

"There is another potential problem," Captain Rawley said. "Most people have never heard of the really small towns around here. People who have ski places up here say they're in Windham because people recognize that name. We have the clerks in all of the neighboring towns searching their records. To find her cabin we need to focus on her grandfather."

"What about neighbors? Would they have noticed an older man living by himself?" Twaddle inquired.

"The trouble is that most of the houses are ski cabins and unoccupied now. Once kids are out of school, about half of the owners come back during the summer," Rawley replied.

"What about security system providers or caretaking services?" Twaddle demanded. "Either one would have permanent phone numbers to call in case of emergency. They might have a number that matches Lisa Markey's in New York City. Or one of them might remember the name of an elderly client who recently passed away.

Surely someone can be found who can give us the address of Lisa Markey's cabin."

Twaddle's voice was calm but he had emphasized every word. *Surely someone can be . . .*

Ben knew that when his partner spoke like that he was beyond frustration and desperately worried that it might be too late to save Alexandra Saunders.

"We are trying all of the above," Rawley insisted. "I am awaiting information."

The car had been idling. Recognizing that they had no idea where to go next, Officer Jennings switched off the ignition.

For ten long minutes there was absolute silence. It was suddenly broken by the cackling of the radio.

"We have it," a terse voice announced. "We received a call from New York City. The sister got the address. We're dispatching two patrol cars."

"What is the address?" Twaddle demanded.

"Twelve Snowden Lane."

"We're five minutes from there," Rawley snapped.

Before Rawley finished, Officer Jennings had started the car, flipped on the siren and was speeding toward Snowden Lane.

Marcus Ambrose knew he could not risk landing at the town heliport. He had hovered for over a half hour on the perimeter of the storm, waiting for it to diminish.

He remembered clearly that there was a church parking lot about a mile south of Lisa's cottage. Checking to be sure the parking lot was empty, he eased the chopper to a landing behind the church, where it would be out of sight from the road. He was pleased that the rain would muffle the sound of the engine.

He reached behind him for a rain slicker and put it on hurriedly.

Then, taking a deep breath, he opened the helicopter door and hopped to the ground. His hand went into his pocket, checking to be sure that the two items he needed were there. Aiming his flashlight ahead of him, he walked swiftly up the small hill and through the wooded area that separated the church parking lot from Lisa Markey's cabin.

There has really never been anyone else, Alexandra kept thinking. She realized she had a crush on Larry that day ten years ago when as an eighteen-year-old she was sent to his studio. Somewhere along the line she had fallen in love with him.

Her eyes welled with tears. Had she always misread him? How often in Venice had he asked her, "What is wrong?" I know he cares about me. He always did. When I thought he didn't care, I should have realized that he needed some time to himself after all those difficult years with Audrey and then her illness.

She heard a creaking sound behind her.

"It's about a quarter mile down this dead-end road," Rawley said. "It's the only house on this road. Turn off the siren. We don't want to warn him."

The dirt road was flooded in some areas and forced Officer Jennings to slow to a crawl. Ben knew that it could become impassable, which would mean they would have to run to the cabin where Alexandra might be.

Lurching and skidding, they finally spotted the cabin ahead. A tree had fallen across the driveway.

The blinding glare of a flashlight was trained on Alexandra's face.

"Just want to be sure it's really you this time," Marcus Ambrose said softly. "Too bad about your friend." He was holding a cord in his hand.

Alexandra pushed aside the blanket and tried to get up. Her feet were tangled in it and she could not move fast enough. In an instant he was behind the chair slipping the cord around her neck. As she struggled to escape, the cord tightened and bit into her flesh.

"No, no, no, please God, no."

Her hands reached up to try to stop the cord from tightening any further. But it was useless. She could not get her fingers under it. She began to black out, her mind filled with the image of her sister's face. They had had so little time together. And Larry. He loved her. She knew he loved her—

She gasped as the cord stopped being pulled tight and she felt something being rubbed on her face. She tried to move but the cord immediately tightened again.

"Hold still. It's time for your final Beauty Mask," Marcus Ambrose whispered.

Officer Jennings swerved around the fallen tree onto the front lawn. The tires sank into the waterlogged soil. As their car came to a halt, the electricity blinked back on. Through the living room window, they could see with frightening clarity the nightmarish scene that was being enacted. Alexandra Saunders was seated in a chair, her blonde hair spilling on her shoulders. Her would-be murderer was holding a cord around her neck with one hand. His other hand was smearing something white on her face.

Ambrose looked up and saw the headlights of the patrol car. Startled, he let go of the cord and fled through the side door heading toward the woods. Rawley and Jennings bolted from the patrol car, chased him to the edge of the woods and wrestled him to the ground.

Twaddle and Ben rushed into the living room, where an unconscious Alexandra was slumped against the side of the chair. In an instant Twaddle had loosened the rope around her neck. Ben pulled her from the chair onto the floor and frantically began administering CPR, forcing air into her tortured lungs . . . forcing her heart to begin beating again.

On Sunday afternoon Detectives Twaddle and Lyons paid a visit to Alexandra in her apartment. Mike answered their ring. With a smile of welcome, he motioned them in.

Alexandra was sitting on the couch, a bandage around her neck. She was wearing a multicolored caftan, her blonde hair loose on her shoulders. Her vivid blue eyes were sparkling. Her complexion was flawless.

What an incredibly beautiful woman, Twaddle thought. The face that launched a thousand ships.

She started to stand up but was restrained by a hand on her arm.

"Take it easy," Larry cautioned. "You're still unsteady on your feet."

She smiled at the detectives. "I don't know how to thank you," she said. "If you hadn't been there . . ."

"I am so glad we were," Twaddle responded.

"I hardly remember anything after he started choking me. . . ."

In an involuntary reaction Larry Thompson put his arm around her.

"You were taken to the hospital in Windham and kept overnight. Do you remember that?" Twaddle asked.

Alexandra nodded. "Sort of. The first thing I really remember clearly yesterday is being on the helicopter coming back here from Windham. And you guys," she glanced at Janice, Mike and Larry, "waiting for me when I was wheeled away from the helicopter. Talk about a support group. I thought I looked bad. You were all a mess!"

"We certainly were," Mike said with a smile. "You were still under sedation but you made it loud and clear that you were not going to another hospital."

Janice had not taken her eyes off her sister but now she asked, "Detective Twaddle, when we met Marcus Ambrose, I was convinced that he was truly concerned about Alexandra. When did you begin to suspect him?"

"He was the last person to see your sister," Twaddle said emphatically. "His suggestion that she might have been running away from paparazzi made sense in one way, but it would have been equally easy for her to have gone up to his office to escape them.

"And from all the descriptions I heard from you," he looked at Larry, "and from Mr. Wilson, and in a twisted way from Mr. Ambrose, I immediately suspected you were having a reaction to medication. As it turns out, I was correct."

"I feel so guilty that Lisa died instead of me," Alexandra said sadly. "I will live with it every day of my life. If only I had warned her that I thought it was possible Marcus Ambrose was drugging me, but I was so out of it that I couldn't be sure. But when his bags were inspected and he was warned about the barbiturates he was carrying, I began to suspect. I turned away as though I wasn't paying attention, but I caught the expression on his face. It was worried. More than that, it was furious. If I had only warned her—but I never thought that he intended to kill anybody."

"We now understand why Ambrose mistook Lisa Markey for you when she was wearing that wig in your apartment," Lyons said. "But I'm still not clear on the remarkable coincidence that Lisa had on the same dress as your sister the night of the murder."

"It wasn't a coincidence," Alexandra said wistfully. "When I bought that dress last Christmas, I got one for me and one for Janice. I wore it a few times and Lisa admired it so much I gave it to her. We agreed she would wear it and the wig to the airport to help Janice and Mike pick her out of the crowd."

"Speaking of picking people out of the crowd," Mike said, "I now know why when we met Marcus Ambrose in his office last week he looked familiar. He must have figured out that our flight was due at 8 A.M. Janice and I weren't the only ones scanning the terminal searching for Alexandra. I am certain that I saw him there."

Alexandra looked at Twaddle. "Marcus Ambrose drugged me, killed Lisa and then tried to kill me. Why?" she asked.

"Mr. Ambrose has an unsavory background," Twaddle told her. "While he has never been charged with a crime, it is believed that he has used his charter airline to smuggle valuable antiques into the country at the same time that he was also working for legitimate customers such as the Wilson Modeling Agency. That was why his baggage was inspected so thoroughly.

"He also had much to gain if the Beauty Mask campaign became a failure. He recently purchased a large number of stock options in another cosmetics company, which in a short time will launch its own product similar to Fowler Cosmetics' Beauty Mask. If he had succeeded in making you ill and delaying the launch of the campaign, those options would have soared in value when the rival product beat Beauty Mask to market."

Larry joined in. "I have good news on that subject. I spoke to Ken Fowler, the chairman of Fowler Cosmetics. When I explained everything that has happened, he immediately agreed to delay the redo of the Venice commercial for another week. He wishes you a speedy recovery."

"I'll be absolutely okay by then," Alexandra said. "I'll put a little makeup on my neck next week and get that commercial over with. After that, I never even want to think of the Beauty Mask stuff again."

Twaddle and Lyons said their good-byes and left the apartment.

Larry Thompson looked at her. "Alexandra, I—"

Before he could continue Alexandra interrupted him. "When

I thought I was going to die, I realized that the three of you are the most important people in the world to me. Larry, any chance you're free the next few days? I'd love it if you'd come with me when I show Janice and Mike around town."

"Alexandra," Larry said, "I am available to you every minute of every day of every year of the rest of my life."

He began to smile and touched her cheek. "Even when you start having wrinkles."

Stowaway

Carol shivered inside her smoke-blue uniform coat and tried to ignore her growing uneasiness. As she glanced around the waiting room of the air terminal she thought that the gaily dressed peasant dolls in the showcases made an incongruous background for the grim-faced policemen who passed in front of them. The handful of boarding passengers, watching the policemen, were standing together, their eyes full of hatred.

As she walked toward them, one of the passengers was saying: "The chase is taking too long. The hunters are not pleased." He turned to Carol. "How long have you been flying, stewardess?"

"Three years," Carol answered.

"You look too young for even that length of time. But if you could have seen my country before it was occupied. This room was always full of gaiety. When I returned to America from my last visit, twenty relatives came to see me off. This time no one dared come. It isn't wise to make a public display of one's American connections."

Carol lowered her voice. "There are so many more policemen today than usual. Do you know why?"

"A member of the underground has escaped," he whispered. "He was spotted near here an hour ago. They'll surely catch him, but I hope I don't see it."

"We'll be boarding in fifteen minutes," Carol answered reassuringly. "Excuse me, I must see the Captain."

Tom had just come in from the Operations Office. He nodded when his eyes met hers. Carol wondered how much longer it would be before her heart stopped racing painfully at every glimpse of him, before she stopped being so aware of his splendid tallness in the dark uniform. She reminded herself sternly that it was time she regarded him as just another pilot and not as the man she had loved so dearly.

She spoke to him, her gray eyes veiled, noncommittal. "You wanted me, Captain?"

Tom's tone was as businesslike as her own. "I was wondering if you've checked Paul."

Carol was ashamed to answer that she'd not yet thought of the purser on the flight since they'd landed in Danubia an hour before. Sick from the effect of the booster shots, Paul had stayed in the crew bunk while the plane was refueled for the return flight to Frankfurt.

"I haven't, Captain. I've been too interested in the hide-and-seek our friends are playing." She inclined her head in the direction of the police.

Tom nodded. "I'd hate to be that poor guy when they catch him. They're positive he's on the field somewhere."

For a moment Tom's voice was familiar, confidential, and Carol looked at him eagerly. But then he became the Captain speaking to the stewardess again. "Please go aboard and see if Paul needs anything. I'll have the ground rep bring the passengers out."

Carol nodded and walked toward the entrance to the runway.

The cold airport seemed desolate in the half darkness of the October evening. Three policemen were entering the plane next to hers. The sight of them made her shiver as she boarded her plane and went forward to find Paul.

He was asleep, so she gently placed another blanket over him and came back to the cabin. Ten minutes more and they'll all be aboard, she thought, checking her watch. She pulled out her hand mirror and ran a comb through the short blonde hair that curled from under her overseas cap.

Just then she realized with a drenching fear that the mirror was reflecting a thin hand grasping the pole of the small open closet behind her seat. *Someone was trying to hide in the recess there!* She glanced frantically out the seat window for help. The police detachment had left the next plane and was heading in her direction.

"Put away the mirror, mademoiselle." The words were quiet, the English clear, the accent a heavy undertone. She heard the hangers being pushed aside. She whirled and faced a thin boy of about seventeen with heavy blonde hair and intelligent blue eyes.

"Please—do not have fear. I will not harm you." The boy glanced out the window at the rapidly approaching police. "Is there another way off this plane?"

Carol's fear changed swiftly. It was for him now that the feeling of disaster swept her. His eyes were frightened and he backed away from the window like a trapped animal, beseeching, urgent, his hand stretched toward Carol, his voice imploring. "If they find me, they will kill me. Where can I hide?"

"I can't hide you," Carol protested. "They'll find you when they search the plane, and I can't involve the airline." She had a clear picture of Tom's face if the police discovered a stowaway on board, especially if she were concealing him.

Feet were ascending the ramp now, heavy shoes clanging on the metal. A loud series of bangs crashed against the closed door.

Carol stared in fascination at the boy's eyes, at the black hopefulness in them. Frantically, she glanced around the cabin. Paul's uniform jacket was hanging in the clothes closet. She pulled it out and snatched his hat off the shelf. "Put these on, quick."

Hope brightened the boy's face. His fingers raced at the buttons and he stuffed his hair under the cap. The banging at the door was repeated.

Carol's hands were wet, her fingers numb. She shoved the boy into the rear seat, fumbled at the catch of the ship's portfolio, and scattered baggage declarations in his lap. "Don't open your mouth. If they ask me your name, I'll say Joe Reynolds and pray they don't check passports."

Her legs seemed too weak to carry her to the cabin door. As she pulled at the handle, the realization of what she was doing swept over her and she thought how pitifully transparent the boy's disguise was. She wondered if she could possibly keep the police from searching the plane. The handle turned and the door swung open. She blocked the entrance and forced an annoyed tone as she faced the policemen. "The steward and I are checking our papers. What's the reason for this?"

"Surely you are aware that a search is being made for an escaped traitor. You have no right to hinder the police in their work."

"*My* work is being hindered. I'll report this to the Captain. You have no right to enter an American plane."

"We are searching every plane in the field," the leader snapped. "Will you step aside? It would be unpleasant to have to force our way in."

Realizing it was no use to argue, Carol quickly sat on the seat next to the boy, her body shifted toward him, her back shielding him from the direct view of the police. His head was bowed over the papers. In the dim light, his uniform was passable, and the absence of a tie was not noticeable in his hunched position.

Carol pulled some declarations off his lap and said: "All right, Joe, let's get this finished. 'Kralik, Walter, six bottles cognac, value thirty dollars. One clock, value—'"

"Who else is aboard?" the leader asked.

"The purser, who's asleep in the crew bunk," Carol said nervously. "He's been very ill."

The inquisitor's gaze passed over "Joe" without interest. "No one else? This is the only American plane here. It is the logical one for the traitor to head for."

The second policeman had checked the lounges, the clothes closet, and the floor under the seats. The third member of the party came back from the flight deck. "There is only one man there, asleep. He is too old to be our prisoner."

"He was spotted near here fifteen minutes ago," the leader snapped. "He must be somewhere."

Carol glanced at her watch. One minute of eight. The passengers must be starting across the field. She had to get rid of the police, hide the boy—in one minute.

She stood up, careful to keep her body directly in front of Joe. By glancing out the opposite window, she could see the waiting room door opening. She said to the leader, "You've searched the plane. My passengers are about to board. Will you please leave?"

"You seem strangely anxious to be rid of us, stewardess."

"My paperwork isn't finished. It's difficult to do it while I'm attending to the passengers."

Steps were hurrying up the ramp. A messenger came in and said to the leader, "Sir, the Commissioner wants an immediate report on the search."

To Carol's relief, all three policemen scurried out.

The ground representative and passengers were at the foot of the ramp as the policemen descended. The crew was entering the plane through the forward entrance.

"Joe!" Carol called. The boy was out of the seat, crouching in the aisle. Carol pulled him into the tail and pointed to the men's lounge. "In there. Take off the uniform and don't open the door for anyone except me."

She stood at the cabin door and forced a smile at the ground rep and passengers. The ground rep handed her the manifest and waited while she greeted the passengers and showed them their seats.

There were six names on the manifest. Five were typed, and the first one, "Vladimir Karlov," had been written in. Next to it were four letters, "exco."

"Extreme courtesy—who's the VIP?" Carol asked the ground rep swiftly.

"A real big shot, the Commissioner of Police in Danubia. He's one of their worst butchers, so handle him with kid gloves. He stopped to talk to the searching party about the escaped prisoner."

The Commissioner—on her flight! Carol felt sick, but as he climbed the ramp she extended her hand, smiling. He was a tall man of about fifty with thin nostrils, tight lips.

"I have been assigned to seat forty."

Carol knew she couldn't let him sit in the rear of the plane. He'd be sure to see "Joe" when she brought him out of the lounge. "It's a beautiful flight to Frankfurt," she said, her smile easy. "It would be foolish not to sit in front of the wing—"

"I prefer a rear seat," he said. "It gives a considerably smoother flight."

"This hop is one of our smoothest runs. The front seats won't be bumpy and will give you a better view."

The Commissioner shrugged and followed her down the aisle. She glanced at the manifest and debated whether to seat him with another passenger. If she did, they might start a conversation and he'd be less likely to be looking around when she brought Joe out of the lounge. But then, remembering the passengers' bitter comments about the search, she decided against it, led him to seat three, placed his bag on the overhead rack, and told him to fasten his seatbelt.

The passenger in seat seven got up and started to walk to the rear.

Carol caught up to him at the door of the men's lounge. "Sir, please take your seat. The plane is starting to move."

The man's face was white. "Please, stewardess, I may be ill. I get a little frightened at takeoff."

Carol took his hand and forced him to let go of the doorknob before he realized it was locked. "I have some pills that will help. Everyone must be in their seat until we're aloft."

After she'd seen him seated, she snapped on the mike. "Good evening, I am your stewardess, Carol Dowling. Please fasten your seatbelts and don't smoke until the sign over the forward door goes off. Our destination is Frankfurt, our anticipated flight time two hours and five minutes. A light supper will be served shortly. Please don't hesitate to ask for anything you want. A pleasant trip, everyone."

When she went to the flight deck, the plane had stopped taxiing and the engines were thundering. She bent over Tom. "Cabin secure, Captain."

Tom turned so quickly that his hand brushed against her hair. She felt a warm glow from the touch and unconsciously raised her hand to her hair.

"Okay, Carol."

The engines were racing—it was hard to catch his words. A year ago he would have looked up at her and his lips would have formed "Love you, Carol," but that was over now. She had an instant of fierce regret that they hadn't somehow made up their quarrel. On sleepless nights, she'd admitted to herself that Tom had tried: he'd made overtures, but she hadn't given an inch. So his attempts at making up had only ended in worse quarrels, and then he'd been stationed in London for six months so they hadn't seen each other. But now they were on a flight together, two polite co-workers giving no hint that things had ever been different.

She started to turn back to the cabin, but Tom motioned her to him. He nodded to the first officer and the engines became subdued. She felt an immense loneliness when he turned away from her. There had been a few moments on this flight when he'd seemed friendly, warm—moments when it looked as though they might be able to talk things through. But this will finish it, she thought. Even if I can get Joe to Frankfurt, Tom will never forgive me.

"Carol, did you speak to the Commissioner yet?"

"Just when I showed him his seat. He's not very chatty."

"Take good care of him. He's important. They're talking about barring Danubia to American planes. If he likes the service, it might help a little. I'll send Dick back to give you a hand with dinner once we're aloft."

"Don't! I mean, it's just a cold supper. With only six passengers, I can manage."

Back in the cabin, she smiled reassuringly at the man afraid of take-offs as she passed him. The plane had reached the runway and the crescendo of engines was deafening. All the passengers, including the Commissioner, were staring out the windows. She went back, tapped on the door of the men's lounge, and softly called to Joe.

Noiselessly, he slipped out. In the dim light, his thin body seemed more like a shadow than a human creature. She put her lips to his ear. "The last seat on the right. Get on the floor. I'll throw a blanket over you."

He moved warily and disappeared into the seat recess. He walks like a cat, Carol thought. Or like a kitten, she amended, remembering the boyish fuzz that had brushed her face.

It was hard to balance in the ascending plane and, steadying herself by one hand on the lounge bulkhead, she took the aisle seat by Joe, flipped a blanket from the overhead rack and threw it over him, shaking it wide. To a casual glance, the blanket might not seem unusual; to a searching glance, it would be odd that anything shapeless could make such a thick mound.

She glued her eyes to the sign over the cabin door. FASTEN YOUR SEATBELTS—NO SMOKING. *Attachez vos ceintures—ne fumez pas.* While the sign was on, she had a reprieve, a safe island. But when it flashed off she'd have to turn on the bright cabin lights that would make a farce out of Joe's hiding place and let the passengers leave their seats.

For the first time she seriously considered what would happen to her for concealing Joe. She thought about what Tom would say and remembered unhappily his reaction last year when she'd caused trouble on his ship.

"But Tom," she'd protested, "what if I did let that poor kid take her dog out of the crate? She was traveling alone, to be adopted by strangers. It was night and the cabin was dark. No one would have known if that woman hadn't gone over to her and got nipped for her trouble."

And Tom had retorted: "Carol, maybe someday you'll learn to obey basic rules. That woman was a stockholder and raised Cain in the front office. I took the blame for letting the dog loose because I knew it wouldn't cost me my job. But after seven years with a clean record, I don't like having a reprimand in my brief now."

She recalled uneasily how she'd flared at him, telling him she was delighted he didn't have a perfect record to live up to anymore—that now, maybe, he'd relax and act human—maybe he'd stop treating the company manual like the Bible. It wasn't hard to remember everything they'd said, she'd relived that quarrel so often.

She tried to picture what Charlie Wright, Northern's station manager at Frankfurt, would do. Charlie was a "company man" too. He liked the planes to arrive and depart on schedule, the passengers to be satisfied. Charlie would definitely be upset at having to report a stowaway to the front office and would undoubtedly suspend her immediately or fire her outright.

Joe's blanket moved slightly and her mind jolted back to the problem of finding a safe hiding place for him. The plane leveled off. As the seatbelt sign died, she rose slowly. Hating to do it, she reached for the switch on the bulkhead and turned the cabin lights from dim to bright.

She started to pass out magazines and newspapers. The man who'd been nervous about takeoff was no longer strained-looking. "That pill helped a lot, stewardess." He accepted a newspaper and fumbled for his glasses. "They must be in my coat." He got up and started toward the rear.

Carol said numbly, "Let me get them for you."

"Not at all." He was passing Joe's hiding place—Carol following, scarcely breathing. The blanket was glaringly out of place in the tidy cabin. The passenger got his eyeglasses, started back down the aisle and stopped. Carol swiftly reflected that this man was the *neat* type—hadn't he straightened his coat on the hanger, smoothed the edges of his newspaper? In just one second he'd pick up that blanket. He was bending, saying: "This must have fallen—"

"Oh, please!" Carol's hand was on his arm, her grip firm. "Please don't bother. I'll get it in a minute." She eased him forward, scolding lightly. "You're our guest. If the Captain saw me letting you tidy up, he'd drop me out the window."

The man smiled, then went amiably to his seat.

Carol's eyes searched the cabin hopelessly. The blanket *was* too obvious. Anytime someone went to the rear of the plane Joe could be discovered.

"Magazine, stewardess."

"Of course." Carol brought a selection to the passenger seated behind the Commissioner, then walked forward. "Would you care to see a magazine, Commissioner Karlov?"

The Commissioner's thin fingers were tapping the armrest, his lips pursed in concentration. "Some piece of information eludes me, stewardess. Something I have been told does not fit. However"—he smiled coldly—"it will come back to me. It always does." He waved away the magazines. "Where is the water fountain?"

"I'll get you a glass of water—" Carol said.

He started to rise. "Don't bother, please. I detest sitting so long. I'll get it myself."

The water fountain was opposite the seat where Joe was hiding. The Commissioner was not a naive observer. He'd be sure to investigate the blanket.

"No!" She blocked the way into the aisle. "The flight's getting bumpy. The Captain doesn't want the passengers to be moving."

The Commissioner looked intently at the unlighted seatbelt sign. "If you will let me pass—"

The plane tilted slightly. Carol swayed against the Commissioner, deliberately dropping the magazines. It *was* getting rough.

If she could just stall him, Tom was sure to flash the sign on. The Commissioner, looking exasperated, picked up a few of the magazines.

Still blocking his way, she slowly picked up the others, carefully sorting them by size. Finally, unable to delay any longer, she straightened up. And the seatbelt sign was flashing!

The Commissioner leaned back and studied Carol intently as she went to the tank, drew him a glass of water, and brought it to him. He didn't thank her but instead observed, "That sign seemed like a direct answer to a plea of yours, stewardess. It must have been important to you that I did not leave my seat."

Carol felt panic, then anger. He knew something was up and it amused him to watch her squirm. She took his barely touched glass. "Sir, I'm going to let you in on a trade secret. When we have a very important passenger on board, a mark is made next to his name on the manifest. That symbol means we're to show every courtesy to that person. You're that passenger on this flight and I'm trying to make your trip as pleasant as possible. I'm afraid I'm not succeeding."

The flight deck door opened and Tom stepped down. The passengers were all seated near the front half of the cabin. Carol stood by the last one. The odds were that Tom merely wanted to say hello to them. He wouldn't bother going all the way through with no one seated in the back.

Tom welcomed the Commissioner, shook hands with the man behind him, pointed out a cloud bank to the two friends playing checkers. Carol studied his movements with vast aching. Every time she saw him a different memory flashed back. This time it was Memorial Day in Gander and their flight was canceled because of a freak snowstorm. Late that night, she and Tom had had a snowball fight. Tom had looked at his watch and said: "Do you realize in two minutes it will be June first? I've never kissed a girl in a snowstorm on June first before." His lips brushed against her cheek and were cold, found her mouth and were warm. "I love you, Carol." It was the first time he had said it.

Carol swallowed against the hurt and came back to reality. She was standing in the aisle and Tom was before her and Joe was in danger and there was no way out.

"Sure you don't want help with dinner, Carol?" His tone was impersonal but his eyes searched hers. She wondered if he had flashes of remembering too.

"No need," she said. "I'll start on it immediately." It would mean going up to the galley and leaving Joe for anyone to discover, but—

Tom cleared his throat and seemed to search for words. "How does it feel to be the only woman on board, Carol—"

The words hung in Carol's mind for seconds before their full import sank in. She gazed from passenger to passenger: the Commissioner, the man afraid of takeoffs, the mild fortyish one, the elderly man sleeping, the two friends at checkers. Men, all men. She'd prayed for a hiding place for Joe, and Tom of all people had pointed it out! The ladies' lounge! Perfect. And so simple.

Now, as Tom studied her, she said casually: "I love being the only woman here, Captain. No competition."

Tom started to go forward and hesitated. "Carol, have coffee with me when we get to Frankfurt. We've got to talk."

It had come. He missed her too. If she said to him now, "I've discovered a stowaway on board," it would be so easy. Tom could take the credit and Danubia would be grateful. It might mean Northern's charter being extended and make up to him for last year's trouble. But she couldn't murder Joe even for Tom's love. "Ask me in Frankfurt if you still want to," she said.

After Tom had gone back to the flight deck, she returned to the seat beside Joe and studied the passengers swiftly. The checker game was absorbing the two players. The elderly man dozed. The fortyish man watched the clouds. The neat one was bent over his newspaper. The Commissioner's head was leaning against the back of the seat. It was too much to hope he was napping. At best he was in deep thought and might not turn around.

She leaned over the blanketed form. "Joe, you've got to get to the rear of the plane. The ladies' lounge is on the left. Go in and lock the door."

Just then she met the Commissioner's glance as he turned in his seat. "Joe, I've got to turn the lights off. When I do, get out of there fast! Do you understand?"

Joe slipped the blanket from his head. His hair was tousled and his eyes blinked in the strong light. He looked like a twelve-year-old roused from a sound sleep. But when his eyes got used to the light, they were the eyes of a man—weary, strained.

His faint nod was all Carol needed to assure her that he understood. She got up. The Commissioner had left his seat and was hurrying toward her.

It took her a second to cross to the light switch and plunge the cabin into darkness. Cries of alarm came from the passengers. Carol made her cries louder than the rest. "I'm sorry! How stupid of me! I can't seem to find the right switch—"

The click of a door closing—had she heard it or merely wanted to hear it?

"Turn on that light, stewardess." An icy voice, a rough hand on her arm.

Carol threw the switch and stared into the face of the Commissioner—a face distorted with rage.

"Why?" His voice was furious.

"Why what, sir? I merely intended to turn the microphone on to announce dinner. See—the mike switch is next to the lights."

The Commissioner studied the panel, uncertainty crossing his face. Carol turned the mike on. "I hope you're hungry, everybody. I'll serve dinner in minutes, and while you're waiting we'll have a cocktail. Manhattans, martinis or daiquiris. I'll be right there to get your orders." She turned to the Commissioner and said respectfully, "Cocktail, sir?"

"Will you have one with me, stewardess?"

"I can't drink while I'm working."

"Neither can I."

What did he mean by that, Carol wondered, passing the cocktail tray. More cat-and-mouse stuff, she decided as she yanked prepared food from the cubbyhole refrigerator in the galley and made up trays. She took special pains with the Commissioner's dinner, folding the linen napkin in creases and pouring the coffee at the last minute to keep it steaming hot.

"Aren't there usually two attendants?" the Commissioner asked as she placed the tray in front of him

"Yes, but the purser's ill. He's lying down."

She served the others, poured second coffees, brought trays to the crew. Tom turned over the controls to the first officer and sat at the navigator's table. "I'll be glad when we get to Frankfurt," he said uneasily. "With this tail wind, we should be in in half an hour. I've been edgy this whole flight. Something seems wrong, but I can't put my finger on it." He grinned. "Maybe I'm just tired and need some of your good coffee, Carol."

Carol pulled the curtain from the crew bunk up slightly. "Paul has certainly been asleep a long time."

"He just woke up and asked me to get his jacket. He wanted to give you a hand. But I made him stay put. He feels rotten."

Joe's fate was hanging in such a delicate balance. If Paul had come back, he'd have seen Joe. If Paul's jacket hadn't been hanging in the cabin, the police would have found Joe. If Tom hadn't said she was the only woman aboard—

"I'll pick up the trays since we've only a half hour to go."

She started collecting trays from the passengers, working her way forward. The Commissioner's tray was untouched. He was staring down at it. A premonition warned Carol not to disturb him. She cleared and stacked the other trays. But then her wristwatch told her they'd land in ten minutes. The seatbelt sign came on. She went for the Commissioner's tray. "Shall I take it, sir? I'm afraid you didn't eat much."

But the Commissioner stood up. "You *almost* got away with it, miss, but I finally realized what's been eluding me. At Danubia the search party said the purser was ill and the stewardess was checking baggage declarations with the steward." His face turned cruel. "Why didn't the steward help you with dinner? Because there isn't any."

His fingers dug into Carol's shoulders. "Our prisoner *did* get on this plane and you've hidden him."

Carol fought rising panic. "Let me go."

"He is on board, isn't he? Well, it's not too late. The Captain must take us back to Danubia. A thorough search will be made."

He pushed her aside and lunged for the door to the flight deck. Carol grasped at his arm but he flung her hand away. The other passengers were on their feet, staring.

Her last hope was these men who with bitterness had watched the search. Would they help?

"Yes, there's an escaped prisoner on board!" she shouted. "He's a kid you'd love to shoot, but I won't let you do it!"

For a moment, the passengers seemed frozen as they clutched seat backs for support in the sloping plane. Carol, in utter despair, thought they wouldn't help. But then, as though they finally understood what was going on, they lunged forward together. The mild one threw himself against the Commissioner and knocked his hand from the doorknob. A checker player pinned his arms behind his back. The plane was circling the field, the airport lights level with the window. A faint bump—Frankfurt!

The passengers released the Commissioner as the flight deck door opened. Tom stood there, angrily taking in the scene. "Carol, what the devil is going on?"

She went to him, shutting her eyes against the Commissioner's fury, and against the impact of her words on Tom. She felt sick, pained. "Captain—" her tongue was thick, she could barely form words "—Captain, I wish to report a stowaway. . . ."

She gratefully sipped the steaming coffee in the station manager's office. The past hour was a blur of airport officials, police, photographers. Only vivid was the Commissioner's demand: "This man is a citizen of my country. He must be returned immediately." And the station manager's reply: "This is regrettable, but we must turn the stowaway over to the Bonn government. If his story checks, he'll be granted asylum."

She stared at her hand where Joe had kissed it before being taken into custody.

He'd said, "You have given me my life, my future."

The door opened slowly and Charlie Wright, the station manager, walked in, followed by Tom. "Well, that's that."

He looked squarely at Carol. "Proud of yourself? Feeling real heroic and dying to see the morning headlines? 'Stewardess hides stowaway in thrilling flight from Danubia.' The papers won't print that Northern won't be welcome in Danubia anymore and will lose a few million in revenue because of you. As for you, Carol, you can head home and there'll be a hearing in New York but—you're fired."

"I expected it. But you've got to understand Tom knew nothing about the stowaway."

"It's a Captain's business to know what goes on in his plane," Charlie shot back. "Tom will probably get away with a stiff calldown unless he gets heroic and tries to take the blame for you. I hear from the grapevine he did that once before."

"That's right," Carol said. "He took the blame for me last year and I didn't have the decency to thank him for it." She looked into Tom's strangely inscrutable face. "Tom, last year you were furious with me, and rightly so. I was completely wrong. This time, I'm truly sorry for the trouble you'll have over this but I couldn't have done otherwise."

She turned to Charlie, fighting tears. "If you're finished, I'm going to the hotel. I'm dead."

He looked at her with some sympathy. "Carol, unofficially I can understand what you did. Officially—"

She tried to smile. "Good night." She went out and started to walk down the stairs.

Tom caught up with her at the landing. "Look, Carol, let's put the record straight—I'm *glad* the boy got through! You wouldn't be the girl I love if you'd handed him over to those butchers."

The girl I love.

"But thank God you won't be flying on my plane anymore. I'd be afraid to sit at the stick wondering what was going on in the cabin." His arms slipped around her.

"But if you're not on my plane, I wish you'd be there to pick me up at the airport. You can hide spies and dogs and anything you darn please in the backseat. Carol, I'm trying to ask you to marry me."

Carol looked at him, the splendid tallness of him and the tenderness in his eyes. Then his lips were warm against hers and he was saying again the words she'd wanted so long to hear, "Love you, Carol."

The waiting room of the terminal was dim and quiet. After a moment, they started down the stairs toward it, their footsteps echoing ahead.

When the Bough Breaks

. . . Michael clutched frantically at the dead tree branch, his small body suspended high in the air. He looked beseechingly at Marion for help, but she was holding a huge telephone receiver because she had to call a man to attend to the tree. Peter was jumping on the dead branch and it broke with a sickening crunch. Peter grabbed the trunk of the tree for support, and Marion stared spellbound as Michael's graceful little body fell swiftly down until it lay crumpled and broken on the terrace. Marion looked at the telephone receiver in her hand but it had turned into a dead branch. She dropped it and screamed, "Michael, Michael!" Her voice a thin, piercing wail . . .

She awoke with Michael's name still on her lips and with Scott's arms holding her tight. Scott's tone was tender.

"The same dream, darling?"

"Yes, yes," she sobbed. "Just the same. Peter and I—we killed him."

Scott shook her gently. "Marion, you've got to stop torturing yourself. Michael fell from a tree. It's happened before and it will again—five-year-olds are natural climbers and sometimes they fall. But blaming yourself or Peter for the accident won't bring Michael back."

"But Peter told me about that dead branch. If anyone else had, I'd have done something about it, but Peter was such a little pest."

She'd said it so many times before, just this way in just these words. She pulled away from Scott and got out of bed. "I'll be all right in a minute. It's just that today—"

"I know," Scott said quietly. "He'd be starting kindergarten. I haven't forgotten."

Marion closed her eyes against the pain. "Why not say it?" she asked tonelessly. "I robbed you of your son. You always told me I was careless about attending to things that needed fixing."

Scott sat on the side of the bed and reached for his bathrobe. "My darling, Michael's been dead three months. It was a tragic accident. You didn't rob me of my son, but you are deliberately taking yourself from me. Each day you seem to escape me a little more. Can't we accept our loss together?"

Marion shook her head drearily. "If I'd only listened to Peter. He was always telling me what to do." She laughed mirthlessly. "He was more like you than your own son."

Scott pulled on his bathrobe. "Marion, until you forgive yourself and Peter you'll never get over losing Michael. Just as you shouldn't blame yourself, you've no right to hate Peter so. He's just a little boy, and God knows Michael loved him."

Marion mechanically brushed her hair back. "If it hadn't been for Peter, he'd be alive today. If Peter hadn't started to follow him out on that branch . . ."

Scott stopped on his way to the shower. "When the real estate agent phones, tell him those people can have the house. Maybe if we go back to the city for a while, it will help."

It was true. If Marion looked out the front windows during the day, she could see children playing in the street. The left windows looked out on thick trees and hedge, but a corner of Peter's house was still visible. The back windows looked over the terrace and the giant elm where Michael . . .

She went down to the kitchen and started breakfast.

Later, after Scott had left, she poured herself more coffee and went back to the dinette table. This was the time of day she'd once loved best, with Michael still in his pajamas, eager with the questions that seemed to store up in his mind during the night. It was the one time of day when he'd been hers alone, because right after breakfast the bell would ring and Michael would slide from his chair, joyously calling, "It's Peter!"

Marion glanced involuntarily at the kitchen door. She felt that if she opened it, Peter would be there—her son's friend Peter, with his sandy hair that had seemed so drab next to Michael's blue-black head; Peter, square and somehow squat-looking when compared with Michael's slimness.

The coffee grew cold as Marion wondered what on earth Michael had seen in Peter. From the day the child had come here to live with his great-aunt, he'd attached himself to Michael. Marion had felt sorry for him. He was surely a lonely child, orphaned and living with a sick old woman, and yet he could be so irritating.

Whenever he and Michael had been out playing and there was an accident, it was always Peter who brought Michael home with a cut or bruise. "We were playing and he fell. I happened to jump on him. I didn't mean to."

Marion had asked him one day: "Peter, do you ever once land on the bottom?"

He had grinned at her, his hazel eyes shining, ignoring her annoyance. "Nope."

On rainy days when he and Michael had played indoors she could always be sure that at least one of Michael's toys would be taken apart. Scott had refused to get upset when she told him about it. "Honey, the kid's an engineer," he had said. "He's got to see what makes things tick. The trouble is he spends most of his time taking things apart. The next step will be to start putting things together. He'll do it—wait and see."

Marion had replied, "In the meantime, Michael won't have a thing left to play with."

Not that Michael had minded. He had adored Peter. Even though Peter technically went home for lunch, he was always back in no time and ended up having dessert with Michael.

If he hadn't been such a nuisance, Marion thought drearily. If he hadn't always tried to tell me what to do. Peter always noticed when something needed fixing. "Mrs. Blaine, your toaster cord is getting worn out. . . . Mrs. Blaine, you shouldn't tie Michael's shoelace in a knot when it breaks. You should get him a new one. . . . Mrs. Blaine . . ."

Inevitably, then, Marion recalled that Saturday in June when she'd been sitting on the terrace reading. The trees were blooming fully, gloriously, and Michael and Peter were playing in the backyard. They'd been getting excited about starting kindergarten in the fall and Michael had come over to ask her. "Are you sure they'll let us in? How will they know we're both five and a half?"

She'd smiled into his serious gray eyes and given him a special, cross-my-heart promise: She would take them both to school and tell the teacher to be sure to let them in. She was deep in the book again before she realized that Peter was standing next to her chair.

"There's a dead branch, you know," he had announced.

"A dead branch?"

"Right up there." He had pointed toward the elm that shaded the terrace. "See?"

He was right. One of the branches had no leaves on it. "Well, we'll have to see about that." She had tried to go back to the book.

"You ought to call the man to cut that branch off. It might fall down and hurt us."

Marion had felt her temper slowly warm. "Peter," she had said finally. "I'll call the man when I get good and ready, but be sure of one thing—if that branch does fall, with your luck you'll be a hundred miles away."

He'd smiled that accepting smile and had gone back to Michael. Afterward she'd glanced up. The branch certainly did look dry, and a local tree-surgery outfit was working across the street. She'd seen the truck. If she called them over . . .

Then she'd picked up her book firmly. No five-year-old was going to give her instructions. That branch had been dead all winter. If it hadn't come down when the winter ice was on it or in the March winds, it certainly would last a few days more.

And then the next day the branch had snapped from the tree when Michael climbed out on it.

She couldn't erase the scene from her mind: Michael's still form on the terrace; the branch sprawled beside him; Peter, his foot still on the part that hadn't snapped, clinging to the trunk of the tree.

It had been her fault, but Peter's too. Michael had climbed out on the dead branch, but if Peter hadn't followed him—Peter, who knew the branch wasn't safe—maybe it wouldn't have snapped. Maybe . . .

Michael was in a coma when they took him to the hospital. He opened his eyes just once and spoke. He stared at her and smiled and then said weakly: "Peter and I have a very good secret. Peter . . ."

Peter. It was his last word.

Marion got up and mechanically began clearing the table and tidying the kitchen. Then she went upstairs and dressed. She'd dismissed her cleaning woman, hoping that the physical work of scrubbing and waxing and vacuuming would wear her out and help her to sleep at night. But without Michael the house stayed unnaturally neat.

She dressed slowly, but it was only quarter past eight when she finished. She twisted her black hair into a French knot and went downstairs.

She wandered out onto the front porch and then wished she hadn't. The neighborhood children—freshly scrubbed and combed, miraculously neat in new clothes and shiny shoes—were hurrying past, excitedly discussing the opening of school. The ones starting kindergarten were obvious. They looked half eager, half fearful, and were clinging to their mothers' hands.

We'd be leaving too, Marion thought dully, and she gripped the porch railing. She didn't have the strength to walk the few steps to the door and go inside. She stood staring as the children passed, in twos and threes and larger groups, until at last they all seemed to be gone. All except one. He was coming down the block alone and was a little late. It was quarter of nine now.

Peter! She tore her eyes from him, looked down and saw the knuckles of her hands turn white as she gripped the railing. Then she forced herself to look back again.

She hadn't seen him since the day of the funeral. He'd been in bed for three days after the accident in deep shock. But when they had come back from the cemetery he was waiting. "Mrs. Blaine," he'd said, "Michael . . ."

She'd heard her own voice—ragged, out of control. "Get him away from me! Get him out of my sight!"

And she had not seen Peter again all summer. He and his ailing great-aunt had gone to a resort.

Peter seemed to have grown taller. He hadn't seen her yet but was walking slowly, staring at his feet. He looked forlorn and alone. She kept her eyes on him, whispering to herself: "I hate that child." But as she said it Peter looked up, met her gaze and smiled. He smiled as though he'd been expecting her but was afraid she'd be late. She could hear Michael's voice saying: "Peter is my friend."

Without thinking about it she walked down the steps of the porch and along the flagstone path to the sidewalk. She felt as though she were being dragged, the way she used to feel when Michael tugged insistently at her hand when he wanted her to hurry. She felt that he was reminding her of the cross-my-heart promise to take Peter and him to school on opening day.

She'd keep that promise. She'd go with Peter. No matter how you felt about a child, you couldn't let a little boy face his first day alone.

She was in front of him. Her lips felt dry and cracked. Scott had said she'd never get over losing Michael till she forgave this child. "Hello, Peter." It was scarcely audible.

His "hello" was matter-of-fact, ignoring the last three months.

"I'll walk you to school," she said.

He nodded and started trotting beside her. "I know, Michael said you promised to." His voice faltered over the name, and she realized with unwilling compassion that Peter must have had a lonely summer too.

Marion glanced down at his empty hands. "Didn't you bring a snack or milk money?" she asked. "The card from school said you were supposed to."

"I know." Peter's voice was resigned. "I reminded my aunt last night but she forgot. She always forgets things." Then his tone became anxious. "I won't be hungry, but do you think I should have brought a leaf?"

"A leaf?" Marion asked.

"Yes. The kids who were in kindergarten last year told Michael and me that if you bring in a leaf or something you can talk about it in Show and Tell. Michael was trying to get a great big one when he fell. I told him there was lots of time, but he wanted to."

Michael had been reaching for a leaf.

Marion closed her eyes, seeing again the scene in the backyard. Then she stopped abruptly and turned to face Peter. "But why did Michael climb on the dead branch? It didn't have any leaves."

Peter looked up at her, puzzled. "He didn't fall off the dead branch. He was on the one above it. When he fell I got scared and

I started out on the dead branch to catch him, and that was when it snapped off. But I was still holding onto the tree."

Marion sank to her knees before Peter and put both her hands on his shoulders. "Peter, please," she said, "this is terribly important. Are you sure that Michael didn't fall from the dead branch? Are you very, very sure?"

Peter looked even more puzzled. "But I told you—he was trying to get a leaf."

She pulled his head against her neck. "Thank you, thank you," she sobbed, and thought: I did not kill my child. I did not kill my child. Oh, Michael. And for the first time since his death the sound of his name brought peace. She felt about him the way she used to when he was asleep at night—warm, tucked in, cared for, without further need of her.

Peter pulled back a little. "Michael and I had a very good secret. I'd better tell you about it."

With his last breath Michael had tried to tell her about that secret. "What is it?"

"Well"—he looked a little proud, a little anxious—"it's just that Michael said that next to you and his daddy I was his very best friend. And if you're not mad at me anymore, can I still be? Because you can be best friends with Mr. Blaine, but I just had Michael."

Marion was suddenly conscious of the bony hardness of Peter's shoulders. He'd got terribly thin over the summer.

"I haven't been much of a friend to Mr. Blaine or anyone," she said unsteadily. "But, Peter, of course you're still best friends with Michael—and with Mr. Blaine and me too, if you want. I'll tell you what—after school I'll be waiting for you and we'll ask the other boys to come back to play with you." She smiled into his shining eyes. "Would you like that?"

Michael's toys were packed in the storage room in the basement. She'd have to dig them out—Peter had always had such fun taking them apart. She gave his hand a quick squeeze. "I'll bet anything," she told him, "that by now you're wonderful at putting things together again."

Voices in the Coalbin

It was dark when they arrived. Mike steered the car off the dirt road down the long driveway and stopped in front of the cottage. The real estate agent had promised to have the heat turned up and the lights on. She obviously didn't believe in wasting electricity.

An insect-repellent bulb over the door emitted a bleak yellowish beam that trembled in the steady drizzle. The small-paned windows were barely outlined by a faint flicker of light that seeped through a partially open blind.

Mike stretched. Ten hours of driving for the past two days had cramped his long, muscular body. He brushed back his dark brown hair from his forehead wishing he'd taken time to get a haircut before they left New York. Laurie teased him when his hair started to grow. "You look like a thirty-year-old Roman Emperor, Curlytop," she would comment. "All you need is a toga and laurel wreath to complete the effect."

She had fallen asleep about an hour ago. Her head was resting on his lap. He glanced down at her, hating to wake her up. Even though he could barely make out her profile, he knew that in sleep the tense lines vanished from around her mouth and the panic-stricken expression disappeared from her face.

Four months ago the recurring nightmare had begun, the nightmare that made her shriek, *"No, I won't go with you. I won't sing with you."*

He'd shaken her awake. "It's all right, sweetheart. It's all right."

Her screams would fade into terrified sobs. "I don't know who they are but they want me, Mike. I can't see their faces but they're all huddled together beckoning to me."

He had taken her to a psychiatrist, who put her on medication and began intensive therapy. But the nightmares continued, unabated. They had turned a gifted twenty-four-year-old singer who had just completed a run as a soloist in her first Broadway musical to a trembling wraith who could not be alone after dark.

The psychiatrist had suggested a vacation. Mike told him about the summers he'd spent at his grandmother's house on Oshbee Lake forty miles from Milwaukee. "My grandmother died last September," he'd explained. "The house is up for sale. Laurie's never been there and she loves the water."

The doctor had approved. "But be careful of her," he warned. "She's severely depressed. I'm sure these nightmares are a reaction to her childhood experiences, but they're overwhelming her."

Laurie had eagerly endorsed the chance to go away. Mike was a junior partner in his father's law firm. "Anything that will help Laurie," his father told him. "Take whatever time you need."

I remember brightness here, Mike thought as he studied the shadow-filled cottage with increasing dismay. I remember the feel of the water when I dove in, the warmth of the sun on my face, the way the breeze filled the sails and the boat skimmed across the lake.

It was the end of June but it might have been early March. According to the radio, the cold spell had been gripping Wisconsin for three days. There'd better be enough coal to get the furnace going, Mike thought, or else the real estate agent will lose the listing.

He had to wake up Laurie. It would be worse to leave her in the car, even for a minute. "We're here, love," he said, his voice falsely cheerful.

Laurie stirred. He felt her stiffen, then relax as he tightened his arms around her. "It's so dark," she whispered.

"We'll get inside and turn some lights on."

He remembered how the lock had always been tricky. You had to pull the door to you before the key could fit into the cylinder. There was a night-light plugged into an outlet in the small foyer. The house was not warm but neither was it the bone-chilling cold he had feared.

Quickly Mike switched on the hall light. The wallpaper with its climbing ivy pattern seemed faded and soiled. The house had been rented for the five summers his grandmother was in the nursing home. Mike remembered how clean and warm and welcoming it had been when she was living there.

Laurie's silence was ominous. His arm around her, he brought her into the living room. The overstuffed velour furniture that used to welcome his body when he settled in with a book was still in place but, like the wallpaper, seemed soiled and shabby.

Mike's forehead furrowed into a troubled frown. "Honey, I'm sorry. Coming here was a lousy idea. Do you want to go to a motel? We passed a couple that looked pretty decent."

Laurie smiled up at him. "Mike, I want to stay here. I want you to share with me all those wonderful summers you spent in this place. I want to pretend your grandmother was mine. Then maybe I'll get over whatever is happening to me."

Laurie's grandmother had raised her. A fear-ridden neurotic, she had tried to instill in Laurie fear of the dark, fear of strangers, fear of planes and cars, fear of animals. When Laurie and Mike met two years ago, she'd shocked and amused him by reciting some of the litany of hair-raising stories that her grandmother had fed her on a daily basis.

"How did you turn out so normal, so much fun?" Mike used to ask her.

"I was damned if I'd let her turn me into a certified nut." But the last four months had proved that Laurie had not escaped after all, that there was psychological damage that needed repairing.

Now Mike smiled down at her, loving the vivid sea-green eyes, the thick dark lashes that threw shadows on her porcelain skin, the way tendrils of chestnut hair framed her oval face.

"You're so darn pretty," he said, "and sure I'll tell you all about Grandma. You only knew her when she was an invalid. I'll tell you about fishing with her in a storm, about jogging around the lake and her yelling for me to keep up the pace, about finally managing to outswim her when she was sixty."

Laurie took his face in her hands. "Help me to be like her."

Together they brought in their suitcases and the groceries they had purchased along the way. Mike went down to the basement. He grimaced when he glanced at the coalbin. It was fairly large, a four-feet-wide by six-feet-long plankboard enclosure situated next to the furnace and directly under the window that served as an opening for the chute from the delivery truck. Mike remembered how when he was eight he'd helped his grandmother replace some of the boards on the bin. Now they all looked rotted.

"Nights get cold even in the summer but we'll always be plenty warm, Mike," his grandmother would say cheerily as she let him shovel coal into the old blackened furnace.

Mike remembered the bin as always heaped with shiny black nuggets. Now it was nearly empty. There was barely enough coal for two or three days. He reached for the shovel.

The furnace was still serviceable. Its rumbling sound quickly echoed throughout the house. The ducts thumped and rattled as hot air wheezed through them.

In the kitchen Laurie had unpacked the groceries and begun to make a salad. Mike grilled a steak. They opened a bottle of Bordeaux and sat side by side at the old enamel table, their shoulders companionably touching.

They were on their way up the staircase to bed when Mike spotted the note from the real estate agent on the foyer table: "Hope you find everything in order. Sorry about the weather. Coal delivery on Friday."

They decided to use his grandmother's room. "She loved that metal-frame bed," Mike said. "Always claimed that there wasn't a night she didn't sleep like a baby in it."

"Let's hope it works that way for me." Laurie sighed. There were clean sheets in the linen closet but they felt damp and clammy. The boxspring and mattress smelled musty.

"Warm me up," Laurie whispered, shivering as they pulled the covers over them.

"My pleasure."

They fell asleep in each other's arms. At three o'clock Laurie began to shriek, a piercing, wailing scream that filled the house. "Go away. Go away. I won't. I won't."

It was dawn before she stopped sobbing. "They're getting closer," she told Mike. "They're getting closer."

The rain persisted throughout the day. The outside thermometer registered thirty-eight degrees. They read all morning curled up on the velour couches. Mike watched as Laurie began to unwind. When she fell into a deep sleep after lunch, he went into the kitchen and called the psychiatrist.

"Her sense that they're getting closer may be a good sign," the doctor told him. "Possibly she's on the verge of a breakthrough. I'm convinced the root of these nightmares is in all the old wives' tales her grandmother told Laurie. If we can isolate exactly which one caused this fear, we'll be able to exorcise it and all the others. Watch her carefully, but remember. She's a strong girl and she wants to get well. That's half the battle."

When Laurie woke up, they decided to inventory the house. "Dad said we can have anything we want," Mike reminded her. "A couple of the tables are antiques and that clock on the mantel is a gem." There was a storage closet in the foyer. They began dragging its contents into the living room. Laurie, looking about eighteen in jeans and a sweater, her hair tied loosely in a chignon, became animated as she went through them. "The local artists were pretty lousy," she laughed, "but the frames are great. Can't you just see them on our walls?"

Last year as a wedding present, Mike's family had bought them a loft in Greenwich Village. Until four months ago, they'd spent their spare time going to garage sales and auctions looking for bargains. Since the nightmares began, Laurie had lost interest in furnishing the apartment. Mike crossed his fingers. Maybe she *was* starting to get better.

On the top shelf buried behind patchwork quilts he discovered a Victrola. "Oh, my God, I'd forgotten about that," he said. "What a find! Look. Here are a bunch of old records."

He did not notice Laurie's sudden silence as he brushed the layers of dust from the Victrola and lifted the lid. The Edison trademark, a dog listening to a tube and the caption *His Master's Voice* was on the inside of the lid. "It even has a needle in it," Mike said. Quickly he placed a record on the turntable, cranked the handle, slid the starter to "On" and watched as the disk began to revolve. Carefully he placed the arm with its thin, delicate needle in the first groove.

The record was scratched. The singers' voices were male but high-pitched, almost to the point of falsetto. The effect was out of synch, music being played too rapidly. "I can't make out the words," Mike said. "Do you recognize it?"

"It's 'Chinatown,'" Laurie said. "Listen." She began to sing with the record, her lovely soprano voice leading the chorus. *Hearts that know no other world, drifting to and fro.* Her voice broke. Gasping, she screamed, *"Turn it off, Mike. Turn it off now!"* She covered her ears with her hands and sank onto her knees, her face deathly white.

Mike yanked the needle away from the record. "Honey, what is it?"

"I don't know. I just don't know."

That night the nightmare took a different form. This time the approaching figures were singing "Chinatown" and in falsetto voices demanding Laurie come sing with them.

At dawn they sat in the kitchen sipping coffee. "Mike, it's coming back to me," Laurie told him. "When I was little. My grandmother had one of those Victrolas. She had that same record. I asked her where the people were who were singing. I thought they had to be hiding in the house somewhere. She took me down to the basement and pointed to the coalbin. She said the voices were coming from there. She swore to me that the people who were singing were in the coalbin."

Mike put down his coffee cup. "Good God!"

"I never went down to the basement after that. I was afraid. Then we moved to an apartment and she gave the Victrola away. I guess that's why I forgot." Laurie's eyes began to blaze with hope. "Mike, maybe that old fear caught up with me for some reason. I was so exhausted by the time the show closed. Right after that the nightmares started. Mike, that record was made years and years ago. The singers are probably all dead by now. And I certainly have learned how sound is reproduced. Maybe it's going to be all right."

"You bet it's going to be all right." Mike stood up and reached for her hand. "You game for something? There's a coalbin downstairs. I want you to come down with me and look at it."

Laurie's eyes filled with panic, then she bit her lip. "Let's go," she said.

Mike studied Laurie's face as her eyes darted around the basement. Through her eyes he realized how dingy it was. The single lightbulb dangling from the ceiling. The cinder-block walls glistening with dampness. The cement dust from the floor that clung to their bedroom slippers. The concrete steps that led to the set of metal doors that opened to a backyard. The rusty bolt that secured them looked as though it had not been opened in years.

The coalbin was adjacent to the furnace at the front end of the house. Mike felt Laurie's nails dig into his palm as they walked over to it.

"We're practically out of coal," he told her. "It's a good thing they're supposed to deliver today. Tell me, honey, what do you see here?"

"A bin. About ten shovelfuls of coal at best. A window. I remember when the delivery truck came how they put the chute through the window and the coal roared down. I used to wonder if it hurt the singers when it fell on them." Laurie tried to laugh. "No visible sign of anyone in residence here. Nightmares at rest, please God."

Hand in hand they went back upstairs. Laurie yawned. "I'm so tired, Mike. And you, poor guy, haven't had a decent night's rest in months because of me. Why don't we just go back to bed and sleep the day away. I bet anything I won't wake up with a dream."

They drifted off to sleep, her hand on his chest, his arms encircling her. "Sweet dreams, love," he whispered.

"I promise they will be. I love you, Mike. Thank you for everything."

The sound of coal rushing down the chute awakened Mike. He blinked. Behind the shades, light was streaming in. Automatically he glanced at his watch. Nearly three o'clock. God, he really must have been bushed. Laurie was already up. He pulled khaki slacks on, stuffed his feet into sneakers, listened for sounds from the bathroom. There were none. Laurie's robe and slippers were on the chair. She must be already dressed. With sudden unreasoning dread, Mike yanked a sweatshirt over his head.

The living room. The dining room. The kitchen. Their coffee cups were still on the table, the chairs pushed back as they left them. Mike's throat closed. The hurtling sound of the coal was lessening. *The coal.* Maybe. He took the cellar stairs two at a time. Coal dust was billowing through the basement. Shiny black nuggets of coal were heaped high in the bin. He heard the snap of the window being closed. He stared down at the footsteps on the floor. The imprints of his sneakers. The side-by-side impressions left when he and Laurie had come down this morning in their slippers.

And then he saw the step-by-step imprints of Laurie's bare feet, the lovely high-arched impressions of her slender, fine-boned feet. The impressions stopped at the coalbin. There was no sign of them returning to the stairs.

The bell rang, the shrill, high-pitched, insistent gong-like sound that had always annoyed him and amused his grandmother. Mike raced up the stairs. Laurie. Let it be Laurie.

The truck driver had a bill in his hand. "Sign for the delivery, sir."

The delivery. Mike grabbed the man's arm. "When you started the coal down the chute, did you look into the bin?"

Puzzled faded blue eyes in a pleasant weather-beaten face looked squarely at him. "Yeah, sure, I glanced in to make sure how much you needed. You were just about out. You didn't have enough for the day. The rain's over but it's gonna stay real cold."

Mike tried to sound calm. "Would you have seen if someone was in the coalbin? I mean, it's dark in the basement. Would you have noticed if a slim young woman had maybe fainted in there?" He could read the deliveryman's mind. He thinks I'm drunk or on drugs. "Don't you get it?" Mike shouted. "My wife is missing. My wife is missing."

For days they searched for Laurie. Feverishly, Mike searched with them. He walked every inch of the heavily wooded areas around the cottage. He sat, hunched and shivering on the deck as they dragged the lake. He stood unbelieving as the newly delivered coal was shoveled from the bin and heaped onto the basement floor.

Surrounded by policemen, all of whose names and faces made no impression on him, he spoke with Laurie's doctor. In a flat, disbelieving tone he told the doctor about Laurie's fear of the voices in the coalbin. When he was finished, the police chief spoke to the doctor. When he hung up, he gripped Mike's shoulder. "We'll keep looking."

Four days later a diver found Laurie's body tangled in weeds in the lake. Death by drowning. She was wearing her nightgown. Bits of coal dust were still clinging to her skin and hair. The police chief tried and could not soften the stark tragedy of her death. "That was why her footsteps stopped at the bin. She must have gotten into it and climbed out of the window. It's pretty wide, you know, and she was a slender girl. I've talked again to her doctor. She probably would have committed suicide before this if you hadn't been there for her. Terrible the way people screw up their children. Her doctor said that her grandmother petrified her with crazy superstitions before the poor kid was old enough to toddle."

"She talked to me. She was getting there." Mike heard his protests, heard himself making arrangements for Laurie's body to be cremated.

The next morning as he was packing, the real estate agent came over, a sensibly dressed, white-haired, thin-faced woman whose brisk air did not conceal the sympathy in her eyes. "We have a buyer for the house," she said. "I'll arrange to have anything you want to keep shipped."

The clock. The antique tables. The pictures that Laurie had laughed over in their beautiful frames. Mike tried to picture going into the Greenwich Village loft alone and could not.

"How about the Victrola?" the real estate agent asked. "It's a real treasure."

Mike had placed it back in the storage closet. Now he took it out, seeing Laurie's terror, hearing her begin to sing "Chinatown," her voice blending with the falsetto voices on the old record. "I don't know if I want it," he said.

The real estate agent looked disapproving. "It's a collector's item. I have to be off. Just let me know about it."

Mike watched as her car disappeared around the winding driveway. *Laurie, I want you.* He lifted the lid of the Victrola as he had five days ago, an eon ago. He cranked the handle, found the "Chinatown" record, placed it on the turntable, turned the switch to the "On" position. He watched as the record picked up speed, then released the arm and placed the needle in the starting groove.

"Chinatown, my Chinatown . . ."

Mike felt his body go cold. *No! No!* Unable to move, unable to breathe, he stared at the spinning record.

"... hearts that know no other world drifting to and fro ..."

Over the scratchy, falsetto voices of the long-ago singers, Laurie's exquisite soprano was filling the room with its heart-stopping, plaintive beauty.

The Cape Cod Masquerade

It was on an August afternoon shortly after they arrived at their rented cottage in the village of Dennis on Cape Cod that Alvirah Meehan noticed that there was something very odd about their next-door neighbor, a painfully thin young woman who appeared to be in her late twenties.

After Alvirah and Willy looked around their cottage a bit, remarking favorably about the four-poster maple bed, the hooked rugs, the cheery kitchen and the fresh, sea-scented breeze, they unpacked their expensive new clothes from their matching Vuitton luggage. Willy then poured an ice-cold beer for each to enjoy on the deck of the house, which overlooked Cape Cod Bay.

Willy, his rotund body eased onto a padded wicker chaise lounge, remarked that it was going to be one heck of a sunset, and thank God for a little peace. Ever since they had won forty million dollars in the New York State lottery, it seemed to Willy, Alvirah had been a walking lightning rod. First she went to the famous Cypress Point Spa in California and nearly got murdered. Then they had gone on a cruise together and—wouldn't you know—the man who sat next to them at the community table in the dining room ended up dead as a mackerel. Still, with the accumulated wisdom of his years, Willy was sure that in Cape Cod, at least, they'd have the quiet he'd been searching for. If Alvirah wrote an article for the *New York Globe* about this vacation, it would have to do with the weather and the fishing.

During his narration, Alvirah was sitting at the picnic table, a companionable few feet away from Willy's stretched-out form. She wished she'd remembered to put on a sun hat. The beautician at Sassoon's had warned her against getting sun on her hair. "It's such a lovely rust shade now, Mrs. Meehan. We don't want it to get those nasty yellow streaks, do we?"

Since recovering from the attempt on her life at the spa, Alvirah had regained all the weight she'd paid three thousand dollars to lose and was again a comfortable size somewhere between a 14 and a 16. But Willy constantly observed that when he put his arms around her, he knew he was holding a woman—not one of those half-starved zombies you see in the fashion ads Alvirah was so fond of studying.

Forty years of affectionately listening to Willy's observations had left Alvirah with the ability to hear him with one ear and close him out with the other. Now as she gazed at the tranquil cottages perched atop the grass-and-sand embankment that served as a seawall, then down below at the sparkling blue-green water and the stretch of rock-strewn beach, she had the troubled feeling that maybe Willy was right. Beautiful as the Cape was, and even though it was a place she had always longed to visit, she might not find a newsworthy story here for her editor, Charley Evans.

Two years ago Charley had sent a *New York Globe* reporter to interview the Meehans on how it felt to win forty million dollars. What would they do with it? Alvirah was a cleaning woman. Willy was a plumber. Would they continue in their jobs?

Alvirah had told the reporter in no uncertain terms that she wasn't that dumb, that the next time she picked up a broom it would be when she was dressed as a witch for a Knights of Columbus costume party. Then she had made a list of all the things she wanted to do, and first was the visit to the Cypress Point Spa—where she planned to hobnob with the celebrities she'd been reading about all her life.

That had led Charley Evans to ask her to write an article for the *Globe* about her stay at the spa. He gave her a sunburst pin that contained a microphone so that she could record her impressions of the people she spoke with and play the tape back when she wrote the article.

The thought of her pin brought an unconscious smile to Alvirah's face.

As Willy said, she'd gotten into hot water at Cypress Point. She'd picked up on what was really going on and was nearly murdered for her trouble. But it had been so exciting, and now she was great friends with everyone at the spa and could go there every year as a guest. And thanks to her help solving the murder on the ship last year, they had an invitation to take a free cruise to Alaska anytime they desired.

Cape Cod was beautiful, but Alvirah had a sneaking suspicion Willy might be right, that this might be an ordinary vacation that wouldn't make good copy for the *Globe*.

Precisely at that moment she glanced over the row of hedges on the right perimeter of their property and observed a young woman with a somber expression standing at the railing of her porch next door and staring at the bay.

It was the way her hands were gripping the railing: Tension, Alvirah thought. She's stuffed with it. It was the way the young woman turned her head, looked straight into Alvirah's eyes, then turned away again. She didn't even see me, Alvirah decided. The fifty- to sixty-foot distance between them did not prevent her from realizing that waves of pain and despair were radiating from the young woman.

Clearly it was time to see if she could help. "I think I'll just introduce myself to our neighbor," she said to Willy. "There's something up with her." She walked down the steps and strolled over to the hedge. "Hello," she said in her friendliest voice. "I saw you drive in.

We've been here for two hours, so I guess that makes us the welcoming committee. I'm Alvirah Meehan."

The young woman turned, and Alvirah felt instant compassion. She looked as though she had been ill. That ghostly pallor, the soft, unused muscles of her arms and legs. "I don't mean to be rude, but I came here to be alone, not to be neighborly," she said quietly. "Excuse me, please." That probably would have been the end of it, as Alvirah later observed, except that as she spun on her heel the girl tripped over a footstool and fell heavily onto the porch. Alvirah rushed to help her up, refused to allow her to go into her cottage unaided and, feeling responsible for the accident, wrapped an ice pack around her rapidly swelling wrist. By the time she had satisfied herself that the wrist was only sprained and made her a cup of tea, Alvirah had learned that her name was Cynthia Rogers and that she was a schoolteacher from Illinois. That piece of information hit with a resounding thud on Alvirah's ears because, as she told Willy when she returned to their place an hour later, within ten minutes she'd recognized their neighbor. "The poor girl may call herself Cynthia Rogers," Alvirah confided to Willy, "but her real name is Cynthia Lathem. She was found guilty of murdering her stepfather twelve years ago. He had big bucks and was well known. All the papers carried the story. I remember it like it was yesterday."

"You remember everything like it was yesterday," Willy commented.

"That's the truth. And you know I always read about murders. Anyhow, this one happened here on Cape Cod. Cynthia swore she was innocent, and she always said there was a witness who could prove she'd been out of the house at the time of the murder, but the jury didn't believe her story. I wonder why she came back. I'll have to call the *Globe* and have Charley Evans send me the files on the case. She's probably just been released from prison. Her complexion is pure gray. Maybe"—and now Alvirah's eyes became thoughtful—"she's up here because she really is innocent and is still looking for that missing witness to prove her story!" To Willy's dismay, Alvirah opened the top drawer of the dresser, took out her sunburst pin with the hidden microphone and began to dial her editor's direct line in New York.

That night, Willy and Alvirah ate at the Red Pheasant Inn. Alvirah wore a beige-and-blue print dress she had bought at Bergdorf Goodman but which, as she remarked to Willy, somehow didn't look much different on her than the print dress she'd bought in Alexander's just before they won the lottery. "It's my full figure," she lamented as she spread butter on a warm cranberry muffin. "My, these muffins are good. And, Willy, I'm glad that you bought that yellow linen jacket. It shows up your blue eyes, and you still have a fine head of hair."

"I feel like a two-hundred-pound canary," Willy commented, "but as long as you like it."

After dinner they went to the Cape Playhouse and thrilled to the performance of Debbie Reynolds in a new comedy being tried out for Broadway. At intermission, as they sipped ginger ale on the grass outside the theater, Alvirah told Willy how she'd always enjoyed Debbie Reynolds from the time Debbie was a kid doing *Singin' in the Rain* with Gene Kelly, and that it was a terrible thing Eddie Fisher ditched her when they had those two small babies. "And what good did it do him?" Alvirah philosophized as the warning came to return to their seats for the second act. "He never had much luck after that. People who don't do the right thing usually don't win in the end." That comment led Alvirah to wonder whether Charley had sent the information on their neighbor by Express Mail. She was anxious to read it.

As Alvirah and Willy were enjoying Debbie Reynolds, Cynthia Lathem was at last beginning to realize that she was really free, that twelve years of prison were behind her. Twelve years ago . . . she'd been about to start her junior year at the Rhode Island School of Design when her stepfather, Stuart Richards, was found shot to death in the study of his mansion, a stately eighteenth-century captain's house in Dennis.

That afternoon Cynthia had driven past the house on her way to the cottage and pulled off the road to study it. Who was there now? she wondered. Had her stepsister Lillian sold it or had she kept it? It had been in the Richards family for three generations, but Lillian had never been sentimental. And then Cynthia had pressed her foot on the accelerator, chilled at the rush of memories of that awful night and the days that followed. The accusation. The arrest, arraignment, trial. Her early confidence. "I can absolutely prove that I left the house at eight o'clock and didn't get home till past midnight. I was on a date."

Now Cynthia shivered and wrapped the light blue woolen robe more tightly around her slender body. She'd weighed 125 pounds when she went to prison. Her present weight, 110, was not enough for her five-foot eight-inch height. Her hair, once a dark blonde, had changed in those years to a medium brown. Drab, she thought as she brushed it. Her eyes, the same shade of hazel as her mother's, were listless and vacant. At lunch that last day Stuart Richards had said, "You look more like your mother all the time. I should have had the brains to hang on to her."

Her mother had been married to Stuart from the time Cynthia was eight until she was twelve, the longer of his two marriages. Lillian, his only birth child, ten years older than Cynthia, had lived with her mother in New York and seldom visited the Cape.

Cynthia laid the brush on the dresser. Had it been a crazy impulse to come here? Two weeks out of prison, barely enough money to live on for six months, not knowing what she could do or would do with her life. Should she have spent so much to rent this cottage, to rent a car? Was there any point to it? What did she hope to accomplish?

A needle in a haystack, she thought. Walking into the small parlor, she reflected that compared to Stuart's mansion, this house was tiny, but after years of confinement it seemed palatial. Outside, the sea breeze was blowing the bay into churning waves. Cynthia walked out on the porch, only vaguely aware of her throbbing wrist, hugging her arms against the chill. But, oh God, to breathe fresh, clean air, to know that if she wanted to get up at dawn and walk the beach the way she had as a child, no one could stop her. The moon, three-quarters full, looking as though a wedge had been neatly sliced from it, made the Bay glisten, a silvery midnight blue. But where the moon did not reach it, the water appeared dark and impenetrable.

Cynthia stared unseeingly as her mind wrenched her back to the terrible night when Stuart was murdered. Then she shook her head. No, she would not allow herself to think about that now. Not tonight. This was a time to let the peace of this place fill her soul. She would go to bed, and she'd leave the windows wide open so that the cool night wind would pour into her room, making her pull the covers closer around her, deepening her sleep.

Tomorrow morning she would wake up early and walk on the beach. She'd feel the wet sand under her feet, and she'd look for shells, just as she had when she was a child. Tomorrow. Yes, she'd give herself the morning to help bridge her reentry into the world, to regain her sense of equilibrium. And then she would begin the quest, probably hopeless, for the one person who would know that she had told the truth.

The next morning, as Alvirah prepared breakfast, Willy drove to get the morning papers. When he returned he was also carrying a bag of still-hot blueberry muffins. "I asked around," he told a delighted Alvirah. "Everyone said to go to the Mercantile behind the post office for the best muffins on the Cape."

They ate at the picnic table on the deck. As she nibbled on her second blueberry muffin, Alvirah studied the early morning joggers on the beach.

"Look, there she is!"

"There *who* is?"

"Cynthia Lathem. She's been gone at least an hour and a half. I bet she's starving."

When Cynthia ascended the steps from the beach to her deck, she was met by a beaming Alvirah, who linked her arm in Cynthia's. "I make the best coffee and fresh-squeezed orange juice. And wait till you taste the blueberry muffins."

"I really don't want—" Cynthia tried to pull back but was propelled across the lawn. Willy jumped up to pull out a bench for her.

"How's your wrist?" he asked. "Alvirah's been real upset that you sprained it when she went over to visit."

Cynthia realized that her mounting irritation was being overcome by the genuine warmth she saw on both their faces. Willy—with his rounded cheeks, strong, pleasant expression and thick mane of white hair—reminded her of Tip O'Neill. She told him that.

Willy beamed. "Fellow just remarked on that in the bakery. Only difference is that while Tip was *speaker* of the house, I was *savior* of the *outhouse*. I'm a retired plumber."

As Cynthia sipped the fresh orange juice and the coffee and picked at the muffin, she listened with disbelief, then awe, as Alvirah told her about winning the lottery, going to Cypress Point Spa and helping to track down a murderer, then going on an Alaskan cruise and figuring out who killed the man who sat next to her at the community table.

She accepted a second cup of coffee. "You've told me all this for a reason, haven't you?" Cynthia said. "You recognized me yesterday, didn't you?"

Alvirah's expression became serious. "Yes."

Cynthia pushed back her bench. "You've been very kind, and I think you want to help me, but the best way you can do that is to leave me alone. I have a lot of things to work out, but I have to do them myself. Thank you for breakfast."

Alvirah watched the slender young woman walk between the two cottages. "She got a little sun this morning," she observed. "Very becoming. When she fills out a little, she'll be a beautiful girl."

"You may as well plan on getting the sun too," Willy observed. "You heard her."

"Oh, forget it. Once Charley sends the files on her case I'll figure out a way to help her."

"Oh my God," Willy moaned. "I might have known. Here we go again."

"I don't know how Charley does it," Alvirah sighed approvingly an hour later. The overnight Express Mail envelope had just arrived. "It looks as though he sent every word anyone ever wrote about the case." She made a tsk-tsking sound. "Look at this picture of Cynthia at the trial. She was just a scared kid."

Methodically, Alvirah began sorting the clippings on the table; then she got out her lined pad and pen and began to make notes.

Willy was reclining on the padded chaise he had claimed for his own, deeply immersed in the sports section of the *Cape Cod Times*. "I'm just about ready to give up on the Mets getting the pennant," he commented sadly, shaking his head.

He looked up for reassurance, but it was clear that Alvirah had not heard him.

At one o'clock Willy went out again, returning this time with a quart of lobster bisque. Over lunch Alvirah filled him in on what she had learned. "In a nutshell, here are the facts: Cynthia's mother was a widow when she married Stuart Richards. Cynthia was eight at the time. They divorced four years later. Richards had one child by his first marriage, a daughter named Lillian. She was ten years older than Cynthia and lived with her mother in New York."

"Why'd Cynthia's mother divorce Richards?" Willy asked between sips of the bisque.

"From what Cynthia said on the witness stand, Richards was one of those men who always belittled women. Her mother would be dressed to go out, and he'd reduce her to tears by ridiculing what she was wearing—that kind of thing. Sounds like he just about gave her a nervous breakdown. Apparently, though, he had always been fond of Cynthia, always taking her out around her birthday and giving her presents.

"Then Cynthia's mother died, and Richards invited the young girl to visit him here at Cape Cod. Actually she wasn't so young by then—she was about to start her junior year at the Rhode Island School of Design. Her mother had been sick for a while, and there apparently wasn't much money left; she said she was planning on dropping out of school and working for a year or two. She claimed that Stuart told her that he'd always planned to leave half his money to his daughter Lillian and the other half to Dartmouth College. But he stayed so angry after Dartmouth let women in as full-time students that he changed his will. She said he told her he was leaving her the Dartmouth portion of his estate, about ten million dollars. The prosecutor got Cynthia to admit that Richards also told her she'd have to wait for him to die to get it; that it was too bad about college, but that her mother should have provided for her education."

Willy put down his spoon. "So there's your motive, huh?"

"That's what the prosecutor said, that Cynthia had wanted the money right away. Anyhow, a guy named Ned Creighton happened to drop in to visit Richards and overheard their conversation. He was a friend of Lillian's, about her age. Cynthia apparently had known him slightly from when she and her mother had lived with Richards at the Cape. So Creighton invited Cynthia to have dinner with him, and Stuart urged her to go.

"According to her testimony, she and Creighton had dinner at the Captain's Table in Hyannis, and then he suggested they go for a ride in his boat, which was anchored at a private dock. She said they were out on the Nantucket Sound when the boat broke down; nothing was working, not even the radio. They were stranded until nearly eleven, when he was finally able to get the motor going again. She apparently had only had a salad at dinner, so once they made shore she asked him to stop for a hamburger.

"She testified that Creighton wasn't very happy about having to stop on the way home, although he did finally pull in at some hamburger joint around Cotuit. Cynthia said she hadn't been on the Cape since she was a child and didn't know the area all that well, so she wasn't sure exactly where they stopped. Anyway, he told her to wait in the car, that he would go in and get the burger. All she remembered about being there was a lot of rock music blaring and seeing teenagers all over the place. But then a woman drove up and parked next to their car, and when she opened her door, it slammed into the side of Creighton's car." Alvirah handed Willy a clipping. "That woman, then, is the witness no one could find."

As Alvirah absentmindedly sipped the bisque, Willy scanned the paper. The woman had apologized profusely and had examined Ned's car for scratches. When she found none, she'd headed into the hamburger joint. According to Cynthia, the woman had been in her mid- to late-forties, chunky, with blunt-cut hair dyed an orange-red shade, and she'd been wearing a shapeless blouse and elastic-waisted polyester slacks.

The clipping went on to recount Cynthia's testimony that Creighton had returned complaining about the line for food and about kids who couldn't make up their minds when they gave an order. She said he'd been obviously edgy, so she didn't tell him at the time about the woman banging the door into his car.

On the witness stand, Cynthia had testified that during the forty-five-minute drive back to Dennis, all of it along unfamiliar roads, Ned Creighton had hardly said a word to her. Then, once they reached Stuart Richards's house, he'd just dropped her off and driven away. When Cynthia went into the house, she'd found Stuart in his study, sprawled on the floor next to his desk, blood drenching his forehead, blood caked on his face, blood matting the carpet beside him.

Willy read more of the account out loud: "'The defendant stated that she thought Richards had had a stroke and had fallen, but that when she brushed his hair back she saw the bullet wound in his forehead, then spotted the gun lying next to him, and she telephoned the police.'"

"She said she thought then that he had committed suicide," Alvirah recounted. "But then she picked up the gun, of course putting her fingerprints on it. The armoire in the study was open, and she admitted that she knew Richards kept a gun in it. Then Creighton contradicted just about everything she had told the police, saying that, yes, he had taken her out to dinner, but that he had gotten her home by eight o'clock, and that all through the meal she had gone on about how she blamed Stuart Richards for her mother's illness and death, and that she intended to have it out with him when she got home. The time of death was established at about nine o'clock, which of course looked bad for her, given Creighton's contrary testimony. And even though her lawyers advertised for the woman she'd met at the burger joint, nobody came forward to verify her story."

"So do you believe Cynthia?" Willy asked. "You know an awful lot of murderers can't face the reality of what they've done and actually end up believing their own lies, or at least go through the motions of trying to confirm them. She could just be looking for this missing witness in an effort to finally convince people of her innocence, even though she's already served her time. I mean, why on earth would Ned Creighton lie about the whole thing?"

"I don't know," Alvirah said, shaking her head. "But you can be sure that somebody is lying, and I'll bet my bottom dollar that it isn't Cynthia. If I were in her boots, I'd set off to try and find out what it was that made Creighton lie, what was in it for him."

With that, Alvirah turned her attention to the bisque, not speaking again until she had finished it off. "My, that was good. What a great vacation we're going to have, Willy. And isn't it wonderful that we took this cottage right next to Cynthia so that I'm here to help her clear her name?"

Willy's only response was the clatter of a spoon and a deep sigh.

The long and peaceful night's sleep followed by the early morning walk had begun to clear the emotional paralysis that Cynthia had experienced from that moment twelve years earlier when she'd heard the jury pronounce the verdict: *Guilty.* Now as she showered and dressed she reflected that these past years had been a nightmare in which she had managed to survive only by freezing her emotions. She had been a model prisoner. She had kept to herself, resisting friendships. She had taken whatever jailhouse college courses were offered. She had graduated from working in the laundry and the kitchen to desk assignments in the library and assistant teaching in the art class. And after a while, when the awful reality of what had happened finally set in, she had begun to draw. The face of the woman in the parking lot. The hamburger stand. Ned's boat. Every detail she could force from her memory. When she was finished she had pictures of a hamburger place that could be found anywhere in the United States, a boat that looked like any Chris-Craft of that year. The woman was a little more clearly defined but not much. It had been dark. Their encounter had lasted only seconds. But the woman was her only hope.

The prosecutor's summation at the end of the trial: "Ladies and gentlemen of the jury, Cynthia Lathem returned to the home of Stuart Richards sometime between 8:00 and 8:30 P.M. on the night of August 2, 1981. She went into her stepfather's study. That very afternoon Stuart Richards had told Cynthia he had changed his will. Ned Creighton heard that conversation, overheard Cynthia and Stuart quarreling. She needed money immediately to pay for her education and demanded he help her. That evening Vera Smith, the waitress at the Captain's Table, overheard Cynthia tell Ned that she would have to drop out of school.

"Cynthia Lathem returned to the Richards mansion that night, angry and worried. She went into that study and confronted Stuart Richards. He was a man who enjoyed upsetting the people around him. He *had* changed his will to include her, but she knew it would be just like him to change it again. And the anger she'd harbored for the way he had treated her mother, the anger that rose in her at the thought of having to leave school, at being turned out into the world virtually penniless, made her go to the armoire where she knew he kept a gun, take out that gun and fire three shots pointblank into the forehead of the man who loved her enough to make her an heiress.

"It is ironic. It is tragic. It is also murder. Cynthia begged Ned Creighton to say that she had spent the evening with him on his boat. No one saw them out on the boat. She talks about stopping at a hamburger stand. But she doesn't know where it is. She admits she never entered it. She talks about a stranger with red-orange hair to whom she spoke in a parking lot. With all the publicity this case has engendered, why didn't that woman come forward? You know the reason. Because she doesn't exist. Because like the hamburger stand and the hours spent on a boat on Nantucket Sound, she is a figment of Cynthia Lathem's imagination."

Cynthia had read the transcript of the trial so often that she had the district attorney's summation committed to memory. "But the woman did exist," Cynthia said aloud. "She does exist." For the next six months, with the little insurance money left her by her mother, she was going to try to find that woman. She might be dead by now, or moved to California, Cynthia thought as she brushed her hair and twisted it into a chignon.

The bedroom of the cottage faced the sea. Cynthia walked to the sliding door and pulled it open. On the beach below she could see couples walking with children. If she was ever to have a normal life, a husband, a child of her own, she had to clear her name.

Jeff Knight. She had met him last year when he came to do a series of television interviews with women in prison. He'd invited her to participate, and she'd flatly refused. He'd persisted, his strong intelligent face filled with concern. "Don't you understand, Cynthia, this program is going to be watched by a couple of million people in New England. The woman who saw you that night could be one of those people."

That was why she finally had agreed to go on the program, had answered his questions, told about the night Stuart died, held up the shadowy sketch of the woman she had spoken with, the sketch of the hamburger stand. And no one had come forward. From New York, Lillian issued a statement saying that the truth had been told at the trial and she would have no further comment. Ned Creighton, now the owner of the Mooncusser, a popular restaurant in Barnstable, repeated how very, very sorry he was for Cynthia.

After the program, Jeff kept coming to see her on visiting days. Only those visits had kept her from total despair when the program produced no results. He would always arrive a little rumpled-looking, his wide shoulders straining at his jacket, his unsettled dark-brown hair curling on his forehead, his brown eyes intense and kind, his long legs never able to find enough room in the cramped visiting area of the prison. When he asked her to marry him after her release, she told him to forget her. He was already getting bids from the networks. He didn't need a convicted murderer in his life.

But what if I weren't a convicted murderer? Cynthia thought as she turned away from the window. She went over to the maple dresser, reached for her pocketbook and went outside to her rented car.

It was early evening before she returned to Dennis. The frustration of the wasted hours had finally brought tears to her eyes. She let them run down her cheeks unchecked. She'd driven to Cotuit, walked around the main street, inquired of the bookstore owner—who seemed to be a longtime native—about a hamburger stand that was a teenage hangout. Where would she be likely to find one? The answer, with a shrug, was, "They come and go. A developer picks up property and builds a shopping center or condominiums, and the hamburger stand is out." She'd gone to the town hall to try to find records of food-service licenses issued or renewed around that time. Two hamburger joint type places were still in business. A third had been converted or torn down. Nothing stirred her memory. And of course she couldn't even be sure they had been in Cotuit. Ned might have been lying about that too. And how do you ask strangers if they know a middle-aged woman with orange-red hair and a chunky build who had lived or summered on the Cape and hated rock-and-roll music?

As she drove through Dennis, Cynthia impulsively ignored the turn to the cottage and again drove past the Richards home. As she was passing, a slender blonde woman came down the steps of the mansion. Even from this distance she knew it was Lillian. Cynthia slowed the car to a crawl, but when Lillian looked in her direction she quickly accelerated and returned to the cottage. As she was turn-ing the key in the lock she heard the phone ring. It rang ten times before it stopped. It had to be Jeff, and she didn't want to talk to him. A few minutes later it rang again. It was obvious that if Jeff had the number he wouldn't give up trying to reach her.

Cynthia picked up the receiver. "Hello."

"My finger is getting very tired pushing buttons," Jeff said. "Nice trick of yours, just disappearing like that."

"How did you find me?"

"It wasn't hard. I knew you'd head for the Cape like a homing pigeon, and your parole officer confirmed it."

She could see him leaning back in his chair, twirling a pencil, the seriousness in his eyes belying the lightness of his tone. "Jeff, forget about me, please. Do us both a favor."

"Negative. Cindy, I understand. But unless you can find that woman you spoke to there's no hope of proving your innocence. And believe me, honey, I tried to find her. When I did the program, I sent out investigators I never told you about. If they couldn't find her, you won't be able to. Cindy, I love you. You know you're innocent. Ned Creighton lied, but we'll never be able to prove it."

Cynthia closed her eyes, knowing that what Jeff said was true.

"Cindy, give it all up. Pack your bag. Drive back here. I'll pick you up at your place at eight o'clock tonight."

Her place. The furnished room the parole officer had helped her select. *Meet my girlfriend. She just got out of prison. What did your mother do before she got married? She was in jail.*

"Good-bye, Jeff," Cynthia said. She broke the connection, left the phone off the hook and turned her back to it.

Alvirah had observed Cynthia's return but did not attempt to contact her. In the afternoon, Willy had gone out on a half-day charter boat and returned triumphantly with two bluefish. During his absence, Alvirah again studied the newspaper clippings of the Stuart Richards murder case. At Cypress Point Spa she had learned the value of airing her opinions into a recorder. That afternoon she kept her recorder busy.

"The crux of this case is why did Ned Creighton lie? He hardly knew Cynthia. Why did he set her up to take the blame for Stuart Richards's death? Stuart Richards had a lot of enemies. Ned's father at one time had business dealings with Stuart, and they'd had a falling out. But Ned was only a kid at that time. Ned was a friend of Lillian Richards. Lillian swore that she didn't know that her father was going to change his will, that she'd always known she would get half his estate and that the other half was going to Dartmouth College. She said she knew he was upset after Dartmouth decided to accept women students but didn't know he was upset enough to finally change his will and leave the Dartmouth money to Cynthia."

Alvirah turned off the recorder. It certainly must have occurred to someone that when Cynthia was found guilty of murdering her stepfather, she would lose her inheritance, and Lillian would receive everything. Lillian had married somebody from New York shortly after the trial was over. She'd been divorced three times since then. So it didn't look as though Ned and she had ever had any romance going. That left only the restaurant. Who were Ned's backers? Motive for Ned to lie, she thought. Who gave him the money to open his restaurant?

Willy came in from the deck, carrying the bluefish fillets he'd prepared. "Still at it?" he asked.

"Uh-huh." Alvirah picked up one of the clippings. "Orange-red hair, chunky build, in her late forties. Would you say that description might have fit me twelve years ago?"

"Now, you know I would never call you chunky," Willy protested.

"I didn't say you would. I'll be right back. I want to talk to Cynthia. I saw her coming in a few minutes ago."

The next afternoon, after having packed Willy off on another charter fishing boat, Alvirah attached her sunburst pin to her new purple print dress and drove with Cynthia to the Mooncusser restaurant in Barnstable. Along the way Alvirah coached her. "Now remember, if he's there, point him out to me right away. I'll keep staring at him. He'll recognize you. He's bound to come over. You know what to say, don't you?"

"I do." Was it possible? Cynthia wondered. Would Ned believe them?

The restaurant was an impressive white colonial-style building with a long, winding driveway. Alvirah took in the building, the exquisitely landscaped property that extended to the water.

"Very, very expensive," she said to Cynthia. "He didn't start this place on a shoestring."

The interior was decorated in Wedgwood blue-and-white. The paintings on the wall were fine ones. For twenty years—until she and Willy hit the lottery—Alvirah had cleaned every Tuesday for Mrs. Rawlings, and her house was one big museum. Mrs. Rawlings enjoyed recounting the history of each painting, how much she paid for it then and, gleefully, how much it was worth right now. Alvirah often thought that with a little practice she could probably be a tour guide at an art museum. "Observe the use of lighting, the splendid details of sunrays brightening the dust on the table." She had the Rawlings spiel down pat.

Knowing Cynthia was nervous, Alvirah tried to distract her by telling her about Mrs. Rawlings after the maître d'hotel escorted them to a window table.

Cynthia felt a reluctant smile come to her lips as Alvirah told her that, with all her money, Mrs. Rawlings never once gave her so much as a postcard for Christmas. "Meanest, cheapest old biddy in the world, but I felt kind of sorry for her," Alvirah said. "No one else would work for her. But when my time comes, I intend to point out to the Lord that I get a lot of Rawlings points in my plus column."

"If this idea works, you get a lot of Lathem points in your plus column," Cynthia said.

"You bet I do. Now don't lose that smile. You've got to look like the cat who ate the canary. Is he here?"

"I haven't seen him yet."

"Good. When that stuffed shirt comes back with the menu, ask for him."

The maître d' was approaching them, a professional smile on his bland face. "May I offer you a beverage?"

"Yes. Two glasses of white wine, and is Mr. Creighton here?" Cynthia asked.

"I believe he's in the kitchen speaking with the chef."

"I'm an old friend," Cynthia said. "Ask him to drop by when he's free."

"Certainly."

"You could be an actress," Alvirah whispered, holding the menu in front of her face. She always felt that you had to be so careful, because someone might be able to read lips. "And I'm glad I made you buy that outfit this morning. What you had in your closet was hopeless."

Cynthia was wearing a short lemon-colored linen jacket and a black linen skirt. A splashy yellow, black and white silk scarf was dramatically tied on one shoulder. Alvirah had also escorted her to the beauty parlor. Now Cynthia's collar-length hair was blown soft and loose around her face. A light beige foundation covered her abnormal paleness and returned color to her wide hazel eyes. "You're gorgeous," Alvirah said.

Regretfully Alvirah had undergone a different metamorphosis. She'd had her Sassoon hair color changed back to its old orange-red and cut unevenly. She'd also had the tips removed from her nails and had left them unpolished. After helping Cynthia select the yellow-and-black outfit, she'd gone to the sale rack, where for very good reasons the purple print she was wearing had been reduced to ten dollars. The fact that it was a size too small for her accentuated the bulges that Willy always explained were only nature's way of padding us for the last big fall.

When Cynthia had protested the desecration of her nails and hairdo, Alvirah simply said, "Every time you talked about that woman, the missing witness, you said she was chunky, had dyed red hair and was dressed like someone who shopped from a pushcart. I've got to be believable."

"I said her outfit looked inexpensive," Cynthia corrected.

"Same thing."

Now Alvirah watched as Cynthia's smile faded. "He's coming?" she asked quickly.

Cynthia nodded.

"Smile at me. Come on. Relax. Don't show him you're nervous."

Cynthia rewarded her with a warm smile and leaned her elbows lightly on the table.

A man was standing over them. Beads of perspiration were forming on his forehead. He moistened his lips. "Cynthia, how good to see you." He reached for her hand.

Alvirah studied him intently. Not bad-looking in a weak kind of way. Narrow eyes almost lost in puffy flesh. He was a good twenty pounds heavier than in the pictures in the files. One of the kind who are handsome as kids and after that it's all downhill, Alvirah decided.

"Is it good to see me, Ned?" Cynthia asked, still smiling.

"That's him," Alvirah announced emphatically. "I'm absolutely sure. He was ahead of me on line in the hamburger joint. I noticed him 'cause he was sore as hell that the kids in front were hemming and hawing about what they wanted on their burgers."

"What are you talking about?" Ned Creighton demanded.

"Why don't you sit down, Ned?" Cynthia said. "I know this is your place, but I still feel as though I should entertain you. After all, you did buy me dinner one night years ago."

Good girl, Alvirah thought. "I'm absolutely sure it was you that night, even though you've put on weight," she snapped indignantly to Creighton. "It's a crying shame that because of your lies this girl had to spend twelve years of her life in prison."

The smile vanished from Cynthia's face.

"Twelve years, six months and ten days," she corrected. "All my twenties, when I should have been finishing college, getting my first job, dating."

Ned Creighton's face hardened. "You're bluffing. This is a cheap trick."

The waiter arrived with two glasses of wine and placed them before Cynthia and Alvirah. "Mr. Creighton?"

Creighton glared at him. "Nothing."

"This is really a lovely place, Ned," Cynthia said quietly. "An awful lot of money must have gone into it. Where did you get it? From Lillian? My share of Stuart Richards's estate was nearly ten million dollars. How much did she give you?" She did not wait for an answer. "Ned, this woman is the witness I could never find. She remembers talking to me that night. Nobody believed me when I told them about a woman slamming her car door against the side of your car. But she remembers doing it. And she remembers seeing you very well. All her life she's kept a daily diary. That night she wrote about what happened in the parking lot."

As she kept nodding her head in agreement, Alvirah studied Ned's face. He's getting rattled, she thought, but he's not convinced. It was time for her to take over. "I left the Cape the very next day," she said.

"I live in Arizona. My husband was sick, real sick. That's why we never did come back. I lost him last year." Sorry, Willy, she thought, but this is important. "Then last week I was watching television, and you know how boring television usually is in the summer. You could have knocked me over with a feather when I saw a rerun of that show about women in prison and then my own picture right there on the screen."

Cynthia reached for the envelope she had placed beside her chair. "This is the picture I drew of the woman I'd spoken to in the parking lot."

Ned Creighton reached for it.

"I'll hold it," Cynthia said.

The sketch showed a woman's face framed by an open car window. The features were shadowy and the background was dark, but the likeness to Alvirah was astonishing.

Cynthia pushed back her chair. Alvirah rose with her.

"You can't give me back twelve years. I know what you're thinking. Even with this proof a jury might not believe me. They didn't believe me twelve years ago. But they might, just might, now. And I don't think you should take that chance, Ned. I think you'd better talk it over with whoever paid you to set me up that night and tell them that I want ten million dollars. That's my rightful share of Stuart's estate."

"You're crazy." Anger had driven the fear from Ned Creighton's face.

"Am I? I don't think so." Cynthia reached into her pocket. "Here's my address and phone number. Alvirah is staying with me. Call me by seven tonight. If I don't hear from you, I'm hiring a lawyer and getting my case reopened." She threw a ten-dollar bill on the table. "That should pay for the wine. Now we're even for that dinner you bought me."

She walked rapidly from the restaurant, Alvirah a step behind her.

Alvirah was aware of the buzz from diners at the other tables. They know something's up, she thought. Good.

She and Cynthia did not speak until they were in the car. Then Cynthia asked shakily, "How was I?"

"Great."

"Alvirah, it just won't work. If they check the sketch that Jeff showed on the program, they'll see all the details I added to make it look like you."

"They haven't got time to do that. Are you sure you saw your stepsister yesterday at the Richards house?"

"Absolutely."

"Then my guess is that Ned Creighton is talking to her right now."

Cynthia drove automatically, not seeing the sunny brightness of the afternoon. "Stuart was despised by a lot of people. Why are you so sure Lillian is involved?"

Alvirah unfastened the zipper on the purple print.

"This dress is so tight I swear I'm going to choke." Ruefully she ran her hand through her erratically chopped hair. "It'll take an army of Sassoons to put me back together after this. I guess I'll have to go back to Cypress Point Spa. What did you ask? Oh, Lillian. She has to be involved. Look at it this way. Your stepfather had a lot of people who hated his guts, but they wouldn't need a Ned Creighton to set you up. Lillian always knew her father was leaving half his money to Dartmouth College. Right?"

"Yes." Cynthia turned down the road that led to the cottages.

"I don't care how many people might have hated your stepfather, Lillian was the only one who *benefited* by you being set up to be found guilty of his murder. She knew Ned. Ned was trying to raise money to open a restaurant. Her father must have told her he was leaving half his fortune to you instead of Dartmouth. She always hated you. You told me that. So she makes a deal with Ned. He takes you out on his boat and pretends that it breaks down. Somebody kills Stuart Richards. Lillian had an alibi. She was in New York. She probably hired someone to kill her father. You almost spoiled everything that night by insisting on having a hamburger. And Ned didn't know you'd spoken to anyone. They must have been plenty scared that witness would show up."

"Suppose someone recognized him that night and said they'd seen him buying the burger?"

"In that case he'd have said that he went out on his boat and stopped afterward for a hamburger, and you were so desperate for an alibi you begged him to say you were with him. But no one came forward."

"It sounds so risky," Cynthia protested.

"Not risky. Simple," Alvirah corrected. "Buh-lieve me, I've studied up on this a lot. You'd be amazed in how many cases the one who commits the murder is the chief mourner at the funeral. It's a fact."

They had arrived back at the cottages. "What now?" Cynthia asked.

"Now we go to your place and wait for your stepsister to phone." Alvirah shook her head at Cynthia. "You still don't believe me. Wait and see. I'll make us a nice cup of tea. It's too bad Creighton showed up before we had lunch. That was a good menu."

They were eating tuna salad sandwiches on the deck of Cynthia's cottage when the phone rang.

"Lillian for you," Alvirah said. She followed Cynthia into the kitchen as Cynthia answered the call.

"Hello." Cynthia's voice was almost a whisper. Alvirah watched as the color drained from her face. "Hello, Lillian."

Alvirah squeezed Cynthia's arm and nodded her head vigorously.

"Yes, Lillian, I just saw Ned. . . . No, I'm not joking. I don't see anything funny about this. . . . Yes. I'll come over tonight. Don't bother about dinner. Your presence has a way of making my throat close. And, Lillian, I told Ned what I want. I won't change my mind."

Cynthia hung up and sank into a chair. "Alvirah, Lillian said that my accusation was ridiculous but that she knows her father could drive anyone to the point of losing control. She's smart."

"That doesn't help us clear your name. I'll give you my sunburst pin so you can record the conversation. You've got to get her to admit that you had absolutely nothing to do with the murder, that she set Ned up to trap you. What time did you tell her you'd go over to her house?"

"Eight o'clock. Ned will be with her."

"Fine. Willy will go with you. He'll be on the floor in the back-seat of the car. For a big man he sure can roll himself into a beach ball. He'll keep an eye on you. They certainly won't try anything in that house. It would be too risky. Next to Willy, my sunburst pin is my greatest treasure," she said. "I'll show you how to use it."

Throughout the afternoon, Alvirah coached Cynthia on what to say to her stepsister. "She's got to be the one who put up the money for the restaurant. Probably through some sham investment companies. Tell her unless she pays up, you're going to contact a top accountant you know who used to work for the government."

"She knows I don't have any money."

"She doesn't know who might have taken an interest in your case. That fellow who did the program on women in prison did, right?"

"Yes. Jeff took an interest."

Alvirah's eyes narrowed, then sparked. "Something between you and Jeff?"

"If I'm exonerated for Stuart Richards's death, yes. If I'm not, there'll never be anything between Jeff and me or anyone else and me."

At six o'clock the phone rang again. Alvirah said, "I'll answer. Let them know I'm here with you." Her booming "Hello" was followed by a warm greeting. "Jeff, we were just talking about you. Cynthia is right here. My, what a pretty girl. You should see her new outfit. She's been telling me all about you. Wait. I'll put her on."

Alvirah frankly listened in as Cynthia explained, "Alvirah rents the next cottage. She's helping me. . . . No, I'm not coming back. . . . Yes, there is a reason to stay here. Tonight just maybe I'll be able to get proof I wasn't guilty of Stuart's death. . . . No, don't come down. I don't want to see you, Jeff, not now. . . . Jeff, yes, yes, I love you. . . . Yes, if I clear my name, I'll marry you."

When Cynthia hung up she was close to tears. "Alvirah, I want to have a life with him so much. You know what he just said? He quoted 'The Highwayman.' He said, 'I'll come to thee by moonlight, though hell should bar the way.'"

"I like him," Alvirah said flatly. "I can read a person from his voice on the phone. Is he coming tonight? I don't want you getting upset or being talked out of this."

"No. He's been made anchorman for the ten o'clock news. But I bet anything he drives down tomorrow."

"We'll see about that. The more people in this, the more chance of having Ned and Lillian smell a rat." Alvirah glanced out the window. "Oh, look, here comes Willy. Stars above, he caught more of those darn bluefish. They gave me heartburn, but I'd never tell him. Whenever he goes fishing I keep a package of Tums in my pocket. Oh, well."

She opened the door and waved over a beaming Willy, who was proudly holding a line from which two limp bluefish dangled forlornly. Willy's smile vanished as he took in Alvirah's bright red mop of unruly hair and the purple print dress that squeezed her body into rolls of flesh. "Aw, nuts," he said. "How come they took back the lottery money?"

At seven-thirty, after having dined on Willy's latest catch, Alvirah placed a cup of tea in front of Cynthia. "You haven't eaten a thing," she said. "You've got to eat to keep your brain clear. Now, have you got it all straight?"

Cynthia fingered the sunburst pin. "I think so. It seems clear."

"Remember, money had to have changed hands between those two—and I don't care how clever they were, it can be traced. If they agree to pay you, offer to come down in price if they'll give you the satisfaction of admitting the truth. Got it?"

"Got it."

At seven-fifty Cynthia drove down the winding lane with Willy on the floor of the backseat. The brilliantly sunny day had turned into a cloudy evening. Alvirah walked through the cottage to the back deck. Wind was whipping the bay into a frenzy of waves that slammed onto the beach. The rumbling of thunder could be heard in the distance. The temperature had plummeted, and suddenly it felt more like October than August. Shivering, she debated about going next door to her own cottage and getting a sweater, then decided against it. In case anyone phoned, she wanted to be right here.

She made a second cup of tea for herself and settled at the dinette table, her back to the door leading from the deck. Then she began writing a first draft of the article she was sure she would be sending to the *New York Globe*. Satisfied, she read aloud what she had written. "'Cynthia Lathem, who was nineteen years old when she was sentenced to a term of twelve years in prison for a murder she did not commit, can now prove her innocence. . . .'"

From behind her a voice said, "Oh, I don't think that's going to happen."

Alvirah swiveled around and stared up into the angry face of Ned Creighton.

Cynthia waited on the porch steps of the Richards mansion. Through the handsome mahogany door she could hear the faint sound of chimes. She had the incongruous thought that she still had her own key to this place, and she wondered if Lillian had changed the locks.

The door swung open. Lillian was standing in the wide hallway, light from the overhead Tiffany lamp accentuating her high cheekbones, wide blue eyes, silvery blond hair. Cynthia felt a chill race through her body. In these twelve years, Lillian had become a clone of Stuart Richards. Smaller of course. Younger, but still a feminine version of his outstanding looks. And with that same hint of cruelty around the eyes.

"Come in, Cynthia." Lillian's voice hadn't changed. Clear, well-bred, but with that familiar sharp, angry undertone that had always characterized Stuart Richards's speech.

Silently, Cynthia followed Lillian down the hallway. The living room was dimly lighted. It looked very much as she remembered it. The placement of the furniture, the Oriental carpets, the painting over the fireplace—all were the same. The baronial dining room on the left still had the same unused appearance. They'd usually eaten in the small dining room off the library.

She had expected that Lillian would take her to the library. Instead, Lillian went directly back to the study where Stuart had died. Cynthia narrowed her lips, felt for the sunburst pin. Was this an attempt to intimidate her? she wondered.

Lillian sat behind the massive desk.

Cynthia thought again of the night she'd come into this room and found Stuart sprawled on the carpet beside that desk. She knew her hands were clammy. Perspiration was forming on her forehead. Outside she could hear the wind wailing as it increased in velocity. Lillian folded her hands and looked up at Cynthia.

"You might as well sit down."

Cynthia bit her lip. The rest of her life would be determined by what she said in these next minutes. "I think I'm the one who should suggest the seating arrangements," she told Lillian. "Your father did leave this house to me. When you phoned, you talked about a settlement. Don't play games now. And don't try to intimidate me. Prison took all the shyness out of me, I promise you that. Where is Ned?"

"He'll be along any minute. Cynthia, those accusations you made to him are insane. You know that."

"I thought I came here to discuss receiving my share of Stuart's estate."

"You came here because I'm sorry for you and because I want to give you a chance to go away somewhere and begin a new life. I'm prepared to set up a trust fund that will give you a monthly income. Another woman wouldn't be so generous to her father's murderer."

Cynthia stared at Lillian, taking in the contempt in her eyes, the icy calm of her demeanor. She had to break that calm. She walked over to the window and looked out. The rain was beating against the house. Claps of thunder shattered the silence in the room. "I wonder what Ned would have done to keep me out of the house that night if it had been raining like this," she said. "The weather worked out for him, didn't it? Warm and cloudy. No other boats nearby. Only that one witness, and now I've found her. Didn't Ned tell you that she positively identified him?"

"How many people would believe that anyone could recognize a stranger after nearly thirteen years? Cynthia, I don't know whom you've hired for this charade, but I'm warning you—drop it. Accept my offer, or I'll call the police and have you arrested for harassment. Don't forget it's very easy to get a criminal's parole revoked."

"A *criminal's* parole. I agree. But I'm not a criminal, and you know it." Cynthia walked over to the Jacobean armoire and pulled open the top drawer. "I knew Stuart kept a gun here. But you certainly knew too. You claimed he had never told you that he'd changed his will and was leaving the Dartmouth half of his estate to me. But you were lying. If Stuart sent for me to tell me about his will, he certainly didn't hide what he was doing from you."

"He did *not* tell me. I hadn't seen him for three months."

"You may not have *seen* him, but you spoke to him, didn't you? You could have put up with Dartmouth getting half his fortune but couldn't stand the idea of splitting his money with me. You hated me for the years I lived in this house, for the fact that he liked me, while you two always clashed. You've got that same vile temper he had."

Lillian stood up. "You don't know what you're talking about."

Cynthia slammed the drawer shut. "Oh, yes, I do. And every fact that convicted me will convict you. I had a key to this house. You had a key. There was no sign of a struggle. I don't think you sent anyone to murder him. I think you did it yourself. Stuart had a panic button on his desk. He didn't push it. He never thought his own daughter would harm him. Why did Ned just *happen* to stop by that afternoon? You knew Stuart had invited me here for the weekend. You knew that he'd encourage me to go out with Ned. Stuart liked company and then he liked to be alone. Maybe Ned hasn't made it clear to you. That witness I found keeps a diary. She showed it to me. She's been writing in it every night since she was twenty. There was no way that entry could have been doctored. She described me. She described Ned's car. She even wrote about the noisy kids on line and how impatient everyone was with them."

I'm getting to her, Cynthia thought. Lillian's face was pale. Her throat was closing convulsively. Deliberately, Cynthia walked back to the desk so that the sunburst pin was pointed directly at Lillian. "You played it smart, didn't you?" she asked. "Ned didn't start pouring money into that restaurant until after I was safely in prison. And I'm sure that on the surface he has some respectable investors. But today the government is awfully good at getting to the source of laundered money. *Your* money, Lillian."

"You'll never prove it." But Lillian's voice had become shrill.

Oh God, if I can just get her to admit it, Cynthia thought. She grasped the edge of the desk with both hands and leaned forward. "Possibly not. But don't take the chance. Let me tell you how it feels to be fingerprinted and handcuffed. How it feels to sit next to a lawyer and hear the district attorney accuse you of murder. How it feels to study the faces of the jury. Jurors are ordinary-looking people. Old. Young. Black. White. Well dressed. Shabby. But they hold the rest of your life in their hands. And, Lillian, you won't like it. The waiting. The damning evidence that fits you much more than it ever fitted me. You don't have the temperament or the guts to go through with it."

Lillian stood up. Her face was frozen in hatred. "Bear in mind there were a lot of taxes when the estate was settled. A good lawyer could probably destroy your so-called witness, but I don't need the scandal. Yes, I'll give you your half." Then she smiled.

"You should have stayed in Arizona," Ned Creighton said to Alvirah. The gun he was holding was pointed at her chest. Alvirah sat at the dinette table, measuring her chances to escape. There were none. He had believed her story this afternoon, and now he had to kill her. Alvirah had the fleeting thought that she'd always known she would have made a wonderful actress. Should she warn Ned her husband would be home any minute? No. At the restaurant she'd told him she was a widow. How long would Willy and Cynthia be? Too long. Lillian wouldn't let Cynthia go until she was sure there was no witness alive, but maybe if Alvirah kept him talking, she'd think of something. "How much did you get for your part in the murder?" she asked.

Ned Creighton smiled, a thin sneering movement of his mouth. "Three million. Just enough to start a classy restaurant."

Alvirah mourned the fact that she had lent her sunburst pin to Cynthia. Proof. Absolute, positive proof, and she wasn't able to record it. And if anything happened to her, no one would know. Mark my words, she thought. If I get out of this, I'm going to have Charley Evans get me a backup pin. Maybe that one should be silver. No, platinum.

Creighton waved his pistol. "Get up."

Alvirah pushed back the chair, leaned her hands on the table. The sugar bowl was in front of her. Did she dare throw it at him? She knew her aim was good, but a gun was faster than a sugar bowl.

"Go into the living room." As she walked around the table, Creighton reached over, grabbed her notes and the beginning of her article and stuffed them in his pocket.

There was a wooden rocking chair next to the fireplace. Creighton pointed to it. "Sit down right there."

Alvirah sat down heavily. Ned's gun was still trained on her. If she tipped the rocker forward and landed on him, could she get away from him? Creighton reached for a narrow key dangling from the mantel. Leaning over, he inserted it in a cylinder in one of the bricks and turned it. The hissing sound of gas spurted from the fireplace. He straightened up. From the matchbox on the mantel he extracted a long safety match, scratched it on the box, blew out the flame and tossed the match onto the hearth. "It's getting cold," he said. "You decided to light a fire. You turned on the gas jet. You threw in a match, but it didn't take. When you bent down to turn off the jet and start again, you lost your balance and fell. Your head struck the mantel and you lost consciousness. A terrible accident for such a nice woman. Cynthia will be very upset when she finds you."

The smell of gas was permeating the room. Alvirah tried to tilt the rocker forward. She had to take the chance of butting Creighton with her head and making him drop the gun. She was too late. A vise-like grip on her shoulders. The sense of being pulled forward. Her forehead slamming against the mantel before she fell to the stone hearth. As she lost consciousness, Alvirah was aware of the sickening smell of gas filling her nostrils.

"Here's Ned now," Lillian said calmly at the sound of door chimes. "I'll let him in."

Cynthia waited. Lillian still had not admitted anything. Could she get Ned Creighton to incriminate himself? She felt like a tightrope walker on a slippery wire, trying to inch her way across a chasm. If she failed, the rest of her life wouldn't be worth living.

Creighton was following Lillian into the room. "Cynthia." His nod was impersonal, not unpleasant. He pulled up a chair beside the desk where Lillian had an open file of printouts.

"I'm just giving Cynthia an idea of how much the estate shrank after the taxes had been settled," Lillian told Creighton. "Then we'll estimate her share."

"Don't deduct whatever you paid Ned from what is rightfully mine," Cynthia said. She saw the angry look Ned shot at Lillian. "Oh, please," she snapped, "among the three of us, let's say it straight."

Lillian said coldly, "I told you that I wanted to share the estate. I know my father could drive people over the edge. I'm doing this because I'm sorry for you. Now here are the figures."

For the next fifteen minutes, Lillian pulled balance sheets out of the file. "Allowing for taxes and then interest made on the remainder, your share would now be five million dollars."

"And this house," Cynthia interjected. Bewildered, she realized that with each passing moment Lillian and Ned were becoming more visibly relaxed. They were both smiling.

"Oh, not the house," Lillian protested. "There'd be too much gossip. We'll have the house appraised, and I'll pay you the value of it. Remember, Cynthia, I'm being very generous. My father toyed with people's lives. He was cruel. If you hadn't killed him, someone else would have. That's why I'm doing this."

"You're doing it because you don't want to sit in a courtroom and take the chance on being convicted of murder, that's why you're doing it." Oh God, Cynthia thought. It's no use. If I can't get her to admit it, it's all over. By tomorrow Lillian and Ned would have the chance to check on Alvirah. "You can have the house," she said. "Don't pay me for it. Just give me the satisfaction of hearing the truth. Admit that I had nothing to do with your father's murder."

Lillian glanced at Ned, then at the clock. "I think at this time we should honor that request." She began to laugh. "Cynthia, I am like my father. I enjoy toying with people. My father did phone to tell me about the change in his will. I could live with Dartmouth getting half his estate but not you. He told me you were coming up—the rest was easy. My mother was a wonderful woman. She was only too happy to verify that I was in New York with her that evening. Ned was delighted to get a great deal of money for giving you a boat ride. You're smart, Cynthia. Smarter than the district attorney's office. Smarter than that dumb lawyer you had."

Let the recorder be working, Cynthia prayed. Let it be working. "And smart enough to find a witness who could verify my story," she added.

Lillian and Ned burst into laughter. "What witness?" Ned asked.

"Get out," Lillian told her. "Get out this minute and don't come back."

Jeff Knight drove swiftly along Route 6, trying to read signs through the torrential rain that was slashing the windshield. Exit 8. He was coming up to it. The producer of the ten o'clock news had been unexpectedly decent. Of course there was a reason. "Go ahead. If Cynthia Lathem is on the Cape and thinks she has a lead on her stepfather's death, you've got a great story breaking."

Jeff wasn't interested in a great story. His only concern was Cynthia. Now he gripped the steering wheel with his long fingers. He had managed to get her address as well as her phone number from her parole officer. He'd spent a lot of summers on the Cape. That is why it had been so frustrating when he had tried to prove Cynthia's story about stopping at the hamburger stand and gotten nowhere. But he'd always stayed in Eastham, some fifty miles from Cotuit. Exit 8. He turned onto Union Street, drove to Route 6A. A couple of miles more. Why did he have the sense of impending doom? If Cynthia had a real lead that could help her, she could be in danger.

He had to slam on his brakes when he reached Nobscusset Road. Another car, ignoring the stop sign, raced from Nobscusset across 6A. Damn fool, Jeff thought as he turned right, then left toward the bay. He realized that the whole area was in darkness. A power failure. He reached the dead end, turned left. The cottage had to be on this winding lane. Number six. He drove slowly, trying to read the numbers as his headlights shone on the mailboxes. Two. Four. Six. Jeff pulled into the driveway, threw open the door and ran through the pelting rain toward the cottage. He held his finger on the bell, then realized that because of the power failure it did not work. He pounded on the door several times. There was no answer. Cynthia wasn't home. He started to walk down the steps, then a sudden unreasoning fear made him go back, pound again on the door, then turn the knob. It twisted in his hand. He pushed the door open.

"Cynthia," he started to call, then gasped as the odor of gas rushed at him. He could hear the hissing coming from the fireplace. Rushing to turn the jet off, he tripped over the prone figure of Alvirah.

Willy moved restlessly in the backseat of Cynthia's car. She'd been in that house for more than an hour now. The guy who'd come later had been there fifteen minutes. Willy wasn't sure what to do. Alvirah really hadn't given specific instructions. She just wanted him to be around to make sure Cynthia didn't leave the house with anyone.

As he debated, he heard the screeching sound of sirens. Police cars. The sirens got closer. Astonished, Willy watched as they turned into the long driveway of the Richards estate and thundered toward him. Policemen rushed from the squad cars, raced up the steps and pounded on the door.

A moment later a sedan pulled into the driveway and stopped behind the squad cars. As Willy watched, a big fellow in a trench coat leapt out of it and took the steps to the porch two at a time. Willy climbed awkwardly out of the car and hoisted himself to his feet in the driveway.

He was in time to grab Alvirah as she staggered from the back of the sedan. Even in the dark he could see the welt on her forehead. "Honey, what happened?"

"I'll tell you later. Get me inside. I don't want to miss this."

In the study of the late Stuart Richards, Alvirah experienced her finest hour. Pointing her finger at Ned, in her most vibrant tones, she pronounced, "He held a gun to me. He turned on the gas jet. He smashed my head against the fireplace. And told me that Lillian Richards paid him three million dollars to set up Cynthia as the murderer."

Cynthia stared at her stepsister. "And unless the batteries in Alvirah's recorder are dead, I have both of them on record admitting their guilt."

The next morning, Willy fixed a late breakfast and served it on the deck. The storm had ended, and once again the sky was joyously blue. Seagulls swooped down to feast on surfacing fish. The bay was tranquil, and children were making castles in the damp sand at the water's edge.

Alvirah, not that much worse for her experience, had finished her article and phoned it in to Charley Evans. Charley had promised her the most ornate sunburst pin that money could buy, one with a microphone so sensitive it could pick up a mouse sneezing in the next room.

Now, as she munched a chocolate-covered doughnut and sipped coffee, she said, "Oh, here comes Jeff. What a shame he had to drive back to Boston last night, but wasn't he wonderful telling the story on the news this morning, and all about how Ned Creighton is talking his head off to the cops? Buh-lieve me, Jeff will go places with the networks."

"That guy saved your life, honey," Willy said. "He's aces high with me. I can't believe I was curled up in that car like a jack-in-the-box when you had your head in a gas jet."

They watched as Jeff got out of the car and Cynthia rushed down the walk and into his arms. Alvirah pushed her chair back. "I'll run over and say hello. It's a real treat to see how they look at each other. They're so in love."

Willy placed a gentle but firm hand on her shoulder. "Alvirah, honey," he begged, "just this once, for five minutes, mind your own business."

Definitely, a Crime of Passion

"'Beware the fury of a patient man,'" Henry Parker Britland IV observed sadly as he studied the picture of his former secretary of state. He had just learned that his close friend and political ally had been indicted for the murder of his lover, Arabella Young.

"Then you think poor Tommy did it?" Sandra O'Brien Britland said with a sigh as she patted homemade jam onto a hot scone, fresh out of the oven.

It was still early morning, and the couple was comfortably ensconced in their king-sized bed at Drumdoe, their country estate in Bernardsville, New Jersey. The *Washington Post*, the *Wall Street Journal*, the *New York Times*, the *Times* (London), *L'Osservatore Romano*, and the *Paris Review*, all in varying stages of being read, were scattered about, some lying on the delicately flowered, gossamer-soft quilt, others spilling over onto the floor. Directly in front of the couple were matching breakfast trays, each complete with a single rose in a narrow silver vase.

"Actually, no," Henry said after a moment, slowly shaking his head. "I find it impossible to believe. Tom always had such strong self-control. That's what made him such a fine secretary of state. But ever since Constance died—it was during my second administration—he just hasn't seemed himself. And it was obvious to everyone that when he met Arabella he just fell madly in love. Of course, what also became obvious after a while was that he had lost some of that steely control—I'll never forget the time he slipped and called Arabella 'Poopie' in front of Lady Thatcher."

"I do wish I had known you then," Sandra said ruefully. "I didn't always agree with you, of course, but I thought you were an excellent president. But then, nine years ago, when you were first sworn in, you'd have found me boring, I'm sure. How interesting could a law student be to the president of the United States? I mean, hopefully you would have found me attractive, but I know you wouldn't have taken me seriously. At least when you met me as a member of Congress, you thought of me with some respect."

Henry turned and looked affectionately at his bride of eight months. Her hair, the color of winter wheat, was tousled. The expression in her intensely blue eyes somehow managed to convey simultaneously intelligence, warmth, wit and humor. And sometimes also childlike wonder. He smiled as he remembered the first time he met her: he had asked if she still believed in Santa Claus.

That had been the evening before the inauguration of his successor, when Henry had hosted a cocktail party at the White House for all the new members of Congress.

"I believe in what Santa Claus represents, sir," Sandra had replied. "Don't you?"

Later, as the guests were leaving, he had invited her to stay for a quiet dinner.

"I'm so sorry," she had replied. "I'm meeting my parents. I can't disappoint them."

Left to dine alone on this final evening in the White House, Henry had thought of all the women who over the past eight years had readily changed their plans in a fraction of a second, and he realized that at last he had found the woman of his dreams. They were married six weeks later. At first the media hype threatened to be unending. The marriage of the country's most eligible bachelor—the forty-four-year-old ex-president—to the beautiful young congresswoman, twelve years his junior, set off a feeding frenzy among journalists. Not in years had a marriage so completely captured the public's collective imagination.

The fact that Sandra's father was a motorman on the New Jersey Central Railroad, that she had worked her way through both St. Peter's College and Fordham Law School, spent seven years as a public defender, then, in a stunning upset, won the congressional seat of the longtime incumbent from Jersey City, already had made her a champion to womankind, as well as a darling of the media.

Henry's status as one of the two most popular presidents of the twentieth century, as well as the possessor of a considerable private fortune, combined with the fact that he appeared with regularity at or near the top of the list of America's sexiest men, made him likewise a favorite source of copy, as well as an object of envy by other men who could only wonder why the gods so obviously favored him.

On their wedding day, one tabloid had run the headline: LORD HENRY BRINTHROP MARRIES OUR GAL SUNDAY, a reference to the once wildly popular radio soap opera that daily, five days a week, for years on end, asked the question: "Can a girl from a mining town in the West find happiness as the wife of England's richest and most handsome lord, Lord Henry Brinthrop?"

Sandra had immediately become known to one and all, including her doting husband, as Sunday. She hated the nickname at first, but became resigned to it when Henry pointed out that for him it had a double meaning, that he thought of her as "a Sunday kind of love," a reference to the lyrics of one of his favorite songs. "Besides," he added, "it suits you. Tip O'Neill had a nickname that was just right for him; Sunday is just right for you."

This morning, as she studied her husband, Sunday thought back

over the months they had spent together, days that until this morning had remained almost carefree. Now, seeing the genuine concern
in Henry's eyes, she covered his hand with hers. "You're worried
about Tommy. I can tell. What can we do to help him?"

"Not very much, I'm afraid. I'll certainly check to make sure the
defense lawyer he has hired is up to the task, but no matter who he
gets to represent him, the prospects look bleak. Think about it. It's a
particularly vicious crime, and when you look at the circumstances
it's hard not to assume that Tom did it. The woman was shot three
times, with Tommy's pistol, in Tommy's library, right after he told
people how upset he was that she had broken up with him."

Sunday picked up one of the papers and examined the picture
of a beaming Thomas Shipman, his arm around the dazzling thirty-
year-old who had helped to dry his tears following his wife's death.
"How old is Tommy?" Sunday asked.

"I'm not sure. Sixty-five, I'd guess, give or take a year."

They both studied the photograph. Tommy was a trim, lean man,
with thinning gray hair and a scholarly face. In contrast, Arabella
Young's wildly teased hair framed a boldly pretty face, and her body
possessed the kind of curves found on *Playboy* covers.

"A May-December relationship if I ever saw one," Sunday
commented.

"They probably say that about us," Henry said lightly, forcing a
smile.

"Oh, Henry, be quiet," Sunday said. Then she took his hand.
"And don't try to pretend that you aren't really upset. We may still be
newlyweds, but I know you too well already to be fooled."

"You're right, I am worried," Henry said quietly. "When I think
back over the past few years, I can't imagine myself sitting in the
Oval Office without Tommy at my side. I'd only had one term in
the Senate before becoming president and in so many ways I was still
very green. Thanks to him I weathered those first months without

falling on my face. When I was all set to have it out with the Soviets, Tommy—in his calm, deliberate way—showed me how wrong I'd be to force a confrontation but then publicly managed to convey the impression that he was only a sounding board for my own decision. Tommy is a true statesman, but more to the point, he is a gentleman, through and through. He's honest, he's smart, he's loyal."

"But surely he's also a man who must have been aware that people were joking about his relationship with Arabella and just how smitten he was with her? Then when she finally wanted out, he lost it," Sunday observed. "That's pretty much the way you see it, isn't it?"

Henry sighed. "Perhaps. Temporary insanity? It's possible." He lifted his breakfast tray and put it on the night table. "Nevertheless, he was always there for me, and I'm going to be there for him. He's been allowed to post bond. I'm going to see him."

Sunday quickly shoved her tray aside, barely managing to catch her half-empty coffee cup before it spilled onto the quilt. "I'm coming too," she said. "Just give me ten minutes in the Jacuzzi and I'll be ready."

Henry watched his wife's long legs as she slid out of bed. "The Jacuzzi. What a splendid idea," he said enthusiastically. "I'll join you."

Thomas Acker Shipman had tried to ignore the army of media camped outside, near his driveway. When he and his lawyer pulled up in front of his house, he had simply stared straight ahead and barged his way from the car to the house, desperately trying not to hear the roar of questions hurled at him as he passed. Once inside, however, the events of the day finally hit him, and he visibly slumped. "I think a scotch may be in order," he said quietly.

His attorney, Leonard Hart, looked at him sympathetically. "I'd say you deserve one," he said. "But first, let me once again reassure you that if you insist, we'll go ahead with a plea bargain, but I'm compelled to once more point out to you that we could put together a very strong insanity defense, and I wish you'd agree to go to trial. The situation is so clear that any jury could understand: you went through the agony of losing a beloved wife, and on the rebound you fell in love with an attractive young woman who at first accepted many gifts from you, then spurned you. It is a classic story, and one that I feel confident would be received sympathetically when coupled with a temporary insanity plea."

As he spoke, Hart's voice became increasingly passionate, as though he were addressing a jury: "You asked her to come here and talk it over, but she taunted you and an argument ensued. Suddenly, you lost your head, and in a blinding rage so intense that you can't even remember the details, you shot her. The gun normally was kept locked away, but this evening you had it out because you had been so upset that you actually had entertained thoughts of killing yourself."

The lawyer paused in his presentation, and in the moment of silence the former secretary of state stared up at him, a puzzled look on his face. "Is that actually how you see it?" he asked.

Hart seemed surprised at the question. "Why, yes, of course," he replied. "There are a few details we have to iron out yet, a few things that I'm not completely clear on. For example, we'll have to explain how you could simply leave Miss Young bleeding on the floor and go up to bed, where you slept so soundly that you didn't even hear your housekeeper's scream when she discovered the body the next morning. Based on what I know, though, I would think that at the trial we would contend that you were in a state of shock."

"Would you?" Shipman asked wearily. "But I wasn't in shock. In fact, after I had that drink, I just seemed to start floating. I can barely remember what Arabella and I said to each other, never mind recalling actually shooting her."

A pained look crossed the lawyer's face. "I think, Tom, that I must beg you not to make statements like that to anyone. Will you promise me, please? And may I also suggest that certainly for the foreseeable future you go easy on the scotch; obviously it isn't agreeing with you."

Thomas Shipman stood behind the drapes as he peered through the window, watching as his rotund attorney attempted to fend off a charge by the media. Rather like seeing the lions released on a solitary Christian, he thought. Only in this case, it wasn't Attorney Hart's blood they were after. It was his own. Unfortunately, he had no taste for martyrdom.

Fortunately, he had been able to reach his housekeeper, Lillian West, in time to tell her to stay home today. He had known last evening, when the indictment was handed down, that television cameras would be camped outside his house, to witness and record every step of his leaving in handcuffs, followed by the arraignment, the fingerprinting, the plea of innocence, and then this morning's less-than-triumphal return home. No, getting into his house today had been like running the gauntlet; he didn't want his housekeeper to be subjected to that too.

He did miss having someone around, though. The house felt too quiet, and lonely. Engulfed by memories, his mind was drawn back to the day he and Constance had bought the place, some thirty years ago. They had driven up from Manhattan to have lunch at the Bird and Bottle near Bear Mountain, then had taken a leisurely drive back to the city. Impulsively, they had decided to detour through the lovely residential streets in Tarrytown, and it was then that they came across the FOR SALE sign in front of this turn-of-the-century house overlooking the Hudson River and the Palisades.

And for the next twenty-eight years, two months, and ten days, we lived here in a state of happily ever after, Shipman thought. "Oh, Constance, if only we could have had twenty-eight more," he said quietly as he headed toward the kitchen, having decided on coffee instead of scotch as the drink he needed.

This house had been a special place for them. Even when he served as secretary of state and had to travel so much of the time, they managed to have occasional weekends together here, and always it was a kind of restorative for the soul. And then one morning two years ago, Constance had said, "Tom, I don't feel so well." And a moment later she was gone.

Working twenty-hour days had helped him numb the pain somewhat. Thank God I had the job to distract me, he thought, smiling to himself as he recalled the nickname the press had given him, "The Flying Secretary." But I not only kept busy; Henry and I also managed to do some good. We left Washington and the country in better shape than it's been in for years.

Reaching the kitchen, he carefully measured out enough coffee for four cups and then did the same with the water. See, I can take care of myself, he thought. Too bad I didn't do more of it after Constance died. But then Arabella entered the scene. So ready with comfort, so alluring. And now, so dead.

He thought back to the evening, two days ago. What had they said to each other in the library? He vaguely remembered becoming angry. But could he actually have been angry enough to carry out such a terrible act of violence? And how could he possibly have left her bleeding on the library floor while he stumbled up to bed? He shook his head. It just didn't make sense.

The phone rang, but Shipman only stared at it. When the ringing stopped, he took the receiver off the hook and laid it on the counter.

When the coffee was ready, he poured a cup and with slightly trembling fingers carried it into the living room. Normally he would have settled in his big leather chair in the library, but not today. Now he wondered if he would ever be able to enter that room again.

Just as he was getting settled, he heard shouting from outside. He knew the media were still encamped on his street, but he couldn't imagine the cause of such a racket. Yet before he even pulled back the drapes far enough to allow him to peer outside, he had guessed what had caused the furor.

The former president of the United States had arrived on the scene, to offer friendship and comfort.

The Secret Service personnel tried valiantly to clear a path for the Britlands as they forged their way through the crowd of reporters and cameramen. With his arm protectively around his wife, Henry paused, indicating his willingness to offer at least a cursory statement: "As always in this great country, a man is innocent until proven guilty. Thomas Shipman was a truly great secretary of state and remains a close friend. Sunday and I are here today in friendship."

Having made his statement, the former president turned and headed toward the porch, ignoring the barrage of questions the reporters hurled at him. Just as they reached the top step leading to the porch, Tom Shipman unlocked and opened the front door, and his visitors glided inside without further incident.

It was only when the door had closed behind the Britlands, and he felt himself enclosed in a firm and reassuring bear hug, that Thomas Shipman began to sob.

Sensing that the two men needed some time to talk privately, Sunday headed to the kitchen, insisting against Shipman's protest that she prepare lunch for the three of them. The former secretary kept saying that he could call in his housekeeper, but Sunday insisted that he leave everything to her. "You'll feel a lot better when you have something in your stomach, Tom," she said. "You guys say your hellos and then come join me. I'm sure you must have everything I need to make an omelet. It'll be ready in just a few minutes."

Shipman, in fact, quickly regained his composure. Somehow just Henry Britland's presence in his home gave him the sense, at least for the moment, that he could handle whatever it was that he would have to face. They went to the kitchen, finding Sunday already at work on the omelet. Her brisk, sure movements at the chopping board brought back for Shipman a recent memory of Palm Beach, and of watching someone else prepare a salad, while he dreamed of a future that now could never be.

Glancing out the window, he realized suddenly that the shade was raised, and that if somebody managed to sneak around to the back of the house, there would be a perfect opportunity to snap a candid photo of the three of them. Swiftly, he moved across the room and lowered the shade.

He turned back toward Henry and Sunday and smiled sadly at the two of them. "You know, I recently got talked into putting an electronic setup on the drapes in all the other rooms, something that would let me close them either by a timer or by a mere click of the control. I never thought I'd need that in here, though. I know almost nothing about cooking, and Arabella wasn't exactly the Betty Crocker type herself."

He paused and shook his head. "Oh, well. It doesn't matter now. And besides, I never did like the damn things. In fact, the drapes in the library still don't work right. Every time you click to either open or close them, you get this loud cracking noise, almost like somebody firing a gun. Oddly appropriate, wouldn't you say? I mean, since there really was a gun fired in there less than forty-eight hours ago. You've heard about events casting their shadows before them? Well . . ."

He turned away for a moment, the room silent except for the

sounds of Sunday getting the omelet ready for the pan. Then Shipman moved to the kitchen table and sat across from Henry. He was reminded almost immediately of the times they had faced each other across the desk in the Oval Office. He looked up, catching the younger man's eye. "You know, Mr. President, I—"

"Tommy, knock it off. It's me. Henry."

"All right, Henry. I was just thinking that we are both lawyers, and—"

"And so is Sunday," Henry reminded him. "Don't forget. She did her time as a public defender before she ran for office."

Shipman smiled wanly. "Then I suggest that she's our resident expert." He turned toward her. "Sunday, did you ever have to launch a defense where your client had been dead drunk at the time the crime was committed, in the course of which he not only shot his . . . ah . . . friend, three times, but left her sprawled out on the floor to bleed to death while he staggered upstairs to sleep it off?"

Without turning from the stove, she responded. "Maybe not quite those circumstances, but I did defend a number of people who had been so high on drugs at the time that they didn't even remember committing the crime. Typically, though, there were witnesses who offered sworn testimony against them. It was tough."

"So they were found guilty, of course?" Shipman asked.

Sunday paused and looked at him, smiling ruefully. "They had the book thrown at them," she admitted.

"Exactly. My attorney, Len Hart, is a good and capable fellow who wants me to plead guilty by reason of insanity—temporary, of course. But as I see it, my only course is to plea bargain in the hope that in exchange for a guilty plea, the state will not seek the death penalty."

Henry and Sunday now both were watching their friend as he talked, staring straight ahead. "You understand," Shipman continued, "that I took the life of a young woman who ought to have enjoyed fifty years more on this planet. If I go to prison, I probably won't last more than five or ten years. The confinement, however long it lasts, may help to expiate this awful guilt before I am called to meet my Maker."

All three of them remained silent as Sunday finished preparing the meal—tossing a salad, then pouring beaten eggs into a heated skillet, adding chopped tomatoes, scallions, and ham, folding the ends of the bubbling eggs into flaps, and finally flipping the omelet over. The toast popped up as she slid the first omelet onto a heated plate and placed it in front of Shipman. "Eat," she commanded.

Twenty minutes later, when Tom Shipman pushed the last bit of salad onto a crust of toast and stared at the empty plate in front of him, he observed, "It is an embarrassment of riches, Henry, that with a French chef already employed in your kitchen, you are also blessed with a wife who is a culinary master."

"Thank you, kind sir," Sunday said briskly. "The truth is, whatever talents I have in the kitchen began during the time I put in as a short-order cook when I was working my way through Fordham."

Shipman smiled as he stared distractedly at the empty plate in front of him. "It's a talent to be admired. And certainly one Arabella didn't possess." He shook his head slowly from side to side. "It's hard to believe I could have been so foolish."

Sunday put her hand on top of his, then said quietly, "Tommy, certainly there have got to be some extenuating circumstances that will work in your favor. You've put in so many years of public service, and you've been involved in so many charitable projects. The courts will be looking for anything they can use to soften the sentence— assuming, of course, that there really is one. Henry and I are here to help in any way we can, and we will stay by your side through whatever follows."

Henry Britland placed his hand firmly on Shipman's shoulder. "That's right, old friend, we are here for you. Just ask, and we will try to make it happen. But before we can do anything, we need to know what really did happen here. We had heard that Arabella had broken up with you, so why was she here that night?"

Shipman did not answer immediately. "She just dropped in," he said evasively.

"Then you weren't expecting her?" Sunday asked quickly.

He hesitated. "Uh . . . no . . . no, I wasn't."

Henry leaned forward. "Okay, Tom, but as Will Rogers said, 'All I know is just what I read in the papers.' According to the media accounts, you had phoned Arabella earlier in the day and begged her to talk to you. She had come over that evening around nine."

"That's right," he replied without explanation.

Henry and Sunday exchanged worried glances. Clearly there was something that Tom wasn't telling them.

"What about the gun?" Henry asked. "Frankly, I was startled to hear that you even had one, and especially that it was registered in your name. You were such a staunch supporter of the Brady Bill, and were considered an enemy by the NRA. Where did you keep it?"

"Truthfully, I had totally forgotten I even had it," Shipman said tonelessly. "I got it when we first moved here, and it had been in the back of my safe for years. Then coincidentally I noticed it there the other day, right after hearing that the town police were having a drive to get people to exchange guns for toys. So I just took it out of the safe and had left it lying on the library table, the bullets beside it. I had planned to drop it off at the police station the next morning. Well, they got it all right, just not in the way I had planned."

Sunday knew that she and Henry were sharing the same thought. The situation was beginning to look particularly bad: not only had Tom shot Arabella, but he had loaded the gun after her arrival.

"Tom, what were you doing before Arabella got here?" Henry asked.

The couple watched as Shipman considered the question before answering: "I had been at the annual stockholders' meeting of American Micro. It had been an exhausting day, exacerbated by the fact that I had a terrible cold. My housekeeper, Lillian West, had dinner ready for me at seven-thirty. I ate only a little and then went directly upstairs because I still wasn't feeling well. In fact, I even had chills, so I took a long, hot shower; then I got into bed. I hadn't been sleeping well for several nights, so I took a sleeping pill. Then I was awakened—from a very sound sleep, I must say—when Lillian knocked on my door to tell me that Arabella was downstairs to see me."

"So you came back downstairs?"

"Yes. I remember that Lillian was just leaving as I came down, and that Arabella was already in the library."

"Were you pleased to see her?"

Shipman paused for a moment before answering. "No, I was not. I remember that I was still groggy from the sleeping pill and could hardly keep my eyes open. Also I was angry that after ignoring my phone calls, she had simply decided to appear without warning. As you may remember, there is a bar in the library. Well, Arabella already had made herself at home by preparing a martini for each of us."

"Tom, why would you even think of drinking a martini on top of a sleeping pill?" Henry asked.

"Because I'm a fool," Shipman snapped. "And because I was so sick of Arabella's loud laugh and irritating voice that I thought I'd go mad if I didn't drown them out."

Henry and Sunday stared at their friend. "But I thought you were crazy about her," Henry said.

"Oh, I was for a while, but in the end, I was the one who broke it off," Shipman replied. "As a gentleman, though, I thought it proper to tell people that it had been her decision. Certainly anyone looking at the disparity in our ages would have expected it to be that way. The truth was, I had finally—temporarily, as it turns out—come to my senses."

"Then why were you calling her?" Sunday asked. "I don't follow."

"Because she had taken to phoning me in the middle of the night, sometimes repeatedly, hour upon hour. Usually she would hang up right after hearing my voice, but I knew it was Arabella. So I had called her to warn her that it couldn't go on that way. But I certainly did not invite her over."

"Tom, why haven't you told any of this to the police? Certainly based on everything I have read and heard, everyone thinks it was a crime of passion."

Tom Shipman shook his head sadly. "Because I think that in the end it probably was. That last night Arabella told me that she was going to get in touch with one of the tabloids and was going to sell them a story about wild parties that you and I allegedly gave together during your administration."

"But that's ridiculous," Henry said indignantly.

"Blackmail," Sunday said softly.

"Exactly. So do you think telling that story would help my case?" Shipman asked. He shook his head. "No, even though it wasn't the case, at least there's some dignity to being punished for murdering a woman because I loved her too much to lose her. Dignity for her, and, perhaps, even a modicum of dignity for me."

Sunday insisted on cleaning up the kitchen while Henry escorted Tommy upstairs to rest.

"Tommy, I wish there were someone staying here with you while all this is going on," the former president said. "I hate to leave you alone."

"Oh, don't worry, Henry, I'm fine. Besides, I don't feel alone after our visit."

Despite his friend's admonition, Henry knew he would worry, as he began to do almost immediately after Shipman went off to the bathroom. Constance and Tommy had never had children, and now so many of their close friends from the area had retired and moved away, most of them to Florida. Henry's thoughts were interrupted by the sounding of his ever-present beeper. Using his cellular phone, he replied immediately. The caller was Jack Collins, the head of the Secret Service team assigned to him. "I'm sorry to bother you, Mr. President, but a neighbor is most anxious to get a message to Mr. Shipman. She says that a good friend of his, a Countess Condazzi who lives in Palm Beach, has been trying to get through to him, but he is not answering his phone and apparently his answering machine is turned off, so she has been unable to leave him a message. I gather that she has become somewhat distraught and is insisting that Mr. Shipman be notified that she is awaiting his call."

"Thanks, Jack. I'll give Secretary Shipman the message. And Sunday and I will be leaving in just a few minutes."

"Right, sir. We'll be ready."

Countess Condazzi, Henry thought. How interesting. I wonder who that can be.

His curiosity deepened when, on being informed of the call, Thomas Acker Shipman's eyes brightened, and a smile formed on his lips. "Betsy phoned, eh?" he said. "How dear of her." But almost as quickly as it had appeared, the brightness faded from his eyes, and the smile vanished. "Perhaps you could send word to my neighbor that I won't be accepting calls from anyone," he said. "At this juncture, there seems to be little point in talking to anyone other than my lawyer."

A few minutes later, as Henry and Sunday were being hustled past the media, a Lexus pulled into the driveway next to them. The couple watched as a woman jumped from the car and, using the stir created by their departure as diversion, managed to get to the house undisturbed, where, using her own key, she entered immediately.

"That has to be the housekeeper," Sunday said, having noted that the woman, who appeared to be in her fifties, was dressed plainly and wore her hair in a coronet of braids. "She certainly looks the part, and besides, who else would have a key? Well, at least Tom won't be alone."

"He must be paying her well," Henry observed. "That car is expensive."

On the drive home, he told Sunday about the mysterious phone call from the countess in Palm Beach. She made no comment, but he could tell from the way she tilted her head to one side and puckered her forehead that she was both disturbed and deep in thought.

The car they were riding in was a nondescript, eight-year-old Chevy, one of the specially equipped secondhand cars Henry kept available for their use, especially helpful in allowing them to avoid detection when they so desired. As always, they were accompanied by two Secret Service agents, one driving while the other rode shotgun. A thick glass divider separated the front seat from the back, allowing Henry and Sunday the freedom to talk without being overheard.

Breaking what for her was an extended silence, Sunday said, "Henry, there's something wrong about this case. You could sense it from the accounts in the paper, but now, having talked to Tommy, I'm certain of it."

Henry nodded. "I agree completely. At first I thought that perhaps the details of the crime might be so gruesome that he had to deny them even to himself." He paused, then shook his head. "But now I realize that this is not a question of denial. Tommy really doesn't know what happened. And all of this is just so unlike him!" he exclaimed. "No matter what the provocation—threats of blackmail or whatever—I cannot accept that even confounded by the combination of a sleeping pill and a martini, Tommy could go so completely out of control as to have killed the woman! Just seeing him today made me realize how extraordinary all this is. You didn't know him then, Sunday, but he was devoted to Constance. Yet when she died, his composure was remarkable. He suffered, yes, but he remained calm throughout the entire ordeal." He paused, then shook his head again. "No, Tommy simply isn't the kind of man who flips out, no matter what the provocation."

"Well, his composure may have been remarkable when his wife died, but then falling hook, line and sinker for Arabella Young when Connie was barely cold in her grave does say something about the man, you'll have to agree."

"Yes, but rebound perhaps? Or denial?"

"Exactly," Sunday replied. "Of course, sometimes people fall in love almost immediately after a great loss and it actually works out, but more often than not, it doesn't."

"You're probably right. The very fact that Tommy never married Arabella after actually giving her an engagement ring—what, nearly two years ago?—says to me that almost from the outset he must have known it was a mistake."

"Well, all of this took place before I came on the scene, of course," Sunday mused, "but I did keep abreast of much of it through the tabloids, which at the time made a big fuss over how in love the staid secretary of state was with the flashy PR person only half his age. But then I remember seeing two photos of him run side by side, one showing him out in public, snuggling Arabella, while the other was taken at his wife's burial and obviously caught him at a moment when his composure had slipped. No one that grief stricken could be that happy only a couple of months later. And the way she dressed— she just didn't seem to be Tommy's kind of woman." Sunday sensed rather than saw her husband's raised eyebrow. "Oh, come on. I know you read the tabloids cover to cover after I'm done with them. Tell me the truth. What did you think of Arabella?"

"Truthfully, I thought of her as little as possible."

"You're not answering my question."

"I try never to speak ill of the dead." He paused. "But if you must know, I found her boisterous, vulgar and obnoxious. She possessed a shrewd enough mind, but she talked so fast and so incessantly that her brain never seemed able to keep up with her mouth. And when she laughed, I thought the chandelier would shatter."

"Well, that certainly fits in with what I read about her," Sunday commented. She was silent for a moment, then turned to her husband. "Henry, if Arabella really was stooping to blackmail with Tommy, do you think it is possible she had tried it before, with someone else? I mean, is it possible that between the sleeping pill and the martini, Tommy passed out, and someone else came in without him knowing it? Someone who had followed Arabella, and who suddenly saw an opportunity to get rid of her and let poor Tommy take the blame?"

"And then carried Tommy upstairs and tucked him into bed?" Henry again raised an eyebrow.

They both fell silent as the car turned onto the approach to the Garden State Parkway. Sunday stared out the window as the late afternoon sunshine turned the trees, with their copper and gold and cardinal-red leaves, aglow. "I love autumn," she said pensively. "And it hurts to think that in the late autumn of his life, Tommy should be going through this ordeal." She paused. "Okay, let's try another scenario. You know Tommy well. Suppose he was angry, even furious, but also was so groggy that he couldn't think straight. Put yourself in his position at that moment: what would you have done?"

"I would have done what Tommy and I both did when we were in a similar state of mind at summit meetings. We would sense that we were either too tired or too angry—or both—to be able to think straight, and we would go to bed."

Sunday clasped Henry's hand. "That's exactly my point. Suppose Tommy actually staggered upstairs under his own steam, leaving Arabella behind. And suppose someone else really had followed her there, someone who knew what she was doing that evening. We have to find out who Arabella might have been with earlier. And we should talk to Tommy's housekeeper. She left shortly after Arabella arrived. Maybe there was a car parked on the street that she noticed. And the countess from Palm Beach who called, who so urgently wanted to talk to Tommy. We've got to contact her; it's probably nothing, but you never know what she might be able to tell us."

"Agreed," Henry said admiringly. "As usual, we're on the same wavelength, only you're farther along than I am. I actually hadn't given any thought to talking to the countess." He reached his arm around Sunday and pulled her closer. "Come here. Do you realize that I have not kissed you since 11:10 this morning?" he asked softly.

Sunday caressed his lips with the tip of her index finger. "Ah, then it's more than my steel-trap mind that appeals to you?"

"You've noticed." Henry kissed her fingertip, then grasped her hand and lowered it, removing any obstruction between his lips and hers.

Sunday pulled back. "Just one more thing, Henry. You've got to make sure that Tommy doesn't agree to a plea bargain before we at least try to help him."

"And how am I supposed to do that?" he asked.

"An executive order, of course."

"Darling, I'm no longer president."

"Ah, but in Tommy's eyes you are."

"All right, I'll try. But here's another executive order: stop talking."

In the front seat, the Secret Service agents glanced in the rearview mirror, then grinned at each other.

Henry was up by sunrise the next morning for a ride around a portion of the two-thousand-acre property with the estate manager.

Back by eight-thirty, he was joined by Sunday in the breakfast room, which overlooked the classic English garden at the back of the house. The room itself was decorated to complement the view, with a wealth of botanical prints set against the background of Belgian linen awning-stripe wall covering. It gave the room a feeling of being constantly filled with flowers and, as Sunday frequently observed, was a long way from the upstairs apartment in the two-family house in Jersey City where she had been raised, and where her parents still lived.

"Don't forget that Congress goes into session next week," Sunday said as she eased into her second cup of coffee. "Whatever I can do to help Tommy, I have to start working on it right now. My suggestion would be that I begin by finding out everything I can about Arabella. Did Marvin finish the complete background check we asked for?"

The Marvin she referred to was Marvin Klein, the man who ran Henry's office, which was situated in the estate's former carriage house. Possessed of a droll sense of humor, Marvin called himself the chief of staff for a government in exile, referring to the fact that following Henry Britland's second term, there had been a groundswell of opinion urging a change in the restriction that a United States president could serve only two terms. A poll at the time showed that 80 percent of the electorate wanted that prohibition amended to read no more than two consecutive terms. Quite obviously, a majority of the American public wanted Henry Parker Britland IV back in residence at 1600 Pennsylvania Avenue.

"I've got it right here," Henry said. "I just read it. It would appear that the late Arabella successfully managed to bury quite a bit of her background. Some of the juicy bits that Marvin's sources were able to come up with include the fact that she had a previous marriage which ended in a divorce that saw her taking her ex to the cleaners, and that her longtime on-again, off-again boyfriend, Alfred Barker, spent some time in prison for bribing athletes."

"Really! Is he out of prison now?"

"Not only is he out, my dear, but he had dinner with Arabella the night she died."

Sunday's jaw dropped. "Darling, how on earth did Marvin ever discover that?"

"How does Marvin ever discover anything? All I know is that he has his sources. And furthermore, it seems that Alfred Barker lives in Yonkers, which as you probably know is not far from Tarrytown. Her ex-husband is said to be happily remarried and does not live in the area."

"Marvin learned all this overnight?" Sunday asked, her eyes bright with excitement.

Henry nodded in answer, as Sims, the butler, refilled his coffee cup. "Thank you, Sims. And not only that," he continued, "he also learned that apparently Alfred Barker was still very fond of Arabella, however improbable that may sound, and had recently been heard bragging to friends that now that she had ditched the old guy, she'd be getting back together with him."

"What does Barker do now?" Sunday asked.

"Well, technically he owns a plumbing supply store, but Marvin's sources say that actually it is a front for a numbers racket, which he apparently runs pretty much on his own. My favorite bit of information, though, is that our Mr. Barker is known to have a violent temper when double-crossed."

Sunday scrunched her face as though deep in thought. "Hmmm. Let's see now. He had dinner with Arabella just before she barged in on Tommy. He hates being double-crossed, which probably means he is also very jealous, and he has a terrible temper." She looked at her husband. "Are you thinking what I'm thinking?"

"Exactly."

"I knew this was a crime of passion!" Sunday said excitedly. "Only it appears that the passion was not on Tommy's part. Okay, so I'll go see Barker today, as well as Tommy's housekeeper. What was her name?"

"Dora, I believe," Henry replied. Then he corrected himself: "No, no—that was the housekeeper who worked for them for years. Great old lady. I believe Tommy said that she retired shortly after Constance died. No, if memory serves me, the one he has now, and that we caught a glimpse of yesterday, is named Lillian West."

"That's right. The woman with the braids and the Lexus," Sunday said. "So I'll take on Barker and the housekeeper. What are you going to do?"

"I'm flying down to Palm Beach to meet with this Countess Condazzi, but I'll be home for dinner. And you, my dear, have to promise me that you'll be careful. Remember that this Alfred Barker is clearly an unsavory character. I don't want you giving the Secret Service guys the slip."

"Okay."

"I mean it, Sunday," Henry said in the quiet, serious tone he had used so effectively to make his cabinet members quake in their boots.

"Oooh, you're one tough hombre," Sunday said, smiling. "Okay, I promise. I'll stick to them like glue. And you fly safely." She kissed the top of his head and then left the breakfast room, humming "Hail to the Chief."

Some four hours later, having piloted his jet to the West Palm Beach airport, Henry arrived at the Spanish-style mansion that was the home of Countess Condazzi. "Wait outside," he instructed his Secret Service detail.

The countess appeared to be in her mid-sixties, a small, slender woman with exquisite features and calm gray eyes. She greeted Henry with cordial warmth, then got straight to the point. "I was so glad to get your call, Mr. President," she said. "I read the news accounts of Tommy's terrible situation, and I have been so anxious to talk to him. I know how much he must be suffering, but he won't return my phone calls. Look, I know Tommy could not have committed this crime. We've been friends since we were children; we went to school together, including college, and in all that time there was never a moment when he so lost control of himself. Even when others around him were being fresh or disorderly, as they tended to be at the prom, and even when he was drinking, Tommy was always a gentleman. He took care of me, and when the prom was over, he took me home. No, Tommy simply could not have done this thing."

"That's exactly the way I see it," Henry said in agreement. "So you grew up with him?"

"Across the street from each other in Rye. We dated all through college, but then he met Constance and I met Eduardo Condazzi, who was from Spain. I got married, and a year later, when Eduardo's older brother died and he inherited the title and the family's vineyards, we moved to Spain. Eduardo passed away three years ago. My son is now the count and lives in Spain still, but I thought it was time for me to come home. Then, after all these years, I bumped into Tommy when he was visiting friends down here for a golfing weekend. It was so wonderful to see him again. The years just seemed to melt away."

And love was rekindled, Henry thought. "Countess . . ."

"Betsy," she instructed firmly.

"All right, Betsy, I have to be blunt. Did you and Tommy begin to pick up where you left off years ago?"

"Well, yes and no," Betsy said slowly. "I made it clear to him how very glad I was to see him again, and I think he felt the same way about me. But you see, I also think that Tommy never really gave himself a chance to grieve for Constance. In fact, we talked about it at length. It was obvious to me that his involvement with Arabella Young was his way of trying to escape the grieving process. I advised him to drop Arabella, and then to give himself a period of mourning, something like six months to a year. But then, I told him, he had to call me and take me to a prom."

Henry studied Betsy Condazzi's face, her wistful smile, her eyes filled with memories. "Did he agree?" he asked.

"Not completely. He said that he was selling his house and was going to move down here permanently." She smiled. "He said that he'd be ready long before six months were up, to take me to the prom."

Henry paused before asking the next question: "If Arabella Young had gone to the tabloids with a story claiming that during my administration and even before his wife's death, Tommy and I had thrown wild, debauched parties in the White House, what would your reaction be?"

"Why, I'd know it wasn't true," she said simply. "And Tommy knows me well enough to be sure that he could count on my support."

On the return flight to Teterboro Airport, Henry let his pilot take over the controls. His time was spent deep in thought. It was becoming increasingly clear to him that Tommy was being set up. Obviously he was aware that his future had promised a second chance at happiness and that he didn't have to kill in order to safeguard that chance. No, it just didn't make sense that he would have killed Arabella Young. But how were they going to prove it? He wondered if Sunday was having any better luck in finding a likely motive for Arabella's murder.

Alfred Barker was not a man who inspired instinctive liking, Sunday thought as she sat across from him in the office of his plumbing supply store.

He appeared to be in his mid-forties, a thick, barrel-chested man with heavily lidded eyes, a sallow complexion, and salt-and-pepper hair, which he combed dramatically across his skull in an obvious effort to hide a growing bald spot. His open shirt, however, revealed a wealth of hair on his chest. The only other distinctive thing she noticed about him was a jagged scar on the back of his right hand.

Sunday felt a fleeting moment of gratitude as she thought of Henry's lean, muscular body, his altogether pleasing appearance, including his famous "stubborn" jaw and the sable-brown eyes that could convey or, if necessary, conceal emotion. And while she frequently chaffed at the omnipresent Secret Service men—after all, she had never been a first lady, so why should she need them now?—at this moment, closeted in this squalid room with this hostile man, she was glad to know that they stood just outside the partially open door.

She had introduced herself as Sandra O'Brien, and it was obvious that Alfred Barker did not have a clue that the rest of her name was Britland.

"So why do you wanna talk to me about Arabella?" Barker asked as he lit a cigar.

"I want to start by saying that I'm very sorry about her death," Sunday said sincerely. "I understand that you and she were very close. But, you see, I know Mr. Shipman." She paused, then explained, "My husband at one time worked with him. And there seems to be a conflicting version of who broke up his relationship with Miss Young."

"What does that matter? Arabella was sick of the old creep," Barker said. "Arabella always liked me."

"But she got engaged to Thomas Shipman," Sunday protested.

"Yeah, but I knew that would never last. All he had was a fat wallet. You see, Arabella got married when she was eighteen to some jerk who was so dumb he needed to be introduced to himself every morning. But Arabella was smart. The guy may have been stupid, but he was worth hanging onto 'cause there were big bucks in the family. So she hung around for three or four years, let him pay for her to go to college, get her teeth fixed, whatever, then waited until his very rich uncle died, got him to commingle the money, and then dumped him. She cleaned up in the divorce."

Alfred Barker relit the tip of his cigar and exhaled noisily, then leaned back in his chair. "What a shrewd cookie she was. A natural."

"And was it then that she started seeing you?" Sunday prodded.

"Right. But then I had a little misunderstanding with the government and ended up in the can for a spell. She got herself a job with a fancy public relations firm, and when a chance to move to their Washington branch came up a couple of years ago, she grabbed it."

Barker inhaled deeply on the cigar, then coughed noisily. "Nope, you couldn't hold Arabella down, not that I ever wanted to. When I got sprung last year, she used to call me all the time and tell me about that jerk, Shipman, but it was a good setup for her, because he was always giving her jewelry, and she was always meeting fancy people." Barker leaned across the desk and said meaningfully, "Including the president of the United States, Henry Parker Britland the Fourth." He paused, once again leaning back in his chair. He looked at Sunday accusingly. "How many people in this country ever sat down at the table and traded jokes with the president of the United States? Have you?" he challenged.

"No, not with the president," Sunday said honestly, remembering that first night at the White House when she had declined Henry's invitation to dinner.

"See what I mean?" Barker crowed triumphantly.

"Well, obviously, as secretary of state, Thomas Shipman was able to provide great contacts for Arabella. But according to Mr. Shipman, he was the one who was breaking off the relationship. Not Arabella."

"Yeah. Well, so what?"

"Then why would he kill her?"

Barker's face darkened, and he slammed his fist on the desk. "I warned Arabella not to threaten him with that tabloid routine. I told her that this time she was running with a different crowd. But it had worked for her before, so she wouldn't listen to me."

"She got away with it before!" Sunday exclaimed, remembering that this was exactly the scenario she had suggested to Henry. "Who else did she try to blackmail?"

"Oh, some guy she worked with. I don't know his name. Some small potatoes. But it's never a good idea to mess around with a guy who's got the kind of clout Shipman has. Remember what he did to Castro?"

"How much did she talk about her efforts to blackmail him?"

"Not much, and then only to me. I kept telling her not to try it, but she figured it would be worth a couple of bucks." Unlikely tears welled in Alfred Barker's eyes. "I really liked her. But she was so stubborn. She just wouldn't listen." He paused, apparently lost for a moment in reflection. "I warned her. There was even this quotation that I showed her."

Sunday's head jerked back in involuntary reaction to Barker's startling statement.

"I like quotations," he said. "I read them for laughs and for insight, or whatever, if you know what I mean."

Sunday nodded her head. "My husband is very fond of quotations. He says they contain wisdom."

"Yeah, that's what I mean! What's your husband do?"

"He's unemployed at the moment," Sunday replied, looking down at her hands.

"That's tough. Does he know anything about plumbing?"

"Not much."

"Do you think he could run numbers?"

Sunday shook her head sadly. "No, mostly he just stays home.

And he reads a lot, like the quotations you were mentioning," she said, trying to get the conversation back on track.

"Yeah, the one I read Arabella fit her so well it was amazing. She had a big mouth. A real big mouth. I came across this quote and showed it to her. I always told her that her big mouth would get her in trouble, and boy it did."

Barker rummaged through the top drawer of his desk, then pulled out a tattered piece of paper. "Here it is. Read this." He thrust a page at Sunday that obviously had been torn from a book of quotations. One entry on the page was circled in red:

Beyond this stone, a lump of clay,
Lies Arabella Young,
Who on the 24th of May
Began to hold her tongue.

"It comes from an old English tombstone. Just like that! Except for the date, is that a coincidence or is that a coincidence?" Barker sighed heavily and then slumped back in his chair. "Yeah, I'm sure gonna miss Arabella. She was fun."

"You had dinner with her the night she died, didn't you?"

"Yeah."

"Did you drop her off at the Shipman house?"

"Nah. I told her she should give it a rest, but she wouldn't listen. So I put her in a cab. She was planning to borrow his car to get home." Barker shook his head. "Only she wasn't planning to return it. She was sure he'd give her anything just to keep her from talking to the tabloids." He fell silent for a moment. "Instead, look what he did to her."

Barker stood up, his face twisted with fresh anger. "I hope they fry him!"

Sunday got to her feet. "The death penalty in New York State is administered by lethal injection, but I get your drift. Tell me, Mr. Barker, what did you do after you put Arabella in a cab?"

"You know, I've been expecting to be asked that, but the cops didn't even bother talking to me. They knew they got Arabella's killer from the start. So, after I put her in the cab, I went to my mother's and took her to the movies. I do that once a month. I was at her house by quarter of nine, and in line to buy tickets at two minutes of nine. The ticket guy knows me. The kid who sells popcorn at the theater knows me. The woman who was sitting next to me is Mama's friend, and she knows I was there for the whole show. So I didn't murder Arabella, but I know who did!"

Barker pounded his fist on the desk, sending an empty soda bottle crashing to the floor. "You wanna help Shipman? Decorate his cell."

Sunday's Secret Service guards were suddenly beside her, staring intently at Barker. "I wouldn't pound the desk in this lady's presence," one of them suggested icily.

For the first time since she had entered the office, Sunday noticed, Alfred Barker was at a loss for words.

Thomas Acker Shipman had not been pleased to receive the call from Marvin Klein, Henry Britland's aide, informing him of the president's request that he delay the plea-bargaining process. What is the use? Shipman wondered, disgruntled by not being able to get on with it. It was inevitable that he would have to go to jail, and he just wanted to get it over with. Besides, this house already had taken on the aspects of a prison. Once the plea bargaining was finished, the media would have a surge of interest in him, but then he would be dropped and they would be on to another poor slob. A sixty-five-year-old man going to prison for ten or fifteen years didn't remain hot copy for long.

The only thing that keeps them churning so much, he thought as he once again peered out at the mass of reporters still camped outside his house, is the speculation about whether or not I'll go to trial. Once that's been resolved, and it's clear that I'm taking my medicine without putting up a fight, they'll lose interest.

His housekeeper, Lillian West, had arrived promptly at eight o'clock that morning. He had hoped to discourage her coming today by putting on the safety chain, but apparently all he succeeded in doing was making her more determined than ever to get in. When her key did not gain her entrance, she had pushed the doorbell firmly and called his name until he let her in. "You need taking care of, whether you think so or not," she had said, sharply brushing aside the objection he had voiced yesterday, that he didn't want her private life invaded by the media, and that, in fact, he really did prefer to be left alone.

And so she had gone about her usual daily chores, cleaning rooms that he would never again get to live in, and fixing meals for which he had no appetite. Shipman watched her as she moved about the house. Lillian was a handsome woman, an excellent housekeeper, and a cordon bleu cook, but her overly bossy tendencies occasionally made him wistfully remember Dora, the housekeeper who had been with him and Connie for some twenty years. So what if she had sometimes burned the bacon; she had always been a pleasant fixture in their home.

Also, Dora had been of the old school, while Lillian clearly believed in the equality of the employee to the employer. Nevertheless, Shipman realized that for the short time he would be in the house before going to prison, he could manage to put up with Lillian's take-over attitude. He would just make the best of it by trying to enjoy the creature comforts of delicious meals and properly served wine.

Recognizing that he could not cut himself off completely from the outside world, and acknowledging that he actually needed to be available to his lawyer, Shipman had turned on the telephone answering machine and had begun taking calls, although screening out those that weren't necessary. When he heard Sunday's voice, however, he gladly picked up the phone.

"Tommy, I'm in the car and on my way to your house from Yonkers," Sunday explained. "I want to talk to your housekeeper. Is she in today, and if not, do you know where I can reach her?"

"Lillian is here."

"Wonderful. Don't let her leave until I have had a chance to visit with her. I should be there in about an hour."

"I can't imagine what she'll be able to tell you that the police haven't already heard."

"Tommy, I've just talked with Arabella's boyfriend. He knew of her plan to extort money from you, and from what he said, I gather that it was a stunt that she had pulled on at least one other person. We've got to find out who that person was. It's entirely possible that someone followed Arabella to your house that night, and we hope that when Lillian left she might have seen something—a car, maybe—that didn't seem significant at the time but could prove to be important. The police never really investigated any other possible suspects, and since Henry and I are convinced that you didn't do it, we're going to sniff around for them. So buck up! It ain't over till it's over."

Shipman hung up and turned to see Lillian West standing in the doorway to his study. Obviously she had been listening to his conversation. Even so, he smiled pleasantly. "Mrs. Britland is on her way here to talk to you," he said. "She and the president seem to feel that I may not be guilty of killing Arabella after all and are doing some sleuthing on their own. They have a theory that might prove to be very helpful to me, and that's what she wants to speak to you about."

"That's wonderful," Lillian West said, her voice flat and her tone chilly. "I can't wait to talk to her."

Sunday's next call was to Henry, on his plane. They exchanged reports on what they had learned so far, he from the countess and she from Alfred Barker. After Sunday's revelation about Arabella's habit of blackmailing the men she dated, she added a cautionary note: "The only problem with all this is that no matter who else might have wanted to kill Arabella, proving that that person walked into Tommy's house undetected, loaded the gun that happened to be lying there, and then pulled the trigger is going to be difficult."

"Difficult maybe, but not impossible," Henry said by way of reassurance. "I'll get Marvin started right away on checking out Arabella's last places of employment, and maybe he can find out who she might have been involved with there."

After saying good-bye to Sunday, Henry sat back to ponder what he had just learned about Arabella's past. He felt a strong sense of unease, but he couldn't quite put it together. He had a growing premonition that something was wrong, but he couldn't put his finger on just what it was.

He leaned back in the swivel chair that was his favorite spot on the plane, other than the flight deck. It was something Sunday had said, he decided, but what was it? With almost total recall, he reviewed their conversation. Of course, he said to himself when he reached that point in his recollection, it was Sunday's observation about the difficulty in trying to prove that some unknown person had walked into Tommy's house, loaded the pistol and pulled the trigger.

That was it! It didn't have to be an outsider. There was one person who could have done that, who knew that Tommy felt both sick and overwhelmingly tired, who knew that Arabella was there, who in fact had let her in. *The housekeeper!*

She was relatively new. Chances were that Tommy hadn't really had her checked out, probably didn't know much of anything about her.

Quickly, Henry phoned Countess Condazzi. Let her still be home, he prayed silently. When her now-familiar voice answered, he wasted no time in getting to the point of his call: "Betsy, did Tommy ever say anything to you about his new housekeeper?"

She hesitated before answering. "Well, yes, but only jokingly."

"What do you mean?"

"Oh, you know how it is," she responded. "There are so many women in their fifties and sixties who are unattached, but there are so few men. When I spoke to Tommy last—it was the morning of the day that poor girl was killed—I said I had a dozen friends who are widowed or divorced who would be jealous because of his interest in me, and that if he showed up down here, he would be the center of attention. I remember that he said that except for me, he intended to steer clear of unattached women, and that, in fact, he had just had a most unpleasant experience in this regard." She paused before continuing. "It seems that only that morning he had told his new housekeeper that he was putting his house on the market and would be moving to Palm Beach. He confided to her that he was finished with Arabella because someone else had become important to him. Later, when he was thinking back over the conversation and her reaction to it, he realized that the housekeeper may have gotten the crazy idea that he had meant her. So he made a special point of informing her that, of course, he would not need her services once the house was sold and, naturally, would not be taking her with him to Florida. He recounted that she at first had seemed shocked and then had become cool and distant." Again the countess paused; then she gasped. "Goodness, you don't think she could have had anything to do with this mess Tommy's in, do you?"

"I'm afraid I'm beginning to, Betsy," Henry replied. "Look, I'll get back to you. I've got to get my man on this right away." He broke the connection and swiftly dialed Marvin Klein.

"Marvin," he said. "I've got a hunch about Secretary Shipman's housekeeper, Lillian West. Do a complete check on her. Immediately."

Marvin Klein did not like to break the law as he would be doing by penetrating private computer records, but he knew that when his boss said "Immediately," the matter had to be urgent.

It was only a matter of minutes before he had assembled a dossier on fifty-six-year-old Lillian West, including her rather extensive record of traffic violations and, more to the point, her employment history. Marvin frowned as he began to read. West was a college graduate, had an M.A., and had taught home economics at a number of colleges, the last one being Wren College in New Hampshire. Then, six years ago, she had left there and taken a job as a housekeeper.

Since then she had held four different positions. Her references—citing her punctuality, her high standard of work, and her cooking ability—were good but not enthusiastic. Marvin decided to check on them himself.

Less than a half hour after Henry's call, Marvin was on the phone to the former president, who was still winging his way back from Florida. "Sir, the records indicate that Lillian West, while employed in various college-level teaching positions, had a history of troubled relationships with her superiors. Six years ago she left her last teaching job and went to work as a housekeeper for a widower in Vermont. He died ten months later, apparently of a heart attack. She then went to work for a divorced executive, who unfortunately died within the year. Before she went to work for Secretary Shipman, her employer was an eighty-year-old millionaire; he fired her but gave her a good reference nonetheless. I spoke to him. He said that while Ms. West was an excellent housekeeper and cook, she also was quite presumptuous and seemed to put no stock in the more traditional relationship between the head of the house and the housekeeper. In fact, he said that it was when he became aware that she had set her mind on marrying him that he decided she would have to go, and shortly after that he showed her the door."

"Did this man report ever having any health problems?" Henry asked quietly as he absorbed the possibilities that were presented by Lillian West's troubled history.

"I did think to ask him that, sir. He said that he is in robust health now, but that during the last several weeks of Ms. West's employment, specifically after he had given her notice, he experienced extreme fatigue, followed by an undiagnosed illness that culminated in pneumonia."

Tommy had spoken of a heavy cold and overwhelming fatigue. Henry's hand gripped the phone. "Good job, Marvin. Thanks."

"Sir, I'm afraid there's more. According to the records, Ms. West's hobby is hunting, and apparently she is very familiar with guns. Finally, I spoke to the president of Wren College, where she had her last teaching job. As he remembered it, Ms. West was forced to resign. He said that she had displayed symptoms of being deeply disturbed but refused all attempts at counseling."

Henry ended the conversation with his aide as a wave of anxiety swept over him. Sunday was on her way right now to see Lillian West, totally unaware of any of the background Marvin had uncovered. She would unwittingly alert the housekeeper to the fact that they were looking into the very strong possibility that someone other than Thomas Shipman had murdered Arabella Young. There was no telling how the woman might react. Henry's hand had never shaken even at summit meetings, but right now his fingers could barely punch the numbers to reach Sunday's car phone.

Secret Service agent Art Dowling answered. "We're at Secretary Shipman's place now, sir. Mrs. Britland is inside."

"Get her," Henry snapped. "Tell her I must speak to her."

"Right away, sir."

Several minutes passed before Agent Dowling was back on the phone. "Sir, there may be a problem. We've rung the doorbell repeatedly, but no one is answering."

Sunday and Tommy sat side by side on the leather couch in the library, staring into the muzzle of a revolver. Opposite them, Lillian

West sat erect and steady as she held the gun. The persistent pealing of the front doorbell did not seem to distract her.

"Your palace guard, no doubt," she said sarcastically.

The woman is crazy, Sunday thought as she stared into the housekeeper's wild eyes. She's crazy and she's desperate. She knows she has nothing to lose by killing us, and she is just nuts enough to do it.

Sunday thought next of the Secret Service agents waiting outside. Art Dowling and Clint Carr were with her today. What would they do when no one answered the door? They'd probably force their way in, she reasoned. And when they do, she will shoot Tommy and me, she thought, her level of alarm increasing. I know she will.

"You have everything," Lillian West said to Sunday, her eyes fixed on her prisoner, her voice low and angry. "You're beautiful, you're young, you've got an important job, and you're married to a rich and attractive man. Well, I just hope that you have enjoyed the time you've had with him."

"Yes, I have," Sunday said calmly. "He is a wonderful man and husband, and I want more time with him."

"Too bad, but that's not going to happen, and it's your fault. This wouldn't be necessary if you'd just left well enough alone. What difference would it make if he"—Lillian West paused, her eyes cutting momentarily to Tommy—"if he went to prison? He's not worth your trouble. He's no good. He tricked me. He lied to me. He promised to take me to Florida. He was going to marry me." She paused again, this time turning her full glare on the former secretary of state. "Of course, he wasn't as rich as the others, but he has enough to get by. I've gone through all his papers here and I know." A smile played on her lips. "And he's nicer than the others too. I liked that especially. We could have been very happy."

"Lillian, I didn't lie to you," Tommy said quietly. "Think back over all that I ever said to you, and I think you'll agree. I do like you though, and I think you need help. I want to see that you get it. I promise that both Sunday and I will do everything we can for you."

"What, by getting me another housekeeping job?" Lillian snapped. "Cleaning, cooking, shopping. No thanks! I traded teaching silly girls for this kind of drudgery because I thought that somebody would finally appreciate me, would want to take care of me. But it didn't happen. After I waited on all of them, they still treated me like dirt." She directed her gaze again at Tommy. "I thought you were going to be different, but you're not. You're just like all the rest."

While they had been talking, the pealing of the doorbell had stopped. Sunday knew that the Secret Service men would be looking for some way to get in, and she had no doubt that they would succeed. Then she froze. When Lillian West had admitted her, she had reset the alarm. "We don't want one of those reporters trying to sneak in," she had explained.

If Art or Clint tries to open a window, the alarm will go off, Sunday thought, and once that happens, Tommy and I are goners. She felt Tommy's hand brush hers. He's thinking the same thing, she realized. My God, what can we do? She had often heard the expression "staring death in the face," but it wasn't until this moment that she knew what it meant. Henry, she thought, Henry! Please don't let this woman take away our life together.

Tommy's hand was closed over hers now. His index finger was insistently jabbing the back of her hand. He was trying to send her a signal. But what? she wondered. What did he want her to do?

Henry stayed on the line, anxious not to break the connection to the Secret Service agent outside Tommy Shipman's house. Agent Dowling was on his cellular phone now, and continued to talk to the former president as he carefully worked his way around the house. "Sir, all the draperies are drawn, in virtually every room. We've contacted the local police and they should be here any moment. Clint is at the back of the house, climbing a tree that has branches that reach near some windows. We might be able to get in undetected through there. The problem is that we have no way of knowing where they are within the house."

My God, Henry thought. It would take at least an hour to get the special equipment over there that would enable us to follow their movement inside the house. I'm just afraid we don't have that time to spare. Sunday's face loomed in his mind. Sunday! Sunday! She had to be all right. He wanted to get out and push the plane to make it go faster. He wanted to order the army out. He wanted to be there. Now! He shook his head. He had never felt so helpless. Then he heard Dowling swear furiously.

"What is it, Art?" he shouted. "What is it?"

"Sir, the draperies in the right front downstairs room just opened, and I am sure I heard shots being fired inside."

"That stupid woman provided me with the perfect opportunity," Lillian West was saying. "I knew I was running out of time, that I wouldn't be able to kill you slowly, the way I wanted. But this was just as good, really. This way I not only punished you but that dreadful woman as well."

"Then you did kill Arabella?" Tommy exclaimed.

"Of course I did," she snapped impatiently. "It was so easy too. You see, I didn't leave that evening. I showed her to this room, woke you up, said good night, shut the door and hid in the coat closet. I heard it all. And I knew the pistol was there, ready for use. When you staggered upstairs, I knew it would be only a matter of minutes before you lost consciousness." She paused and smiled mischievously. "My sleeping pills are much more effective than the ones you were used to, aren't they? They have special ingredients." She smiled again.

"And a few interesting viruses as well. Why do you think your cold has improved so much since that night? Because you haven't let me in to give you your pills. If you had, your cold would be pneumonia by now."

"You were poisoning Tommy?" Sunday exclaimed.

Lillian West stared indignantly at the younger woman. "I was punishing him," she said firmly. Then she turned again to Shipman. "Once you were safely upstairs, I went back into the library. Arabella was rummaging around on your desk and was flustered at first by having me catch her. She said she was looking for your car keys, said that you weren't feeling well and had told her to drive herself home, that she would be back with the car in the morning. Then she asked me what I was doing back there, since I had told you both good night. I said I had come back because I had promised to turn your old pistol in at the police station but had forgotten to take it. The poor fool stood there and watched me while I picked it up and loaded it. Her last words were, 'Isn't it dangerous to load it? I'm sure Mr. Shipman didn't intend that.'"

Lillian West began to laugh, a high-pitched, almost hysterical cackle. Tears ran from her eyes and her body shook, but through it all she kept the gun trained on them.

She's working up to killing us, Sunday thought, for the first moment fully realizing that there was little hope for escape. Tommy's finger was still jabbing the back of her hand. "'Isn't it dangerous to load it?'" West repeated, mimicking Arabella's last words, her own voice cracking with loud, raucous laughter. "'I'm sure Mr. Shipman didn't intend that!'"

She rested her gun hand on her left arm, steadying it. The laughter ended.

"Would you consider opening the draperies?" Shipman asked. "At least let me see sunlight one more time."

Lillian West's smile was mirthless. "Why bother with that? You're about to see the shining light at the end of the tunnel," she told him.

The draperies, Sunday thought suddenly. That was what Tommy had been trying to get across to her. Yesterday when he had lowered the shade in the kitchen he'd mentioned that the electronic device that worked the draperies in this room was defective, that it sounded a lot like a gunshot when it was used. Sunday looked around carefully. The control for the drapes was lying on the armrest of the couch. She had to get to it. It was their only hope.

Sunday pressed Tommy's hand by way of indicating that she finally understood. Then, as a prayer raced through her mind, she reached out and with a lightning-fast movement pressed the button that would open the drapes.

The sound, loud as a gunshot, just as promised, made Lillian West whirl her head around. In that instant, both Tommy and Sunday leapt from the couch. Tommy threw himself at the woman's lower body, but it was Sunday who slammed West's hand upward just as she began to pull the gun's trigger. As they struggled, several shots were fired. Sunday felt a burning sensation in her left arm, but it did not deter her. Unable to wrest the gun from the woman, she threw herself on top of her and kicked at the chair so that it toppled over with all three of them on it, just as the shattering of glass signaled the welcome arrival of her Secret Service detail.

Ten minutes later, a handkerchief wrapped securely over the superficial wound on her arm, Sunday was on the phone to a totally unnerved ex-president of the United States.

"I'm fine," she said for the fifteenth time, "just fine. And Tommy is fine too. Lillian West is in a straitjacket and on her way out of here. So stop worrying. Everything has been taken care of."

"But you could have been killed," Henry said, not for the first time. He didn't want to break the phone connection. He didn't want to let his wife stop talking. This had been too close. He couldn't bear the thought that he might ever not be able to hear her voice.

"But I wasn't killed," Sunday said briskly. "And, Henry, we were both right. It was definitely a crime of passion. It was just that we were a little slow in figuring out whose passion was the cause of the crime."

The Man Next Door

The man next door had known for weeks that it was time to invite another guest to the secret place, the space he had fashioned out of the utility room in the basement. It had been six months since Tiffany, the last one. She had lasted twenty days, longer than most of the others.

He had tried to put Bree Matthews out of his mind. It didn't make sense to invite her, he knew that. Every morning as he followed his routine, washing the windows, polishing the furniture, vacuuming the carpets, sweeping and washing the walk from the steps to the sidewalk, he reminded himself that it was dangerous to choose a next-door neighbor. *Much* too dangerous.

But he couldn't help it. Bree Matthews was never out of his mind for an instant. Ever since the day she had rung his bell and he had invited her in, he had known. That was when his growing need to have her with him became uncontrollable. She had stood in his foyer, dressed in a loose sweater and jeans, her arms folded, one high-arched foot unconsciously tapping the polished floor as she told him that the leak in her adjoining town house was originating from *his* roof.

"When I bought this place I never thought I'd have so much

trouble," she had snapped. "The contractor could have redone Buckingham Palace for what I paid him to renovate, but whenever it rains hard, you'd think I lived under Niagara Falls. Anyway, he *insists* that whoever did your work caused the problem."

Her anger had thrilled him. She was beautiful, in a bold, Celtic way, with midnight-blue eyes, fair skin, and blue-black hair. And beneath that she had a slim athlete's body. He guessed her to be in her late twenties, older than the women he usually favored, but still so very appealing.

He had known that even though it was a warm spring afternoon, there was no excuse for the way perspiration began to pour from him as he stood a few inches from her. He wanted so much to reach out and touch her, to push the door closed, to lock her in.

He had blushed and stammered as he explained that there was absolutely no possibility that the leak was coming from his roof, that he'd done all the repairs himself. He suggested she call another contractor for an opinion.

He had almost explained that he had worked for a builder for fifteen years and knew that the guy she had hired was doing a shoddy job, but he managed to stop himself. He didn't want to admit that he had any interest in her or her home, didn't want her to know that he had even noticed, didn't want to give anything about himself away. . . .

A few days later she came up the street as he was outside planting impatiens along the driveway, and stopped to apologize. Following his advice, she had called in a different contractor who confirmed what she had suspected: the first one had done a sloppy job. "He'll hear from me in court," she vowed. "I've had a summons issued for him."

Then, emboldened by her friendliness, he did something foolish. As he stood with her, he was facing their semidetached town houses and once again noticed the lopsided venetian blind on her front window, the one nearest his place. Every time he saw it, it drove him crazy. The vertical blinds on his front windows and those on hers lined up perfectly, which made the sight of that lopsided one bother him as much as hearing a fingernail screech across a blackboard.

So he offered to fix it for her. She turned and looked at the offending blind as if she had never seen it before, then she replied, "Thanks, but why bother? The decorator has window treatments ready to put in as soon as the damage caused by the leaks is repaired. It'll get fixed then."

"*Then*," of course, could be months from now, but still he was glad she had said no. He had definitely decided to invite her to be his next guest, and when she disappeared there would be questions. The police would ring his bell, make inquiries. "Mr. Mensch, did you see Miss Matthews leave with anyone?" they would ask. "Did you notice anyone visiting her lately? How friendly were you with her?"

He could answer truthfully: "We only spoke casually on the street if we ran into each other. She has a young man she seems to be dating. I've exchanged a few words with him from time to time. Tall, brown hair, about thirty or so. Believe he said his name is Carter. Kevin Carter."

The police would probably already know about Carter. When Matthews disappeared they would talk to her close friends first.

He had never even been questioned about Tiffany. There had been no connection between them, no reason for anyone to ask. Occasionally they ran into each other at museums—he had found several of his young women in museums. The third or fourth time they met he made it a point to ask Tiffany her impression of a painting she was looking at.

He had liked her instantly. Beautiful Tiffany, so appealing, so intelligent. She believed that because he claimed to share her enthusiasm for Gustav Klimt, he was a kindred spirit, a man to be trusted. She had been grateful for his offer of a ride back to Georgetown on a rainy day. He had picked her up as she was walking to the Metro.

She had scarcely felt the prick of the needle that knocked her out. She slumped at his feet in the car, and he drove her back to his place. Matthews was just leaving her house as he pulled into the drive; he even nodded to her as he clicked the garage door opener. At that time he had no idea that Matthews would be next, of course.

Every morning for the next three weeks, he had spent all his time with Tiffany. He loved having her there. The secret place was bright and cheerful. The floor had a thick yellow pad, like a comfortable mattress, and he had filled the room with books and games.

He had even painted the windowless bathroom adjacent to it a cheery red and yellow, and he had installed a portable shower. Every morning he would lock her in the bathroom, and while she was showering he would vacuum and scrub the secret place. He kept it immaculate. As he did everything in his life. He couldn't abide untidiness. He laid out clean clothes for her every day too. He also washed and ironed the clothes she came in, just as he had with the others. He had even had her jacket cleaned, that silly jacket with the name of cities all over the world. He didn't want to have it cleaned, but noticing that spot on the sleeve drove him crazy. He couldn't get it out of his head. Finally he gave in.

He spent a lot of money cleaning his own clothes as well. Sometimes when he woke up, he would find himself trying to brush away crumbs from the sheets. Was that because he remembered having to do that? There were a lot of questions from his childhood, things he couldn't fully remember. But maybe it was best that way.

He knew he was fortunate. He was able to spend all his time with the women he chose because he didn't have to work. He didn't need the money. His father had never spent a cent on anything besides bare essentials. After high school, when he began working for the builder, his father demanded he turn over his paycheck to him. "I'm saving for you, August," he had said. "It's wasteful to spend money on women. They're all like your mother. Taking everything you have and leaving with another man for California. Said she was too young when we got married, that nineteen was too young to have a baby. Not too young for *my* mother, I told her."

Ten years ago his father died suddenly, and he had been astonished to find that during all those years of penny-pinching, his father had invested in stocks. At thirty-four, he, August Mensch, was worth over a million dollars. Suddenly he could afford to travel and live the way he wanted to, the way he had dreamed about during all those years of sitting at home at night, listening to his father tell him how his mother neglected him when he was a baby. "She left you in the playpen for hours. When you cried, she'd throw a bottle or some crackers to you. You were her prisoner, not her baby. I bought baby books, but she wouldn't even read to you. I'd come home from work and find you sitting in spilled milk and crumbs, cold and neglected."

August had moved to this place last year, rented this furnished and run-down town house cheaply, and made the necessary repairs himself. He had painted it and scrubbed the kitchen and bathrooms until they shone, and he cleaned the furniture and polished the floors daily. His lease ran out on May 1, only twenty days from now. He had already told the owner he was planning to leave. By then he would have had Matthews and it would be time to move on. He would be leaving the place greatly improved. The only thing he would have to take care of was to whitewash all the improvements he had made to the secret place, so no one would ever guess what had happened there.

How many cities had he lived in during the last ten years? he wondered. He had lost track. Seven? Eight? More? Starting with finding his mother in San Diego. He liked Washington, would have stayed there longer. But he knew that after Bree Matthews it wouldn't be a good idea.

What kind of guest would she be? he wondered. Tiffany had been both frightened and angry. She ridiculed the books he bought for her, refusing to read them. She told him her family had no money, as if that was what he wanted. She told him she wanted to paint. He even bought an easel and art supplies for her.

She actually started one painting while she was visiting, a painting of a man and woman kissing. It was going to be a copy of Klimt's *The Kiss*. He tore it off the easel and told her to copy one of the nice illustrations in the children's books he had given her. That was when she had picked up an open jar of paint and thrown it at him.

August Mensch didn't quite remember the next minutes, just that when he looked down at the sticky mess on his jacket and trousers, he had lunged at her.

When her body was pulled out of a Washington canal the next day, they questioned her ex-boyfriends. The papers were full of the case. He laughed at the speculation about where she had been the three weeks she was missing.

Mensch sighed. He didn't want to think of Tiffany now. He wanted to dust and polish the room again to make it ready for Matthews. Then he had to finish chiseling mortar from the cinder blocks in the wall that separated his basement from hers.

He would remove enough of those blocks to gain entry into Matthews's basement. He would bring her back the same way. He knew she had installed a security system, but this way it wouldn't do her any good. Then he would replace the cinder blocks and carefully re-cement.

It was Sunday night. He had watched her house all day. She hadn't gone out at all. Lately she had stayed in on Sundays, since Carter stopped coming around. He had seen him there last a couple of weeks ago.

He brushed away an invisible piece of dust. Tomorrow at this time she would be with him; she'd be his companion. He had bought a stack of Dr. Seuss books for her to read to him. He had thrown out all the other books. Some had been splattered with red paint. All of them reminded him how Tiffany had refused to read to him.

Over the years, he had always tried to make his guests comfortable. It wasn't his fault that they were always ungrateful. He remembered how the one in Kansas City told him she wanted a steak. He had bought a thick one, the thickest he could find. When he came back he could see that she had used the time he was out to try to escape. She hadn't wanted the steak at all. He'd lost his temper. He couldn't remember exactly what happened after that.

He hoped Bree would be nicer.

He'd soon know. Tomorrow morning he would make his move.

"What is *that*?" Bree muttered to herself as she stood at the head of the stairs leading to her basement. She could hear a faint scraping sound emanating from the basement of the adjacent town house.

She shook her head. What did it matter? She couldn't sleep anyway. It was irritating, though. Only six o'clock on a Monday morning, and Mensch was already on some do-it-yourself project. Some neat-as-a-pin improvement, no doubt, she said to herself, already in a bad temper. She sighed. What a rotten day it was going to be. She had a lousy cold. There was no point getting up so early, but she wasn't sleepy. She had felt miserable yesterday and had stayed in bed all day, dozing. She hadn't even bothered to pick up the phone, just listened to messages. Her folks were away. Gran didn't call, and a certain Mr. Kevin Carter never put his finger on the touch tone.

Now cold or no cold, she was due in court at 9 A.M. to try to make that first contractor pay for the repairs she had to do to the roof he was supposed to have fixed. To say nothing of getting him to pay for the damage inside caused by the leaks. She closed the basement door decisively and went into the kitchen, squeezed a grapefruit, made coffee, toasted an English muffin, settled at the breakfast bar.

She had begun to refer to this town house as the dwelling-from-hell, but once all the damage was repaired she had to admit it would be lovely.

She tried to eat her breakfast, but found she couldn't. I've never testified in court, she thought. That's why I'm nervous and down. But I'm sure the judge will side with me, she reassured herself. No judge would put up with having his or her house ruined.

Bree—short for Bridget—Matthews, thirty, single, blue-eyed and dark-haired, with porcelain skin that wouldn't tolerate the sun, was admittedly jumpy by nature. Buying this place last year had so far been an expensive mistake. For once I should *not* have listened to Granny, she thought, then smiled unconsciously thinking of how from her retirement community in Connecticut her grandmother still burned up the wires giving her good advice.

Eight years ago she was the one who told me I should take the job in Washington working for our congressman even though she thought he was a dope, Bree remembered as she forced herself to eat half of the English muffin. Then she advised me to grab the chance to join Douglas Public Relations when I got that offer. She's been right about everything except about buying this place and renovating it, Bree thought. "Real estate's a good way to make money, Bree," she had said, "especially in Georgetown."

Wrong! Bree frowned grimly as she sipped coffee. My Pierre Deux wall hangings are stained and peeling. And it's not wall*paper*, mind you, not when you spring for seventy dollars a yard. At that price the stuff becomes wall*hanging*. She frowned as she remembered explaining that to Kevin, who had said, "Now, that's what I call pretentious." Just what she needed to hear!

Mentally she reviewed everything she would tell the judge: "The Persian carpet that Granny proudly put on the floor of her first house is rolled and wrapped in plastic to be sure no new leaks can damage it further, and the polish on the parquet floors is dull and stained. I've got pictures to show just how bad my home looks. I wish you'd look at them, Your Honor. Now I'm waiting for the painter and floor guy to come back to charge a fortune to redo what they did perfectly well four months ago.

"I asked, pleaded, begged, even snarled at that contractor, trying to get him to take care of the leak. Then when he finally did show up, he told me that the water was coming from my neighbor's roof, and I believed him. I made a dope of myself ringing his bell, accusing poor Mr. Mensch of causing all the problems. You see, Your Honor, we share a common wall, and the contractor said the water was getting in that way. I, of course, believed him. He is supposed to be the expert."

Bree thought of her next-door neighbor, the balding guy with the graying ponytail who looked embarrassed just to say hello if they ran into each other on the street. The day that she had gone storming over, he had invited her in. At first he had listened to her rant with calm, unblinking eyes, his face thoughtful—as she imagined a priest would look during confession, if she could see through the screen, of course. Then he had suddenly started blushing and perspiring and almost whispered his protest that it couldn't be his roof, because surely he would have a leak too. She should call another contractor, he said.

"I scared the poor guy out of his wits," she had told Kevin that night. "I should have known the minute I saw the way he keeps his place that he'd never tolerate a leaking roof. The polish on the floor in his foyer almost blinded me. I bet when he was a kid he got a medal for being the neatest boy in camp."

Kevin. That was something else. Try as she might, she couldn't keep him from coming to mind. She would be seeing him this morn-ing, the first time in a while. He had insisted on meeting her in court even though they were no longer dating.

I've never brought anyone to court, she thought, and going there is definitely not my idea of a good time, particularly since I absolutely do not want to see Kevin. Pouring herself a second cup of coffee, she settled back at the breakfast bar. Just because Kev helped me file the complaint, she thought, he's going to be Johnny-on-the-spot in court today, which thank you very much I don't need. I do not want to see him. At all. And it's such a gloomy day all around. Bree looked out the window at the thick fog. She shook her head, her mouth set in a hard line. In fact, her irritation with Kevin had become so pronounced she practically blamed him for the leaking roof. He no longer called every morning, or sent flowers on the seventeenth of every month, the seventeenth being the day on which they had their first date. That was ten months ago, just after Bree had moved in to the town house. Bree felt the hard line of her mouth turning down at the corners, and she shook her head again. I love being independent, she thought ruefully, but sometimes I hate being alone.

Bree knew she had to get over all this. She realized that she was get-ting in the habit of regularly rearguing her quarrel with Kevin Carter. She also realized that when she missed him most—like this past Sat-urday, when she had moped around, going to a movie and having dinner alone, or yesterday when she stayed in bed feeling lonely and lousy—she needed to reinforce her sense of being in the right.

Bree remembered their fight, which like most had started out small and soon took on epic, life-changing proportions. Kev said I was foolish not to accept the settlement the contractor offered me, she recalled, that I probably won't get much more by going to court, but I wouldn't think of it. I'm pigheaded and love a fight and always shoot from the hip. Telling me that I was becoming irrational about this, he said that, for example, I had no business storming next door after that shy little guy. I reminded him that I apologized profusely, and Mr. Mensch was so sweet about it that he even offered to fix that broken blind in the living room window.

Somewhat uncomfortably, Bree remembered that there had been a pause in their exchange, but instead of letting it go, she had then told Kevin that he seemed to be the one who loved a fight, and why did he have to always take everybody else's side? That was when he said maybe we should step back and examine our relationship. And I said that if it has to be examined, then it didn't exist, so good-bye.

She sighed. It had been a very long two weeks.

I really wish Mensch would stop that damn tinkering or whatever he's doing in his basement, she thought, hearing the noise again. Lately he had been giving her the creeps. She had seen him watching her when she got out of the car, and she had felt his eyes following her whenever she moved about her yard. Maybe he did take offense that day and is brooding about it, she reasoned. She had been thinking about telling Kevin that Mensch was making her nervous—but then they had the quarrel, and she never got the chance. Anyway, Mensch seemed harmless enough.

Bree shrugged, then got up, still holding her coffee cup. I'm just all around jumpy, she thought, but in a couple of hours this will be behind me, one way or the other. Tonight I'll come home early, go to bed and sleep off this damn cold, and tomorrow I'll start to get the house in shipshape again.

Again the scraping sound came from the basement. Knock it off, she almost said aloud. Briefly debating going down to see what was causing the noise, she decided against it. So Mensch has a do-it-yourself project going, she thought. It's none of my business.

Then the scraping noise stopped, followed by hollow silence. Was that a footstep on the basement stairs? Impossible. The basement door that led outside was bolted and armed. Then what was causing it? . . .

She whirled around to see her next-door neighbor standing behind her, a hypodermic needle in his hand.

As she dropped the coffee cup, he plunged the needle deep into her arm.

Kevin Carter, *J.D.*, felt the level of his irritability hit the danger zone. This was just another example of Bree's total inability to listen to reason, he thought. She's pigheaded. Strong-willed. Impulsive. So where in hell was she?

The contractor, Richie Omberg, had shown up on time. A surly-looking guy, he kept looking at his watch and mumbling about being due on a job. He raised his voice as he reiterated his position to the lawyer: "I offered to fix the leak, but by then she'd had it done at six times what I coulda done it for. Twice I'd sent someone to look at it and she wasn't home. Once the guy who inspected it said he thought it was coming from the next roof, said there hasta be a leak there. Guess that little squirt who rented next door fixed it. Anyhow, I offered to pay what it woulda cost me."

Bree had been due in court at nine o'clock. When she hadn't showed up by ten, the judge dismissed the complaint.

A furious Kevin Carter went to his job at the State Department. He did not call Bridget Matthews at Douglas Public Relations, where she worked, nor did he attempt to call her at home. The next call between them was going to come from her. She owed him an apology. He tried not to remember that after she had gotten her day in court, he had planned to tell her that he missed her like hell and please, let's make up.

Mensch dragged Bree's limp body through the kitchen to the hallway that led to the basement stairs. He slid her down, step by step, until he reached the bottom; then he bent down and picked her up. Clearly she hadn't bothered to do anything with her basement. The cinder-block walls were gray and dreary, the floor tiles were clean but shabby. He had made the opening in the wall in the boiler room where it would be least noticed. He had pulled the cinder blocks into his base-ment, so now all he had to do was to secure her in the secret place, come back to get her clothing, then replace and re-mortar the blocks.

The opening he had made was just large enough to slide her body through and then crawl in after her. In his basement he picked her up again and carried her to the secret place. She was still knocked out, so there was no resistance as he attached the restraints to her wrists and ankles, and, as a precaution, tied the scarf loosely around her mouth. He could tell from her breathing that she had a cold. He certainly didn't want her to suffocate.

For a moment he reveled in the sight of her, limp and lovely, her hair tumbling onto the mattress, her body relaxed and peaceful. He straightened her terry-cloth robe and tucked it around her.

Now that she was here, he felt so strong, so calm. He had been shocked to find her in the kitchen so early in the morning. Now he had to move quickly: to get her clothes and her purse, to wipe up that spilled coffee. It had to look as if she disappeared after she left the house.

He looked at the answering machine in her kitchen, the blinking light indicating there had been seven calls. That was odd, he thought. He knew she hadn't gone out at all yesterday. Was it possible she didn't bother to answer the phone all day?

He played the messages back. All calls from friends. "How are you?" "Let's get together." "Good luck in court." "Hope you make that contractor pay." The last message was from the same person as the first: "Guess you're still out. I'll try you tomorrow."

Mensch took a moment to sit down at the breakfast bar. It was very important that he think all this through. Matthews had not gone out at all yesterday. It seemed as though she also hadn't answered her phone all day. Suppose instead of just taking her clothes to make it look as though she'd left for work, I tidied up the house so that people would think she hadn't reached home at all Saturday night. After all, he had seen her come up the block alone at around eleven, the newspaper under her arm. Who was there to say she had arrived safely?

Mensch got up. He already had his latex gloves on. He started looking about. The garbage container under the kitchen sink was empty. He took a fresh disposable bag from the drawer and put in it the squeezed grapefruit, coffee grinds, and pieces of the cup Bree had dropped.

Working methodically, he cleaned the kitchen, even taking time to scour the pot she had left on the stove. How careless of her to let it get burned, he thought.

Upstairs in her bedroom, he made the bed and picked up the Sunday edition of the *Washington Post* that was on the floor next to it. He put the paper in the garbage bag. She had left a suit on the bed. He hung it up in the closet where she kept that kind of clothing.

Next he cleaned the bathroom. Her washer and dryer were in the bathroom, concealed by louvered doors. On top of the washer he found the jeans and sweater he had seen her wearing on Saturday. It hadn't started raining at the time, but she had also had on her yellow raincoat. He collected the sweater and jeans and her undergarments and sneakers and socks. Then from her dresser he selected more undergarments. From her closets he took a few pairs of slacks and sweaters. They were basically nondescript, and he knew they would never be missed.

He found her raincoat and shoulder bag in the foyer by the front door. Mensch looked at his watch. It was seven-thirty, time to go. He had to replace and re-mortar the cinder blocks. He looked around to be sure he had missed nothing. His eye fell on the lopsided venetian blind in the front window. A knife-like pain went through his skull; his gorge rose. He felt almost physically ill. He couldn't stand to look at it.

Mensch put the clothing and purse and garbage bag on the floor. In quick, determined steps he reached the window and put his gloved hand on the blind.

The cord was broken, but there was enough slack to tie it and still level the blind. He breathed a long sigh of relief when he finished the task. It now stopped at exactly the same level as the other two and as his, just grazing the sill.

He felt much better now. With neat, compact movements he gathered up Bree's coat, shoulder bag, clothing, and the garbage bag.

Two minutes later he was in his own basement, replacing the cinder blocks.

At first Bree thought she was having a nightmare—a Disney World nightmare. When she woke up she opened her eyes to see cinder-block walls painted with evenly spaced brown slats. The space was small, not much more than six by nine feet, and she was lying on a bright yellow plastic mattress of some sort. It was soft, as though it had quilts inside it. About three feet from the ceiling a band of yellow paint connected the slats at the top to resemble a railing. Above the band, decals lined the walls: Mickey Mouse. Cinderella. Kermit the Frog. Miss Piggy. Sleeping Beauty. Pocahontas.

She suddenly realized that there was a gag over her face, and she tried to push it away, but could only move her arm a few inches. Her arms and legs were held in some kind of restraints.

The grogginess was lifting now. Where was she? What had happened? Panic overwhelmed her as she remembered turning to see Mensch, her neighbor, standing over her in the kitchen. Where had he taken her? Where was he now?

She looked around slowly, then her eyes widened. This room, wherever it was, resembled an oversized playpen. Stacked nearby were a series of children's books, all with thin spines except for the thick volume at the bottom. She could read the lettering: *Grimm's Fairy Tales*.

How had she gotten here? She remembered she had been about to get dressed to go to court. She had tossed the suit she had planned to wear across the bed. It was new. She wanted to look good, and in truth, more for Kevin than for the judge. Now she admitted that much to herself.

Kevin. Of course he would come looking for her when she didn't show up in court. He'd know something had happened to her.

Ica, her housekeeper, would look for her too. She came in on Mondays. She'd know something was wrong. Bree remembered dropping the coffee cup she was holding. It shattered on the kitchen floor as Mensch grabbed her and stuck the needle in her arm. Ica would know that she wouldn't leave spilled coffee and a broken cup for her to clean up.

As her head cleared, Bree remembered that just before she had turned and seen Mensch, she had heard a footstep on the basement stairs. Her mouth went dry at the thought that somehow he had come in through the basement. But how? Her basement door was bolted and armed, the window barred.

Then sheer panic swept through her. Clearly this hadn't just "happened"; this had been carefully planned. She tried to scream, but could only make a muffled gasping cry. She tried to pray, a single sentence that in her soul she repeated over and over: *"Please, God, let Kevin find me."*

Late Tuesday afternoon Kevin received a worried phone call from the agency where Bree worked. Had he heard from her? She never showed up for work on Monday, and she hadn't phoned. They thought she might have been stuck in court all day yesterday, but now they were concerned.

Fifteen minutes later, August Mensch watched through a slit in his front window drapery as Kevin Carter held his finger on the doorbell to Bree Matthews's town house.

He watched as Carter stood on the front lawn and looked in the living room window. He half expected that Carter would ring his doorbell, but that didn't happen. Instead he stood for a few minutes looking irresolute, then looked in the window of the garage. Mensch knew her car was there. In a way he wished he could have gotten rid of it, but that had been impossible.

He watched until Carter, his shoulders slumped, walked slowly back to his car and drove away. With a satisfied smile, Mensch walked down the foyer to the basement steps. Savoring the sight that would greet him, he descended slowly, then walked across the basement, as always admiring his tools and paints and polishes, all placed in perfect order on shelves, or hanging in precise rows from neatly squared pegboard.

Snow shovels hung over the cinder blocks that he had removed to gain entry into Matthews's basement. Beneath them the mortar had dried, and he had carefully smeared it with the dry flakes he had kept when he separated the blocks. Now nothing showed, either here or on Bridget Matthews's side. He was sure of that.

Then he crossed through the boiler room, and beyond it, to the secret place.

Matthews was lying on the mat, the restraints still on her arms and legs. She looked up at him and he could see that underneath the anger, fear was beginning to take hold. That was smart of her.

She was wearing a sweater and slacks, things he had taken from her closet.

He knelt before her and removed the gag from her mouth. It was a silk scarf, tied so that it was neither too tight nor caused a mark. "Your boyfriend was just looking for you," he told her. "He's gone now."

He loosened the restraints on her left arm and leg. "What book would you like to read to me today, Mommy?" he asked, his voice suddenly childlike and begging.

On Thursday morning Kevin sat in the office of FBI agent Lou Ferroni. The nation's capital was awash with cherry blossoms, but as he stared out the window he was unaware of them. Everything seemed a blur, especially the last two days: his frantic call to the police, the questions, the calls to Bree's family, the calls to friends, the sudden involvement of the FBI. What was Ferroni saying? Kevin forced himself to listen.

"She's been gone long enough for us to consider her a missing person," the agent said. Fifty-three years old and nearing retirement, Ferroni realized that he'd seen the look on Carter's face far too often in the past twenty-eight years, always on the faces of those left behind. Shock. Fear. Heartsick that the person they love may not be alive.

Carter was the boyfriend, or ex-boyfriend. He'd freely admitted that he and Matthews had quarreled. Ferroni wasn't eliminating him as a suspect, but he seemed unlikely and his alibi checked out. Bridget, or Bree, as her friends had called her, had been in her house on Saturday, that much they knew. They had not been able to locate anyone who saw or spoke to her on Sunday, though, and she hadn't shown up for her court appointment on Monday.

"Let's go over it again," Ferroni suggested. "You say that Miss Matthews's housekeeper was surprised to find the bed made and dishes done when she came in Monday morning?" He had already spoken with the housekeeper, but wanted to see if there were any discrepancies in Carter's story.

Kevin nodded. "I called Ica as soon as I realized Bree was missing. She has a key to Bree's place. I picked her up and she let me in. Of course Bree wasn't there. Ica told me that when she went in on Monday morning she couldn't understand why the bed was made and the dishes run through the dishwasher. It just wasn't normal. Bree never made the bed on Monday because that's when Ica changed it. So that meant the bed had not been slept in Sunday night, and that Bree could have vanished any time between Saturday and Sunday night."

Ferroni's gut instinct told him that the misery he was seeing in Kevin Carter's face was genuine. So if he didn't do it, who did that leave? Richie Ombert, the contractor Matthews was suing, had had several complaints filed against him for using abusive language and threatening gestures toward disgruntled customers.

Certainly the renovation business caused tempers to flare. Ferroni knew that firsthand. His wife had been ready to practically murder the guy who built the addition on their house. Ombert, though, seemed worse than most. He had a nasty edge, and for the moment he was a prime suspect in Bridget Matthews's disappearance.

There was one aspect of this case Ferroni was not prepared to share with Carter. The computer of VICAP, the FBI's violent criminal apprehension program, had been tracking a particular pattern of disappearing young women. The trail started some ten years ago in California, when a young art student disappeared. Her body showed up three weeks later; she had been strangled. The weird part was that when she was found she was dressed in the same clothes as when she had disappeared, and they were freshly washed and pressed. There was no sign of molestation, no hint of violence beyond the obvious cause of death. But where had she been those three weeks?

Shortly afterward the VICAP computer spat out a case in Arizona with striking similarities. One followed in New Mexico, then Colorado . . . North Dakota . . . Wisconsin . . . Kansas . . . Missouri . . . Indiana . . . Ohio . . . Pennsylvania . . . Finally, six months ago, there in D.C., an art student, Tiffany Wright, had disappeared. Her body was fished out of a Washington canal three weeks later, but it had been there only a short time. Except for the effect the water had had on her clothes, they were neat. The only odd note were some faint spots of red paint, the kind artists use, still visible on her blouse.

That little clue had started them working on the art student angle, looking among her classmates. It was the first time there had been any kind of stain or mark or rip or tear on any of the women's clothes. So far, however, it had led nowhere. Odds were that the disappearance of Bridget Matthews was not tied to the death of Tiffany Wright. It would be a marked departure in the serial killer's method of operation for him to strike twice in one city, but then maybe he was changing his habits.

"By any chance is Miss Matthews interested in art?" Ferroni asked Carter. "Does she take art lessons as a hobby?"

Kevin kneaded his forehead, trying to relieve the ache that reminded him of the one time in his life he had had too much to drink.

Bree, where are you?

"She never took art lessons that I know of. Bree was more into music and theater," he said. "We went to Kennedy Center pretty frequently. She particularly liked concerts."

Liked? he thought. Why am I using the past tense? No, God, no!

Ferroni consulted the notes in his hand. "Kevin, I want to go over this again. It's important. You were familiar with the house. There may be something you noticed when you went in with the housekeeper."

Kevin hesitated.

"What is it?" Ferroni asked quickly.

Through haggard eyes, Kevin stared at him. Then he glumly

shook his head. "There *was* something different; I sensed it at the time. But I don't know what it was."

How many days have I been here? Bree asked herself. She had lost count. Three? Five? They were all blending together. Mensch had just gone upstairs with her breakfast tray. She knew he'd be back within the hour for her to begin reading to him again.

He had a routine he followed rigidly. In the morning, he came down carrying fresh clothing for her, a blouse or sweater, jeans or slacks. Obviously he had taken the time to go through her closet and dresser after he had knocked her out. It appeared that he had only brought casual clothes that were washable.

Next he would unshackle her hands, connect the leg restraints to each other at the ankle, then lead her to the bathroom, drop the clean clothes on a chair and lock her in. A minute later she'd hear the whir of the vacuum.

She had studied him closely. He was thin but strong. No matter how she tried to think of a way to escape, she was sure she couldn't manage it. The ankle restraints forced her to shuffle a few feet at a time, so she clearly couldn't outrun him. There was nothing that she could use to stun him long enough for her to get up the stairs and out the door.

She knew where she was—the basement of his town house. The wall on the right was the one that they shared. She thought of how upset she had been about the stained wallpaper on that wall. No, not wall*paper*—wall*hanging*, Bree reminded herself, fighting back a hysterical wave of laughter.

By now the police are looking for me, she thought. Kevin will tell them how I accused Mensch of causing the leak in the roof. They'll investigate him, then they'll realize there's something weird about him. Surely they can't miss that?

Will Mom and Dad tell Gran that I'm missing? Please God, don't let them tell her. It would be too much of a shock for her.

She had to believe that somehow the police would start to investigate Mensch. It seemed so obvious that he must have kidnapped her. Surely they would figure it out? But, of course, trapped here in this cell she had no idea what anyone outside might be thinking. Someone would have missed her by now—she was certain of that—but where were they looking? She had absolutely no idea, and unless Mensch radically altered his routine, there would be no opportunity to let them know she was here. No, she would just have to wait and hope. And stay alive. To stay alive she had to keep him appeased until help came. As long as she read the children's books to him, he seemed to be satisfied.

Last night she had given him a list of books by Roald Dahl that he should get. He had been pleased. "None of my guests were as nice as you," he told her.

What had he *done* to those women? Don't think about that, Bree warned herself fiercely—it worries him when you show that you're afraid. She had realized that the one time she broke down sobbing and begged him to release her. That was when he told her that the police had rung his bell and asked when the last time was that he had seen Miss Matthews.

"I told them I was on my way back from the supermarket Saturday, around two o'clock, and I saw you go out. They asked what you were wearing. I said it was overcast and you had on a bright yellow raincoat and jeans. They thanked me and said I was very helpful," he said calmly, in his sing-song voice.

That was when she became almost hysterical.

"You're making too much noise," he told her. He put one hand on her mouth, while the other encircled her throat. For a moment she thought he was going to strangle her. But then he hesitated and said,

"Promise to be quiet, and I'll let you read to me. Please, Mommy, don't cry."

Since then she had managed to hold her emotion in check.

Bree steeled herself. She could sense that he'd be back any moment. Then she heard it, the turning of the handle. Oh, God, please, she prayed, let them find me.

Mensch came in. She could see that he looked troubled. "My landlord phoned," he told her. "He said that according to the contract he has the right to show this place two weeks before the lease is up. That's Monday, and it's Friday already. And I have to take all the decorations down from here and whitewash the walls and also the walls of the bathroom and give them time to dry. That will take the whole weekend. So this has to be our last day together, Bridget. I'm sorry. I'll go out and buy some more books, but I guess you should try to read to me a little faster. . . ."

At ten o'clock on Friday morning, Kevin was once again in Lou Ferroni's office in the FBI building.

"Thanks to the publicity, we've been able to pretty much cover Miss Matthews's activities on Saturday," Agent Ferroni told him. "Several neighbors reported they saw her walking down the street at about two o'clock on Saturday. They agree that she was wearing a bright yellow raincoat and jeans and carrying a shoulder bag. We know the raincoat and bag are missing from her home. We don't know what she did on Saturday afternoon, but we do know she had dinner alone at Antonio's in Georgetown and went to the nine o'clock showing of the new Batman film at the Beacon Theater."

Bree had dinner alone on Saturday night, Kevin thought. So did I. And she genuinely likes those crazy Batman films. We've laughed about that. I can't stand them, but I had promised to see that one with her.

"No one seems to have seen Miss Matthews after that," Ferroni continued. "But we do have one piece of information that we find significant. We've learned that the contractor she was suing was in the same movie theater that night at the same showing. He claims he drove straight home, but there's no one to back up his story. He apparently separated from his wife recently."

Ferroni did not add that the contractor had mouthed off to a number of people about what he'd like to do to the dame who was hauling him into court over what he termed "some silly leak."

"We're working on the theory that Miss Matthews did not get home that night. Was she in the habit of using the Metro instead of her car?"

"The Metro or a cab if she was going directly from place to place. She said trying to park was too much of a nuisance." Kevin could see that Ferroni was starting to believe that Richie Ombert, the contractor, was responsible for Bree's disappearance. He thought of Ombert in court this past Monday. Surly. Aggravated. Noisily elated when the judge dismissed the complaint.

He wasn't acting, Kevin thought. He seemed genuinely surprised and relieved when Bree didn't show up. No, Ombert is not the answer. He shook his head, trying to clear it out. He suddenly felt as though he were being smothered. He had to get out of here. "There are no other leads?" he asked Ferroni.

The FBI agent thought of the briefly considered theory that Bree Matthews had been abducted by a serial killer. "No," he said firmly, then added, "How is Miss Matthews's family? Has her father gone back to Connecticut?"

"He had to. We're in constant touch, but Bree's grandmother had a mild heart attack Tuesday evening. One of those horrible coincidences. Bree's mother is with her. You can imagine the state she's in. That's why Bree's father went back."

Ferroni shook his head. "I'm sorry. I wish I thought we'd get good news." He realized that in a way it would have been better if they thought the serial killer had Matthews. All the women he had abducted had lived for several weeks after disappearing. That would at least give them more time.

Kevin got up. "I'm going to Bree's house," he said. "I'm going to call every one of the people in her phone book."

Ferroni raised his eyebrows.

"I want to see if anyone spoke to her on Sunday," Kevin said simply.

"With all the publicity these last few days about her disappearance, any friend that spoke to her would have come forward, I'm sure of that," Ferroni told him. "How do you think we traced her movements on Saturday?"

Kevin did not answer.

"What about her answering machine? Were there any messages on it?" Kevin asked.

"Not from Sunday, or if there had been, they were erased," Ferroni replied. "At first we thought it might be significant, but then we realized that she could have called in and gotten them just by using the machine's code."

Kevin shook his head dejectedly. He had to get out of there. He had promised to phone Ica after his meeting with Ferroni but decided to wait and call her from Bree's house instead. He realized he was frantic to be there, that somehow being around her things made him feel nearer to Bree.

Her neighbor, the guy with the ponytail, was coming down the block when Kevin parked in front of the house. He was carrying a shopping bag from the bookstore. Their eyes met, but neither man spoke. Instead the neighbor nodded, then turned to go up his walk.

Wouldn't you think he'd have the decency to at least *ask* about Bree? Kevin thought bitterly. Too damn busy washing his windows or tending his lawn to give a damn about anyone else.

Or maybe he's embarrassed to ask. Afraid of what he'll hear. Kevin took out the key Ica had given him, let himself into the house, and phoned her.

"Can you come over and help me?" he asked. "There's something about this place that's bugging me. Something's just not quite right, and I can't figure out what it is. Maybe you can help."

While he waited, he stared at the phone. Bree was one of the few women he had ever known to consider the phone an intrusion. "At home we always turned off the ringer at mealtime," she had told him. "It's so much more civilized."

So civilized that now we don't know if anyone spoke to you on Sunday, Kevin thought. He looked around; there's got to be a clue here somewhere, he told himself. Why was he so sure that the contractor wasn't the answer to Bree's disappearance?

Restlessly he began to walk around the downstairs floor. He stopped at the door of the front room. The contrast to the cheery kitchen and den was striking. Here as in the dining room, because of the water damage, the furniture and carpet were covered with plastic and pushed to the center of the room.

The wallpaper—or wall*hanging* (as Bree had insisted it be called)—a soft ivory with a faint stripe, was stained and bubbled.

Kevin remembered how happy Bree had been when all the decorating was supposedly finished three months ago. They'd even talked around the subject of marriage, in the same sentence mentioning her town house and the marvelous old farmhouse he had bought for Virginia weekends.

Too darn cautious to commit ourselves, Kevin thought bitterly. But not too cautious to have a fight over nothing. It had all been so silly.

He thought about sitting with her in that same room, the warm ivories and reds and blues of the Persian carpet repeated up the newly reupholstered couch and chairs. Bree had pointed to the vertical metal blinds.

"I hate those damn things," she had said. "The last one doesn't even close properly, but I wanted to get everything else in before I choose draperies."

The blinds. He looked up.

The doorbell rang, interrupting his train of thought. The handsome Jamaican woman's face mirrored the misery he felt. "I haven't slept two hours straight this week," she said. "Looks to me as though you haven't either."

Kevin nodded. "Ica, there's something about this house that's bothering me, something I ought to be noticing. Help me."

She nodded. "It's funny you should say that, 'cause I felt that way too, but blamed it on finding the bed made and the dishes done. But if Bree didn't get home on Saturday night, then that would explain those things. She never left the place untidy."

Together they walked up the stairs to the bedroom. Ica looked around uncertainly. "The room felt different when I got here Monday, different from the way it usually feels," she said hesitantly.

"In what way?" Kevin asked quickly.

"It was . . . well, it was way too neat." Ica walked over to the bed. "Those throw pillows, Bree just tossed them around, like the way they are now."

"What are you telling me?" Kevin asked. He grabbed her arm, aware that Ica was about to tell him what he needed to know.

"The whole place felt just—too neat. I stripped the bed even though it was made because I wanted to change the sheets. I had to dig and pull the sheets and blankets loose, they were tucked in so tight. And the throw pillows on top of the quilt were all lined up against the headboard like little soldiers."

"Anything else? Please just keep talking, Ica. We may be getting somewhere," Kevin begged.

"Yes," Ica said excitedly. "Last week Bree had let a pot boil over. I scoured it as best I could and left a note for her to pick up some steel wool and scouring powder; I said I'd finish it when I came back. Monday morning that pot was sitting out on the stove, scrubbed clean as could be. I know my Bree. She never would have touched it. She told me those strong soaps made her hands break out. Come on, I'll show it to you."

Together they ran down the stairs into the kitchen. From the cupboard she pulled out a gleaming pot.

"There isn't even a mark on the bottom," she said. "You'd think it was practically brand-new." She looked excitedly at Kevin. "Things weren't right here. The bed was made too neatly. This pot is too clean."

"And . . . and the blind in the front window has been fixed," Kevin shouted. "It's lined up like the ones next door."

He hadn't known that he was about to say that, but suddenly he realized that was what had been bothering him all along. He had sensed the difference right away, but the effect had been so subtle, it had registered only in his subconscious. But now that he had brought it into focus, he thought of the neighbor, the quiet guy with the ponytail, the one who was always washing his windows or trimming his lawn or sweeping his walk.

What did anyone know about him? If he rang the bell, Bree might have let him in. And he had offered to fix the blind—Bree had mentioned that. Kevin pulled Ferroni's card from his pocket and handed it to Ica. "I'm going next door. Tell Ferroni to get over here fast."

"Just one more book. That's all we'll have time for. Then you'll leave me again, Mommy. Just like she did. Just like all of them did."

In the two hours she had been reading to him, Bree had watched Mensch regress from adoring to angry child. He's working up the courage to kill me, she thought.

He was sitting cross-legged beside her on the mat.

"But I want to read all of them to you," she said, her voice soothing, coaxing. "I know you'll love them. Then tomorrow I could help you paint the walls. We could get it done so much faster if we work together, so I can keep reading to you."

He stood up abruptly. "You're trying to trick me. You don't want to go with me. You're just like all the others." He stared at her, his eyes shuttered and small with anger. "I saw your boyfriend go into your house a little while ago. He's too nosy. It's good that you're wearing the jeans. I have to get your raincoat and shoulder bag." He looked as if he was about to cry. "There's no time for any more books," he said sadly.

He rushed out. I'm going to die, Bree thought. Frantically she tried to pull her arms and legs free of the restraints. Her right arm swung up and she realized that he'd forgotten to refasten the shackle to the wall. He had said Kevin was next door. She had heard that you can transfer thoughts. She closed her eyes and concentrated: *Kevin, help me. Kevin, I need you.*

She had to play for time. She would have only one chance at him, one moment of surprise. She would swing at his head with the dangling shackle, try to stun him. But what good would that do? Save her for a few seconds? *Then* what? she thought despondently. How could she stop him?

Her eyes fell on the stack of books. Maybe there was a way. She grabbed the first one and began tearing the pages, scattering the pieces, forcing them to flutter hither and yon across the bright yellow mattress.

I must have known that today was the day, Mensch thought as he retrieved Bree's raincoat and shoulder bag from the bedroom closet. I laid out jeans and the red sweater she was wearing that Saturday. When they find her it will be like all the others. And again they will ask the same question: Where was she for the days she was missing? It would be fun to read about it. Everyone wanting to know, and only he would have the answer.

As he came down the stairs, he stopped suddenly. The doorbell was ringing. The button was being held down. He laid down the pocketbook and the coat and stood frozen momentarily with uncertainty. Should he answer? Would it seem suspicious if he didn't? No. Better to get rid of her, get her out of here fast, he decided.

Mensch picked up the raincoat and rushed down the basement stairs.

I know he's in there, Kevin thought, but he's not answering. I've got to get inside.

Ica was running across the lawn. "Mr. Ferroni is on his way. He said to absolutely wait for him. Not to ring the bell anymore. He got all excited when I talked about everything being so neat. He said if it's what he thinks it is, Bree will still be alive."

It seemed to Kevin that he could hear Bree crying out to him. He was overwhelmed by a sense of running out of time, by an awareness that he had to get into Mensch's house immediately. He ran to the front window and strained to look in. Through the slats he could see the rigidly neat living room. Craning his neck, he could see the stairway in the foyer. Then his blood froze. A woman's leather shoulder bag was on the last step. Bree's shoulder bag! He recognized it; he had given it to her for her birthday.

Frantically he ran to the sidewalk where a refuse can stood waiting to be emptied. He dumped the contents onto the street, ran back with the can and overturned it under the window. As Ica steadied it for him, he climbed up, then kicked in the window. As the glass shattered, he kicked away the knife-like edges and jumped into the room. He raced up the stairs, shouting Bree's name.

Finding no one there, he clattered down the stairs again, pausing only long enough to open the front door. "Tell the FBI I'm inside, Ica."

He raced through the rooms on the ground floor and still found no one.

There was only one place left to search: the basement.

Finally the ringing stopped. Whoever had been at the door had gone away. Mensch knew he had to hurry. The raincoat and a plastic bag over his arm, he strode across the basement, through the boiler room and opened the door to the secret room.

Then he froze. Bits of paper littered the yellow plastic. Matthews was tearing up his books, his baby books. "Stop it!" he shrieked.

His head hurt, his throat was closing. He had a pain in his chest. The room was a mess; he had to clean it up.

He felt dizzy, almost as if he couldn't breathe. It was as if the mess of papers was smothering him! He had to clean it up so he could breathe!

Then he would kill her. Kill her slowly. He ran into the bathroom, grabbed the wastebasket, ran back and began scooping up the shredded paper and mangled books. His frenzied hands worked quickly, efficiently. In only ten minutes there wasn't a single scrap left.

He looked about him. Matthews was cowering against the mattress. He stood over her. "You're a pig, just like my mommy. This is what I did to her." He knelt beside her, the plastic bag in his hands. Then her hand swung up. The shackle on her wrist slammed into his face.

He screamed, and for an instant he was stunned, then with a snarl he snapped his fingers around her throat.

The basement was empty too. Where was she? Kevin thought desperately. He was about to run into the garage, when from somewhere behind the boiler room he heard Mensch howl in pain. And then there came a scream. A woman's scream. Bree was screaming!

An instant later, as August Mensch tightened his hands on Bree Matthews's neck, he felt his head yanked back and then there was a violent punch that caused his knees to buckle. Dazed, he shook his head and then with a guttural cry sprang to his feet. Bree reached out and grabbed his ankle, pulling him off balance as Kevin caught him in a hammer grip around the throat. Moments later, pounding feet on the basement stairs announced the arrival of the FBI. One minute later Bree, now in the shelter of Kevin's arms, watched as Mensch was manacled with chains at his waist and hands and legs, looking dazed.

"Let's see how *you* like being tied up," she screamed at him.

Two days later, Bree and Kevin stood together at her grandmother's bedside in Connecticut. "The doctor said you'll be fine, Gran," Bree told her.

"Of course I'm fine. Forget the health talk. Let's hear about your place. I bet you made that contractor squirm in court, didn't you?"

Bree grinned at Kevin's raised eyebrows. "Oh, Gran, I decided to accept his settlement offer after all. I've finally realized that I really hate getting into fights."

Haven't We Met Before?

Westchester County Assistant District Attorney Jack Carroll presented his credentials to the guard at Haviland Hospital for the Criminally Insane and waited for the gate to swing open.

It was the right kind of day to visit a place for psychopathic killers, he thought wryly: wet and raw, with a persistent dampness that chilled the spirit as well as the body. And in all probability, this was a fool's errand. It was the fourth time in as many months that he had come here to question William Koenig, who had been declared incompetent to stand trial for the attempted murder of twenty-four-year-old Emily Winters. His defense was that she had caused his death in another incarnation.

It was Jack Carroll's hunch that Koenig was more than a would-be killer. With every fiber of his being he was convinced that Koenig was responsible for the string of unsolved homicides that had plagued Westchester for the last eight years.

And there's not a shred of evidence, Jack reminded himself grimly as he pulled into the hospital parking lot. As usual, the frustration of that thought sent a dart of pure anger through him.

Fortunately, his boss, the DA, was willing to go along with him. "I think you're wasting your time, Jack," he'd said bluntly, "but in the three years you've been here, your hunches have been damn good. If you can manage to nail Koenig on even one of those homicides, I'll personally pin a medal on you."

Jack got out of the car, locked it and with rapid steps followed the path to the hospital's main entrance. It was a new facility, deceptively bland with windows that were barely more than slits. There were no bars, but even a monkey couldn't get through that amount of space, he decided.

Inside the building, the large reception area was tastefully decorated. He might have been entering an upscale business office. As always when he was here, Jack hoped the fact that tight security wasn't readily apparent was not a sign that it didn't exist.

Koenig was going to meet his new psychiatrist today. Rhoda Morris, the one who had been assigned to him since his commitment eight months ago, had left for the private sector. Jack was not sorry about the change. In his opinion, Koenig had had Dr. Morris buffaloed. He hoped the new psychiatrist, Dr. Sara Stein, would be older and more experienced.

When he was ushered into her office, he immediately liked what he saw. Dr. Stein was a pleasant-looking, full-figured woman who looked to be in her late fifties, with gray hair and even features in a face dominated by warm and intelligent brown eyes. He felt her scrutiny and hoped her first impression of him was favorable as well.

He knew she was seeing a twenty-eight-year-old, sandy-haired six-footer with a boyish face. He only hoped she wouldn't mistake him for a recent college graduate, the way some people did.

She did not. "I'm glad to meet you, Mr. Carroll," she said briskly. "As you know, I haven't yet met William Koenig. After reading the file and learning of your interest in him, I decided to have my first session with him with you present. Of course, he knows why you are here."

Jack drew a deep breath. "Doctor, I'm here because I think William Koenig may be the most dangerous inmate under this roof."

"We discussed him at the staff meeting this morning. The consensus is that his psychotic tendencies may have been fueled by his experimenting with past-life regression. But as you may have suspected, my colleagues do not agree with you that Koenig is a multiple killer."

"Dr. Stein, he may not be. On the other hand, if I'm right and we can get to the truth, the families of at least four homicide victims will have some sense of closure."

He paused for a moment and then continued: "Let me give you an example. Two years ago an elderly woman in Dobbs Ferry was asphyxiated during a fire that had been deliberately set in her home. Her family is making life hell for a twelve-year-old neighborhood kid who had started a campfire in the nearby woods a few days earlier. They're accusing him of being an arsonist."

"They need someone to blame," she observed. "But that will have a terrible effect on an innocent child. Let's get Koenig in here."

"Doctor, try to get him to talk about other lives he may remember. If we knew about them I believe we could begin to understand why he might have selected other victims for retribution."

She nodded and turned on the intercom. "We're ready for Koenig," she said.

"William, Assistant District Attorney Carroll wants to talk with you."

"I've explained to your assistant, Doctor, that I will talk to him only through you," Koenig said patiently. "I will answer his questions through you. I understand that my answers may be used against me. I do not want to have a lawyer present. I also understand that I can stop answering questions at any point. I do not expect the confidentiality of a doctor-patient relationship in this matter. You are new here, but I have met Mr. Carroll a number of times before. I will not speak to him directly again. Is there anything else?"

Dr. Stein glanced at Jack Carroll, who shook his head.

"No, nothing else, William," she said.

"Then I think we should proceed. The state is paying you handsomely to probe my mind, Doctor. Why don't you start earning your money?"

William Koenig smiled gently to take the sting out of his words. He was quietly counting the hours until this evening but wanted nothing in his demeanor to suggest that this was his last day here. His escape plan was foolproof.

William hoped that the weather would continue to be gray and rainfilled at least through tomorrow. His manacled hands clasped in his lap, a restraining strap across his waist, the guard studying him through the heavily glassed door, he sat in silent contempt across the desk from his new psychiatrist, Dr. Stein, and his old adversary, Jack Carroll.

Behind his seemingly anxious-to-please smile, he was thinking that Stein was dowdy, with her hair slipping from where she'd twisted it into a bun. She didn't wear makeup, either. His last psychiatrist had been pretty. He'd liked her—she was so engagingly naive.

Carroll was a nice-looking guy, the kind who probably had all the girls after him in school. He was smart too, the only one smart enough to wonder if maybe he, William Koenig, was responsible for a string of unsolved homicides.

But all they could prove was that last February he had tried to strangle Emily Winters.

"William, I hope you'll be comfortable with me and help me to understand you. In your own words, will you tell me why you attacked Emily Winters?"

William knew perfectly well that Stein had studied his file backward and forward. Even so, it was flattering to see the interest in her eyes when he told her—in his own words, as she put it—that in 1708, in his life as Simon Guiness, he had been hanged in London because of the false testimony of Kate Fallow, a woman who had become obsessed with him.

"She killed her husband, then made it look as though he had been a victim of a random attack on the road to their estate," William explained gravely. "Then, when I rejected her, she went to the magistrate and claimed that I had stabbed her husband because I coveted her."

He shivered as he spoke, remembering the misery that followed. They had believed Kate Fallow. For months he had rotted in a damp and dirty prison until execution ended his life as Simon Guiness.

"When did you first know that you had a past life, William?"

"I learned that about myself when I was in high school. I became interested in parapsychology and succeeded in hypnotizing myself and finding my own path into all that had gone before."

William realized that Dr. Stein did not believe that he had the power to hypnotize himself. "It's not hard if you concentrate," he said impatiently. "You sit in front of a mirror in a dark room with just one candle burning. With a pen or crayon, put a dot in the center of your forehead to indicate your third eye. Then stare at that dot in the mirror." His voice lowered. "You will see the change beginning as you find your way into the past."

"Change, William?"

"You will see it in the mirror," he whispered. "Your present image will dissolve and disappear, as mine did. Other faces will appear, faces of the people you were in previous lives."

He glanced over at Jack Carroll. "I've explained all this to him," he told the doctor. "I bet he's tried to see if he could hypnotize himself. Tried and failed. He's too sensible. He doesn't get it."

"Will I know what happened to those people in my past lives if I am able to hypnotize myself?" Dr. Stein asked.

"Oh, yes, Doctor, you will remember all the details."

"How many lives do you remember, William?"

William stared at the green wall behind Dr. Stein's desk. Moss green. He was very proud that he understood shades, not just colors. They all tried to trick him into telling about the other lives he had lived, about punishments he had meted out to people who had hurt him in the past.

If you only knew, William thought. There were eleven others. A smile played around his lips as he recalled the first, the old woman he'd followed home from the railroad station because he realized she was the witch who had put a curse on him in Salem. He had waited until he was sure she was asleep and then set fire to her house. Fire for fire.

He chose his words carefully. "The face that was clear to me at the time I happened to come across the woman you call Emily Winters was that of Simon Guiness. Knowing the terrible fate I suffered as Simon, you can understand why the sight of a young woman with red-gold hair and wide blue eyes upset me so much."

"Did seeing a woman with that appearance always upset you, William?"

"Oh, no, it began a little over three years ago—after I had relived my life as Simon Guiness."

"Tell me about finding Emily."

He remembered how he had spotted her from the street. She was waiting on a window table in the restaurant. "I studied her, to be absolutely sure it was Kate," he reminisced. "Then I went into the restaurant. It wasn't very crowded, so I was able to observed her very carefully. . . ."

William's voice trailed off as he remembered the thrill of realizing he had finally tracked down Kate Fallow. "When she passed my table, I touched her arm," he confided. "She looked terrified, then frightened. I'm certain that she sensed danger, even though I apologized."

"Did you say anything to her, William?"

"I asked, 'Haven't we met before?'"

"Then you waited outside until she left the restaurant?"

"Yes, she began to walk home. I followed her from a distance. I saw her turn into a gated area. It was easy to climb the fence out of sight of the guard. I caught up with her at the driveway of a lovely home not unlike the mansion I lived in as Simon Guiness. I thought it was a rather inappropriate dwelling for a woman who makes her living as a waitress. Later I learned that she is a law-school student who works evenings and house-sits for a couple named Adamson, the absent owners of that dwelling."

"You broke into the house."

"That is too crude a word. I waited for hours and observed that an upstairs bedroom had an open window, which meant it would not be alarmed. It was easy to climb the tree nearby and slip inside from there."

"It was Emily's bedroom?"

"Yes. She was asleep. The moon was quite bright, and I was able to study her for a long time. The memories came flooding back of her persistent efforts to win my attention when we lived on neighboring estates in England."

Jack Carroll listened with mounting fury. Emily had told him that she'd sensed Koenig when he came in the window. She knew she couldn't get away in time, that her only hope was to push the panic button on the side of the bed. The security-conscious Mr. Adamson had ordered that each bed be equipped with one. It was wired into the station of the private guards who patrolled the gated community. They knew instantly what room she was in, and they had a key to the house.

"I was so afraid, Jack," she'd told him, her voice a monotone. "I sleep with the lights on now, and I'm afraid to open the windows. I could tell he was going to kill me when he bent over and whispered, 'Haven't we met before?'—the same question he'd asked me in the restaurant."

Somehow Emily had managed to stay coolheaded, Jack thought. She'd told Koenig that she was sure they had met, but wouldn't he talk to her about it and refresh her memory?

"He was so scary," Emily had recalled. "His face got all red, the veins of his neck stood out. He told me how I'd tried to waylay him in the fields, how I'd bragged to him about killing my husband for him. Then he said it was time—and put his hands around my throat."

The security guards had burst in just as Koenig had begun to squeeze her throat. "His fingers were so powerful," Emily had whispered. "So many nights now I wake up feeling them."

At his arrest, William's hysterical rantings that Emily had caused his death in another life had resulted in a media circus.

"You attacked Emily Winters because she looked like Kate Fallow?" Dr. Stein prodded.

"She didn't *look* like her," William said with a touch of irritation. "She *was* Kate Fallow. I recognized her and immediately became my former self, Simon Guiness. Simon had a right to be angry—you should see the justice of that, Dr. Stein. How would *you* feel about someone who caused you to be executed?

"I will tell you that I regret I did not awaken Emily sooner. If I were doing it again, I would wrap a noose around her neck so I could enjoy seeing her experience the fear and anguish I experienced at my own execution. As I tightened the rope, I would explain to her exactly why she had to die."

He was rewarded by the visible tensing of Jack Carroll's body. He sensed that a personal relationship had developed between Carroll and the woman they called Emily Winters.

"Was Emily the only woman you saw who was Kate?" Dr. Stein asked.

"A few times after I recalled my life as Simon Guiness, I saw women with red hair and I got close to them. But one of them had dyed hair. Another didn't have the same shade of eyes. Kate's were very blue. A particular shade of blue. There's a name for it: periwinkle, a sort of blue-violet shade.

"You may be interested to learn that Kate has reappeared in other lifetimes, but obviously has managed to evade judgment. When I studied her that night, I knew she was Kate Fallow, but another name also kept running through my mind. Eliza Jackson. As that lifetime becomes clearer to me, Doctor, I will discuss it with you."

He's playing games with her, Jack Carroll thought. He's managed to convince everyone here that he's crazy, and he is—but crazy like a fox. If we just had some indication of who he believes he was in other lives, we might be able to start matching victims to him.

"You've seen yourself in other past lives?" Dr. Stein asked.

"I've seen faces and sensed that I lived as a knight in King Arthur's time, and in Egypt during the Roman occupation, and as a minister in sixteenth-century Germany, but none of those lives was filled with detail. I am sure that means that only my life as Simon Guiness was unjustly terminated."

William Koenig smiled to himself. His other lives had been very clear, and in all of them the people who had caused him injustices had been punished. Except for the woman they called Emily Winters, but he knew where to find her tonight. When his cousin had visited him in prison, Koenig had told him that he wanted to write a letter of apology to Emily. The cousin had checked and discovered she was in her last year of law school, still working at the restaurant, still living at the Adamsons'.

He felt Dr. Stein's eyes studying him. Jack Carroll's eyes were always impassive, but he knew that under the bland exterior Carroll was furious. Carroll wanted answers. Koenig wondered if Carroll would have Dr. Stein ask the usual questions:

"Did you have anything to do with the fire in Rosedale that killed an elderly woman eight years ago?"

"Five years ago in March, someone of your description was seen leaving the York Cinema in Mamaroneck, where a cashier was later found murdered. Did you ever encounter that cashier in another life?"

"Did you ever call yourself Samuel Esinger and make an appointment with Jeffrey Lane, a real estate agent in Rye?"

The old woman was the witch from Salem. He'd recognized the cashier as the seventeenth-century pirate who had set him adrift in 1603. Lane had been his younger brother in Glasgow in 1790 and murdered him for the estate.

Dr. Stein could sense Carroll's frustration. As he had explained, "I refuse to believe it's sheer coincidence that someone of Koenig's general description was seen in the area where homicides of totally unconnected people took place."

General description, the doctor thought. That suits him. Medium height, medium build, plain features, dirty-blond hair. As Carroll had pointed out, different glasses, a wig, or even a cap or ski hat could alter Koenig's appearance. Only his eyes were compelling: not so much blue as almost colorless. And he was strong. Cords of muscles bulged in his neck and hands. He worked out in his cell for hours at a time.

According to his file, both his mother and his father had been brooding and reclusive. When he was growing up, other children were forbidden to play with him. There were too many accidents when he was around. He'd gone to high school in White Plains and been considered a creep by his classmates.

William had graduated from high school, left Westchester County, and drifted from job to job around the country. His records showed him to be highly intelligent but unable to control his temper. Outbursts of violence against coworkers had led to several brief confinements in mental hospitals. He had returned to White Plains, a time bomb ready to explode, and he did explode the night he attacked Emily Winters.

Dr. Stein noted that William was a voracious reader. Several of the psychiatrists believed that Simon Guiness, the person he claimed to have been in a past life, was a fictional character he had read about. But except for Assistant DA Carroll, no one believed that William was a serial killer.

It was obvious there was no information to be gleaned from him today. It was also obvious that he was baiting Carroll.

"Our time is just about up, William," Dr. Stein said. "I'll see you on Thursday."

"I look forward to it. You seem to be very kind. Who knows? Maybe in another incarnation you were my friend. I'll try to find out if that might be true. I wish you would try as well."

"How is Emily Winters doing?" Dr. Stein asked Jack after Koenig had been removed.

"She's gone to counseling a few times, but I think she should go regularly. Recently, she did something that I thought was dangerous. She went to a parapsychologist and had herself regressed to a former lifetime."

"She wanted to see if she really was Kate Fallow?"

"Yes."

"The power of suggestion would play a great role in any memory like that."

"She didn't remember being Kate Fallow. But she tells me she has a tape of a life she described under hypnosis—when she lived in the South during the Civil War."

"Did she play the tape for you?"

Jack shook his head. "I told her I thought it was absolute non-sense and that she should stick with the trauma counselor and not mess up her head."

"I understand she goes to Fordham Law School. But why wait-ressing?" Stein asked. "And why live in White Plains?"

"Emily's paying her own way through law school and doesn't want a load of loans on her back. She plans to be a public defender—which isn't the biggest paycheck a lawyer can get. She gets her main meals—and excellent tips—at the restaurant. Finally, the grand-mother who raised her isn't going to live much longer. She's in a White Plains nursing home, so this way Emily can run in to see her almost daily."

Sara Stein did not miss the warmth in Jack Carroll's eyes when he talked about Emily Winters. "You're seeing her on a personal basis," she suggested, "which may, of course, affect your response to Wil-liam Koenig."

"Enough to want to be very sure that if he's ever declared sane, he'll stand trial for enough homicides to need all the lifetimes he can find to serve his sentence."

That evening William made his carefully planned escape. The friendly and careless new guard was an easy target. William left him wrapped in blankets on the bed in his cell, his face turned to the wall. The elderly orderly in the locker room didn't live long enough even to glimpse his attacker.

He left the grounds in the orderly's car, dressed in the orderly's clothes and carrying his identification. On the way to Emily's house he made a stop at a hardware store to purchase a rope. The slip-knot was in place by the time he abandoned the car in the municipal parking lot and went on foot to the exclusive neighborhood where a guard stood at the gate. A few hundred yards down, he scaled the fence with the ease of long practice and, sliding behind bushes and trees, made his way to the Adamson residence, where Emily was still living.

He had realized the elderly couple she worked for might have returned home, but a quick glance showed no car in the garage. It will be just Kate and me, he thought. She was due home anytime now. As soon as she opened the door, he'd push in behind her. If necessary, he'd kill her immediately. But he'd give her a chance to disarm the security system, so they could talk. She'd probably do that. Of course, there was always the possibility she'd disarm it in a way that would send a panic signal, yet he'd be listening for anyone trying to get into the house. This time, no matter how fast they were, they would not find her alive.

"The veal chop is wonderful," Emily assured the indecisive customer who could not make up his mind between the veal and the swordfish.

"Do you mean that it's better than the swordfish?"

Oh dear God, Emily thought. She didn't know why she was so nervous today. She had the feeling of something hanging over her, of something terrible about to happen. She felt in her soul that it was inevitable that one night she would awaken from sleep and again see William Koenig, his eyes glazed, his hands outstretched, his fingers reaching for her throat.

Or she'd hear footsteps behind her and turn and he'd be there. Once again he'd ask in that quiet, eerie voice, "Haven't we met before?"

"Maybe I will try the veal."

"I know you'll enjoy it." Emily turned, glad to get away from the window table, glad to retreat to the kitchen, where no one could see her from the street. She felt so vulnerable near the windows, ever since she'd learned that William Koenig had studied her from the dark.

Maybe I should have changed jobs, she thought. "But if he ever gets out, he'll find you anywhere you go," a subconscious voice whispered. This job, this situation suited her. She'd be finished with law school in May and had already been promised a job in the public defender's office. Jack teased her about that. "You'll be trying to get people out of jail, and I'll be trying to put them in. Should be pretty interesting."

They were right for each other. They both knew it, but it was unspoken. There was plenty of time, and he was smart enough to understand that what with school, the waitressing job, house-sitting, and Gran, she wasn't ready for another level of involvement.

She handed the order to the chef's assistant, smiling to herself at what Jack had told her. "I feel as though we're dating in my mother's era. The movies, dinner, bye-bye."

They'd had only one serious misunderstanding. She'd been annoyed that Jack didn't want to listen to the tape that had been made when she was hypnotized and regressed. Maybe it is the collective unconscious. Maybe it's something I read somewhere, she said to herself. But it was compelling to listen to her own voice claiming she had lived in the South during the Civil War.

Not that I put any stock in it, but you can see how people get caught up in the idea of reincarnation, she thought.

The last table of four finally cleared at ten-thirty. Jack had phoned earlier. He'd been up to see William Koenig and suggested meeting her for a nightcap. She was sorely tempted, but she had an exam coming up in two days and a lot of reading still to do.

Emily said good night to Pat Cleary, her boss, and smilingly agreed to stop by the restaurant tomorrow and pick up a hot lunch to take to the nursing home for her grandmother.

"I know you see her on Thursdays in the late morning," Pat said genially, "and we all know that nursing-home food isn't the sort that comes from a good pub."

Her car, parked in the restaurant lot, started with its usual protesting screech. Maybe next year at this time, when I finally finish law school, I can actually get myself a car that travels on more than prayers, Emily promised herself.

Jack drove a Toyota. He'd told her that when he graduated from law school three years ago, his father had presented him with a Jaguar. "Broke my heart, but I thought it would look a little peculiar for an assistant DA to arrive at court in a Jag," he said.

The guard waved her through the security gate. It was a joke between them that with all the pricey cars that rolled through here, hers was the only one that qualified as a possible candidate for Rent-a-Wreck.

She always put it in the garage. The Adamsons had made it clear they did not want it in view of the neighborhood.

Emily walked quickly along the path from the garage to the kitchen door. This was the most frustrating moment of her day. Once inside, and with the instant-security button pushed, she knew that no door or window could be disturbed without the alarm blasting. That would bring the security guards to the house within seconds.

And besides, William Koenig was in a padded cell, or however they kept maniacs confined in that new facility.

She put her key in the door and turned it. As the lock clicked and the handle turned, she felt a firm hand cover her mouth. The door opened, and she was propelled inside the house. "Haven't we met before?" Koenig whispered.

Jack Carroll went back to his office, his mood angry and disgruntled. Snap out of it, he told himself. He had a case to prepare for trial, and the boss would hardly thank him if he messed it up because he'd been spending time on his hunch about Koenig.

It would have been nice to be able to look forward to meeting Emily for a drink, but he did understand that she had to burn the midnight oil. When Jack reflected on his privileged upbringing in Rye and the struggle Emily had always known, he felt humbled. Her parents dead. Raised by a grandmother who'd been ailing for years and was now terminally ill. Partial scholarships to good schools and lots of hard work. And now, instead of going for the big bucks, Emily wanted to spend her life taking care of people who needed legal assistance and could not pay for it.

And she's the one who had to have that nut attack her, Jack fumed to himself. He admitted that after seeing Koenig today, what he really wanted to do was put his arms around Emily and make sure she was alive, close, safe, out of danger.

The hours passed as he immersed himself in preparing his opening statement for the trial that would begin next week. In other small offices, other assistant DAs were doing the same thing. Brothers all are we, they joked to one another.

And sisters, the women assistant DAs would remind them.

At eleven-fifteen his phone rang. Dr. Stein sounded surprised when he answered. "Mr. Carroll," she said, "I didn't really expect to find you at the office."

The strain in her voice made Jack's throat close. "What's happened?"

"It's Koenig. The guard assigned to his unit has been found strangled in Koenig's cell. The orderly who cleans around the locker room was found in the closet. We're searching the grounds, but we think Koenig got away in the orderly's car. He's been gone at least two hours. Does he know where Emily Winters lives now?"

"He might. I'll call her and get protection around her." Jack jiggled the disconnect and dialed Emily's number. Emily, answer, please answer, he begged. As soon as he heard her voice, he'd tell her to bolt and lock the doors. Then he'd call the private security guards and have them rush over until he could get the squad cars there. Until he could get to Emily himself.

The phone rang twice. With a vast sense of relief he heard it being picked up.

"Emily?"

"No, Mr. Carroll, it is I, Simon Guiness, Kate is with me. She has agreed with me that, yes indeed, we have met before."

The panic button on the security panel was the star-shaped button. It would have been easy to hit it with the tip of her finger as she disarmed the system, but Emily had made an instant decision not to do it. He was watching her too closely. He'd have known, and the rope he had slipped around her neck would have been tightened.

She had only one chance, and that was to get him to talk. It would have taken him at least half an hour to get from the hospital to here. By now they must know he had escaped. By now Jack would be on his way to her.

"That was a wise decision. You have bought yourself a few minutes' more existence in this lifetime."

They were both in the kitchen. It was a large room with a fireplace at the far end, faced by a couch and two comfortable chairs, with a television set to one side. When the Adamsons were home, Mr. Adamson would frequently tell Emily that with all the rooms in this great barn of a house, this spot was his favorite. They often ate dinner there, with Mrs. Adamson doing the cooking. He would sit content, reading the paper and watching the news.

Emily realized that she was in shock. Why else would she be

thinking of the Adamsons as William Koenig guided her to Mr. Adamson's chair and stood behind her? She felt the rough rope scrape the skin of her throat.

Please God, she thought, don't let me show him how scared I am. He needs that. Let me try to keep him talking to me. Jack will be here. I know he will.

She struggled to remember all that Jack had told her about Koenig. "I know you are going to kill me," she said, "and I know I caused your death. But it was because I loved you so much, Simon, and you rejected me. A woman scorned can surely be forgiven because of such great love."

"I did scorn," Koenig agreed. "But that was no reason to lie."

Emily's mouth was so dry she didn't know whether or not she could force the words from her throat. "But you see, Simon, you encouraged me. Don't you remember? I know I flirted with you, but you said you desired me. You were the most handsome man in the village. All the girls wanted you."

"I didn't realize that." Koenig sounded pleased.

Keep him talking, she warned herself. Keep him talking.

"Am I the first person you have punished for offenses against you in your lifetimes?"

"Oh no, Kate. You are the eleventh."

"Tell me about the others."

Jack is right, Emily thought. He is a serial killer. If I can just get him to boast.

The phone rang. When Koenig answered and spoke to Jack, Emily knew that she had only seconds to live. Jack would call the security guards and they would break in.

Koenig knew that too. He hung up and smiled at her. "If you're wondering if I expect to get away, of course I don't. They'll take me back to Haviland. But that's all right. It's not a bad place, and you're the last one I needed to find. My revenge is complete. Stand up."

He pulled at the noose as she stood. Emily began to gasp. Oh God, please, she prayed.

"Stand on that chair." He indicated the kitchen chair under the crossbeam.

"No."

She felt a vicious yank. Do it! she screamed to herself. Buy another second or two. Maybe they'll get here in time.

With seemingly effortless movement he tossed the end of the rope over the crossbeam. "Scared, aren't you? My sole regret, Kate, is that I believe I also knew you in another, different lifetime. Your name was Eliza Jackson. I'd like to have known what happened between us then."

Emily felt herself begin to black out. "I remember that lifetime," she whispered. "I *was* Eliza Jackson. I went to a parapsychologist. He hypnotized me, and when I regressed, I told him I was Eliza Jackson."

"I don't believe you."

"There's a tape in that drawer. The recorder is next to it. Please, listen. We did know each other in 1861."

"I'm not letting go of the rope. Even if they try to break in, it will be too late for you." He reached into the drawer and pulled out the tape recorder. With one hand he dropped in the cassette and pushed the "On" button.

Emily saw faces at the window: the security guards. But Koenig had seen them too. With a lightning gesture he wrapped the end of the rope around his left hand, braced himself and began to pull it toward him.

Emily couldn't breathe. Her hands clawed at the rope around her neck as she felt herself being pulled up, her feet rising from the chair.

"My name is Eliza Jackson." The tape was rolling, the volume high.

William Koenig froze, dropped the rope and rushed to the recorder as Emily's voice, dreamy and reflective, filled the room.

"We *did* meet in another lifetime!" Koenig shrieked.

The second hesitation was all that was needed. The window shattered. The guards were in the room.

One grabbed Koenig. The other gently lifted Emily from the floor, where she had tumbled when Koenig let go of the rope, and removed the noose from around her throat.

Koenig was being clapped into restraints. "I want to hear the rest of the tape!" he screamed. "I need to know what you did to me as Eliza Jackson!"

Emily looked straight into Koenig's eyes. "I don't know what Eliza Jackson may have done to you," she told him, "but I do know this: She just saved my life."

The Funniest Thing Has Been Happening Lately

Fred Rand did not need to read the list of the four people whom he was compelled to kill to know their names. They had been engraved on his soul for fifteen years. He had come back to Long Island from Florida hoping to learn that they had suffered in some way, that their comfortable, self-centered world had been altered, that life had treated them harshly.

I would have accepted that, he thought. I could have made it do. I would have gone back to St. Augustine and lived out my life.

But to his dismay, they were all functioning very well, very well indeed.

Genevieve Baxter. Known to her friends as Gen. She was the first on the list who would be punished, because she would be the easiest. She had contributed to the chain of events that ended in the tragedy that had destroyed his life. Gen was now seventy-five years old and had been a widow for several years, a sadness but, under careful consideration, nothing he would deem as sufficient punishment. He had been following her on and off for the past few weeks and had a very fair idea of her present activities.

From all appearances, Gen was leading a busy, contented life.

Two of her children lived in nearby towns. She was active in the affairs at her church, Our Lady of Refuge.

There is no refuge for me, he thought.

Six grandchildren.

Gen lived in the house she had shared with her husband. One of those pleasant imitation Tudors that had been a favorite middle-class design in Long Island suburbs in the 1950s.

He knew. He had lived in one of them only a few towns away until fifteen years ago.

This afternoon he had stood at the next checkout counter from Gen Baxter in the supermarket and heard her talking to the clerk. She was planning to go to her granddaughter's ballet recital tonight.

She would never see another one.

Vinnie D'Angelo. The second person on the list. Vinnie had been reprimanded for dereliction of duty after it happened. That hadn't stopped him from being promoted a year later. He'd retired as head of security at the Long Island Mall, the very place where his goofing off had cost a life. He spent winters in North Carolina now. But in March he came back to Babylon and put his boat in the water. Vinnie was an avid fisherman.

Babylon was only half an hour away. He'd watched Vinnie at the dock, his step jaunty as he cast off the lines and revved up the motor.

He already had his plan in place. He'd take a boat out, get close to where Vinnie was fishing, and pretend to be stalled. Then when Vinnie, helpful Vinnie, offered to tow him in, he would have his chance to even the score.

Lieutenant Stuart Kling of the Manhasset police force might be the hardest one to corner. He'd been a brash young cop anxious to fill his quota of speeding tickets when he could have prevented a murder. He would not get the chance to prevent his own death.

And finally . . . regretfully . . . Lisa Monroe Scanlon. After following her for several weeks he had impulsively decided to speak to her. He'd pretended to be astonished when he passed her in the Island shopping center. Her three children were with her. Seven-year-old twin boys and a baby girl. He still wasn't sure if it had been a good idea to make that contact, but he'd kept the conversation very casual, even to the point of saying he was only up from Florida on business and going back the next day.

Lisa had become an interior decorator, married Tim Scanlon, and was now balancing work and children. "Busy, but lots of fun," she'd said, smiling.

Lots of fun. I bet, he'd thought.

And her parents were fine. Doting grandparents.

Isn't that grand?

The acid in his throat had almost choked him as he'd walked back to his car.

If Lisa hadn't been so happy, so fulfilled—that was the word, *fulfilled*—he might have changed his mind. Smiling, happy Lisa had been the catalyst.

Tonight was Genevieve Baxter's turn.

Gen Baxter locked the door and turned the alarm on. It was almost ten-thirty and she was tired. She'd attended her nine-year-old granddaughter Laurie's ballet recital. Afterward the family had gone out for pizza.

The last few days had been warm for March, but tonight had turned sharply colder and the arthritis in her hands and ankles was sending throbbing pain throughout her limbs. I feel every day of my age, she thought ruefully as she changed into a warm nightgown, tied the sash of her robe, slid her feet into comfortable old slippers and went back downstairs.

The hot cup of cocoa was a longtime tradition. Sip it propped in bed with a book or watching the eleven o'clock news.

At the foot of the stairs Gen hesitated. It had been three years that she'd been alone in the house, but until lately she'd never felt nervous. The house was so familiar that she was sure she could go through it blindfolded and never make a misstep, but for some reason tonight was different.

Oh stop it, she told herself. You're imagining things. Why would anyone want to follow me? Of course it was silly. She knew that. It was just that she'd had an impression of being near the same person a couple of times in the last few weeks.

I never was good at remembering faces unless I see them regularly, she reflected as she measured the cocoa into a cup and filled it with milk, then placed the cup in the microwave oven. That's why today when that man was in line at the next checkout counter I knew that I'd seen him at least three or four times lately and that maybe I should recognize him.

Today she'd been so sure that he was following her that she'd sat in the car until she saw him carry out his groceries and walk across the parking lot. She'd watched him load the groceries in the trunk of his car and start to drive toward the exit at the other end of the mall.

I'll follow him, she thought, just until I'm able to make out his license number and jot it down.

The paper with the number was in her pocketbook. She'd almost talked to Mark, her son, about it at the ballet tonight, but it was such a happy night and he was so proud of Laurie being the swan princess in the recital that she hadn't wanted to throw a shadow on the evening.

Anyway the family would all joke and say that Mom is just trying to pick up a fellow, Gen told herself.

The microwave beeped to indicate that the two minutes were up. With a potholder she took the cup out, put it on a saucer and started for the stairs. Charlie always used to say he didn't know why I don't blister my tongue the way I like everything so hot, she thought with an affectionate smile.

Charlie. She missed him all the time in the quietly constant way that widows her age miss the husband they'd shared their lives with for so many years. But as Gen turned out the kitchen light and walked down the dimly lit hall to the staircase, she felt a wild primal need for Charlie to be there with her. She needed him.

And then it began. The handle of the front door was turning.

"Who is it?" The involuntary question died on her lips. The lock was clicking. She heard it release. The door opened.

The man at the checkout counter was coming toward her.

He did not bother to close the door but left it open and stood staring at her, his hands at his sides. He didn't even seem to notice when the alarm began to shriek. Tall and gaunt with thinning black hair, his face had a dazed expression as though he had wandered in by mistake and was frightened.

But then he said, "You should have tried to help her, you know," and his hands were suddenly claws, snapping around her neck. Gen sank to her knees, gasping for breath that was no longer granted her. As the cup of cocoa fell from her hands and through waves of blackness she felt splashes of heat burning her skin, she realized who her assailant was. In the moment before she died, a flash of pure anger permeated her soul that he would dare to blame her for something she could not have foreseen.

Fred made his escape cutting around the house and through the backyard to the garden apartment development where he had parked his car.

He was driving down the street when a squad car screamed past him, probably called by the security monitoring service that re-

sponded to the alarm at Gen Baxter's home. A few minutes later, as
he turned onto the highway, he relived the moment Gen Baxter had
died. Just before her eyes became fixed and staring, he'd seen an expression in them. What was it? Anger. Yes, and reproach. How dare
she reproach him? How dare she be angry at him? She had helped to
kill his only child and had now paid the price for that terrible deed.

Back in the motel, he poured a drink from the bottle of scotch
that was his bedside companion. He stripped to his shorts and got
into bed, but for hours lay sleepless. He had expected Genevieve
Baxter's death to give him a measure of release, but he sensed immediately that release would only come when all four were dead.

Tomorrow it would be Vinnie D'Angelo. The weather prediction
was good, so he was bound to go out in his boat. Then in the next
day or two, Stuart Kling would pay for his role in the tragedy. He
would be a little harder, a little more challenging. Fred smiled to
himself, a sad, tired smile. Planning Kling's death would keep his
mind occupied, keep the demons away. Or at least he hoped so.

Detective Joe O'Connor of the Nassau Police Department had
known Mrs. Genevieve Baxter since he was a kid. He'd gone to high
school with her son Mark and had even dated her daughter Kay
when they were teenagers. He asked to be assigned to investigate the
Baxter murder.

Now, three days after the funeral, he sat having coffee with Mark
in the kitchen of the home that had become a crime scene. "I can't
help thinking how much you look like your mother," Joe told him.

A hint of a smile turned up the corners of Mark's lips. "I guess so.
I hope so." Forty-three years old, he was a handsome man with blue-
gray eyes, a well-shaped nose, sensitive mouth and firm chin. His
sandy hair was streaked with gray. He was clenching and unclench-
ing the coffee cup he was holding.

"Mark, it doesn't make sense." Joe's beefy frame was hunched forward, his dark eyes narrowed in frustration barely in check. "There was no robbery. This guy broke in, strangled your mother, and got out. Was he some nut who just happened to pick this house, or is there some reason he wanted to kill her?"

"Who in the name of God would want to kill my mother?" Mark asked wearily. "She always kept the front door locked. How could he have forced it open so easily? It's obvious she was just about to start upstairs with the cocoa. She must have heard or seen him trying to get in. She never even had time to push the panic button. It was right there in the vestibule next to the door."

"That lock was probably the one that came with the house forty-some-odd years ago," O'Connor told him. "The guy had to have had a professional tool that jammed and released it in ten seconds. I think your mother was targeted. Maybe the guy who did it is a nut, but I don't believe this is a random murder. Mark, you've got to help me. First, start thinking. Did your mother say anything about anyone bothering her with phone calls or maybe mention that a repairman was at the house lately? You know what I mean. When you go through her clothes and mail, keep an eye out for anything that in any way seems unusual."

Mark nodded. "I understand."

The next day he called O'Connor at headquarters. "Joe, something did occur to me. The last time I saw my mother was at Laurie's ballet recital. You know that. Then we went out for pizza and she started to say—I remember her exact words—'The funniest thing has been happening lately,' and unless I'm imagining it now, Mom looked worried. But then the waitress came and took our order and some people came up to the table to congratulate Laurie on her dancing and that was it. Mom didn't bring it up again."

Something was going on that had her worried, Joe thought. I knew it. "Mark, whatever it might have been, you couldn't have prevented what happened to her a few hours later," he said, "but this is exactly what I meant when I asked you to keep alert for anything that seems unusual. And remember, watch for any repair bills that might come in the mail in these next few weeks."

Fred was at the pier in Babylon waiting for Vinnie D'Angelo to show up, and suddenly he decided to call Helen in Atlanta. Even though they had divorced ten years go, as Jenny had kept them together in life, by her death she also had created an unbreakable bond between them. It was the one thing they had ever really shared, the joy she had given, the grief she had left.

"Where are you, Fred? You didn't sound good when I spoke to you last month."

Last month, February 28, had been the fifteenth anniversary of Jenny's death.

"Oh, thought I'd come back up to the old neighorhood. Sentimental journey, I guess. Hasn't changed much. Visited Jenny's grave. Put some flowers on it."

"Fred, are you taking your medicine?"

"Sure. Love my medicine. Makes me feel happy all the time."

"Fred, go home. See your doctor."

"I'll see him when I get back. Everything okay with you, Helen?"

"It's okay."

"Still like your job?" After Jenny died, they'd moved to Florida and Helen had gone to nursing school. She was now a pediatric nurse in a hospital in Atlanta.

"I love it. Take care of yourself, Fred."

"Yeah. I rented a boat. I'm going fishing today."

"Now, that's good. How's the weather up there?"

"Couldn't be better." Suddenly he was eager to end the conversation. He could see Vinnie D'Angelo, fishing gear in hand, heading for his boat. "Gotta go, Helen. Be well."

He had attempted to pass time in Florida by buying a top-of-the-line thirty-five-foot Chris-Craft and taking up fishing. Now his hands felt sure on the wheel as he followed D'Angelo's boat out from the marina. It was still so early in the season that there were few other boats out, and as he had hoped, D'Angelo went a good distance from the others.

An hour later he was drifting past D'Angelo's boat. He was sunning on the deck, his rod fixed in place in a bracket. "Any chance of a tow?" Fred called. "This thing conked out on me."

It was even easier than killing Gen Baxter. In his boat, D'Angelo the retired hotshot head of security was a jovial Good Samaritan. Hail-fellow-well-met; come aboard; have-a-beer; you-should-know-better-than-to-rent-from-that-jerk; all-his-boats-are-worn-out-tubs!

It was when D'Angelo was bending to get a beer out of the cooler that Fred took the hammer out of his windbreaker and struck the blow. D'Angelo slumped over, blood gushing from the back of his head. He was a thick-bodied man and it was a struggle to drag him up and then shove him over the side of the boat.

Fred sat down and had a beer, then found a towel, mopped up the blood and threw the towel in the water. He got back into his rented boat and sped away, enjoying the sequence he knew would follow.

On the days he'd observed Vinnie's habits, he'd seen that Vinnie fished until one o'clock and then drove to his house about fifteen minutes away. Probably had lunch with his wife. Nice and cozy for the two of them.

Around two o'clock she'd probably call the boat to see what was keeping him. No answer. Then she'd call the manager's office at the pier. No, Vinnie isn't back. His slip is empty. Probably they'd notify the coast guard or ask someone to go looking for him. Or maybe by then someone in a passing boat would have wondered that there didn't seem to be anyone on board a boat that had been anchored in the same spot for so long. Maybe even one of good old Vinnie's buddies would have pulled alongside and taken a look to see if he was okay.

I know all about the ritual of learning that someone is missing, Fred thought. I know all about the waiting.

He returned the rented boat, got into his car, and drove to the motel to shower and change his clothes. The motel was in Garden City, far enough away from Manhasset where Gen had lived, and Babylon where Vinnie had lived, and Syosset where Stuart Kling lived, to make him confident he wouldn't run into anyone who might know he'd been hanging round observing Baxter or D'Angelo.

Stuart Kling was next. He was a lieutenant in the Nassau County police. No more prowling around in a squad car on the highway for Stu. No more books of traffic tickets to fill. Fred had already figured the best way to get him. Nice and simple. Kling worked out in the gym early mornings three days a week. He wouldn't be armed going in or coming out of there.

Fred tore a page out of his daily reminder notebook, in block letters printed: "TRAFFIC TICKET TO HELL," and put it carefully in the pocket of the jacket he would wear in the morning.

He'd throw it on Stu's body after he shot him.

In Atlanta, Helen Rand was about to leave for the hospital when she received the phone call from her ex-husband. As always, speaking to him was an unsettling experience. In the fifteen years since Jenny's murder, she had managed to create a new life for herself. The intensive nurses training course had kept her busy and exhausted those first few years, then the job in the hospital in St. Augustine, combined with studying for her master's degree at night.

And finally ten years ago when she knew she could no longer live with Fred, she took the job in Atlanta and filed for divorce.

At first he'd called her constantly, not because he missed her, but because he needed to be sure that she still shared his heartache about losing Jenny. It was typical of him, she thought, to call to tell her he had visited Jenny's grave.

A year ago he had told her he was seeing a psychiatrist and taking medication for depression. But there was something else. About six months ago when he called, he began talking about the trial and cursing the people who testified at it. Jenny's murderer had been a twenty-six-year-old ne'er-do-well who had been hanging around the mall trying to urge young women to get into the van that belonged to the service station where he had a part-time job.

One of them had complained to the security guard who was going off duty. Instead of detaining him, the guard had shoved the guy into his van and told him to get out of the mall. Under cross-examination the guard had admitted that he hadn't wanted to be detained. He was meeting his bowling team.

Another witness had been that nice woman who'd cried when she talked about seeing Jenny being pulled off the highway with a flat tire. "I drove onto the breakdown lane to see if I could help her," she'd explained, "but then the van from the gas station pulled in ahead of her car and I thought she had phoned for help, so I didn't stay."

If the guard at the mall had done his job, if the woman had stayed to be sure Jenny was all right, if the cop who actually saw her getting into the van had checked to be sure she was all right instead of going after the speeder, if Lisa had gone shopping with Jenny that day . . . If . . . If . . . If . . .

And the biggest *if* was the one that was never spoken.

Whenever she talked to Fred now, Helen felt as though all the terrible pain and anger she tried so hard to put behind her poured back into her soul. Stop it, stop it, she told herself. But maybe I should call his psychiatrist, she thought as she reached for her jacket. Fred mentioned his name once or twice. What was it? Raleigh? Renwood? Raines?

She lived in an apartment building ten blocks from the hospital in downtown Atlanta, and unless it was pouring rain she walked both ways.

Today was a bit overcast, but early spring was in the air and Helen felt better as soon as she stepped outside. She would be sixty her next birthday, but knew she looked at least five years younger. Her hair was salt and pepper and cut short with the natural wave framing her face. When she was young she'd worn it long. Old friends from her days at St. Mary's Academy always said that at eighteen Jenny had been a mirror image of her.

Jenny. Eighteen, never going to see nineteen.

Jenny. Eighteen, going on eternity.

Jenny. Eighteen and accepted at Georgetown, the college she and Lisa had planned to attend together and take by storm.

I didn't think I could ever get up in the morning again after she died, Helen thought, her mind still awash in the remembered pain Fred's phone call had triggered. But then, Fred's terrible inability to accept or cope had forced her to be strong for his sake. Until she could no longer put up with his . . . say it, she thought . . . his *dishonesty*.

Unconsciously, she walked more quickly as though hoping to outpace her thoughts. Resolutely she made herself think of her life as it was now, Atlanta, the new friends, the pediatrics intensive care unit where she was part of the team that helped keep the flicker of life alive in a dying child. And in the last year, after all this time, Gene, sixty-three years old, a widower, the director of Orthopedic Surgery. They were seeing each other regularly.

Raleigh. Renwood. Raines. What was that psychiatrist's name?

Something was shouting at her to get in touch with him. She knew what she'd do. There had to be a list of psychiatrists who practiced in or around St. Augustine. She'd ask Gene to see if any of the doctors in the psychiatric section could check for her. Then if they could identify the right one, she could phone and explain that she was Fred Rand's ex-wife and worried that he might be on the verge of some sort of breakdown.

If she would talk to Fred's doctor, maybe he could call Fred on his cell phone. At least it was worth a try.

Or maybe she should just stay out of it. Fred always calmed down eventually, and she didn't even know where he was staying. He probably wouldn't answer his cell phone anyway. He almost never did.

Early the next morning Stuart Kling did an extra half hour at the gym. He showered and changed into sweats. From there he planned to go straight to headquarters. Feeling particularly pleased with himself that he'd finally shed the five pounds he'd been trying to lose since Christmas, his step was light as he walked out the side entrance of the gym to the parking lot.

He heard rather than saw the window being lowered on the van that was parked next to his car. An instinct of nearby danger made him whirl around, his car key in hand. Stuart Kling had a nearly infallible memory for faces, and in the final moment before he died, he identified his murderer. His finger plunged involuntarily on the remote control in his hand and the trunk of the car sprang open as he crumpled to the ground. A sheet of paper fluttered from the van and was anchored by the blood that poured from the wound in his chest.

"TRAFFIC TICKET TO HELL" was what the stunned employee of the gym who ran out at the sound of the gunshot and reached Kling first was able to read before the printed letters on the paper became too stained to distinguish. Frantically the employee rushed to get the number on the license plate of the van as it roared out of the parking lot, but the plate was missing.

Three days after his meeting with Detective Joe O'Connor, Mark Baxter found a torn edge of a checking account deposit slip with a license plate number jotted on it in the large handbag his mother had regularly carried unless she was dressing up for a particular event.

It was in the zippered section where she always kept her checkbook and wallet, and somewhat crumpled. In the past few days, as well as phoning O'Connor about his mother's ambiguous reference to "something funny happening lately," Mark had called him about a new handyman a neighbor had told him his mother has been using, a new deliveryman from the dry cleaner and several emails he found on her computer from a distant cousin who asked about getting together when he was in town.

He was beginning to feel somewhat foolish because O'Connor had checked out all the leads and they had led exactly nowhere. It's probably been buried there for months, he thought, vaguely remembering that a neighborhood kid had slightly dented his mother's car when he parked too close to her in the church parking lot. But she'd decided to let it go because she was trading the car in anyway and didn't want the kid to get in trouble with his parents.

He crumpled the deposit slip, tossed it in the wastebasket and went home. The house where he had been raised, the house that had always been warm and welcoming, was now the scene of his mother's murder, and the less time he spent in it, the better. On the way to his law office he listened to the radio and heard the news that Nassau County police lieutenant Stuart Kling had been murdered as he was leaving the gym where he regularly worked out.

Kling, Mark thought. Poor guy. Why does that name sound familiar? The newscaster was saying that the prime suspect was a man Kling had arrested six years earlier who had just been released from a psychiatric hospital. I never used to think it was a lousy world, Mark thought, but I'm beginning to wonder.

His first appointment was at eleven o'clock. Because of his rearranged schedule since his mother's death, he had a busy day, but underlying all the meetings two things kept throbbing from below the level of conscious thinking. He should at least pass the license number he'd found in his mother's pocketbook over to Joe O'Connor, and why did Stuart Kling's name feel as though it should have great importance to him?

Tomorrow would finish it. Lisa Monroe Scanlon. After tomorrow she wouldn't be alive to go into that handsome house in Locust Valley, that symbol of the early success of two talented young people. Tim Scanlon was a stockbroker, and at thirty-eight a vice president of a prestigious financial giant. Fred had looked in the window of Lisa's interior decorating studio. Couches draped with a variety of expensive upholstery samples, chairs and antique tables. A mantel with candlesticks, a delicate painted clock. Floral prints on the walls.

She did all right for herself, Fred thought. A husband, a family, a business. And her parents reveling in their adorable grandchildren, while my grandchildren were never called into existence.

That day Jenny had gone to pick up Lisa. They had planned to go shopping together, but then Lisa changed her mind.

If she had gone with Jenny, if there had been two of them in the car when the tire went flat, Jenny would be alive today.

That night as Fred listened to the news reports of the shooting death of Lieutenant Stuart Kling, he cleaned and loaded the gun he would use to complete his task. He knew exactly when he would go into the house. Tomorrow morning. Tim Scanlon left at quarter past seven. The twins got on the school bus at 8:05. The bus was at the corner of their street, just a few houses down. The three mornings he'd watched, Lisa had walked with them to the corner and then scurried back home. She always left the door slightly ajar.

If she did that tomorrow, he'd slip inside and be waiting for her. If she didn't, he'd ring the bell and tell her he'd stopped with a gift for her. She'd let him in. After all, he was Mr. Rand, Jenny's father.

Then when the babysitter arrived at nine o'clock, she would find Lisa's body.

And I will go home, Fred thought. And visit Dr. Rawlston, my psychiatrist, and tell him that I do feel I am making progress in my struggle to accept my daughter's death. I will tell him that seeing my daughter's grave made a profound sense of peace come over me and I am sure it will stay with me. I will tell him that I no longer hate the people who caused Jenny's death.

I gave him their names, he thought. That wasn't wise. For some reason he was suddenly uneasy. The euphoria that began the moment he squeezed the trigger and watched Stuart Kling crumple on the ground was evaporating. He had a feeling of people waiting in the shadows, approaching him.

His cell phone rang. He did not answer it. He guessed it might be Helen. He knew she suspected that something different was going on inside him. He knew he had talked too much to her about the people who had caused Jenny's death.

She had urged him to call his psychiatrist. Would she have called Dr. Rawlston? Between them would they decide to call the police and suggest that Fred Rand was a deeply troubled man and perhaps certain people should be warned if he tried to contact them? And then they would learn that three of those certain people were already dead.

Abruptly Fred finished loading the gun, put it in his briefcase, stood up and began to pack. It was time to get out of here. He'd drive to Locust Valley now. The house next to Lisa's was obviously used only as a summer home. He could park in the back and never be noticed.

Even if it meant that he would be caught, he had to complete the job.

At eight-thirty, Fred Rand checked out of the motel in Garden City, got in his car and drove forty minutes to Locust Valley. Just after he turned off the highway, he stopped at a small restaurant and had dinner, remembering to slip a few rolls in his pocket in case he felt like nibbling during the night. At ten o'clock he was parked deep in the shadows of the house next to the Scanlon home. Tonight the sleep that had been denied him in the quite comfortable bed in the motel came easily when he leaned his head back and tilted the seat to a reclining position.

He awoke at dawn and waited.

Mark Baxter slept restlessly. Kling. Stuart Kling. Why should he know that name? He woke up, puzzled over it and went back to sleep. This time he dreamed that his mother was in the bank and making a deposit. But instead of the amount on the check she was depositing, she had written a license number and was trying to make the clerk accept it.

At seven o'clock when Mark grabbed a cup of coffee and kissed his wife and daughter good-bye, he did not drive to his office. Instead he turned the car in the direction of his late mother's home. He knew that he had to fish the license number out of the wastebasket, give it to Detective Joe O'Connor and tell O'Connor that for some reason he should be remembering a connection with the murdered Nassau County police lieutenant.

Helen Rand had a sleepless night. She spent it berating herself that she had not attempted to reach Fred's psychiatrist. At dinner she had talked about her concern to Gene and he had told her Bruce Stevens, a psychiatrist friend of his, could undoubtedly track down a psychiatrist with a name like Rawlings or Raines or Renwood in the St. Augustine area.

When Gene dropped her off, Helen had actually tried through the telephone information operator to obtain the psychiatrist's number, but without the exact name, she got exactly nowhere.

At seven-fifteen she called Gene at the hospital. "Please call Dr. Stevens, Gene. I don't know why, but I'm suddenly terribly worried."

At eight o'clock she was speaking to Dr. Richard Rawlston who practiced in Ponte Vedre, some fifteen miles from St. Augustine.

Quickly she explained her concerns to him, then waited, hoping against hope that he would, if not dismiss them, at least tell her that in his opinion there was no serious threat that Fred would do something rash.

"You say Fred is in Long Island now and you don't believe he is taking his medication, Mrs. Rand?"

"That's right."

There was a long pause, then the psychiatrist said, "I had been quite concerned about Fred, but then he told me that he was going on a cruise with friends and feeling much better. If that was a lie and he is in Long Island, I think there are three people who might need protection. I have their names. They are all people whom he blames for not preventing your daughter's death. A security guard, an elderly woman, and a police officer."

"Yes, those are the people he blamed."

"Do you know where Fred is staying, Mrs. Rand?"

"No, I don't."

"Then I think I have no recourse but to call the Nassau County police and notify them of our concern. I would like to give them your number in case they want to talk with you."

"Of course. I'm off duty today. I'll be here."

Helen hung up the phone. And waited.

Mark was in Joe O'Connor's office when the call from Dr. Rawlston came in. They had just traced the license number that Genevieve Baxter had jotted down on the deposit slip. It belonged to a Volvo that had been rented by Fred Rand of St. Augustine, Florida.

"He took my mother's life because . . ." Mark broke into sobs. "He blamed her! He blamed her!"

"And Stuart Kling and Vinnie D'Angelo, whose body washed in yesterday afternoon. They suspected foul play in D'Angelo's case," Joe said grimly.

"If only Mother had told me that night," Mark said.

"You don't know how many 'if only's' we hear in this business." O'Connor picked up the phone. "Put out an all-points bulletin . . . armed and dangerous . . ."

At seven-fifteen Fred watched as Tim Scanlon left his home. Hidden in the heavy foundation shrubbery outside the kitchen window, he saw Tim drop quick kisses on his family, could even hear him calling from the vestibule, "Remember, I'll be a little late tonight, honey."

No you won't, Fred thought. You'll be back here in a couple of hours. After you get the call about Lisa.

In her bathrobe, her hair twisted up on the back of her head, Lisa looked very young, he thought, almost as young as she'd been in the days when she and Jenny were always together.

You'll be together soon, Fred thought.

The news that Fred had killed the three people in Long Island left Helen in absolute shock. For an hour she sat motionless, unable to grasp the awfulness of his crime. But then she realized that through the horror she was also feeling a terrible sense of being warned. Jenny's voice was shouting to her.

At ten of eight, she called Dr. Rawlston back. Her voice frantic with fear she asked, "Doctor, did Fred ever say anything about blaming Jenny's friend Lisa for her death?"

"No. He did tell me Lisa was her friend and was supposed to go shopping with her that day but changed her mind. But that was all he said."

"There's a reason he might have held back, something he's never been able to face. I've got to call the Nassau police. Who did you speak to there?"

Mark was just about to leave when Helen Rand phoned. He watched as the furrows on O'Connor's face deepened. "You say her married name is Scanlon and you think she lives in Locust Valley. We'll get right on it." O'Connor hung up and looked at him. "There may be someone else on his list, Mark."

"Okay, you two, have a good day." With a final kiss, Lisa watched her twins climb onto the bus and hurried back home. Ever since the morning she'd locked herself out, she not only unlocked the door when she went to the corner with the twins but also left it slightly ajar.

For those two minutes she left fifteen-month-old Kelly in the playpen with plastic blocks she couldn't possible swallow and a rubber ball. Anything she could put in her mouth was out of reach.

But this morning, it was clear that something had frightened Kelly. She had pulled herself to her feet and was wailing, "*Mammmaaaaa!*"

Lisa picked her up. "Hey. What's your problem?"

I'm her problem, Fred thought. He was in the vestibule closet, aware he didn't have to rush. He could wait five or ten minutes and savor his generosity in granting Lisa a few minutes more of life.

And he certainly wouldn't kill her while she was holding the baby. He wanted to see her more clearly and carefully pushed the door open a fraction wider, then realized it had made a noise. Had she noticed?

Lisa heard a familiar faint creaking of the vestibule door opening. There's someone here. That's why the baby is frightened, she thought. What should I do?

Don't let him know you're aware of him. Pick up the baby and walk toward the door. Push the panic button.

Oh, God, please help me.

She *had* noticed. He could tell by the sudden rigidity of her body. "Lisa," he said softly.

Lisa spun around.

"Put the baby back in the playpen and then walk away from it. I don't want anything to happen to her. Sometimes bullets ricochet, you know."

Jenny's father was standing there, a gun in his hand. Why was he here? She knew. Because he hates me. He hates me because I'm alive and Jenny is dead. She had felt strange after she met him that day. She remembered how she had prattled on and on about her life and watched his eyes grow bleak and angry. He was going to kill her.

She tried not to show how afraid she was. "Please, I'll do anything you say. Let me put the baby down and let's walk into the kitchen."

"That's very motherly of you. Too bad you weren't as good a friend."

Lisa held Kelly tightly, kissed her and started to put her back in the playpen. Kelly wrapped her arms around her neck. "No, no, no."

Gently Lisa tried to disengage them.

"Hurry up, Lisa." Fred heard the wail of a siren. A police car was pulling into the driveway. "Hurry up," he shouted.

Frantically Lisa bent over the playpen, pulled the baby's arms from around her neck and dropped her onto the plastic matting. The rubber ball rolled forward. A sudden incongruous image of Jenny and herself, the stars of the softball team, she pitching, Jenny catching, jumped into her mind and she knew she might have a chance to save herself. In one lightning movement Lisa scooped up the ball, bolted away from the playpen, whirled around, and with a powerful thrust of her arm threw the ball at Fred. The ball hit his hand and the barrel of the gun leapt up as he pulled the trigger.

The bullet passed inches over her head and lodged in the wall. Before he could aim again the police were in the house wrestling him to the ground.

Fifteen minutes later, Detective Joe O'Connor called Helen Rand. "Thanks to you, Lisa is okay, Mrs. Rand," O'Connor said. "Our guys got there in the nick of time. Lisa told us that she didn't think she had a chance but then when she saw the ball in the playpen it reminded her of playing softball with Jenny. She felt as though Jenny was telling her what to do."

"Fred?"

"Under arrest. Violent. Not sorry he killed them. Blamed them for Jenny's death. You know that."

Helen's long-held control snapped. "He's blaming them! Do you know who killed my daughter? Fred did. He had family money but he was always cheap. Jenny was his only child. He bought her a car when she was eighteen. Sure he did. An old car with bald tires. That's why Lisa's father wouldn't let her ride in it that day. I begged Jenny not to set foot in it, but he told her to go ahead. He'd replace the tires when Sears had a sale. Tell him something for me. Tell him he killed his own child."

She choked back a sob. "I should have made him face the truth a long time ago. He was heartbroken after Jenny died. I felt so sorry for him but I should have made him face it."

"Mrs. Rand, you couldn't have made him believe Jenny's death was his fault. People like your ex-husband always blame everyone except themselves. And always remember that if you hadn't phoned me, Lisa would be dead now. You saved her life."

"No," Helen whispered. "You're wrong. You just told me yourself. Jenny saved Lisa's life." She managed a smile. "Jenny was one terrific kid and it looks as though even now, wherever she is up there, she hasn't changed a bit."

The Tell-Tale Purr

There comes a time when in the name of common decency grand-mothers ought to die. I confess that in the early stages of my life I had a halfhearted affection for my grandmother but that time is long since past. She is now well up in her eighties and still exceed-ingly vain even though at night her teeth repose in a water glass by her bed. She has a constant struggle every morning to get her contact lenses popped into her myopic eyes and requires a cane to support her arthritic knees. The cane is a custom-made affair designed to re-semble the walking stick Fred Astaire used in some of his dances. Grandma's story is that she danced with him when she was young and the cane/walking stick is her good-luck charm.

Her mind is still very keen and seems to become keener even as her eccentricities grow. She, who always proudly considered herself frugal, is spending money like water. Thanks to several investments her husband, my grandfather, made, she is downright wealthy and it has been with great pleasure that I have observed her simple life-style. But now it is different. For example, she just put an elevator, which cost forty thousand dollars, in her modest home. She is sure she will live to be one hundred and is contemplating building a state-of-the-art gym in the backyard because she read in a Harvard medical report that exercise is good for arthritis.

I submit to you that a better cure for her arthritis is to put an end to it forever. This I propose to do.

You must realize that I am her sole grandson and heir. Her only child, my mother, departed this earth shortly after I graduated from college. In the twenty-six years since then I have married and divorced twice and been involved in many ill-fated ventures. It is time for me to stop wasting my time on useless enterprises and enjoy a life of comfort. I must help to make that possible.

Obviously her demise would need to seem natural. At her advanced age, it would not be unlikely to have her pass away in her sleep, but if someone holding a pillow were to help that situation occur there is always the danger of a bruise that might make the police suspicious. Police always look for motive and I would be a living, breathing motive. I am uncomfortable about the fact that when under the influence of wine I was heard to say that the only present I wanted from my grandmother for my next birthday was a ticket to her funeral.

How then was I to help my grandmother sail across the River Styx without arousing suspicion?

I was quite simply at a loss. I could push her down the stairs and claim she fell but if she survived the fall, she would know that I caused it.

I could try to disable her car but that ancient old Bentley she drives with the skill of Mario Andretti would probably survive a crash.

Poison is easily detectable.

My problem was solved in a most unexpected way.

I had been invited to have dinner at the home of a successful friend, Clifford Winkle. I value Clifford's superb wines and gourmet table far more than I value Clifford. Also I find his wife, Belinda, insipid. But I was in the mood for a splendid dinner in comfortable circumstances and looked forward to the evening with pleasure.

I was seated with Clifford and his wife, enjoying a generous scotch on the rocks that I knew had been poured from a two-hundred-dollar bottle of single malt reserve, when their little treasure, ten-year-old Perry, burst into the room.

"I've decided, I've decided," he shouted, spittle spraying from the space between his upper front teeth.

The parents smiled indulgently. "Perry has been reading the complete works of Edgar Allan Poe this week," Clifford told me.

The last time I was a guest I had endured Perry's endless description of a book he had read about fly-fishing, and how by reading it, he could really, really understand all about baiting and casting and catching and why fly-fishing was really, really special. I wanted desperately to interrupt him and tell him I had already seen *A River Runs Through It*, Robert Redford's splendid film on the subject but, of course, I did not.

Now Perry's all-consuming passion was obviously Edgar Allan Poe. "'The Tell-Tale Heart' is my favorite," he crowed, his short red hair spiking up on the crown of his skull, "but I could write a better ending, I know I could."

Barefoot boy with cheek out-Poes Poe, I thought. However, I wanted to show some small degree of interest. I was down to my last sip of the two-hundred-dollar scotch and hoped that by directing attention to myself, Clifford might notice my empty glass and not neglect his duty as my host. "In high school I wrote a new ending to 'The Cask of Amantillado,'" I volunteered. "I got an A in my English class for it. I remember how it began." I cleared my throat. "'Yes. I killed him. I killed him a long fifty years ago. . . .'"

Perry ignored me. "You see in the 'The Tell-Tale Heart' the guy killed the old man because he can't stand looking at his eye. Then he buries the old man's heart but when the cops come he thinks he hears the heart beating and goes nuts and confesses. Right?"

"Right!" Clifford affirmed enthusiastically.

"Exactly. Um-hmm," Belinda agreed, beaming at her whiz kid.

"In my book, the guy kills the old man, but another guy watches him do it, then helps him cut up the body and bury the heart under the floor. When the cops come in, the murderer laughs and jokes with them and thinks he's getting away with it. Then when the cops go, the friend comes back and as a joke says he can hear the old man's heart beating. Isn't that good?"

Fascinating, I thought. If only Poe had lived to meet Perry.

"But then the murderer, 'cause he doesn't know it's a joke, believes he really is hearing the heart, and you know what?"

"What?" Clifford asked.

"I can't guess," Belinda gushed, her eyes wide, her hands clutching the arms of her chair.

"The murderer dies of fright because of the heart he thinks he's hearing."

Perry beamed at his own brilliance. Send for the Nobel Prize, I thought, not realizing there was more to come.

"And the twist is that his friend was going to split the money the old man had hidden somewhere in London and now he realizes he'll never know where to find it so he's punished for the crime too." Perry grinned triumphantly, an ear-to-ear grin that made all the freckles on his cheeks bond together in a henna-tinted mass.

It was I who led the applause and my reaction was genuine. *The sound had scared the murderer to death.* My grandmother's fear of cats rushed into my mind. She shakes and trembles to the point of almost fainting at the sight or sound of one. It goes back, I am told, over eighty years ago when a rabid cat attacked her in the garden. She still bears a scar on her left cheek from that long-ago encounter.

My grandmother has a new elevator.

Suppose . . . just suppose, Grandma got stuck in her new elevator in the dark during a power failure. And then she hears the sounds of cats yowling and hissing and howling and purring. She hears them scratching at the door of the elevator. She is sure they will break through. She cowers, shrieking, against the back of the elevator, then crumples onto the floor, the memory of that long-ago attack overwhelming her. No, it is not a memory. It is happening. She is sure that the cat is poised to attack her again, not just one cat but all the cats in this crazed, menacing pack, foaming at the mouth, teeth bared.

There is only one way to escape the panic. She is frightened into heart failure and her death would be blamed on her being trapped, alone, at night, in the new elevator.

I was so excited and thrilled at this solution to my problem that I hardly tasted the excellent dinner and was uncommonly responsive to Perry who, of course, dined with us and never shut up.

I planned my grandmother's death very carefully. Nothing must arouse even the slightest suspicion. Fortunately there are frequent power failures in her area of northern Connecticut during wind storms. She has talked of installing a home generator but so far that has not happened. Still, I knew I had to move swiftly.

Night after night for the next few weeks, I roamed through the nearby towns, slithering through dark alleys and around abandoned buildings, any place where wild cats gathered. I tossed pieces of meat and cheese to get them fighting with one another, their teeth bared, their ungodly yowls rumbling from their throats, getting it all on tape. One night I was attacked by a cat who, frantic for the food in my hand, sprung on me, her front claw ripping my left cheek in the same spot my grandmother was scarred.

Undeterred, I kept on my mission, even recording cats in animal shelters, where I caught the plaintive meows of discarded felines bewildered by their fate. At the home of a neighbor I secretly caught on tape the contented purring of her cherished pet.

A cacophony of sound, a work of genius. That was the result of my labors.

As I was engaged in my nocturnal wanderings, by day I was also lavishing attention on my grandmother, visiting her at least three times a week, enduring at mealtime the vegetarian regime that was her latest quirk to stay alive until her hundredth birthday. Seen with such frequency, the annoying habits she was developing became increasingly hard to take. She began avoiding my eyes when I spoke to her as though she were aware everything I said was a lie. She also took on a nervous mannerism of pursing then releasing her lips, which gave the impression she was always sucking on a straw.

Grandma lived alone. Her housekeeper, Ana, a kind Jamaican woman, arrived at 9 A.M., prepared Grandma's breakfast and lunch, tidied the house, then went home and returned to prepare and serve dinner. Ana was very protective of Grandma. She had already confided to me her distress that Grandma might somehow get trapped in the elevator when she was alone. "You know how when it gets very windy, she gets power failures that can last for hours," Ana worried. I assured her that I too was troubled by that possibility. Then, I impatiently waited for the weather to cooperate and a good wind storm to come along. It finally happened. The weather report was for heavy winds during the night. That evening I had dinner with Grandma, a particularly difficult dinner, what with the vegetarian menu, Grandma's averted eyes, her twitching mouth and then the dismaying news that she was meeting an architect concerning her idea for building a personal gym. It was clearly time to act.

After dinner, I kissed Grandma good night, went into the kitchen, where Ana was tidying up, then drove away. At that time, I only lived three blocks from Grandma. I parked my car and waved to my next-door neighbor, who was just arriving home. I felt it was fortuitous that, if necessary, he could testify that he had seen me enter my own modest rental cottage. I waited an hour and then slipped out my back door. It was already dark and chillingly cold, and it was easy to hurry undetected back to Grandma's house. I arrived through the wooded area, checking to be sure that Ana's car was gone. It was, and I slipped across the lawn to the window of the den. As I had expected, I could see Grandma, hunched up on her recliner, an old fur lap robe wrapped around her, watching her favorite television show.

For the next ten minutes she stayed there, then, as I had expected, promptly at nine o'clock, the fur robe dragging behind her, she turned off the television and made her way to the front of the house. In a flash, key in hand, I was at the basement door and inside. As soon as I heard the rumble of the elevator, I threw the switch, plunging the house into silence and darkness.

I crept upstairs, my feet noiseless in my sneakers, my flashlight a thin beam. From the sound of my grandmother's cries for help I could detect that the elevator was only a few feet off the floor. Now for the tricky part. I placed my tape recorder on the vestibule table behind a book I had left for Grandma. I reasoned that Ana, if indeed she noticed it, would think nothing of it being there. I had developed a habit of bringing books and little gifts for Grandma.

And then I turned on the tape. The sound that thundered from it was a litany from cat hell, meowing, clawing, scratching and howling, their shrieks interwoven with the sudden incongruous rattle of purring contentment.

There was absolute silence from the elevator.

Had the recording done its job already? I wondered. It was possible, but I wouldn't know for sure until the morning. The tape was twenty minutes long and would play repeatedly until midnight. I was sure that would be sufficient.

I let myself out of the house and walked home at a quick pace, bracing against the sharp wind that was now making tree branches bend and dance. Chilled to the bone, I went directly to bed. I confess I could not fall asleep. The mental image of my grandmother's stiffening body inside her elevator kept me from restful slumber. But then as I allowed myself to imagine finally getting my hands on all her money, my frame of mind improved and from dawn till eight o'clock I enjoyed a refreshing slumber.

But then as I began to prepare breakfast, several possibilities occurred to me. Suppose Grandma's face was frozen into a frightened mask? Would that make anyone suspicious? Worse yet, suppose for some reason the recording had not automatically turned off!

My original plan had been to await Ana's phone call, the one that would convey the sad news that Grandma had been trapped in the elevator and must have had a heart attack. At the frightening possibility that the tape just might still be playing, I leapt up from the breakfast table, threw on some clothes and rushed over, arriving as Ana was opening the front door. To my vast relief there was no sound from the recorder.

The morning was overcast, which meant that the vestibule was dark. As Ana greeted me she tried to turn on the light. Then she frowned. "My God, there must have been another power failure." She turned and made a beeline for the stairs to Grandma's bedroom. I, on the other hand, raced down to the basement and threw the master switch on the panel. The whir of the elevator rewarded me. I rushed up the stairs and was there when Ana yanked open the elevator door. Grandma was on the floor wrapped in her mink fur lap robe. She opened her eyes and blinked up at us. With the fur wrapped around her head, the strands of fur resting on her cheek, for all the world she had the face of a cat. Her mouth pursed in and out as though she were sipping milk. "Grandma . . ." My voice failed. With Ana's help, she was struggling to her feet, her hands on the floor, her back arched to help regain her balance.

"Eerr . . . eerr . . ." she sighed. *Or was she saying "Purrrr . . . purrrr"?*

"Eerrr, that's the best sleep I've had in years," Grandma said contentedly.

"Weren't you frightened trapped in there?" Ana asked incredulously.

"Oh, no, I was tired and I just made the best of it. I tried calling out but there was no one to hear me. I decided not to waste my voice."

The recording had been playing. I had heard it myself.

Grandma was eyeing me. "You look terrible," she said. "I don't want you worrying about me. Don't you know I'll live to be one hundred? That's my promise to you. So I was stuck in the elevator. The carpet is thick. I lay down and was nice and warm under the robe. In my dreams I was hearing this faint purring sound like water lapping against the shore."

Afraid I would give myself away, I stumbled downstairs and grabbed my recorder from the table, then realized that in my haste I had knocked a small object off the table. I bent down and picked it up. It was a hearing aid. I started to lay it down and saw there was another one on the table.

Ana was coming down the stairs. "How long has Grandma been wearing hearing aids?" I demanded.

"They're just what I'm coming for. She leaves them on that table every night. She's so vain that I guess she didn't tell you that her hearing has been going steadily downhill and she's practically deaf now. She's been studying lip reading and is quite good at it. Haven't you noticed the way she always looks at your lips when you're talking? She finally got the hearing aids but uses them only for television in the evening and always leaves them right here."

"She can't hear?" I asked, dumbfounded.

"Only a few sounds, deep ones, nothing shrill."

That happened five years ago. Of course, I immediately destroyed the tape, but in my sleep I hear it playing over and over. It doesn't frighten me. Instead it keeps me company. I don't know why. There's something else that's a little strange. I cannot look at my grandmother's face without seeing the face of a cat. That's because of those whiskers on her cheeks and lips, the odd pursing movements of her mouth, the narrow intense eyes that are always focused on my lips. Also, her bedchamber of choice is now the elevator where, for naps and at night, she curls up on the carpeted floor wrapped in her mink lap robe. Her breathing has even taken on a purring sound.

I can hardly keep my wits about me as I await my inheritance. I do not have the courage to try to precipitate its arrival again. I live with Grandma now, and as time passes, I believe I am beginning to resemble her. The scar on her cheek is directly under her left eye; mine is in the same spot. I have a very light beard and shave infrequently. At times my beard looks just like her whiskers. We have those same narrow green eyes.

My grandmother loves very warm milk. She's taken to pouring it into a saucer to cool it before she laps it up. I tried it and now I like it that way too. It's purr-fect.

Mary Higgins Clark

The Melody Lingers On

Out now in print and eBook

Lane Harmon, assistant to a renowned interior designer,
is used to meeting the rich and famous in their opulent
homes. But when she is called to the Bennett house,
she knows this job will be different. Parker Bennett
has been missing for two years – since just before the
discovery that billions of dollars had vanished from a
fund he managed. The scandal has not died and a cloud
of suspicion remains around his name. Did he commit
suicide or was his disappearance staged?

His wife is convinced Parker is innocent – and alive. But
there are people after him who are determined to learn
the truth at any cost. And the more Lane gets drawn into
the Bennett's world of glamour and intrigue, the most she
puts her life and those of her family in jeopardy . . .

**With the hair-raising skill that has made her a
multi-million copy global phenomenon,
Mary Higgins Clark combines a huge financial
scandal and a breathtaking tale of deception and
betrayal into one of her finest novels yet.**

LIKE YOUR FICTION A LITTLE ON THE DARK SIDE?

Like to curl up in a darkened room all alone, with the doors bolted and the windows locked and slip into something cold and terrifying...half hoping something goes bump in the night?

Me too.

That's why you'll find me at The Dark Pages - the home of crooks and villains, mobsters and terrorists, spies and private eyes; where the plots are twistier than a knotted noose and the pacing tighter than Marlon Brando's braces.

Beneath the city's glitz, down a litter-strewn alley, behind venetian blinds where neon slices the smoke-filled gloom, reading the dark pages.

Join me: **WWW.THEDARKPAGES.CO.UK**

AGENT X

@dark_pages